A SPY
IN THE
STRUGGLE

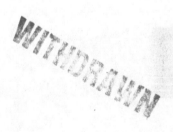

Also by Aya de León

A Spy in the Struggle

Side Chick Nation

The Accidental Mistress

The Boss

Uptown Thief

A SPY
IN THE
STRUGGLE

AYA de LEÓN

www.kensingtonbooks.com

DAFINA BOOKS are published by

Kensington Publishing Corp.
119 West 40th Street
New York, NY 10018

All Kensington titles, imprints, and distributed lines are available at special quantity discounts for bulk purchases for sales promotion, premiums, fund-raising, and educational or institutional use.

Special book excerpts or customized printings can also be created to fit specific needs. For details, write or phone the office of the Kensington Sales Manager: Kensington Publishing Corp., 119 West 40th Street, New York, NY 10018. Attn. Sales Department. Phone: 1-800-221-2647.

The Dafina logo is a trademark of Kensington Publishing Corp.

ISBN-13: 978-1-4967-2859-3
ISBN-10: 1-4967-2859-9
First Kensington Trade Paperback Printing: January 2021

ISBN-13: 978-1-4967-2861-6 (ebook)
ISBN-10: 1-4967-2861-0 (ebook)
First Kensington Electronic Edition: January 2021

10 9 8 7 6 5 4 3 2 1

Printed in the United States of America

For Sam Greenlee

Acknowledgments

This book is a work of fiction, but it was inspired by my experience as part of the Free My People Youth Leadership Movement in Roxbury, MA. Thanks to Alexander, Adjoa, Arnetta, Bernard, Curtis, Caroline, Donna, Darcelle, Eric, Joyce, Joeritta, Jessica, Kevin, Lisa, Mark, Mark, Nakeia, Pamela, Richard, Raeesha, Salaama, Tamu, Tutu, Tarkpor, and all the other fabulous and brilliant young people and adults whose names I can't recall after so many years, but Free My People definitely changed my life! Thanks also to my Antioch teachers, Alma Luz Villanueva and Leonard Chang. my VONA teacher Elmaz Abinader, and my consultant Wendy Tokunaga. Thanks also to Sisters in Crime and their great webinar with Jerri Williams from the FBI. Thanks also to Altos de Chavon in the Dominican Republic, where I worked on an early draft of the book. Thanks to the many activists who consulted with me over the years, especially Ira Armstrong, Ian Kim, Van Jones, and Naomi Klein. Thanks above all to all the real-life movements out there fighting for racial and climate justice, especially the Movement for Black Lives and the Sunrise Movement. And of course, thanks as always to my family: Anna, Stuart, Coco, Larry, Paci, Neens and Dee, my agent Jenni Ferrari Adler, and the fabulous squad at Kensington: Esi Sogah, Vida Engstrand, Michelle Addo, and Norma Perez-Hernandez.

"My situation was unique . . . being an African American woman working undercover is exceptionally stressful. . . . When I wasn't on assignment . . . I would stay in bed, isolated and alone, for days.

—From *Clean Dirt: A Memoir of Johnnie Mae Gibson, FBI Special Agent*

Three things cannot long stay hidden: the sun, the moon, and the truth.

—Buddha

Part 1

Chapter 1

"So, you were the whistleblower," the man on the FBI interview panel said.

Yolanda Vance knew he meant it as a compliment. People always did. But after everything that had happened, she wished she had kept her mouth shut.

Yolanda had been a first-year associate at the Manhattan firm of Van Dell, Meyers and Whitney, working for a senior partner in securities. Early one morning, her boss instructed her to take a stack of documents to the shredder.

He looked like he had slept in his designer suit. He was practically yelling as he shoved the papers into her chest.

As a former basketball player, Yolanda deftly grabbed the stack of documents and pivoted toward the copy room, the same way she would have done on the ball court.

Why did he have a junior attorney shredding papers? Couldn't his secretary do it?

As she walked down the hallway, one of the sounds became consistently louder. That sound, that buzz, had been a background hum ever since she came in just after six. Yolanda had mistaken it for the grind of a distant garbage truck or some heavy outdoor construction machinery. But as she approached, she detected a pulse to it, a rise and fall like mechanical breathing: the monstrous snore of the shredder.

Beside the machine were a few massive towers of papers and a young man in shirtsleeves feeding it as quickly as he could. Various people were adding to the pile, including the senior partner's secretary, who hustled from the file room with a whole box of papers.

Why were they shredding all these documents?

Then she heard a scuffle below and went out to the mezzanine. It was filled with all the other staff. Over the railing she watched as the gleaming marble floor of the entryway was suddenly obscured by a swarm of blazers and windbreakers with large yellow letters.

FBI.

Yolanda would be damned if this senior partner planned to make her an accessory to whatever the hell this was. Instead of shredding the papers, she slipped them under her shirt.

The basement floor of the law office had previously been an Olympic-sized pool. The firm's designers had transformed it into a sunken waiting room with couches on the cobalt tile floor, but they kept the round, beveled-glass windows high up in the walls.

Yolanda waited to be interviewed with others in her department. She sat stiffly on the designer leather couch. Under her navy-blue merino wool sweater, against her tight stomach, were the fifty-something un-shredded pages that the partner had ordered her to destroy.

The FBI agent who called her to his desk was a middle-aged man with half glasses.

"Your firm is under investigation for securities fraud," the agent said.

Yolanda looked around and saw several of the partners, including the one she worked for. He was being escorted to the conference room where they were interviewing senior partners and higher-ranking staff in the securities division.

"These allegations are in connection with—" the agent broke off as Yolanda pulled the papers out from under her sweater.

"So tell us, Miss Vance, why would you like to work for the Federal Bureau of Investigation?" asked the agent who had called her a whistleblower. He raised his pale eyebrows slightly. The other two agents wore slack expressions that Yolanda couldn't read.

Her starched white shirt was soaked at the armpits under a tailored designer navy suit. Usually she only perspired when she worked out. The moisture at her scalp caused the roots of her permed and pressed hair to curl slightly. She was grateful that the panel at this second interview was all white. Neither of the crisp thirtyish men nor the dowdy older woman would decode the panic signal in the humid waves at her hairline.

Yolanda faced them squarely, having prepared for the question. She couldn't tell the truth: *I don't really want to work for the FBI.* "I've always wanted to practice law," she began. That was true. Watching reruns of *Perry Mason* in middle school, she had always wanted to be an attorney. To stand in a courtroom and bellow beneath thick eyebrows: *But you DID go to the beach house and THAT'S when you killed him, Mrs. Lowell!* Then to watch the woman on the stand, eyes wide, cupid's bow mouth open in horror, crumple at the accusation, weep, confess.

But that didn't answer the question of why she wanted to work for the FBI in particular. She couldn't tell them that she had applied six months ago as a backup plan that she never thought she'd need. But she couldn't get a job in corporate law since she had turned over those un-shredded papers from Van Dell, Meyers and Whitney.

If she had a little more time, she would have been able to find work in a different type of law, or maybe something out of state. But she was two months behind in rent for her Queens studio apartment. When she left Detroit, she had promised herself that as an adult, she would always have a stable place to live. She needed a job now. Yesterday.

Lester Johnakin's Book of Positive Thinking was the closest thing Yolanda had to religion since she was a kid. In high school, she had become disillusioned with Johnakin, but his words still came to her in times of stress. "Let the world know why you are the right person to receive the outcome you desire."

She spoke with a confidence she'd learned to fake during her teens. She wasn't a young woman on the verge of homelessness; she was a confident Harvard Law School graduate who was ready to be an asset to the Bureau.

"Attorneys at the FBI make significantly less than in corporate law," the woman on the interview panel explained.

"I understand," Yolanda said. What good was the high salary at Van Dell, Meyers and Whitney when she had lost her job after six months when the firm went down for their crooked practices? When a choice not to break the law made her a pariah in her legal field? She had checked the FBI pay scale and retirement benefits. Even if they moved her around from one city to another, it would be comforting to practice with the law on her side.

After the interview, she walked two blocks with her confident strut before she allowed herself to lean against a building and exhale. She looked up at the cloudy Manhattan sky and prayed for the first time in decades: "Dear God or Whatever, please let the FBI hire me." Her unemployment had ended, and she had $28.62 in her bank account. "Please God. Please." Praying felt ridiculous to her. As she headed to the subway, she peeled off her jacket and exposed her sodden shirt to the autumn wind.

* * *

During Yolanda's second week of FBI training at Quantico, she found herself struggling with marksmanship. She had never shot a gun before. One of her fellow trainees kept boasting about all the guns his family had. Her first day at the shooting range, he situated himself next to her and started shooting before she had her earphones on. She jumped and the earphones fell out of her hand. Her second time at the range, she made sure to get there early, but she was still jittery and anxious. Her first two weeks of evaluations for marksmanship were mediocre. She came to dread the range.

"Not used to dealing with guys so much, eh?" the instructor asked her one day. Special Agent Donnelly was in her fifties, with short graying hair and rimless glasses.

"Excuse me?" Yolanda asked.

"I saw your file," she said. "Women's high school and college. By the time you were in school with boys, you were at Harvard Law. Those guys must have been more mature than this asswipe."

"If you can see he's a jerk, why don't you stop him?" Yolanda asked.

"This isn't law school," Donnelly said. "Criminals don't raise their hands and wait to get called on. You'll need to shoot when you're shaken. When you've got blast concussion. When you're pissed. He's helping replicate field conditions."

"But I'm not trying to be in a real situation with guns and blast concussion," Yolanda said. "I'm an attorney."

"Well, you can quit if you want," Donnelly said. "But you're an athlete. You're smart as hell. Don't let that dick bring you down. I'm committed to making sure all the women graduate from this cohort. Not by coddling you, but by teaching you to kick ass."

Donnelly reminded Yolanda of her basketball coach. Same pep talk: half affirmation and half challenge.

Next time at the firing range, "that dick" pulled the same thing with another woman. Yolanda turned to him and complained loudly. When he shrugged that he couldn't hear, she motioned for him to pull off his earphones. He waited for that set of tests to end, and finally slid one of the earphones back to hear better. When he did, Yolanda shot off five rounds very quickly and close to him. He jumped, eyes wide.

Meanwhile, the other woman put her headphones on and shot off several rounds, as well.

Yolanda's shots were wild. But for the first time, she felt the gun as an extension of her arm, not a hostile accessory. After that, she improved steadily.

New Jersey wasn't New York, but it would do for now. When she decided to escape from her middle school in Detroit, she hadn't dreamed of the FBI. It wasn't visions of New Jersey that had motivated her to sacrifice everything for achievement in prep school, in college, in law school. It had always been the glamour of Manhattan. And by high school, it was the opulence of corporate law. She'd lived the dream for those six months at Van Dell, Meyers and Whitney. She recalled walking from the subway to their Midtown offices in the most gorgeous and comfortable suede boots in the entire world. She'd had a beautiful one-bedroom apartment in Chelsea, with a vaulted ceiling and a river view. During the winter, she had an ankle length cashmere coat to bundle her up every time she left the apartment.

But now all her suede and cashmere was boxed in the back of her closet. She wore neat suits to work every day. Her salary was half what she had made at Van Dell, Meyers and Whitney. But she wouldn't be losing her job because the New Jersey branch of the FBI got shut down as an accessory to securities fraud. And her government job had provided a steady income and a decent place to live for a year.

Besides, she could easily get to New York. She went into

the city most weekends to a blues club in the Village. Blues was nostalgic. It connected Yolanda to her early childhood in Georgia, before her family moved to Detroit. She was getting into the groove and letting the good times roll. Life was going unexpectedly well.

Late one afternoon, Yolanda was in her FBI cubicle in the New Jersey field office when her boss walked in. Special Agent Sanchez, a gray-haired veteran FBI attorney, was the head of the white-collar division where she worked. The office was square and windowless, but she liked working for Sanchez. He was smart, fair, and he valued her mind.

She had just identified a possible link between their money laundering suspect and a Russian mob operation and had been looking forward to telling her boss.

When he entered, she had smiled and opened her mouth to give Sanchez the update, but then another man had walked in. She didn't recognize this fortyish man with a pale blond crew cut. Ex-military, she surmised from the rigidity with which he held his body.

"Agent Vance," her boss said. "This is Agent Rafferty of the Counter Terrorism Squad in the San Francisco office."

Rafferty looked her up and down with no hint of a leer, more of a disapproval. She dressed for men like him, offering him neat, bobbed hair, masculine colors, clothes never tight on her almost boyish figure. Her lips had the natural fullness of a fifties starlet, but she wore them with only a matte balm. Her eyes were large, with long lashes, and she wore neither liner nor shadow.

"Agent Vance, we have a West Coast assignment for you," Rafferty began. "I'm the case agent on a surveillance operation."

"Surveillance?" Yolanda asked. "But I'm an attorney, sir."

She looked to Sanchez, his mouth turned down in a barely visible frown.

"There's a key industry in Northern California with a

vital national security contract," Sanchez said. "A black identity extremist group is threatening to undermine the contractor. It is unusual to have a new recruit go undercover. But San Francisco thinks you'll be a good fit. You did extremely well in the Academy, and your work has been excellent in the short time you've been on my squad."

"I appreciate that, sir," Yolanda said.

"Unfortunately for us," Sanchez continued, "you are being reassigned to San Francisco. Rafferty will take it from here."

"Yes, sir," she said, her jaw clenching.

Sanchez escorted her and Rafferty to a conference room, and he began the initial briefing on the operation.

"Agent Vance," Rafferty began. "We selected you for your connection with the city of Holloway. The Cartwright College link and previous exposure to the subject population distinguishes you in this case, not your skills and track record. In all honesty, I would prefer a more experienced agent."

Yolanda sat silent. *Then why don't you goddamn go and get one?* She wanted to say. *Nobody asked you to come up here and blow up my life.*

"But this is an unusual case, because many of the subjects in the organization are teenagers," Rafferty went on. "I see that you coached at the Teen Center in Holloway. Connections like that don't come along often for agents, and we're determined to exploit this opportunity."

"Teenagers?" Yolanda asked, unable to contain her incredulity. "Sir?"

"Unfortunately, yes," he said. His mouth was tight, as if he had tasted something unpleasant. "The short version is that the black identity extremist organization Red, Black and GREEN! is harassing Randell Corporation, an important industrial contractor with the US government. Our office has made several unsuccessful attempts to monitor their operations."

For the first time, Yolanda regretted coaching girls' basketball, even though she had really enjoyed it. Initially, she had just wanted to look more well-rounded for law school applications.

"I won't let you down, sir," Yolanda said coolly when the interview concluded.

"I'm really sorry about this, Vance," Sanchez said after Rafferty had left.

I don't fucking believe it, was the line in Yolanda's head. But instead she asked, "Will I be able to come back to New Jersey when this is over?"

"I'm putting in the transfer request today," Sanchez said. "I want you back on my squad after you finish the assignment, Vance. You can count on it."

Yolanda felt somewhat reassured. She could come back. She would come back. She just had to spy on some black extremist teenagers.

Chapter 2

Yolanda read the case file on the flight from Newark. Since she had lived in Holloway for all four years of college, she only needed to skim a lot of the background material on the town. But one article she read closely. It had been published six months before in one of the Bay Area's independent weekly newspapers:

Holloway, CA: How a Has-Been Town Became a Hotbed of Black Eco-Activism

Holloway, California. Population 400,000. A small Northern California city at the end of the BART subway line, just past Richmond. Like its Bay Area neighbors—Richmond and Oakland—Holloway attracted many African American migrants from the South to work in shipyards for World War II. But after the war, those transplants found themselves in a dead-end.

However, on Holloway Avenue, a few relics of the town's former glory survived the riots of the late 1960s. Above the old plywood boards that were nailed over the door and broken windows, a sign with peeling yellow and blue paint still invited pedestrians into Netta's High Class Hideaway, formerly a legendary blues nightclub. For a while in the early 1990s, some local heroin users removed the boards from the back door and used the place as a shooting gallery. A few dirty needles in dusty corners had escaped the hasty and slipshod cleaning of the overworked public health division. No one in the community knew who owned the place, abandoned since the riots. Down the street, another sign had survived: Jimmy Earle's Legendary BBQ.

Today, Holloway Avenue boasts a string of fast food joints, several bars, and a few cheap Chinese food places. For nightlife, Holloway residents have to travel ten miles to Oakland or across the Bay Bridge to San Francisco. In response to repeated shootings, the City of Holloway won't grant permits to any nightclubs.

In the late 1990s, the mayor had begun to push Plan 2000!—an initiative to build a gated biotech research facility that promised to bring thousands of jobs to Holloway. Plan 2000! did bring thousands of jobs, just not to many Holloway residents. The mostly white researchers would zip off the 80 freeway and through the heavily guarded gates, while the clerical workers would take the short walk from the Holloway BART subway stop.

Only the unskilled and custodial jobs ended up going to Holloway residents. Initially, there was some community outcry, but after a handful of protests, the town sunk back into its usual disappointment. RandellCorp isn't the only gated community in Holloway. On the top of the hill, Cartwright College has stood for over 150 years, an elite women's school with a barbed wire fence around a rustic campus. Eucalyptus trees and brick walls screen the campus from the view of residents. The 27 bus line brings workers from downtown Holloway to and from the campus— cafeteria workers in hairnets, gardeners who maintain the pristine grounds—but the female students rarely venture off campus. Unless they have cars, in which case they can hop on a nearby freeway on- ramp and bypass the town completely.

To the people of Holloway, RandellCorp be- came like Cartwright College, a fading insult in the landscape of neglect.

However, a few years after Randell was built, the cancer rate in Holloway began to soar. In Randell's fifth year, Randell was caught dumping toxic chemical waste in an abandoned railroad yard not far from an elementary school. Randell agreed to pay a fine and clean up the site. Mean- while, there were allegations of other dumping sites. And although those sites did show evidence of toxic contamination, there was no conclusive evidence to tie them to Randell.

Meanwhile, environmental researchers re- leased several studies in which the data clearly in- dicated that the cancer rate had A) grown significantly since RandellCorp began operation and B) risen in proportion to the residents' prox- imity to the railroad yard and other alleged dump- ing sites. However, for every meticulously researched independent study that led to damning conclusions, a government-funded study would appear, tracing the cancer to other causes. An op- ed in the West County Herald questioned the habits of the town's predominantly African American residents, encouraging them to "eat a lower carb diet" and "exercise more regularly." One study cited the cuts in physical education at Holloway High as a factor in poor health outcomes and another blamed the increased cancer rates on video games.

Two years ago, when a KPFA/Pacifica radio Top 10 list identified the Randell-cancer link as one of the most underreported stories of the year, the issue caught the interest of a national environmental group. Planet Greener, headquartered in Maryland, had long been criticized for a lack of diversity in its senior staff and board of directors. More recently, they had gotten a slew of bad press for having installed oil and natural gas drilling on several of their nature preserves. In response to donor questions about their drilling practices, Planet Greener insisted that the wells were necessary to raise funds for their Minority Community Outreach programs, which they would be unveiling shortly. Although there had been no previous public information on these programs, they began appearing soon afterwards in low-income communities around the nation—one in nearly every state. During that year, Planet Greener hired Marcus Winters, a black activist from Richmond, to develop a community gardening program for youth in Holloway.

Winters, a veteran community organizer, started a youth leadership project that quickly connected community gardening to Holloway's lack of green space to food justice to environmental racism and police violence. He began to train the teens to organize a multigenerational campaign against Randell. The youth activists picked the name "Red, Black and GREEN!" explaining that Red stood for Indigenous people, Black for African Americans, and Green for the environment. But these are also the Pan African liberation colors, associated with many radical African American movements, which was not at all what Planet Greener's leadership had in mind. However, Marcus Winters seemed to have a thriving youth project on a very modest budget, and it was the most successful of their Minority Community Outreach Programs.

Many of the teens came from Holloway's St. Anthony housing projects, or from the working-class neighborhood that surrounded the projects, a combination of concrete block apartment buildings and small, single-family homes. The projects are widely known as "The Stats," both a convenient nickname, and for its statistics: high concentration of nearby liquor stores, high infant mortality rate, teen pregnancy rate, incarceration rate, addiction rate, HIV rate, dropout rate, and murder rate.

Although Red, Black and GREEN! has had an impact on the teens in the city, it'll take a lot more than a youth empowerment project to truly make Holloway much greener.

"Welcome to San Francisco, Miss Vance," the agent shook her hand with a firm grip. "I'll be taking you to the apartment the Bureau has for you in Holloway."

As Yolanda stepped out of the airport, the feel and smell of the Northern California air brought back her first trip to the area.

At seventeen, she had come from the Alice Lloyd Prep School to Cartwright College, for the summer pre-freshman program. She'd had a cheap duffel on one shoulder and her school backpack on the other, with everything she owned in those two canvas bags. Except her winter coat—a blue, nylon jacket with polyester fill—that didn't fit in the duffel.

All those years ago, she had stepped outside the airport doors into an unusually warm day, completely unsure of where to go. So she had first greeted San Francisco sweating and lost, a nomad, wearing too many layers and all her belongings on her back.

Take time to notice how far you've come. As usual, Lester Johnakin's words still came to her.

Every time she flew back into SFO it was better. The autumn of her sophomore year, she came back from her New York summer internship with designer clothes she had bought for wholesale prices on West 27th Street in Manhattan and suitcases on wheels she had bought cheap on the street in Harlem. The following summer, she had returned from Chicago with a stylish new haircut and enough money to pay for a shuttle to Cartwright instead of public transportation.

The agent led her to a dark sedan with government plates. She slid into the back, and they pulled away from the curb. Moments later, they came around a freeway curve, and Yolanda saw the dark San Francisco Bay stretching before them.

The hum of the car lulled her. Yolanda dozed as the sedan sped down the freeway to the Bay Bridge, cruising above the dark water, and then turned north.

Yolanda awoke when they took the Holloway freeway exit. The white letters on the green highway sign indicated a right turn to go up the hill to Cartwright College. Instead, the driver hung a left and headed into the flatlands.

Yolanda peered at the empty streets as they drove into a neighborhood of apartment buildings and vacant lots. The road ahead of them sparkled with broken glass. A side street had single story homes beneath silhouettes of trees, all pruned into gnarled shapes to avoid telephone wires.

In the dim streetlights, she could see that some of the houses had well-kept gardens, while others had cars parked on overgrown lawns. All first-floor windows had security bars.

The sedan slowed in the middle of a block, just past a pale bungalow with neatly manicured hedges, and a boarded up two-story house. The agent pulled up beside a gray stucco apartment building that rose in a solid block above its neighbors.

They unloaded the luggage and walked to a façade tagged with graffiti. The agent opened the front door with a key, and they entered a musty foyer with grimy brown carpet. A yellowing plastic runner led up the stairs. The agent helped Yolanda carry her bags up to the second floor, and down the narrow hallway to a one-room apartment. He used the second key on the ring to open the apartment door and reached easily for the light switch.

The bare bulb in the ceiling fixture illuminated a small studio, with a single bed, tiny couch, a video monitor, and a desk on one side. A small table with two chairs barely fit in the kitchenette.

The wooden desk turned out to be deceptively simple. The agent used the third key on the ring to open the top desk drawer, which revealed a laptop computer that popped up. The second two drawers opened to reveal a printer/scanner/copy machine that could also print color photos.

The apartment had the impersonal impact of the rooms she'd lived in at boarding school, at Cartwright, and at the FBI academy. Even in New Jersey, she had been living in an extended stay hotel.

She put her suitcases in the tiny closet, but the door didn't quite close. It seemed closed, but then it opened back up a moment later, she had to really press her shoulder against it.

At least the place was clean. Yolanda detected no odors of cooking or cigarettes or daily living, only a mild lingering citrus scent of some detergent. Yolanda's sense of smell was extremely sensitive. She could smell cigarette smoke half a block away. She could walk into a bathroom fifteen minutes after someone washed their hands and know whether they used peppermint or rose scented soap.

The agent handed her the keys and left. She locked the door behind him.

The bedside clock said 2:20. 5:20 AM East Coast time— she'd usually be waking up at this hour.

She unpacked her suitcase and changed for bed. The polyester bedspread was a southwestern theme in faded turquoise, sandy brown, and burnt orange.

She was tired after the flight from Newark, but she lay awake for a long time in the bed, simmering with outrage. How the hell did these assholes send her to a ghetto to infiltrate some outfit with black teenagers?

She took a deep breath. Focus. Practicing as an FBI attorney was the goal now. Whatever the hell was needed to wrap up this assignment, she would do it so she could get on with her life. Either go back to her job in Jersey or someplace else that wasn't an insult to all she had worked for. And then, after she settled into her resolve, she lay awake some more, wondering if the FBI could hear her breathing.

The next morning, an agent came to pick Yolanda up in a car with a Lyft sticker. He drove her past the storefront church where Red Black and GREEN! held their meetings.

Yolanda hadn't been in a church for over two decades. But the stained-glass window with the image of a black Jesus brought it all back.

As the agent drove her to FBI headquarters in San Francisco, Yolanda recalled their church in Georgia. Her father would get so riled up when he preached, sweat dripping from his face, using a handkerchief to mop his forehead. The square of fabric started out crisp and white but ended up a sodden rag.

The year her father died, the police in their small town had fatally shot three young black people, two young men and a young woman. Her father, a young pastor, had turned the church he'd inherited from his own father into an activist ministry.

Every week, the congregation would pray for the victims and their families. He would call down the blood of Jesus to protect other young people in the community. "The blood!" he would shout, raising a dual specter of the protective blood of Jesus and the blood that had been shed by black people in police shootings.

"Just because we up here in the church—hah!" he said. "Don't try to tell me these police shootings are the will of God. Well! That this is part of God's plan. Saaay-tan! Yes, Satan has a plan, too. And I just might call that plan out today . . . *Racism!*"

The organist would punctuate the key words of the sermon with sharp notes.

"Racism is the work of the devil," her father went on. "Now don't you go out of here saying Pastor Vance said white folks was the devil, or the police was the devil. Police are just men. Hah! Just men, with guns in their hand. In their holsters. In their police vehicles. But Satan! Has put hate in some of these men's hearts. Using that manmade weapon to do the will of the devil. And take innocent black lives. So when we march, we march against the devil. When we call for the firing of the Chief of Police, we're calling out the devil. When we hold a candlelight vigil, we trying to drive out the devil with our light. I wish I had one or two witnesses in here."

"Amen!" the congregation yelled back.

"Yes, Lord!"

"Hallelujah!"

Her father would go on, encouraged by the call and response. "I know some folks been telling me I'm getting too political up in the church. But did y'all ever hear of the Civil Rights Movement? If we worship Jesus, then we need to be like Jesus, who fought for justice. Oh I wish some of the saints could hear me right now. Don't take my word for it. The Biiiiible says so."

"Praise Him!"

By the end of his sermon, his suit and robe would be soaked with sweat and his voice would be hoarse, but the congregation would be on its feet, screaming and dancing, as the drums played a fast one/two beat and people got filled with the Holy Spirit.

Preschool-age Yolanda had sat in the front row next to her mother. Her wide eyes fixed on her father. She couldn't quite understand what he meant, but she could feel his power. The charismatic rapture with which he held the entire church. Smiling with pride that this was her very own daddy.

"You need to understand," Rafferty explained at Yolanda's first briefing. "These Red, Black and GREEN! kids are very persuasive. They know just how to distort information and manipulate emotions to gain people's sympathy."

"I went to boarding school, sir," Yolanda said. "I coached basketball. I know how to handle manipulative teenagers."

They were in the conference room of the San Francisco office with a female agent named Peterson. She had long chestnut-colored hair in a bun and a firm handshake. Rafferty had explained that Peterson would be the handling agent for the undercover operation—Yolanda's "go-to girl." Yolanda glanced at Peterson when he said it and caught the slightest downward tic at the corner of Peterson's mouth.

"The long version of your cover is in the file," Rafferty explained. "But the short version is that you've been hired by a San Francisco law firm. You're living in Holloway and studying for the July bar in California."

Yolanda was supposed to be herself, excluding only the FBI, and the fact that she had been the whistleblower at Van Dell, Meyers and Whitney.

Peterson interjected. "Red, Black and GREEN! is trying to recruit more adults, so this upcoming community meeting is a perfect place to make contact. You want to be just the kind of person they're looking for—a Cartwright alum with a flexible schedule who is concerned about the environment—"

Rafferty cut her off: "Operation HOLOGRAM stands for Holloway Green Amateurs. We can't have these teenagers mucking around with our national security. The Environmental Protection Agency has dismissed every complaint against Randell as having no merit. And the corporation paid for the cleanup of that one railroad yard issue. So this organization is not only radicalizing these kids, but it's also teaching them to be victims, whiners, looking for someone to blame."

Yolanda knew just what he meant. She thought of her freshman year roommate at Cartwright College. That white girl, a self-styled revolutionary, walked into the room with her "luggage," three black garbage bags. Later it turned out she had a trust fund.

"These clips are from RBG's last community meeting," Rafferty said.

RBG? Yolanda caught Peterson's eye. Yolanda mouthed "Ruth Bader Ginsburg?"

Peterson chuckled silently and shook her head. "RBG stands for Red, Black, and GREEN!" Peterson said.

The screen showed an image of several teenage girls laughing.

A fortyish man stepped into the picture and Rafferty leaned forward. Peterson paused the video again.

"RBG leader, Marcus Winters," Rafferty said. The man on the screen had African features in a pale face. His short afro was graying at the temples. Winters stood frozen with an overflowing manila folder in his hand. Yolanda scrutinized his rumpled, button down shirt with a faint stain on the pocket, his worn jeans, and off-brand sneakers.

As the image began to move again, Winters rifled through the folder. He handed several papers to one of the girls and then leaned in close to speak with her.

"Bingo! Right there!" Rafferty pointed, and Peterson paused the image, blowing up the shot of the young woman's face. Her upward glance at Winters made her eyes look particularly wide.

"That look tells everything," Rafferty said. "That's how Winters operates. He picks smart kids, skims cream off the top, and coaches them on exactly what to say. He insists he's not the one pulling the strings, but it's all right there."

"There are a few other adults," Peterson said, "But we don't have them on video yet—"

Rafferty interrupted "Take the video home to study, as well as this dossier on Winters and the RBG adults. Tomorrow you'll make contact at their next meeting."

He handed her a thick pair of files.

"Call if you have questions," Rafferty explained as Peterson ejected a small drive from a port in the side of the computer. "I'll expect a report first thing Friday morning."

After Rafferty walked out, Peterson handed Yolanda the tiny drive.

"Thanks," Yolanda said. "By the way, is Special Agent Donnelly still in San Francisco?"

Peterson's eyebrows rose. "You know Donnelly?" she asked. "Friends in high places."

"She was my shooting instructor at Quantico," Yolanda said. "I didn't realize she was a bigwig."

"She's on par with Rafferty's supervisor," Peterson said. "She heads the white collar division."

"Special Agent Vance," Donnelly greeted her warmly in the San Francisco office. "I knew you'd make it through."

"Agent Vance is working Operation HOLOGRAM," Peterson said. "Her first day."

"The Cartwright College connection," Donnelly snapped her fingers. "Of course. You gotta let me take you out for a drink one of these days." She handed Yolanda her card.

"I'm impressed," Peterson said as they headed for the elevator. "She's not that friendly with everyone."

Yolanda shrugged and slid Donnelly's card into her jeans pocket.

To: Special Agent Rafferty
From: Special Agent █████████████
Re: ASSIGNMENT OF NEW AGENT TO OPERATION HOLOGRAM
    With all due respect to you as the case agent, I would like to take a moment to go on record as saying that I think Special Agent Vance lacks experience for this assignment. I know I don't need to tell you that this is a particularly sensitive assignment, due to ██

██

Although I respectfully disagree with your decision, I understand that I was removed from the operation because I did not establish an effective rapport with the subjects in my brief tenure on this case. While I realize that Vance's youth is an asset in terms of rapport, I believe her inexperience is a significant liability. Perhaps I could work directly with Vance on this assignment, as a mentor of sorts.

To: Special Agent ██████████
From: Special Agent Rafferty
Re: Re: ASSIGNMENT OF NEW AGENT TO OPERATION HOLOGRAM

My decision is final and closed for discussion. Mentorship is out of the question. I want you strictly behind the scenes.

Chapter 3

The next morning, Yolanda put on her running clothes. She jogged three miles uphill to the college, and the path around the perimeter would be another four miles.

By the time she flashed her alumni ID at the gate, she was loose and sweating. Her body recalled the shape of the perimeter path that she had run nearly every morning for four years.

In New York and even New Jersey, she had run on treadmills and urban concrete, but this was her favorite: clean air, dappled shade, and year-round green. A gated women's college with no catcallers. Few men on campus other than faculty and staff.

As she came around a curve, she easily passed a trio of middle-aged women in sweat suits. She continued up the slight incline and past the large oak tree. Ahead, she could see a few joggers. She would overtake the pair of young Asian girls in a couple of minutes, but the black woman far ahead might be trouble.

Yolanda put on a burst of speed and caught up to the two girls, just as the she hit the bridge over the creek. She crossed it in three long bounds. *Eat! My! Dust!* She thought, as her footfalls echoed off the wooden planks.

At the top of the next hill, the field stretched out ahead of her. In the distance sat the president's residence, a white Victorian with a wraparound porch and colorful garden.

Ahead on the path, she noticed the black woman jogger was tall and muscular. Yolanda matched her strides to the other woman in time and length. As she sped up, she felt a satisfying burn in her muscles, and slowly closed the gap between them.

Yolanda focused on the far distance. The woman became a blur of white tank top, blue shorts, black afro, and dark brown skin in her vision, a spot she needed to run past.

As Yolanda edged closer, a cluster of young women came jogging in the other direction. The black girl didn't even hear Yolanda come up behind her, and didn't see her until she had passed. Yolanda put on a burst of speed to open a strong lead and then settled into her rhythm.

Nearly five minutes later, she could hear running footfalls behind her. She assumed it was the black girl.

Yolanda accelerated to keep her lead, but the girl sped up accordingly. The footfalls seemed to be gaining.

Yolanda didn't break her rhythm to turn around. Still, the footsteps gained. As they came around the curve behind the faculty housing, nearly the halfway point of the four miles, Yolanda needed to be careful. This girl was clearly a strong runner, and Yolanda couldn't risk sprinting here and losing her wind for the next two miles.

Whenever Yolanda picked up her pace, the other girl matched her. Finally, as they passed the faculty housing, and the path drew closer to the road, a car went by and the girl passed her at a sprint. She'll run herself out, Yolanda thought. Either that or she's done with her run. But at ten or so yards ahead, the girl slowed down considerably.

But when the jogger turned around, Yolanda almost stumbled. Her adversary was a man. A rarity on Cartwright's campus, and Yolanda didn't think she'd seen a black man in the entire four years she attended the school.

He began to jog backwards, smiling at her. "Well?" he asked. "Are you just gonna let me beat you?"

Yolanda blinked, wiping sweat from her eyes.

"Oh come on," he said. "Don't pretend we haven't been racing for that last mile."

"Sorry, I can't hear you," Yolanda touched her ear and shook her head.

He slowed down a little bit to get closer and spoke in a louder voice: "I said," he began, still jogging backwards. "Don't pretend—" He turned around to look behind him.

In the second he turned, Yolanda opened up into a full-out sprint, and passed him as he was turning around. He sped up and nearly caught up with her, staying just close enough to be within earshot of her panting voice.

"This is a really hard pace to maintain," he gasped. "Most people can't keep this up."

"Especially if they're talking," Yolanda tossed over her shoulder.

"How far are you running?" he asked.

"Front gate," she managed between breaths.

"It's on, then!" he shot forward, and Yolanda was barely able to hold on to her lead. They had another half-mile to go.

When they came around the corner, and the front gate swam into view, each put in an all-out effort. He was taller, but she had better training, and they crossed the gate side-by-side, with Yolanda slightly in front.

"Great run," he said, still panting as they slowed down to a trot. "What's your name?"

"Yolanda," she said, still trying to catch her breath.

"Olujimi," he said, putting a hand on his chest. "Pleasure racing with you."

She searched his voice for a West African accent to match the name, but couldn't detect one.

"Too bad you lost," he said.

"In your dreams," Yolanda said, laughing as she jogged out the gate.

Olujimi had picked up a towel off the fence and was wiping the sweat from his face. His dark skin was clear and he had a fantastic smile. "Feel free to come back for a rematch," he called across the fence. "I run most days around noon."

Yolanda shrugged as she jogged across the street. She could feel him watching her, but resisted the urge to turn around. She smiled all the way home.

Chapter 4

At one AM, the bar that had formerly been Netta's High Class Hideaway was shutting down. The bartender, a black woman in her fifties, came out to smoke on the back stoop. It wasn't even a stoop, just a concrete block with a low railing and three steps down. She'd hoped to close early, but that one insistent drunk needed to tell her all about his problems with his wife over rounds of watery beer. As near as she could tell from the story, it was really his ex-wife, but this fact hadn't yet sunk in.

Before she could even light a cigarette, her breath looked like smoke in the icy air. She lit up and could feel her body relax as the smoke hit her lungs. As she inhaled, she heard something skittering over near the dumpster. Fucking rats. But as she looked down into the alley, she saw something much bigger. A huddled form slumped against the building next door.

A homeless person? She took another lungful of smoke. On cold nights, they slept on the grate to stay warm. She took another drag and peered through the gloom of the alley. The form was so still. Sometimes they huddled under bulky coats or blankets, but not this one. Thin clothes. No rise. No fall.

"Oh Lord." She stubbed out her cigarette and went in to call 911.

When two officers responded an hour later, the bartender had closed up and left, but the figure remained.

Deaver, the older officer, was a beefy-built cop with a ruddy face.

"See?" he told his partner. "Your strongest light source is your headlamps."

Rodriguez nodded. As the rookie and younger partner, he was used to Deaver's running commentary.

"But the dumpster's still casting too many shadows," Deaver said. "So we gotta go in with the flashlights."

In their thick-soled shoes, he and Rodriguez walked down the alley among the rustle of rats. Slowly, Deaver turned his beam to illuminate first a foot, then a leg and a chest with no sign of breathing. Finally, they found themselves looking at an African American woman of indeterminate age. Her hair—a blonde, synthetic weave—fell over her face. She lay on her side, half in and half out of a thin, red sweatshirt, a needle still sticking out of the bare arm that jutted out below her body.

"Heroin OD," Deaver pronounced, and snapped off his light.

"Shouldn't we feel for a pulse?" Rodriguez asked.

"I'm not gonna touch her," Deaver said.

As Rodriguez approached the woman, he could hear Deaver calling the coroner. The woman's red sweatshirt clashed with the trendy green shirt and name brand jeans with glossy green trim on the front pockets. If not for the needle, she would have looked like a discarded Christmas mannequin in red and green with the gold hair. Rodriguez dutifully put two fingers under her nostrils. He felt nothing but still night air.

Turning away from Deaver, he crossed himself.

"What'd I tell you?" Deaver asked. "We'd get these all the time when this place was a shooting gallery."

Deaver rattled on about Holloway Avenue twenty years before. While they waited, Rodriguez angled the flashlight beam so he could see the face under the curtain of hair. She was younger than he had originally thought, and her soft, unlined face was distorted in a grimace of pain.

"I've never seen a heroin OD before," Rodriguez said. "But shouldn't she look . . . peaceful?"

Deaver looked at the face. "Who knows with these junkies? Sometimes they realize they're about to OD, but it's not like they can get the stuff back out of their veins."

Rodriguez shut off the light, and the woman's face was again bathed in shadow.

The image unsettled Rodriguez: lips pulled taut, showing nicotine-stained teeth, her light brown contact lenses staring up, glassy and opaque.

Rodriguez had seen several dead bodies on the force, all shootings of young black men. He never got used to seeing the dead, always crossed himself. But he'd gotten used to the rhythm of homicide investigations: cordoning off the area, questioning witnesses, seeing the forensics team gather evidence.

Half an hour later, the coroner came. He put on a latex glove to touch her neck for a nanosecond and declared her "dead several hours."

No one bothered to take photographs or inspect the scene before they loaded her into the coroner's van. As the white doors banged shut, Rodriguez couldn't get the woman's face, the howling mouth of pain, out of his mind.

Chapter 5

The next evening, Yolanda mapped her 1.2 mile walk to the Red, Black and GREEN! community meeting. Her block was alive with young people talking and laughing in the warm weather. In front of the bungalow next door, a young man murmured insistently on a cell phone, while a young woman on the porch cornrowed a preschool boy's hair.

The block dead-ended into Holloway Avenue, and had a bustling liquor store at the corner. A cluster of young men stood around. One of them said, "baby got ass for days," as a pair of young women strutted past. The girls grinned, but another young woman huddled into her jacket and darted inside, steeled against the "hey, why don't you smile?"

At the next corner, passengers stepped off the #17 bus. A young mother struggled to get her stroller down onto the sidewalk, and a man in a mechanic's uniform leaped up to help. An older woman stepped off the bus, her back advertised SPIC N' SPAN CLEANING OF POINT RICHMOND. A pair of girls in Holloway High athletic uniforms sped off the bus, dribbling a basketball.

As RBG's church came into view, Yolanda began scanning the faces, looking for subjects to match with the names and photos of key members from the file. She saw only blacks and Latinos. *Latinxs,* she reminded herself to stay current. Although one pale young woman might possibly be white. The girl had sandy brown hair oiled and pulled back in a tight ponytail and hoop earrings.

As Yolanda approached the storefront church, she saw RBG had planted raised beds in all the curb strips on the block. Kale and tomato plants.

A burst of laughter erupted from the knot of teenagers on the street. A young man smoked a cigarette, and a young woman pushed him, playfully. He staggered back to catch himself, and the cigarette's ash fell onto the sidewalk, scattering among the blackened gum spots and broken glass.

"Look what that fool messaged me," one young woman said, brandishing her phone.

A twinge of anxious nostalgia hit Yolanda. She had never been the teen girl in that knot. She casually surveyed the faces. None of them matched the photos she had been studying so carefully. Over the last twenty-four hours, she had watched the video over and over without sound and listened to the audio without visuals to memorize the voices. She made the photos into flash cards, with profiles written onto sticky notes on the back.

She had memorized the broad planes of the group leader's face and the words on the canary yellow sticky note:

Marcus Winters
40 years old
divorced
two sons and a daughter
former union organizer
teenage participant in the Black Radical Congress
former member of the Communist Party
high school dropout
never attended college

Yolanda wondered how he could lead an organization with no degree. She had highlighted this fact on the bottom of the sticky note. Like in her high school senior year. For the championship basketball game, she posted the article about the other team captain's ankle injury. Yolanda wanted to remind herself that she was the strong one, uninjured, victory imminent. Yolanda had marched into the game confident, and her school had won.

On the wall was a poster with the title SAY THEIR NAMES, and a long list of hundreds of black people killed by police, and the years they had died. At the bottom was an ellipsis (. . .) letting people know that the list would only grow. The poster had been made a couple years previously. Someone had taken a marker and written "DEFUND POLICE."

Yolanda recognized one of the printed names in particular. Dante Clark. He, along with Kisha James and Michael Lawson, were the three teens that the police had shot back in Georgia during her childhood. Dante Clark had always been a notorious case, because the officers managed to shoot him over thirty times in the back while he was allegedly threatening them with a knife that was never found.

As a kid, she had always taken her father's word for their innocence, for the police's guilt. But in eighth grade, she'd done a google search on another topic and the name of her hometown had popped up by coincidence. She found a number of articles that painted a very different picture of the shot teens. Yolanda's father had conjured images of child angels lying in the coffins with their wings folded over them. The newspaper articles revealed a mug shot of Dante Clark, who had actually been nearly twenty at the time of the shooting, and had been in juvenile hall for disturbing the peace, auto theft, and assault. There were two arrests of the underage Michael Lawson for selling drugs, although no convictions.

And Kisha James had been arrested for trespassing, shoplifting, and smoking marijuana. In that moment, Yolanda reevaluated everything she had thought about her father. He hadn't been a crusader for justice in the community. He'd been a charlatan who had taken advantage of a community that wanted someone to blame for their problems. She saw it every day around her in middle school in Detroit. Kids who didn't apply themselves. Were always whining and wanted handouts. No work ethic. So these three kids had been hoodlums, like the boys who grabbed her behind in the hallways at school, or the girls who called her a stuck-up bitch because she was in advanced classes, or raised her hand in class when she knew the answer.

When she was a little girl watching her father preach, she had no idea how black teens acted, but now she knew all too well. Why did people make excuses for these kids? In middle school, she saw how her peers mouthed off to the principal, to the security guards at the school. She watched them get into fights. Cuss out teachers. They didn't seem to care. If those black teens had gotten shot in Georgia, she wasn't going to say that they deserved to die, but if you get belligerent with a white cop with a loaded gun, what do you expect?

"Is you new here?" a young voice asked. Yolanda returned from her recollection to see a boy of about eight standing in front of her.

Yolanda had prepared her explanation for a teenager. How young were these kids gonna be? "I saw a flyer," she said. "I thought I'd come check it out."

"What starts with F and ends with U-C-K?" the boy asked.

"Excuse me?" Yolanda asked.

A teenage girl grabbed the kid. "I told you not to bother anybody." Yolanda recognized the thickset, light-skinned girl as Sheena McHale. "You supposed to be doing your homework with Carlos." Sheena turned him around and gave him a push toward the far end of the room. "Go find him."

The boy walked off, dragging his feet, then turned suddenly. "Fire truck!" he said, grinning at Yolanda. "Fire truck starts with F and ends in U-C-K!"

Yolanda smiled back, and he disappeared into the crowd.

"Sorry about my little brother," Sheena said. "I'm supposed to be the welcoming committee, not him. I'm Sheena."

"Yolanda Vance," she said, and they shook. FBI agents often used an alias, but since Yolanda was there as a Cartwright graduate, she needed to use her real name.

"It wasn't such a bad joke," Yolanda said.

Sheena rolled her eyes. "At least he can spell," she said, and handed Yolanda a flyer. "Ten Things I Hate About Randell Corporation."

As Sheena greeted an older black couple, Yolanda drifted along with the sparse crowd into the storefront church sanctuary. Rows of folding chairs lined the battered linoleum floor. The only remarkable feature was the stained-glass Black Jesus that she had seen from the street. Yolanda found a seat where she could see the entire room. She spotted most of the teenagers from the file, but not Winters. Several teens were setting up a flip chart and a video camera. Yolanda checked her watch. 7:05. When were they going to start?

Yolanda kept her eye on the group's teen leader, Dana Whitfield. At 7:30, Dana tapped on the microphone. By then, the room was packed with people, about half were high school age. A few minutes before, Marcus Winters had rushed in, bicycle helmet in one hand, briefcase in the other. His light-skinned face was flushed, and his right pant leg was held up in a strap.

He had put on weight since the video had been taken in the fall. His belly and face were slightly fuller, and his eyes looked puffy.

Several other adults drifted in, and Yolanda realized with a start that she knew one of the women. Kenya, a tall woman with extension braids and an African-print jumpsuit. They had played basketball together at Cartwright. And then they had run into each other in New York.

Yolanda opened her mouth to call to Kenya when a sudden memory made her breath catch. She had seen Kenya at her favorite blues club. Maybe six months ago. Kenya was in New York for vacation, and they'd had a couple drinks. Lester Johnakin said never to keep good news a secret. Yolanda was feeling very good news about her recently acquired job in New Jersey. At the time, she wasn't on any track to work undercover. She had told Kenya about the drama with Van Dell, Meyers and Whitney, and that she'd bounced back with a great new job. As an attorney. She didn't say FBI, but she definitely said something about working for the government. That would be sufficient to blow her cover.

Yolanda shrank back. She couldn't let Kenya see her.

Slowly, she retreated toward the rear of the sanctuary, putting as much distance between herself and her former classmate as possible. She leaned against the back wall, slouching into her sweatshirt. Then she ran her fingers through her hair, combing it forward on the side that faced Kenya, obscuring her cheek and the line of her jaw.

Through a curtain of hair, she saw that Kenya was sitting with two other black women she didn't recognize. Yolanda was still focused on them when she heard the thud of tapping on a microphone.

"Good evening everybody," Dana spoke into the microphone. Her shoulder-length hair was in dreadlocks, pulled back from her heart-shaped face. She wore jeans and a "Red, Black and GREEN!" t-shirt. Unlike Winters, she looked more vibrant than in the video, more confident. Yolanda noted that Winters hadn't briefed her beforehand. Dana had sat laughing with friends, until Winters arrived and gave Dana a thumbs-up from across the room.

"We all know why we're here tonight," Dana began. "Because our community deserves better. Because, in the words of Fannie Lou Hamer, 'we're sick and tired of being sick and tired.'"

A murmur of approval rose in the church.

"How many of you know at least one person with cancer?"

All the hands in the audience went up.

"I know more than just one," a young man called out.

"So we're sick of being sick," Dana said. "And how many of you, or your folks, have to travel at least an hour to get to and from work every day?"

The majority of the adults' hands shot up. Yolanda noticed Kenya's two friends put their hands up.

"And that's if we're lucky enough to even have a job," Dana said. "When the recession hit, it hit our community hard. But why aren't there jobs right here in Holloway? Jobs for *us*. Because a certain company moved in promising thousands of jobs." The congregation murmured its agreement. "And they brought jobs. For white people who don't even live here."

Yolanda had coached kids like that during college. They sneered at her because she went to Cartwright. "Success," she had always told them, "is not just a white thing."

Dana went on: "So these white professionals drive through our town, on an overpass built specially for them, running over our neighborhoods, over our broke-down schools, speeding through our town like a fast-food drive-through. Yes, I'd like a one hundred thousand dollar a year job with full benefits please. Can you supersize that?"

A ripple of laughter ran through the church.

"Oh, wait a minute," Dana said. "My bad. We did get some jobs. One of my cousins works in the mailroom. I bet the maintenance crew looks like us. Too bad nobody in my family is qualified to be a chemical engineer or a data analyst."

"Then the pandemic hit," Dana went on. "And those Randell employees could work from home while they sheltered in place. But our people didn't get those jobs. Nope. Our people were essential workers who had to travel at least an hour on public transportation to clean hospitals in San Francisco. Our people already had high asthma rates from the air quality in our city. Our people already had diabetes from the food deserts that we live in."

Murmurs of agreement from the room.

Dana nodded. "And how many of you know at least one person who died from COVID?"

Again, all the hands went up.

"So our people were the ones dying, while the employees at Randell who live in cozy white suburbs worked from home." She banged a hand on the podium. "Randell has been here twenty years! They could have set up programs to prepare us for those jobs. How dare you set up shop here and not create one job training program. Not donate a single dollar to the science department at our high school. Not a cent for professional development for people who live a block from your mega lab. They don't even bother to send their listings to the employment counseling office in Holloway. And this crooked city administration gave them the world's sweetest deal. They get cheap land, a freeway, a place to dump their toxic waste, and don't have to pay a cent in taxes. As far as I can see, that lab is a big middle finger to our community. And it's not enough to have a handful of custodian jobs—"

"And they killed my grandbaby!" a white-haired woman yelled from the middle of the church. "She was a janitor, and they killed her!"

At the mic, Dana faltered.

"They killed her!" the woman yelled, skirting the edge of shrillness.

Eyes wide, Dana shrugged and motioned with upturned palms for Marcus Winters to help.

"Sister," Winters said, rising from his seat. His voice was loud enough to carry without the microphone. "Would you like to testify about what happened with your granddaughter?"

"That's why I came to this meeting tonight," the woman insisted. She stood up, waving an arthritic hand with each word. "The police won't tell me nothing. They say she was on drugs, but I know they a lie."

"Can you come to the microphone?" Winters asked.

"I don't need no microphone," she said. "I'm just gon' say what I told the police. And they couldn't give me no answers."

One of the adults from the file photos approached the woman. A black woman in her fifties with long dreadlocks. Yolanda identified her as Sharon Martinez.

"Tell us about your granddaughter," Sharon said.

"Her name was Anitra," the woman said, her dark brown face crumpling as she held back tears. "She was a good girl. Didn't get into no trouble til a few years back. I know she was smoking that crack cocaine, but she didn't never steal or nothing. Put her own self in treatment. How they gonna say she still using drugs? I'm telling you, my baby was clean from them drugs almost two years. They a lie. They a goddamn lie."

The woman's face blazed as she spoke, jabbing a finger into the air for emphasis. Her red polyester blouse was buttoned incorrectly, leaving a gap through which her bra flashed white.

"Who said she was using drugs?" Sharon asked.

"The police," the woman insisted angrily. "They said it was a heron overdose. Ain't no overdose. She didn't never even use heron."

Heron? Yolanda figured that must be slang for heroin.

Marcus Winters now stood at the podium, beside Dana. "Sister," he asked the elderly woman. "What's your name?"

"Mrs. Dorothea Jenkins," she said, sucking her teeth as if he should have already known.

"Sister Jenkins, we're gonna help you get justice with Randell," Winters promised, then turned to the crowd. "This is why we need to have these community forums, because nobody else is telling the truth about what Randell is doing in our community."

Yolanda saw a look pass between Winters and Sharon Martinez.

"Sister Jenkins," Winters went on, "I'm gonna put you in the capable hands of our group's Wellness Coordinator to get the whole story."

He turned to the audience. "How many people want to know the truth about what happened to Mrs. Jenkins's granddaughter?"

The crowd roared back that they did. Sharon escorted Mrs. Jenkins to the aisle.

"We got you, Sister Jenkins!" somebody called after her.

"How many people want to know the truth about what other dirt Randell is doing in our community, dirt that our own young people have dug up?"

The crowd shouted its encouragement.

"All right," Winters said, nodding his approval. "I'm gonna turn it back over to Dana Whitfield, spokesperson for Red, Black and GREEN!"

As Dana took the mic, Yolanda looked back to where Kenya had been sitting, but suddenly couldn't see her. She glanced around, and saw Kenya walking up the aisle, directly toward her. Reflexively, Yolanda pulled the drawstring to the hoodie, and the fabric contracted over her face, leaving mostly just the lock of forward-combed hair visible. She must look ridiculous. But hopefully more like an antisocial teenager than a former classmate who was now working for the FBI.

Kenya strolled up the aisle, her eyes roaming over the crowd. Yolanda could see the exact moment when Kenya's eyes swept around to her, and the split second when her eyes moved on, unrecognizing.

Her ex-teammate walked past, asking the teen at the door which way to the restroom.

Yolanda stayed in her spot, just inside the door, listening both to the kids on stage, and the two women in the hallway outside.

Mrs. Jenkins was crying quietly now, and Yolanda could hear the occasional murmur of comfort from Sharon.

"She was doing so good," Mrs. Jenkins choked out. "She got that job at Randell and look like she was gonna be all right. Her brother in jail, so I just prayed. My whole church praying for them and then she got clean, but now they say they found her with a needle in her arm?"

A burst of laughter in the sanctuary drowned out the rest of her words, and Yolanda looked toward the podium to see two teenagers with a flip chart.

She recognized both from the video. The girl, Nakeesha, had on a glossy black sweater over a pair of tight jeans. Carlos, a Latino kid, wore a button down plaid shirt over dark pants.

"So this," Carlos said, pointing to the taller of the two black bars on a graph "is the total amount of emissions caused by a single gallon of fossil fuel gas, but this," he indicated another bar that was barely visible, "this is the amount of emissions from a gallon of Randell Lab's designer 'Emerald Standard Fuel.'"

"Looks good, right?" Nakeesha said. "Like they really doing something for the planet, right?"

"It's what they call a renewable biodiesel fuel," Carlos said.

"And Randell been going around advertising they gone green," Nakeesha said. "Commercials with pictures of trees and grass. Celebrities driving they cars through mountains with this gas. But as usual, the only green Randell really cares about is money."

"Because this is the real environmental impact of Emerald Standard Fuel," Carlos said. He took a red marker and made the second bar on the graph nearly as tall as the first one. "They collect some of the biofuel sources in the United States. But they don't want to pay US real estate prices or US construction prices to build the refinery. Or pay US workers minimum wage to work in the refinery."

"So instead they ship the fuel all the way to the fuel refinery they built in Southeast Asia, y'all," Nakeesha said. "Then they refine it and ship it all the way back. And they don't use renewable fuels for all that shipping."

"So the celebrities in their commercials aren't lying that their biodiesel Mercedes is burning a hundred percent clean fuel," Carlos said. "But the amount of fossil fuels that are getting burned to produce that clean fuel is ultimately the same as if they had just gotten regular gas."

"And this is what we trying to bring home to y'all," Nakeesha said. "Even when Randell looks like they trying to do the right thing, they still up on something fraudulent. Not only did they admit to dumping toxic waste in our neighborhoods, they also destroying the planet with products that pretend to be fighting the climate crisis."

"And that's the bottom line," Carlos said. "These shady corporations are never going to be the solution to the climate emergency. We need to let Indigenous people and frontline affected communities of color take the lead. The solutions have been clear for years: keep these fossil fuels in the ground. Transition into clean energy like solar power, wind power, consume less, and stop destroying the trees and mangrove swamps and wetlands and other natural ways the earth already has of getting carbon emissions out of the air."

"She what?" Sharon's sharp voice cut through the presentation of the two teens, and Yolanda tuned back into the conversation on the other side of the wall.

"It was all up her arm," Mrs. Jenkins said.

"That's not possible," Sharon said. "We'll definitely look into it."

At that point, Mrs. Jenkins began to cry again. "You lose your baby," she sobbed. "And you know it ain't right, and you gotta fight wit' so many folks but you jus keep on going til somebody finally listens and when they do, you stop fighting for a minute and you realize that she's gone."

Kenya walked back in and headed down the aisle to her seat. Yolanda looked at the floor and held her breath as she passed.

"My grandbaby's gone." Mrs. Jenkins said from the hallway.

Loud applause broke out in the sanctuary, drowning out the elderly woman.

By the time Yolanda could hear her again, Mrs. Jenkins's crying had turned to gasps and hiccups.

"Thank you," Nakeesha was saying at the front of the room, as she bowed grandly.

"And, thanks to our teacher, Jimmy Thomson," Carlos added.

"We love you, Jimmy," Nakeesha waved to the camera as they stepped away from the podium.

The rest of the evening consisted of teenagers complaining about Randell. While Yolanda had found the case against Emerald Standard Fuel compelling, the complaints had the opposite effect.

Yolanda had been in a bad situation, too. She was poor as

a kid. She went to a terrible school in Detroit. But what did she do? She worked hard and got a scholarship to a boarding school. And she bounced back from Van Dell, Meyers and Whitney. Bad situations didn't have to define you. You want better, so you do better.

After the meeting broke up, a crush of people moved toward the exit. Yolanda kept an eye on Kenya, who was chatting with her two friends.

"So what did you think?" Sheena, the teen from the welcome committee asked Yolanda.

"I had no idea all that was going on here," Yolanda said. Kenya was getting her purse and heading up the aisle.

"I've got another riddle!" Sheena's brother said, coming up to them.

Swiftly, Yolanda knelt down beside him, turning her back to Kenya.

"What's long and hard and full of semen?" the little boy asked.

"Boy, if you don't—!" Sheena grabbed his arm and looked down at Yolanda. "A submarine."

"Why you gotta spoil my joke?" he asked.

"You are such a little pervert," Sheena steered him out through the door.

Yolanda lingered inside, trying to make sure that Kenya would be gone. She followed some of the last stragglers out. In front of the church, the crowd had thinned. Mrs. Jenkins was gone, and there was no sign of Kenya.

Marcus honked the horn of a van parked in front, as a dozen teens piled in. "Come on guys, I wanna get to bed."

Yolanda hurried down the church steps and turned onto Holloway Avenue. Not until she closed the apartment door did she stop looking over her shoulder, convinced that Kenya would appear behind her, calling her name.

She emailed a report to Rafferty that she had identified every single face from the file, and she reported the development with Mrs. Jenkins. Then she went online to find out more about Kenya.

Her former teammate apparently had just started teaching history and coaching girls' basketball at the middle school in Holloway.

Not good.

Part 2

Chapter 6

The following day, Yolanda ran up to Cartwright. Before she left the apartment, she checked the location of the middle school where Kenya taught and steered clear of it on her route. By 12:15, she was jogging through the gates. Olujimi said noon. She wanted to give him a head start, and still beat him.

About halfway around the path she saw him. How had she ever mistaken him for a woman? Broad shoulders, narrow hips, high butt, long sinewy legs. He jogged with his shirt off today.

She stalked him, keeping her distance. He had a rhythm going—graceful, hypnotic. When they were fifty yards from the finish, on a softer patch of ground that would make less noise, she sprinted by him.

"What the—!" she heard his bark of indignation as she streaked past.

He pushed for an all-out run, but she had been preparing for this, was in the zone, unruffled, and beat him, undeniably, by at least a couple yards.

Afterwards, she extended her hand for a high five, her eyes avoiding his sweat-soaked chest.

"Good race," she said with a grin.

"More like crooked race," Olujimi reached toward her

hand, but instead of slapping her five, he held it for a moment. "So you know I demand a rematch, right?"

"What?" she feigned innocence. "I beat you fair and square." Extracting her hand, she began to walk along the path to cool down.

"You snuck up on me," he said.

"You should be more aware of your surroundings," she said. "You got too comfortable here on the Cartwright campus."

"You deliberately jogged in my blind spot," he said.

"You had a huge head start," she said. "I not only beat you, but made better time."

"Fine," he said. "Next time we need to set a start time, and start together."

"Okay," she accepted the challenge.

"How about tomorrow at seven?" he said.

"In the morning?" she asked.

He shook his head. "At night. After a pre-race dinner. To discuss rules, governance, etcetera."

"Uh," she faltered. "I don't—I mean—I shouldn't—"

His face fell. "Oh God, you're not an undergraduate here, are you? That would be really inappropriate."

Yolanda laughed. "Not for years," she said. "I'm a Cartwright alum." She explained about the law firm in San Francisco and studying for the bar.

"You don't want to go into corporate law," he urged her. "Who needs all that money and power when you could be a broke but heroic college professor like me?"

"You're too late to dissuade me. I've already accepted the position." She shrugged.

"It's never too late. You could sabotage," he said. "You know, intentionally fail the bar."

Yolanda laughed so hard she nearly snorted.

"Corporate lawyers are a bunch of crooks," he said. "How about that scandal with Van Dell, Meyers and Whitney?"

"Point taken," she said. "That was my first job out of law school, which explains why I'm in California now."

"Well, if corporate law did you wrong, how you gonna come back for more punishment?"

"I don't like to lose," she said.

Olujimi smiled. "Well, now that I've determined you're not a student, I can tell you very directly how much I'd love to take you out sometime."

"I'm flattered," Yolanda said. "And you're very attractive yourself, but I'm not . . ." she shrugged, unsure what to say. "I'm not really in a position to date right now."

"You're married?"

"No."

"Boyfriend?" She shook her head. "Girlfriend?"

"No, I just—I'm studying for the bar, and can't really handle any—distractions."

"Okay," he smiled. "Well, when you pass the bar, I hope you'll let me take you out to celebrate and distract you."

She shrugged noncommittally. "I'll think about it."

In the distance, the tower bells chimed.

"I gotta go catch a shower so I can make it to class," he said reluctantly. "I hope I'll at least see you again here on campus."

"Bet on it," Yolanda grinned, as she walked away, then called to him. "I can take time from studying to deliver a few ass whippings."

"Just wait, little girl," he said. "I'm gonna take my vitamins before I see you again."

She jogged out the front gate feeling buzzed, competitive, and sexy. Like the middle school basketball coach she'd been determined to impress. This set up worked well for her: the motivational crush.

Red, Black and GREEN! held its regular Sunday meetings in the church basement as opposed to the sanctuary. A flight of stairs led down to a large, low-ceilinged room with a worn linoleum floor. A few small, dingy, high windows were dark in the early winter evening. Several naked fluorescents illuminated the room with a blue-white glow, though half the tubes were burnt out.

The large circle of seats in the center consisted of raggedy sofas, worn office chairs with broken wheels, and a piano bench.

An institutional kitchen gleamed through an open door on one side.

Suddenly, a flash of childhood memory blossomed in Yolanda's mind: Sunday dinners in a church basement. Sitting on her mother's lap. Long tables with plastic tablecloths and brown faces eating chicken and yams. Yolanda blinked away the memory. She hadn't lived in Georgia in twenty years. But as the brown faces drifted into the basement meeting, one part of her mind began to recognize certain Southern inflections in speech.

"I'm so glad you could make it!" Sheena McHale approached Yolanda. She had a bright pink streak in her long curly hair today, and it matched her pink sweat suit and sneakers. "Let me show you around," Sheena said.

Sheena led Yolanda to an open door in the opposite wall from the kitchen. "This is our office. It's a mess, like always."

The windowless, one-room office had a long folding table in the center, covered with papers, books, and fast food wrappers. Two mismatched desks stood chairless, one with an old Mac on it and the other a desktop PC. The Latino teen sat on a milk crate in front of the PC, playing a video game where a ball hit different bubbles and sent jewels cascading down.

Sheena dug through a pile on the table, pulling out several booklets, and handing them to Yolanda.

"Carlos," Sheena said. "You know Marcus doesn't like anybody to play on his computer."

"I keep his computer alive," Carlos said. "I'm above the law here."

"All our stuff is hella broke down," Sheena said. "We have two computers because only one has internet." She pointed to the PC that Carlos was playing on. "This one is supposed to be just for Marcus. He keeps all the program files on there and the teens are not supposed to use it." She looked pointedly at Carlos, but he seemed oblivious to all but the computer game. A gold bubble hit something, and shimmering rubies flew all over the screen.

A pile of sleeping bags sat against the far wall.

"So much work out of this little office." Yolanda said.

"Marcus meets with Planet Greener every month," Sheena said, as she walked Yolanda back out to the circle of chairs. "But we pretty much do our own thing."

"I can't wait to read these newsletters," Yolanda said. The group's brochure had been in the file, and she'd read it twice. The newsletters were new.

"I've got an article in one of those," Sheena said brightly. "It's—Darnell!" Sheena turned abruptly from Yolanda. "Darnell, you better give me back my five dollars!" She stalked off after him.

The meeting was supposed to begin at six PM. Yolanda sat facing the door. If Kenya came in, there'd be nowhere to hide in this intimate setting.

By 6:20, the crowd had grown to about twenty-five people, mostly teens. As Yolanda waited, she tried reading the two newsletters. Sheena's article was on violence in the media. Yolanda kept looking from the page to the door, certain Kenya would come in and her cover would be blown.

The snatches of the articles she read just irritated her. These kids complained about everything from police brutality to poor quality schools. But the Bay Area had tons of prep schools. Smart kids like Dana or Sheena could get scholar-

ships. As for violence in the media, if they didn't like what
was on TV, they should turn it off.

The meeting finally started at 6:32. The seats were full,
and latecomers had to pull out folding chairs. At that point,
Kenya probably wasn't coming, but Yolanda couldn't relax.

Dana sat next to Nakeesha on the couch, its orange plaid
upholstery fraying, exposing foam stuffing. The bright fabric
of the young women's clothing seemed incongruous against
the faded orange background. Dana had on an Indonesian
batik blouse in shades of purple over her jeans, and Nakeesha wore a bright blue top with sparkling blue nails to
match.

A flip chart had the question, "What brought you here?"
Everyone was supposed to share their answers briefly with
their neighbors.

"Nakeesha," Dana turned to the girl on the couch next to
Yolanda. "Can you model what it means to share briefly?"

"Not your whole life story, y'all," Nakeesha said. "Like I
might say, my name is Nakeesha, and I'm a Scorpio, and I'm
single," she said smiling. "But for real, I joined because too
many of my friends have got shot over stupid shit, and
school's a waste of my time. Red, Black and GREEN! is the
only good thing happening in Holloway. Except for me being
single again."

"Thank you," Dana said. "Like I would say my name is
Dana, and I joined Red, Black and GREEN! because it was
the only place adults really listened to what I had to say and
took me seriously. So you have a minute to share with your
neighbor."

Yolanda turned to Nakeesha, but she had paired up with
another teenager. She turned to find the young man Darnell
on her other side, who was partnered up with Marcus.

"Hey sister, join us," Marcus said. "I'm Marcus Winters
and I joined Red, Black and GREEN! because I wanted my
kids—wanted all kids—to have a climate on earth that is fit

for human habitation, and I wanted to support young people of color, the folks with the most at stake in the future of our planet, to be active in fighting for climate justice. In other words, I was born by the river in a little tent."

Confusion must have shown in Yolanda's face.

"Sam Cooke," Darnell said. "It's been a long time coming, but he knows his change is gonna come."

"We have this running commentary with soul music lyrics," Marcus said.

Yolanda smiled and nodded. When it was her turn, she offered her name and her well-rehearsed speech: "I recently moved back to Holloway. I'm really concerned about the climate crisis and I've heard a lot of bad things about Randell Corp. But I'm new to all this, so mostly I'll be listening."

After the partner check-in, Sharon Martinez stood up in the center of the circle.

She was the "wellness coordinator" who had spoken with Mrs. Jenkins. According to the file, she had gone to UC Berkeley, which explained her hippie style skirt and blouse. Although she had dreadlocks, her hair had a wavy texture, and around the edges were loose curls that had escaped from the locks.

"Welcome everyone," she began. "We're gonna start with meditation."

Yolanda had a sudden recollection: the smell of incense drifting into the hallway. Walking into the house, elbow and knee scraped from falling off her bike. She was maybe ten? Eleven?

"Close your eyes, put your feet flat on the floor," Sharon said, her voice low and lulling.

The bike had been Yolanda's best friend in the entire state of Colorado. Yolanda would ride out to the desert, pretending she was on an uninhabited island, or another planet.

"Feel the breath in your chest, your nose, the back of your throat."

That day, she had ridden far from home, and down a street past two white boys. When she looped back by, one of them poked a stick into the spokes of her back wheel. As she'd fallen into the dust, the stick had broken. She had gotten back up on the bike as they approached.

"Exhaling all the stress and tension, all the frustration and conflicts of the day."

Yolanda had fought, hit one of them with the stick and ran into the other with the bike. She rode home, the bent spoke making a whirring sound as the back wheel of the bike wobbled beneath her.

"And breathing in. Breathing in abundance, ease, peace, compassion."

She had run into the house, bleeding, tears running down her dusty cheeks. The incense smell greeted her. Through the door to the bedroom, she could see her mother's broad back, red and orange blouse, soft material flowing over her mother's iced coffee-colored shoulders. Her mother chanting: "*Nam-Myoho-Renge-Kyo,*" over and over, so fast that Yolanda couldn't make out any of the words. She learned at some point that it was supposed to mean "Devotion to the Mystic Law of the Lotus Sutra," but in her mother's mouth it translated to, "Don't bother me while I'm meditating."

"Keeping the focus on the breath. When you notice yourself drifting, no judgment, just bring your awareness back."

Yolanda had washed her scraped limbs with alcohol and bit down on the sting.

"Meditation is about being present in the moment. About awareness. Noticing. Noticing your breath."

Her mother didn't even notice the X of bandages on her elbow, the pale shade of flesh tone that didn't match anything on Yolanda's body, except the palms of her hands and the soles of her feet.

Yolanda did her own laundry, washing the blood out of the knee of her jeans.

"So for group introductions tonight, just tell us your name and the city where you were born," Sharon said. "I'll start. Sharon Martinez, and I was born in Mayagüez, Puerto Rico."

Yolanda was surprised. She didn't have an accent. But a lot of the people's birth towns surprised her. Most of the kids were born in nearby towns that had hospitals: Richmond. Vallejo. But the older adults were born in Arkansas or Louisiana. Marcus was born in Brooklyn.

When it was her turn, Yolanda said, "Yolanda Vance. Carson, Georgia."

After the introduction, Dana unveiled the agenda on a flip chart. Yolanda pushed herself to focus.

A "Cancer and COVID Watch" project would collect information on Holloway residents. And their research continued.

"Our last item is Dorothea Jenkins," Dana explained. "About her granddaughter, Anitra." She turned to Sheena.

Sheena nodded, pulling on the two ties in the hood of her pink sweatshirt.

"Me and Sharon met with Mrs. Jenkins," Sheena pulled the ties all the way down and the hood puckered at the back of her neck. She recapped the facts of the granddaughter's death and the reasons Mrs. Jenkins was skeptical. Heroin wasn't Anitra Jenkins's drug of choice, she hated needles, and there had been a sudden abscess.

"What's an abscess?" Darnell asked.

"Kind of like a big cold sore," Sharon said. "But on her arm."

"Uuugh," Nakeesha said.

Sharon said, "People who shoot drugs get them if the drugs or the needles are dirty. It's a bacterial skin infection."

"But Mrs. Jenkins lives with Anitra," Sheena continued. "Grandma would have noticed if she was getting high or if she had a big sore."

"Parents think they know when you're high, but they don't know," Darnell said. Several of the teens laughed, and Nakeesha fist bumped him.

"Anitra was drug tested weekly," Sharon said. "Her test from a few days before came up clean. No one gets an abscess that size, that fast, even if she shot dirty dope right after the test."

"Then what the hell happened?" Nakeesha demanded.

"We don't know," Sharon explained. "She worked the evening custodial shift, five to ten. She didn't come home that night and Mrs. Jenkins got worried."

"Man," Nakeesha said. "I bet they got chemicals in Randell that will fuck you up. Make yo shit come out looking crazy."

"Don't make a joke outta this, Nakeesha," Sheena said. "We sat with Mrs. Jenkins. Her granddaughter is dead."

"So?" Nakeesha said. "My daddy is dead. And I'll joke about his dead ass all I want."

"Come on folks," Sharon said. "Let's stay on task, okay?"

Nakeesha shrugged. Sheena folded her arms across her chest.

"Around one AM," Sharon continued, "the police found her body in an alley behind Netta's."

"Behind the old shooting gallery?" Darnell asked. "Nah. If she want heron, she gotta get it from the Stats. Then why go across town to shoot up in a empty alley?"

"Exactly!" Sheena said.

"So something ain't right here," Marcus Winters said. "And Randell is in the middle of it."

"So we're gonna take action," Sheena said. "Tomorrow at five PM, we're gonna go down to the police station and demand some answers."

After the meeting broke up, Yolanda stood around awkwardly as others clustered to talk.

Next to her, Nakeesha yelled across the room.

"Carlos! Carlos, did you upload the video of our presentation at the forum for Jimmy?"

"You don't need to yell, Nakeesha," he said. "I'm standing right here."

"So did you upload it or what?" she asked.

"Yeah, and I sent him the link," Carlos said.

Yolanda approached the young man.

"Carlos?" she put out her hand. "I'm Yolanda Vance."

He shook her hand mechanically. "Yeah, I saw you at the forum."

"Did I hear you have a video of your presentation? It was great."

"Thanks," he said, not meeting her eyes. "Jimmy really did a lot but couldn't be there. I wanted to record it for him."

"Could you send me the link?" Yolanda asked. "My neighbors really need this information."

"Sure," he said. "I left my phone in the office."

The two of them walked back to the small room. He sat down on the milk crate and opened his phone. For a moment the screen was frozen in his music app. Yolanda made note of the artists: Mos Def, Nishonna, Lupe Fiasco, Deza, Cardi B and Bad Bunny. Apparently, he had also been watching the movie *Ghost Dog*.

Finally, the phone began to respond to his commands.

"Is your air drop on?" he asked.

Yolanda shrugged, and he asked to see her phone.

As he tinkered with the air drop settings, Yolanda pulled a keychain from her pocket with a single key. She dropped it silently onto the worn carpet. Peterson had given it to her as a temporary listening device.

"Yolanda," Sharon said. "I'm glad I caught you. You're Everett Vance's daughter, right? The minister?"

Yolanda gaped at her.

"I did some national organizing about police violence back

in the day," Sharon said. "I even visited Carson, Georgia once. Don't blink or you'll miss it, right?"

"Right," Yolanda said.

"I was sorry to hear about his passing," Sharon said. "He was like Black Lives Matter, years ahead of its time."

Yolanda smiled and nodded, but internally it hit her like a punch to the gut.

"I don't—" Yolanda began. She needed to pull it together. Play it off in front of this woman. "His death hit us hard. I didn't realize anyone here would know him."

"Sorry to bring up a tough subject," Sharon said. "Grief can last a long time. Let me know if you need support."

"No thanks," Yolanda said quickly. "I just don't usually talk about it."

"Of course," Sharon said. "Just glad to know you and I are already connected."

Yolanda felt a tap on her shoulder. "Here's your phone," Carlos said.

Yolanda took it and exited quickly from the office. On her way out, she kicked the key further under the chair.

That night she uploaded the video files for Peterson and Rafferty, and reported that she had dropped the key bug. She didn't mention that Sharon Martinez had known her father.

Chapter 7

Yolanda was five and had just recently come to understand what dead was. Not like sleeping. Your body just stopped working. You didn't breathe. You were gone. There had been a raccoon dead on the road. She had seen dead animals before, but not this close. It wasn't bloody or mangled, but it was so still. Even if it hadn't been in the road, a place where no animal would stop and lie inert, she would have known it was never going to move again.

Two weeks later, the night of her father's car accident, there had been a thunderstorm. The roads were wet and dark. The knocking at the door hadn't woken her, but a wail from her mother had. She came out of the bedroom crying and her mother had picked her up. They had gone to the hospital, and she had clung anxiously to her mother.

The adults around her spoke in hushed tones. *Critical condition. Lucky he's not dead. Jaws of life.* And long, long prayers, during which she dozed off to reassuring words like, "We trust you to hold him in your mighty hands, Lord," and "I claim him completely healed and restored," they said. "Nothing is too difficult for you to fix."

She woke later to whispered voices:

"The sheriffs did this," one of the assistant pastors said.

"He wasn't far from the station. I told him not to go over there without us."

"But that doesn't make sense, Deacon," her mother had said. "If he was coming home from the sheriff's, he would have been headed north on that road, not south . . . are you awake baby?" Her mother had come over then. Patted her back. Soothed her into sleep on the chairs in the waiting room.

And later the voice of the doctor. "He did show an elevated blood alcohol level, Mrs. Vance."

And then he had died. The doctor came in. Her mother was calm one minute then sobbing and shrieking the next.

"Lord Jesus," one of the church mothers wailed.

Yolanda screamed and ran to her mother. The church mother held them both as they cried. Apparently, her father was not in God's capable hands. Apparently, there were things too big for God to handle, or as the minister who preached at the funeral suggested, it was simply her father's time to go and be with the Lord.

My father
who art in heaven . . .

The next day, Yolanda arrived at the police station at five PM.

Like all of Holloway's municipal buildings, it was built right after the 1906 earthquake. A gray block with cement columns and wide marble steps in front. Its heavy wooden door was framed in a rounded archway.

Yolanda felt agitated and frazzled. She hadn't slept well. Memories of Georgia loomed in her mind, and when she finally fell into a hazy sleep, she heard her father preaching a ghostly sermon in her dreams.

As Yolanda neared the police building, the RBG van drove up.

"Hey sis!" Marcus Winters called. He double-parked and stepped from the van.

She greeted him, struggling to keep her eyes from wandering over his shoulder. She looked in both directions, visions of Kenya appearing with "FBI" falling from her mouth in the first sentence.

Yolanda tried to focus as Marcus walked her to the corner, where the teens were clustered on the side of the building. Dana and Sheena sat on the steps talking. Nakeesha, Darnell, and two other teens sat on the banister of a wheelchair ramp.

"Thanks for coming today," Marcus said. "And to our Sunday meeting."

"I really want to get involved," Yolanda said.

"We need adults," Winters said, smiling. "Mostly it's just me and Sharon. And Jimmy, when he can make it."

"Such great kids," Yolanda said. "I'll help any way I can."

Yolanda felt a hand on her shoulder, and then a voice spoke in her ear: "I'm still looking forward to that rematch."

She turned around to see Olujimi. "Fancy meeting you here," he said brightly.

She blinked, utterly disoriented, unable to process him in the new context.

"You two know each other?" Marcus asked.

"She's my nemesis on the runner's path," Olujimi laughed.

Yolanda's chest, her stomach, her intestines, turned to fire, burning her torso from the inside.

"Did you recruit her?" Marcus asked. "I been trying to get you to bring some Cartwright folks down here."

"I didn't even know she was involved with RBG. Shows how little I've been around lately."

How had this happened? How had she let herself flirt with a member of the group? She wasn't sure if this was worse than Kenya or not. At least if her former teammate blew her cover, she could return to New Jersey, a failure at undercover work. But now she had to somehow figure out how to stay on the case, despite her mortification.

"Glad you made it today, man," Marcus said, and they embraced, fists on their chests between them. "I'll be right back after I park the van."

By the time Marcus walked off and Olujimi turned back to Yolanda, she had pulled her face together.

"So how did you like my kids at the forum?" he asked eagerly.

"Your kids?" Yolanda asked.

"Not the politically correct word," he said. "How do you like the empowered young people I'm mentoring? Things are not what they seem, right?"

Yolanda scanned their two conversations. What had she said to him? Anything that would compromise her case? Her cover?

"Disturbing statistics, I know," he said soberly. "Total Greenwashing."

Greenwashing. Emerald Standard Fuel. Right.

"I had no idea you could market a green fuel that wound up with the same amount of carbon emissions as regular gas," Yolanda managed.

"So mad I couldn't be there," Olujimi went on. "But glad I snuck off campus for this police visit. With a Cartwright professor involved, they can't just dismiss the group as Black Identity Extremists. Using the privilege for good, you know?"

Yolanda nodded like she agreed. But everyone knew that extremists always found gullible allies at universities.

"So does this mean you're going to join Red, Black and GREEN?" he asked. "I mean, not like I'm asking out of ulterior motives of wanting to get to know you or anything."

Yolanda laughed along in the awkward moment.

"I have this effect on women," he said. "I throw game;

they laugh—which is why I'm single—nearly having a heart attack keeping up with beautiful women runners—" he broke off. "Actually, only one woman really—"

"Jimmy!" Nakeesha ran up to them. "Did you see the video?"

"Amazing! I was just telling Yolanda. Have you two met?" he asked.

"I seen her at the meetings," Nakeesha waved her hand dismissively in Yolanda's direction.

Olujimi made introductions.

Yolanda put out her hand automatically. Nakeesha nodded absently and turned toward the other teens.

"Carlos!" she yelled. The young Latino kid stood in the knot of teenagers, wearing an Oakland Raiders jacket. "Jimmy's here!"

She pulled the professor toward Carlos.

Olujimi smiled as Nakeesha led him away. "I'll talk to you later, I hope," he said to Yolanda.

"Hold up," Nakeesha said as she walked Olujimi away. "Was the doc trying to talk to the new girl?"

Yolanda couldn't hear what else they said.

How come he wasn't in the FBI file? She had read all the RBG materials, watched the entire video, memorized all the photographs. Jimmy? Olujimi? Thank God she found out before the flirting got worse.

"Hey Yolanda," Sheena waved her over to the group of young people.

"Hey."

"Thanks for coming out today," Dana said. The teens had been discussing something but stopped once Yolanda arrived. She remembered how girls at boarding school did the same.

The three of them watched as Sharon, RBG's wellness coordinator, pulled up in a beat-up white hatchback.

"She's got Mrs. Jenkins," Sheena said.

Yolanda followed the two girls across the neatly manicured lawn and the sidewalk.

Sheena opened the passenger side door and helped Mrs. Jenkins out. The elderly woman's suit was made of a synthetic fabric that mimicked raw silk, and it was correctly buttoned. On her head was a large black church crown with a small veil. She reminded Yolanda of church women in Georgia.

Dana and Sheena helped Mrs. Jenkins across the sidewalk, while Sharon parked. Yolanda stood alone on the clipped grass of the curb strip.

A moment later, Marcus yelled to everyone, "Let's huddle!"

Yolanda joined as Mrs. Jenkins leaned on a glossy black walking stick.

"Did anybody forget a key at the meeting last night?" Sharon called to the group as she trudged over.

"Oh, that's mine," Yolanda said, taking it. She slid it regretfully into the pocket of her jeans.

"First off, thanks for coming, Mrs. Jenkins," Marcus began.

"No, baby, I thank God for y'all. My church just said pray about this situation. I love my Jesus, but I know when it's time to raise hell!" She shook her fist in the air.

"Amen, Mrs. Jenkins," Nakeesha said.

"Here's the plan," Marcus said. "Mrs. Jenkins takes the lead, asks for information about her granddaughter. The rest of us stay quiet. I promised your parents you wouldn't get arrested. We don't want them to say we're being violent or disruptive. No matter what they say, stay cool."

The teens nodded. Yolanda noted how Winters took charge.

"After Mrs. Jenkins is done, Dana will talk, and we'll see what happens. We don't expect much today. But we have a long-term strategy."

"Burn the station down?" Nakeesha asked.

"No!" Winters said. "Don't even hint at anything like

that. We're demanding answers from all the institutions: police, coroner, mayor, and Randell. So later we can show how nobody would give us an answer. We don't expect the police to help us."

"Sure don't," Darnell mumbled. "They the last folks I would call if I was in trouble."

"Anybody else wanna add anything?" Marcus asked.

"I'm sorry for your loss, Mrs. Jenkins," Nakeesha said. "And glad to help you get justice."

"Excuse me," a tall police officer approached the group. "Can I help you? No loitering here."

"No, problem officer," Mrs. Jenkins said. "We was just on our way inside."

The group walked up the marble steps. Yolanda walked behind Carlos, watching his broad, sloping shoulders.

"How're you doing today, Carlos?" she asked.

"Cool," he said without turning. Yolanda bit back her next line: *hey, I watched* Ghost Dog *last night.*

As they filed through the door, she kept her focus forward. But in her peripheral vision, she could see Jimmy trying unsuccessfully to catch her eye.

In the front lobby, afternoon sun bounced off marble-patterned linoleum. The walls were lined with notices: REWARD! FOR INFORMATION LEADING TO . . . RESIDENTS IN THE EAST HOLLOWAY AVENUE CORRIDOR SHOULD BE AWARE THAT . . .

Jimmy held a small video camera low and unobtrusively.

He walked up next to Yolanda and murmured, "I can build a castle from a single grain of sand. I can make a ship sail on dry land."

She laughed nervously.

"I meant the Al Green version, not the Temptations," he grinned.

From somewhere in her subconscious, the song title bubbled up: "I can't get next to you."

A gray-haired officer sat behind a large battered front

desk, beside the door to the interior of the station. He prickled to attention and picked up a phone when RBG arrived. As he spoke quietly into it, he didn't take his eyes off the group.

Mrs. Jenkins approached him. "Good afternoon, young man."

He hung up. "Good afternoon, ma'am."

"My name is Dorothea Jenkins, and my grandbaby was murdered last week," she said.

"I'm sorry to hear that," he said.

"Unfortunately," she said, "your officers did a very inferior job of investigating, so we come to speak to the chief."

"The chief is very busy, ma'am. Do you have an appointment?"

"I called and they told me the same thing, that he's busy, but I came down anyway. And I brought friends, because I believe he would want to know that his officers are allowing a murderer to go free."

"Ma'am, I've called my supervisor, and he'll be with you shortly."

Yolanda could see the teens resisting the desire to speak. Nakeesha made a zipping motion across her lips and Darnell jiggled his foot.

The supervisor arrived, a short, thickset man in a uniform that was a little too tight. "Ma'am, I've called Melanie Coleman down here. She's our public relations liaison."

"We don't need a media handler," Marcus said, breaking his quiet rule. "We need answers."

"Good afternoon," a neat, blonde woman in a burgundy suit approached. Her black designer briefcase matched her pumps. "I'm Mel Coleman. So sorry for your loss, Mrs. Jenkins. Please, come to the conference room. By all means, bring your friends. Let's talk."

"I don't believe this," Jimmy murmured to Marcus.

"Sir," Mel Coleman said to Jimmy. "Are you with the press?"

"I'm co-editor of a cable access show," Jimmy said. "But also a professor at Cartwright."

"How lovely."

She led them through the door past the desk, and into a small windowless room with a conference table that could seat eight. She seated herself opposite Mrs. Jenkins, and the rest of the group wavered in the awkward moment of deciding who would sit and who would stand.

"Ladies first," Darnell said.

Some of the young women sat, but Dana didn't budge. "Ladies choice. I'll stand."

"Why don't the adults sit?" Sheena asked. "Aren't y'all tired on account of being old or something?"

"I don't really think—" Sharon began.

"Oh my god!" Nakeesha rolled her eyes. "Sit down Sheena," she said.

"But—" Sheena hesitated.

"Sit ya ass down," Nakeesha said.

When Sheena took a chair, Nakeesha sat on her lap. Dana took another chair and pulled Darnell onto her lap.

"Go, youth leadership," Marcus said.

Everyone sat but Jimmy, who continued to stand with the camera.

"I apologize that we don't have more chairs," Mel Coleman said. "But above all, Mrs. Jenkins, I'm sorry this has been such an ordeal."

Mel Coleman leaned forward toward Mrs. Jenkins, her forehead puckered in sympathy. She had a hand under her chin with one finger across her lips, as if the pain of the ordeal were too much to speak of.

"Miz Coleman—" Mrs. Jenkins began.

"Call me Mel," the blonde woman smiled.

"Miz Coleman, my grandbaby was found dead in a alley. They said she had a needle in her arm, but my grandbaby didn't shoot heron."

"I don't know the details of the arrest Mrs. Jenkins, but you can be sure that I'll follow up on this."

"When, Miz Coleman? When will you follow up? There's a murderer running loose in Holloway, and don't nobody seem to care."

"I care, Mrs. Jenkins. And you can be sure I'm going to do everything in my power to follow up."

"Can we at least get a copy of the police report?" Marcus asked.

"I'm sorry," Mel said. "I am not in a position to supply that information."

"Then what exactly are you going to do to follow up?" Marcus asked.

She ignored him. "Mrs. Jenkins, when someone has suffered a loss like yours, they deserve support. It's wonderful to have friends, but you also deserve professional support."

"This is bullshit," Sharon said. "I'm a licensed therapist. We didn't come to the police station to get Mrs. Jenkins into a support group. We want answers. Why don't the facts of Anitra Jenkins's death match your department's explanation?"

"I'm so glad you've already made contact with a therapist," Mel said to Mrs. Jenkins. "Here are additional resources." She pulled a pink sheet out of her briefcase. The heading said, "In this difficult time for you and your family . . ."

"Now, let me get some information to follow up as promised," Mel said. She asked a few basic questions and promised again to "follow up." Then she escorted Mrs. Jenkins and the group back out of the station.

None of them spoke until they were outside.

"Man, I'd like my foot to follow up with her ass," Nakeesha said.

"I thought you adults weren't gonna talk," Dana said.

"I'm sorry," Marcus said.

The group walked two blocks to the van. In the gutter alongside the curb was a trail of garbage, and the bright wrapper from a candy bar glinted up at them. They passed a storefront building with peeling paint.

"I didn't expect Ms. Coleman," Marcus said. "She threw off my game."

"You mean Mrs. Coulter," Carlos said.

"Who?" Nakeesha asked.

"Sci-fi," Carlos said. "Creepy character from *The Golden Compass*."

"I apologize too," Sharon said. "I just got so pissed when she came with the bullshit counseling referrals."

"Since when does Holloway PD have a public relations liaison?" Jimmy asked.

"I've seen her before," Marcus said. "They trot her out for press conferences when they shoot black teens in the back. I'm surprised she happened to be there today. It's not like they knew we were coming."

Yolanda had the sudden thought. *They did know,* she thought. *I reported it to the FBI.*

The specter of her report having summoned Mel Coleman was even more disorienting than running into Jimmy. It was like an inability to separate reality from dreaming in this FBI case. From now on, she wouldn't know who would always have been there, and whom she had conjured up.

The teens climbed listlessly into the van.

"I gotta go, y'all," Olujimi said. "See you Sunday."

"Bye Jimmy," the young people chorused.

He turned to Yolanda. "Maybe I'll catch you at the runner's path?"

"We'll see," she said with a shrug.

He walked across the street to an old blue Mercedes with a BIODIESEL bumper sticker.

"Yolanda, you need a ride?" Marcus asked. "Join us for dinner and debrief?"

"Sure," she said, and climbed into the van.

The teens sat one to a seat. The nearest available seat was across from Nakeesha. The teen sat with her arms folded, giving Yolanda a hard look. "Are you gonna stick around?" Nakeesha asked. "Or are you just here writing a paper or something."

"I—I plan to stick around," Yolanda said, sliding into the opposite seat. "I mean if that's okay with you all."

"Speaking of adults who disappear," Darnell said. "Marcus, it's been a minute since we seen ya boy from back in the day."

"Who's sposed to be my boy from back in the day?" Marcus asked.

"You know," Nakeesha jumped in, mimicking a gravelly male voice: "the *white* man just wanna keep us down. And you spoiled ass kids have no idea! Well back in my day, they beat us if we let our pants sag down."

The rest of the young people cracked up.

"He ain't my boy," Marcus explained. "My uncle just knew that cat from around the Panthers in Oakland."

"Whatever," Nakeesha said. "You need to bring some better adults to the group. Yolanda don't count. She still on probation."

"Don't take it personally," Marcus said to Yolanda. "They warm up to new people slowly."

"It's always the same damn thing," Sheena agreed. "Hella people come for the big community meetings, but on the weekly, it's the same old tired adults as always."

Marcus steered the van around a large pothole in the street. "So when are you young people gonna bring some new adults?" he asked.

"My mama comes whenever she can get off work," Dana said. "Lately that's not so often."

"You all have aunties and uncles," Marcus said. "Older cousins? Neighbors? This is a youth empowerment organization. Come on, youth. Be empowered."

A wail of disapproval rose in the small van.

"Who am I gonna bring to a meeting?" Nakeesha asked. "Half my family in jail; the other half working two jobs to support everybody kids."

"Picture my auntie coming in from the suburbs to our raggedy-ass church," Sheena laughed. "She only goes to churches where the pastor rolls up in a Rolls. She ain't tryna come to Holloway."

"If you want to feel God's love," Nakeesha said, her voice growling like a Southern preacher, "you can feel it in the Eye-talian leather of these seats in my luxury vee-hicle."

The laughter rang out as Marcus parked at a fast food joint.

Yolanda's eyes glanced from the restaurant to Marcus.

"Don't judge," Marcus said to Yolanda. "There's no farmer's market today and this is the only place I can afford."

The menu was mostly chicken, except a pork fajita sandwich the teens liked. A few of them knew the young woman at the counter.

They finally got their food. Everyone sat down in molded plastic seats at a long counter that looked out onto Holloway Avenue.

"Nobody tell Planet Greener we ate here, okay?" Marcus said.

"That shit at the police station was crazy," Darnell said.

"Yeah," Dana agreed. "They did the one thing we didn't expect. Talk to us. Be sympathetic."

"Natural fact is, I can't pay my taxes," Nakeesha said.

"Excuse me?" Yolanda said. "I didn't quite catch that."

"Marvin Gaye," Darnell said. "Make me wanna holler."

Yolanda nodded. She had bought a Caesar salad with

chicken, but was surprised when she opened the plastic container to find three pieces of romaine on top of a pile of iceberg lettuce beneath.

"You know Mel Coleman was all bullshit," Marcus said.

"Yeah, but on camera it'll look like she cares," Dana said.

"What? That lady so fake, you could tell a mile away," Darnell insisted.

"Dana's right," Marcus said. "She'll look sincere on camera. What do you think, Yolanda?"

"She used all the right words," Yolanda said. "She kills your case that the police won't give you answers. She's the reasonable doubt."

"Oh right, you're a lawyer," Marcus said. "Jimmy told me."

"Only in the Tri-State Area," Yolanda said. "I'm studying for the California bar."

"Speaking of studying," Marcus said. "Would you be willing to come in and tutor the youth one day a week?"

"Sure," Yolanda said. "I'd love a break from bar review." She picked at her salad. It had crispy fried nuggets and waxy American cheese.

"Did you go to Cartwright law school?" Dana asked.

"They don't have a law school," Yolanda said. "I went to Harvard Law."

"Harvard?" Marcus almost choked on a spicy southwest chicken nugget. "You went to Harvard Law? Oh my God. Can I even sit at the same table with you?"

"It's no big deal," Yolanda said, suddenly uncomfortable.

"What did you study?" Marcus asked. "Corporate law? Wealthy tax evasion? Fire and brimstone?"

"Marcus," Sharon said. "Give the woman a break. She's obviously not like that."

"For all we know, she's in the enemy camp," Marcus said. "Sent to spy on us."

Yolanda felt a quick clutch of panic in her chest, the cheap food in her mouth tasting metallic.

"Come on, Marcus," Sharon said. "Not everyone's a Red Diaper Baby like you."

"That's a Black Red Diaper Baby," Marcus said.

"You went to Harvard," Sharon said to Yolanda. "All the more reason for you to tutor the kids."

"To some degree Marcus is right," Yolanda said evenly. "I studied corporate law, and I worked for Van Dell, Meyers and Whitney in New York."

"The firm that got indicted?" Dana asked.

"Yep," Yolanda said. "A bunch of us got laid off. That's how I ended up back in California."

"Did you steal hella money?" Nakeesha asked.

Yolanda laughed. "No, I definitely did not."

"Can you teach us how to steal hella money?" Nakeesha asked.

"It's easy to steal," Sheena said. "It's not getting caught that's the hard part."

"My daddy already taught me that lesson," Nakeesha said.

Yolanda didn't have an answer for that.

By the time they left the fast food joint and walked into the parking lot, it had gotten dark. Through the plate glass window, they could see a teenager wiping down the tables with a rag. Soon, the dining area would close. Patrons could order the same menu at the drive thru, across bulletproof glass.

Yolanda rode with Sharon, Dana and Sheena, the kids who didn't live in the Stats. Sharon was headed back to Richmond, the town next door. She dropped off Dana and Sheena first. They lived in small, one-story houses a few blocks apart. As Sharon pulled away from the curb, she turned to Yolanda.

"It's been so great to have another adult around the last couple of days."

"I haven't done much," Yolanda said.

"You're doing fine," Sharon said. "I saw that Carlos actually spoke to you already. That's probably a world record."

Sharon turned the car back onto Holloway Avenue and turned north toward Yolanda's house.

"Were you serious about tutoring?" Sharon asked. "Maybe on a Monday or Wednesday? Marcus just really needs support."

They stopped at a red light, and a large SUV pulled up beside them, blasting music so loud that it was hard to hear. After the light changed, the SUV screeched off, and Sharon continued.

"I come in on Tuesdays to do the teen discussion group. Jimmy comes in on Thursdays to do the science project, but the kids come in after school, pretty much every day of the week. This time of year, there's not a lot to do in the garden beyond watering and a little bit of weeding. And there's no real place for kids to go in Holloway."

"I could do Wednesdays," Yolanda said.

"Great!" Sharon said. As they waited at another light, Sharon took a Kaiser Permanente card from her purse. "Call me if you need anything. I'll tell Marcus you're on board."

Yolanda took the card and put it in the pocket of her jeans.

As they pulled up in front of the apartment, Sharon narrowed her eyes. "Did they remodel this building?"

Yolanda shrugged. "I moved in pretty recently."

"I thought it was in the middle of this same block . . ." Sharon murmured, looking at the buildings on either side.

"The front does seem a little more modern than the inside," Yolanda said.

"Gentrification," Sharon said. "I could have sworn this guy lived in one of these apartments. What was his name? Red Dog? Mad Dog?"

"Mad Dog?" Yolanda asked.

"A young man who joined Red, Black and GREEN! a year ago," Sharon said.

"Is he still around?" Yolanda asked. There had been no mention of a Red or Mad Dog in the file.

"No," Sharon sighed. "He was new to Holloway. And he got killed in a drive-by shooting."

"I'm sorry for your loss," Yolanda said.

"We never really got to know him," Sharon said. "He only came to a couple of meetings before he got shot. It was really his family's loss. I heard he had a daughter."

Yolanda nodded sympathetically, as an uneasy sensation rose in her gut. Why was there someone else connected to the case who didn't seem to be in the file?

Chapter 8

Although he was not in the file, the young man was certainly the previous inhabitant of the FBI apartment. As a Bureau operative, he had assumed he was under surveillance. To him, a bugged phone and a monitoring anklet were still better than prison. In exchange for two years' early release, all he had to do was go to some meetings and act mad about being black in America.

A week after the operative had arrived at the apartment, he stood outside a nearby liquor store, talking on the pay phone and swigging gin from the bottle. Across the street, a Jeep idled in the shadows beneath the broken streetlight in front of the vacant lot.

"You can't call me on the cell, cause I swear they listening."

The operative leaned further into the booth as a trio of young men stepped out of the liquor store.

"Girl, I told you, I can't come to LA," the operative said. "You can bring the baby. I just need you to get that bus ticket and come on up here."

The three young men shuffled across the parking lot in their low-slung jeans, unwrapping a bottle of malt liquor and tossing the bag into the gutter. As they passed the operative talking in the shadowy phone booth, the Jeep pulled away from the curb with its lights off and accelerated. The driver pointed an automatic handgun out of the window and took aim.

As the first shot rang out, one of the young men screamed in pain, as a shot caught him in the arm. The other two threw themselves down onto the concrete, as a second shot whizzed past. It hit the operative, who had attempted to dive for cover behind a garbage can.

The Jeep sped off, as the two young men scrambled toward their wounded friend, leaning anxiously over him.

"You okay man?"

"I'll be aight," he gasped. "They only got me in the arm." The youngest of the three, his little brother, began to cry.

"The fuck you crying for?" the older brother asked. "Pull yourself together, nigga. You gotta take my gun to the house before any cops get here."

Gingerly, the younger teen reached for the gun in his older brother's waistband, as they heard the distant sirens.

"Hurry up, nigga!" The pressure just made the kid more anxious, and his hands shook.

The third young man grabbed for the gun and thrust it into the boy's hands. "Go on, now!" He gave him a shove. Stumbling into motion, the kid ran back across the vacant lot toward their apartment.

Only when the sirens were nearby did the liquor store owner step outside to see what had happened.

"Is your friend okay?" the owner asked. "I called the ambulance and the police when I heard the shots."

"They just hit me in the arm," the wounded kid said through clenched teeth.

The police cars came down the street, their headlights illuminating the entire block.

"How about your other friend?" the store owner asked.

"What the fuck?" the young man began. "That lil nigga still here?"

Only as the police car drew closer did the two young men see what the store owner meant. The operative's legs stuck out from behind the garbage can. His low-slung denim shorts reached to mid-calf, but a telltale house arrest anklet made a distinctive lump under his left sock. The phone receiver from the booth dangled off the hook, an operator informing them that if they would like to make a call, they would need to hang up and dial again.

The unhurt young man moved closer, as the police lights illuminated the man's face.

"I ain't neva seen that nigga before in my life," the young man scoffed, attempting to look tough in the face of death.

The fatal shot had hit the FBI operative in the neck. His face was clearly recognizable as someone that nobody in the neighborhood knew.

Chapter 9

Yolanda's next Red, Black and GREEN! meeting began with a dizzying barrage of hugs. Sheena practically jumped on her when she arrived, flinging her arms around Yolanda. Startled, Yolanda only began to hug back after Sheena was letting go, creating a gawky, half-tangle.

Dana hugged her next, and Yolanda thought of it as an exercise. *Reach, embrace, pressure, release.* Like weightlifting. She had a rhythm going by the time Sharon and Nakeesha hugged her.

With Darnell, she went through the motions, but her body felt rigid and awkward with the physical closeness to his adult male body. Carlos didn't hug anyone but Sharon.

By the time the meeting started, she was buzzing with more physical contact than she'd had since hand-to-hand combat training.

She was definitely not a hugger. Even in her many college athletic wins, she accepted hugs reluctantly, so she would be the last girl her teammates would hug, turning first to each other in the elation of victory.

Yolanda celebrated by herself first, glad to be left alone. She practiced "savoring the moment." Positive thinking guru Lester Johnakin encouraged her to stand with her back against a wall, arms outstretched at her sides, palms forward. *I am savoring this moment. I am savoring this victory. I am victorious.*

Her teammates knew she had her own private thing. But after she stepped away from the wall, smiling, they would each come and hug her, really more reaching around and patting her on the back: *good game.*

The last genuine hug she had given to anyone had been to a girl named Dale at boarding school, when she had bought Yolanda some designer clothes. Impulsively, Yolanda had thrown her arms around the wealthy girl, thinking Dale an embodiment of Johnakin's philosophy *positive people attract positive resources.* And his *theory of the committed wish* that anything you set your mind to desiring completely could be yours.

Prior to that, Yolanda had soured on hugs at eleven, during her mother's Sufi period in Colorado. Her mother had followed her latest boyfriend, Andrew, from San Francisco. Andrew had taken them to Sufi rituals of prayer and ecstatic dance.

The events brought two-dozen people together every Saturday for what they called Zikr and dancing. Yolanda and her mother were the only brown faces in the bright yoga studio with wooden floors and a burbling rock fountain.

Yolanda dreaded the greetings, with pair after pair of white arms squeezing her, chest after chest she was smothered against, sometimes with their beads pressing into the side of her face or her painful budding breasts crushed against one body after another. She would come home smelling of a combination of their oils—sandalwood, patchouli, musk—and unwashed skin.

First, they would begin with chanting as their fingers moved along prayer beads in their hands. That part wasn't so bad. But then they got to the dancing.

In college English class, she would have a classmate from Libya. The teacher held up the girl's essay as an example because it was so effective in its detail, but also how much it showed the perspective of the writer. The girl would read it aloud, about her family's Zikr ritual (she spelled it "Dhikr"). She described a powerful experience of connection—to her family, community, and God—one that she missed in college because the Muslim community in Holloway was more conservative. She would pray sometimes with a few friends, but it wasn't the same. Her family's tradition didn't include ecstatic dancing. It seemed the traditional version of the ritual was a more subtle connected experience of looking within.

But those white people's interpretation of Sufi dancing in Colorado was anything but subtle. Their prayer was more of a chant, loud and intense. And afterwards the dancing began.

Yolanda recalled long skirts, gauzy tunics, bright headwraps, flushed faces, endorphin smiles. Yolanda always started out in the dancing circle with everyone else. She enjoyed the drums, the music and rhythms, but as the dancing became more wild and unleashed, she would slip away. Away from white bodies spinning, headwraps untangling, greasy brown hair revealed, sweat staining cotton fabric, the room hot and musty. In a corner in the hallway, next to the philodendron plant, she would pull her book out of her sock, Johnakin's *Small Book of Positive Thinking*.

You have the power to create your life. You alone decide your fate.

She would read the book and visualize. Visualize herself rich and independent. In New York City, an executive of some kind. Powerful and glamorous.

Yolanda would read and visualize until she could tell by the slowing cadence of the music that the dance was winding down. She would put the small book back into her sock and return to the main room. Finding her mother, she would begin to dance beside her, as if she had been there the whole time.

Yolanda was learning the rhythm of the RBG meetings. Each week, before the meditation, they did introductions and talked about something going well in their lives. *The FBI thinks I'm doing a good job on my assignment here. I'm hoping to get back to New Jersey soon.* Each week she studied a few hours of California law, and invented a fake victory in her bar review prior to the meeting.

She was unprepared, however, when Nakeesha announced that Yolanda was going to tutor them for the next few Wednesdays after school, "so y'all had better come."

Everybody looked at her expectantly.

"Do you want to say something about the benefits of college?" Sharon asked Yolanda.

"Not just elite colleges," Marcus said. "There are many different types of education."

"Can you let the woman speak?" Sharon asked.

Yolanda swallowed and stood up. "I—um—am glad to talk about the importance of college.

"I grew up with a single mom," she said. "We didn't have a lot of money, but she had gone to college, and always taught me the importance of education. As black people, others may underestimate us, but if we apply ourselves to learning, we can overcome all obstacles."

The next natural thing out of her mouth would be something about taking responsibility and not blaming anyone when you met obstacles. Or, worse than blaming any one person, blaming something vague and generic, like racism. Racism didn't make you turn in your homework late. Racism didn't force you at gunpoint into the park to smoke marijuana with your friends. But she knew that line of thinking wouldn't be appreciated. She shifted gears.

"And colleges are great for activism," she added. "Every social justice cause you can imagine has a group in college." She needed a sort of conclusion, to bring this home.

"So no matter what your grades or aspirations," Yolanda said, "consider higher education. Whether it's junior college or four-year, public or private, Ivy League or vocational, it doesn't make a difference. What matters is that you take yourself and learning seriously. And believe in your dreams."

She sat down among a smattering of applause. Sharon was smiling, but Marcus's expression was unreadable. Yolanda herself wore a polite smile, but inside she thought: this is a load of bullshit. Of course it matters what college you go to. Nobody pays a hundred thousand dollars a year to get a piece of paper that doesn't mean anything. Obviously.

Later that night, she included the talking points of her speech in her report to the FBI. She also reported the news that RBG had an attorney working to get an order to exhume the body of Anitra Jenkins.

Officer Joaquín Rodriguez sat in bed that night unable to sleep. His wife, Isabel, lay snoring quietly beside him, only the tangle of her dark hair visible on the pillow.

He hadn't had a sleepless night like this since he was a kid on his grandfather's farm in Mexico. Rodriguez loved being around so many animals. In their LA apartment, they couldn't even have a cat. On the farm, he and his brother milked the cows each morning, occasionally squirting a bit of milk into their mouths.

But it troubled him on those nights when they would eat goat. He didn't care about the chickens they ate every day. Chickens were stupid. The pigs were dirty and unfriendly, so the pork didn't bother him either. But the goats were like pets.

On the first night when his abuela made birria for them,

he had noticed one of the goats missing the day before. Even a summer-only farm boy knows what that means. He promised himself not to eat any, but the long day outside running and climbing trees had left him famished. He tried to eat only the rice and beans, the bread, but the delicious smell of the dish lured him, first into one little sip of the broth. Just the broth, not the meat itself. But then he tasted the tiny fibers of meat on his tongue and realized that it was too late. He was already eating the meat. He had seconds of the dish, half of him savoring the spicy, savory chunks of messy stew, half of him feeling like a cannibal.

Sundays, at church, he would pray to the Virgen de Guadalupe for forgiveness, but all his promises to avoid even chicken for a week as penance or never again eat red meat were in vain.

Those long-ago nights after he ate goat meat, like that night in Holloway, he would lie awake, unable to find rest in his mind, although his body was tired. In Mexico, he was weary from physical activity. In Holloway, he was beat from a long evening on second shift.

By the time he was thirteen, he had finally accepted the death of the goats as part of the cycle of life. But how could he make sense of this young woman's death? It had seemed all wrong, but he'd said nothing. Now a group of angry blacks came in last week demanding answers. And who was this blonde liaison woman? This was not part of the cycle of life. Guilt lay on his chest like a concrete slab.

"You still awake?" his wife asked him in Spanish. "What's wrong?"

"Nothing." He lay back down, hiding his sleeplessness behind closed eyes.

The following morning, Monday, Yolanda was called in to Rafferty's office for a special meeting.

When she arrived at his office, Rafferty wasn't there. Peterson greeted her, sitting in one of the two chairs across from the desk, and they both looked out at the foggy San Francisco morning. In the watery gray light, Yolanda could just see the burnt orange tips of the Golden Gate Bridge.

"You ever wonder about the desk?" Peterson asked. "Why he doesn't turn it to face the window?"

"It's a power move," Yolanda replied. "He wants to show all of us what he has, even if he doesn't even bother to enjoy it."

Peterson nodded slowly. "I think you're right. By the way, it's great to have another woman on the team."

"Those ex-military types seem most comfortable surrounded by guys," Yolanda said, diplomatically.

"Tell me about it," Peterson said. "Once, I had a date after work and wore a more feminine suit with my hair partway down. Rafferty looked like he was facing a firing squad."

Yolanda had only seen Peterson in dowdy suits that hid her curves. She always had her thick auburn hair back in an austere bun.

"I'll bet," Yolanda said.

"You know," Peterson said. "I was the one who found your file after the con got shot."

"The con?" Yolanda asked.

"Sorry," Peterson said. "The operative from prison. I forget his name. Rafferty had looked up all the young black agents after the kids rejected the first special agent. There was nobody black who was young enough. So that's how the Bureau ended up making the deal with what's his name— the con."

"Mad Dog?" Yolanda said, recalling Sharon's words. "Red Dog?"

"Right," Peterson said. "Red Dog. After he got killed, Rafferty was racking his brain, but I was the one who kept searching periodically for new agents. Eventually your name popped up."

"What was the first special agent's name again?" Yolanda asked. She had scoured those files. She memorized every person involved. There was no mention of a prison operative or a previous special agent.

"You can look it up in the file . . ." Peterson trailed off.

Yolanda hedged: "Those files were so thick—"

Peterson cocked her head to the side. "Come on, Vance. Save the innocent act for your subjects. It seriously wasn't in the file?"

Yolanda shook her head.

Peterson gritted her teeth. "I can't believe that fucker."

"You mean Rafferty?" Yolanda asked. "What didn't he tell me?"

Peterson took a deep breath. "You didn't hear it from me," she said in a whisper. "First they sent a special agent, but he didn't fit. Then they sent the prison operative. He got killed in a drive-by shooting."

"One of the subjects mentioned that," Yolanda said. "But who was the agent and why didn't he fit?"

Peterson frowned. "I never understood why they picked him. Just because he was black? Sorry, African American? I know the Bureau does a lousy job recruiting minorities, but were they that clueless? These kids needed someone to talk to them about the latest rap stars, not some Hoover era dinosaur stuck in reliving the FBI's glory days of busting up the Black Panther Party."

"Is he still involved in the operation?" Yolanda asked. "Does he work out of this office?"

The door opened and Rafferty walked in. He sat down, with his back to the view of the Golden Gate Bridge and handed Yolanda an authorization memo.

"You need to get those listening devices installed," he said. "You're still fresh from training, but Peterson will give you the equipment and answer any technical questions you have." He barely glanced at her as he spoke, rifling through the papers on his desk.

He continued: "Your reports look good. Anything to add?" He still didn't make eye contact.

"No, sir," she said.

He dismissed them.

Yolanda followed Peterson to her cubicle. The redhead handed Yolanda a key to the RBG office.

"The issue isn't getting in," Peterson explained. "The issue is finding a time to be in there alone. Between the RBG meetings, the church activities on weekends, and the homeless teens sleeping there, the place is never empty."

Peterson gave her several "listening devices" to plant in the office, the main room, and on the landline phone. She was also given a USB plug-in that would automatically copy the contents of Marcus's hard drive.

"Usually, we can gain access through the internet, but since Marcus's computer isn't online, we need your help here."

Yolanda took the device, which looked like a simple USB drive.

Peterson was punching buttons on her computer.

"About that other thing you were saying . . ." Yolanda began.

"Ancient history," Peterson said. "We need to focus on the current op. Familiarize yourself with this equipment. When I get back, let me know if you have any technical questions. And Vance," she said pointedly. "Please don't look at my computer."

When Peterson stepped away, Yolanda saw that the screen was open to a memo.

To: Special Agent Rafferty

From: Special Agent Peterson

Re: Operation HOLOGRAM

I am forwarding an audio file of the conversation re: RBG. The young stakeholders seem to have rejected Special Agent ████████████

TRANSCRIPTION

FEMALE TEEN 1 (FT1): Marcus, I don't know if me and Sheena [sic] can come to the Sunday meeting if we can't get a ride home.

MARCUS WINTERS (MW): I told you all, the van's in the shop. You want me to ride you both on my bike?

FEMALE TEEN 2 (FT2): When's Sharon getting back from Puerto Rico?

MALE TEEN 1 (MT1): What about that old guy? He has a nice car.

FT1: I don't want a ride from him. He creeps me out.

FEMALE TEEN 3 (FT3): I know what you mean. Something about him is . . . is . . . wrong. I can't explain it.

FT 1: He's fake. He smiles at us, but it's just his mouth, you know? Plus, he seems hella [sic] like . . . like the principal at school or something. He asks stupid questions like, "how was school today, young lady?"

FT 3: One minute he's like the schoolmaster in some Jane Austen story, and the next minute he goes on these tirades about the white man that sound like something out of some old Blaxploitation movie, like—

FT 1: I'm saying! "The white man is trying to keep us down, brothers and sisters!"

[Laughter]

MW: He's been around for decades. People in Oakland knew him from the Black Panther days.

MALE TEEN 2 (MT2): I don't trust him.

FT 2: That's what's up. Like why he want to [sic] be around a bunch of teenagers when he seem [sic] so uncomfortable?

Why he want to [sic] ride us somewhere in his car? "Would you like some candy little girl?"

MT 1: Naw. I don't think he [sic] some Chester the Molester type.

FT 1: Fine. You get in that crazy nigger [sic] car, then.

MW: Language!

FT 3: Marcus, just fix the van, okay?

Chapter 10

Yolanda walked in to the RBG offices on Wednesday with the faux leather briefcase half full of homework stuff: legal pads, pens, pencils and a calculator. The other half, beneath the briefcase's divider, was jammed with electronic surveillance equipment, a dust rag, latex gloves, a shoe bag, and a rolled up gray hoodie sweatshirt. Yolanda also had a couple of adhesive bugs in her pocket, for easy access.

She arrived half an hour early, and Carlos let her in.

"Hi," she said awkwardly. "How are you doing?"

Carlos shrugged. "Cool."

"Are you here for tutoring?" she asked hopefully.

"I got my GED," Carlos said. "I'm here helping Marcus fix his computer." He walked into the office, and Yolanda looked around the large outer room. All the places that would work to plant bugs in here were too high for her to reach without standing on a chair.

She walked into the office to find Carlos and Marcus huddled together at the computer.

"But I tried rebooting and that didn't help," Marcus said.

"Okay, let's defrag the hard drive," Carlos said.

"How long is that gonna take?" Marcus asked, exasperated.

"Have you eaten anything?" Carlos asked. "Go get food. It'll be done when you get back."

Marcus pulled his chair back from the computer and seemed surprised to see Yolanda.

"Right, it's Wednesday," he said, wearily. "The teens won't be here for another forty-five minutes. You wanna grab some food?"

"Sure," Yolanda said, and followed him out. They walked to a Chinese restaurant, and Yolanda ordered chicken chow mien through bulletproof glass.

"Carlos can read me like a book," Marcus said. "My blood sugar was so low, no wonder I almost smashed the computer." He chuckled. "I can't believe it's 3:15, and I'm just now having lunch."

"Did you eat breakfast?" Yolanda asked.

"Does a chocolate bar count?"

Yolanda rolled her eyes.

"I know," Marcus said. "My diet is atrocious. I preach healthy food, but I'm a hypocrite. It'll be better after harvest time in our community garden. Anyway, thank you so much for coming to help out."

Yolanda smiled. "My pleasure."

"Hopefully, you'll keep coming on Wednesdays with us after we get back into the dirt."

As they ate, Marcus ranted about his stress level, and how Project Greener wasn't helping them enough.

"I was so naïve. I thought they wanted to start a program in Holloway because they actually had the epiphany that they needed to really develop African-American leadership in the climate movement," he said between mouthfuls. "Now I see it was really just a PR stunt. They got bad press for drilling on what was supposed to be a nature preserve. What did they expect? You can't preserve nature and drill in it at the same time. But we're turning their little charity PR stunt into black climate leadership development whether they support us or not."

She recalled the drilling issue from the article in the file. A conservation agency extracting oil and gas on a nature preserve did seem unethical. But Yolanda also felt tempted to quote Lester Johnakin, to point out how Marcus's negative attitude was certainly part of the problem. No one wants to help a whiner. But she just listened. Twenty minutes later, they were back at the office.

Dana and Sheena had arrived. Yolanda eavesdropped on the two girls gossiping while Carlos and Marcus worked on the computer.

"Why won't it save the fucking document?" Marcus was asking, exasperated, when Nakeesha and Darnell walked in.

Yolanda cleared her throat. "So, welcome everybody," she began. "I've thought a lot about how best to approach tutoring. I was thinking in addition to individual meetings, I could offer an overview of the college application process—"

"Don't worry," Dana said. "Sharon's got that on lock. And we figured out how we want the tutoring to go. Since there's only one of you, we'll just take turns getting tutored. Twenty minutes each, and we can do homework or have free time when it's not our turn."

"And quiet free time," Sheena said to Nakeesha. "Which means sophomores shouldn't be trying to talk to juniors who need to get those grades for college."

"And no streaming videos!" Marcus yelled from the office. "We don't have the bandwidth."

So Yolanda just sat at the small table, and the teenagers rotated into the chair beside her. They brought math, science, and essays. Mostly she was able to be helpful, but so often they would interrupt her. "Yeah, I know that part, but what about . . ."

It was jarring. She wasn't used to teens talking to adults as equals. They needed her help, yet they were comfortable directing how she helped them. It was utterly beyond her experience.

Yolanda and Darnell were hunched over a math problem when Nakeesha interrupted them.

"Six o'clock, everybody!" Nakeesha said. "We can make noise again."

And that was it. Darnell stood up, heedless of not having finished the equation. The teens alternated between chatting and texting, leaving Yolanda alone with her carefully prepared how-to-approach-college-applications lesson, and a briefcase full of bugs.

She thought of the previous agent. Was she supposed to magically fit in here because she was black and under thirty? She hadn't fit in with black teenagers even when she was one. She didn't fit anywhere. Not with the black kids in Detroit. Not with the white girls in prep school. Not with the jock girls on any team. Not with the other women in law school. She always dreamed that the next set of people at the next place would "get" her. Sanchez and his squad in New Jersey had been the closest she'd come to feeling at home since she'd left Georgia.

And now she was wasting her time with these kids. As the adult, shouldn't she have been more in charge? As the group broke up, she looked for opportunities to plant any of the bugs, but at six thirty, Marcus and Carlos were still hard at work, so she headed out with Sheena.

As they walked out onto Holloway Avenue, Sheena's bus was at the stop.

"Wait!" Sheena called to the driver and ran the twenty or so feet to the corner. It turned out the bus was in the final stages of lifting a wheelchair on board.

In the moment of delay, Sheena ran back to Yolanda and hugged her. "Thanks for doing this. We really need the help."

"No problem," Yolanda called out, as Sheena ran back to board the bus.

* * *

The next week, tutoring was more challenging.

"I still don't get it," Nakeesha was saying. She slammed the math book down and sat back in the chair, folding her arms and smacking her gum.

Yolanda wasn't sure how else she could explain it. Nakeesha obviously had a sharp mind. She listened to the kids making up raps on the spot, and Nakeesha always had the rhymes that followed a strong storyline and rhymed unexpected and multisyllabic words. Why couldn't she get this?

Yolanda recalled her own strategies from college.

"Take a deep breath," Yolanda said. "Relax your mind."

"I don't see how that's gonna help anything," Nakeesha said, her jaw tight.

"Oh my god, just try it," Sheena said from the couch.

Nakeesha sucked her teeth, but she closed her eyes and took several deep breaths.

When she opened her eyes, Yolanda smiled brightly.

"Good job," Yolanda said. "Now let's go back to the first math problem. You tell me how you got the answer and we'll build from there."

Nakeesha shrugged. "It was obvious," she said. But then she began to explain it. As she shared her language for the concepts, Yolanda was able to help her apply it to the harder problems. When she got frustrated, Yolanda coached her to breathe and pick the equations back up after she'd relaxed.

"I got it!" she said, after they checked the answer for the problem she had struggled with. "That's right math! You can't defeat me/I solved you completely/So the word on the street be/I be flowing mathematically/Cause I be shining like a black sun/on every decimal and fraction/solving every equation/like a mental—"

"Oh my god, some of us are trying to work here," Sheena said.

"Haters tryna block my elation," Nakeesha said, but much more quietly.

Suddenly, they heard a series of foghorn-like computer bleats coming from the office, and Marcus began cursing.

Sheena threw her book down with a growl of annoyance.

Marcus appeared in the office doorway. "Where the hell is Carlos?" he asked, his voice almost drowned out by the computer's noise.

"He ain't here, obviously," Sheena said. "Nothing here but a whole damn lot of noise."

"I can't deal with this fucking computer!" Marcus yelled. "How am I supposed to get anything done on a computer that keeps crashing?"

"I'm going to the library," Sheena announced, and stomped out.

"See you Sunday," Yolanda called after her.

"And I shouldn't even have to rely on Carlos," Marcus said. "These damn white people at Planet Greener all have decent working computers, but say they can't afford something better for us? I'm up to my ass in fucking grant deadlines."

"Can we help?" Yolanda asked, walking over to him.

"No," Marcus said. "I just need a damn laptop. I'm gonna go to the Copy Spot in El Cerrito." He pulled his USB drive from the machine and stormed out of the office.

After the door slammed, Nakeesha asked, "What do we do?" But she didn't get off the couch.

"Can we shut it off?" Darnell asked.

"No way," Nakeesha warned. "He really goes crazy if we mess with it."

"Let's at least turn the sound down," Dana said. She walked to the computer and found the audio button. As the noise faded, they all relaxed, although the urgent red error messages continued to flash silently on the screen.

Half an hour later, Carlos came in, and Dana explained what happened.

"I told him not to—" Carlos began. "Whatever." He rolled his eyes. "I'll fix it."

Yolanda went back to Dana's essay. Five minutes later, Carlos came back out of the office.

"See you guys tomorrow," Carlos called on his way out the door. "If you see Marcus, tell him to read my instructions next time."

"I ain't saying shit to Marcus," Nakeesha said. "Cause I don't appreciate him raising his voice at us."

As the teens began to pack up, Yolanda realized the building might finally be empty.

She said her goodbyes and stepped out into the gloomy evening. Crossing the street, she entered a women's clothing store.

With one eye on the church, she flipped through rows of clothing. She pretended to admire synthetic dresses in bright colors with sparkly embroidery, and jeans made of stretch material to be worn skintight.

The fabric felt itchy. And the shoes looked like instruments of torture.

She could still recall the press of the hugs from the teenagers. They were whiners, but not so bad once she spent more time with them. Of course, that wouldn't get in the way of her work. The government couldn't have a bunch of kids interfering in a classified project. The teens she had known in prep school were mean girls. These girls meant well, but one wrong message to a friend about "guess what I heard about Randell?" and the real terrorist enemies of the US would have a strategic target to bomb. It was for their own good.

The store's doorbell clanged as a pair of young women entered. Yolanda shivered in the breeze the girls had let in and put on the gray hoodie from the briefcase.

She kept peeking past the big butt mannequins in the window, across the street to the church steps. Within ten minutes, all the teens had exited the church. It was 6:38. The homeless youth were welcome to come in any time after seven PM.

Yolanda thanked the young woman at the counter and jaywalked back across the street in the gathering dusk. By the time she stood at the door of the church, she had twenty minutes.

Her hands were shaking as she used the key Peterson had given her. In the church basement, Yolanda squeezed into the alcove under the stairs, the most secluded spot in the room. She crouched between two stacks of folding chairs, opened the briefcase, and put on the latex gloves.

Without the fluorescents, the only illumination came from the dim entry light over the stairs, and the boxy basement's high windows.

She crossed to the quarter of the room had been walled off to form RBG's office. The door had a button lock and a deadbolt that fit the same key.

She unlocked them both, and opened the door slowly, half expecting that she had made a mistake, and someone would be in there. But the office sat empty.

She quietly rolled the office chair to the nearest window and locked the wheels in place. As she climbed up onto the chair, she heard a car honk outside and nearly toppled off. She pressed a hand onto her chest, as if she could stop her heart from beating so hard. She took a deep breath. It wouldn't do to fall and get knocked out, and have some homeless teens discover her unconscious body beside a briefcase full of electronic surveillance equipment.

She steadied herself on the chair, reaching up to the window frame. She was careful to dust first, as Peterson had reminded her, or the device wouldn't stick. Then she gingerly peeled off the paper to expose the adhesive and affix one of the dark listening devices, each one the size of her little finger's top digit.

Before she went into the main room, she plugged the USB device into the back of Marcus's computer.

The main room was bigger and left her more exposed. She hurried to plant the devices, rolling the chair from window to window. With each installation, it got easier. She planted devices on top of the door frames as well, grateful for the diagonal slant of the moldings that hid them easily.

When she went back into the office, it was 6:49. Pulling out her tools, she unscrewed the receiver of the desk phone and installed devices in the mouthpiece and earpiece. She dropped the screw while putting it back together and cursed as she crawled around on the carpet with her flashlight until she finally found it.

Suddenly, she heard a noise. She froze and listened, but it was just someone walking into the church above.

She looked at her watch. 6:58 PM.

When she brought the office chair back to retrieve the USB device, she saw the flashing message on the computer's screen.

ALERT! SECURITY BREACH! A fiery warning blinked red and orange at her.

Should she leave it? The homeless kids could be here any minute. She recalled Dana turning off the sound on the computer. She felt around on the back of the unit and pressed the button that turned the monitor off. Then she yanked her USB device from the machine.

As she headed out of the office, into the main room, she heard the jingle of keys.

There was no time to lock the inner office door behind her. Silently, she sprinted across the main room to the alcove below the stairs and dove between the folding chairs.

Three laughing boys walked in, two black, one Latino.

They crossed the large main room and walked to the office door.

"It's open," the shortest one said, and they all looked around.

Yolanda held her breath, hoping the shadows would cover her. Hoping the traffic outside would camouflage the thudding of her heart.

The Latino kid spoke up, his voice worried. "We all saw it was open, right? They better not blame us."

"Computer's still here," the taller black kid said, walking into the office.

Yolanda felt in her pocket to make sure she had her flashlight and her screwdrivers, as well as the USB device. Quietly, she slid the tools and her briefcase into a plastic bag. The bag was from a chain store that sold athletic shoes. It had strings that she could wear like a backpack.

"We gotta be sure to lock it when we leave for school," the short boy said. Then all three disappeared into the office, bolting the door behind them.

Her heart still banging against her ribs, Yolanda pulled her hood over her head and stepped out from the alcove, the shoe bag on her back. Even if someone saw her, she'd look more like a young man from the neighborhood than an adult woman. She crept across the room and up the stairs to the street level landing. Carefully, she opened the door a crack. Outside, it was fully dark, and Holloway Avenue was bustling. She slipped out the door and locked it behind her, joining the foot traffic. In the center pocket of her pullover hoodie, she peeled off the latex gloves.

As she walked home, her heartbeat and breathing slowed to normal, she was relieved but also slightly giddy from the episode. She had done it. She had succeeded where a veteran agent had failed—whoever that guy was. As for the fact that her USB device was detected? Like Johnakin said, don't take credit for anyone else's failures or successes.

When she got home, she stood against the wall of her living room, arms outstretched.

I am savoring this moment. I am savoring this victory. I am victorious.

In bed that night, she was still savoring her victory when the image of the homeless teens floated into her mind. She was surprised at how normal they had looked. She had been expecting them to look—scruffy, somehow.

Yolanda realized with a start that she hadn't lived at home in high school, either. Except she'd been at boarding school. But after she left Detroit, her mom had moved into an ashram. They didn't allow kids, so she hadn't really had a place to live either. What if things hadn't worked out at the Alice Lloyd Academy?

She drew on all of her willpower to interrupt those negative thoughts and go back to savoring her victory.

Chapter 11

At 10:15 the next day, Yolanda received a phone call summoning her to the Field Office. She arrived around 11:45 and was ushered into the conference room. Seated around the table were Peterson, Rafferty and James Campbell, the Assistant Special Agent in Charge of the San Francisco Field Office, whom she had only met once, on her first day.

Unlike Rafferty, who was ex-military, Campbell had dark hair moussed back, and his hands were manicured.

In the center of the table was a computer with large speakers.

Campbell and Rafferty were talking. Rafferty glanced up at her without changing his expression, then went back to what he was doing.

Yolanda stood behind Peterson and scribbled a note on her legal pad.

"What's up?" Yolanda had scrawled.

Peterson wrote back. "Something from the listening devices."

The two men kept playing snippets of what sounded like Sharon's voice and winding it back.

Finally, Campbell stopped the recording and walked over to Yolanda.

Her heart was banging against her ribs when he stood and reached out his hand. "Good work, Vance. I know you're still wet behind the ears, but you're operating like a pro. Have a seat and listen to this."

Yolanda shook his hand as Peterson hit a button on the keyboard, and Yolanda heard a faint hiss in the speakers. Then the ringing tone of a phone.

Meanwhile, Peterson pulled the computer itself toward her and plugged in the USB device Yolanda had used on Marcus's computer.

"Hello?" a female voice came over the speakers.

"Sharon, this is Marcus," he said.

"Hey honey, how's your day going?"

"Someone broke into my computer, Sharon."

"Marcus, you know the kids don't have computers, they're bound to sneak in for the internet—"

"No Sharon, this is some whole other shit. I always find Instagram windows open. But this is the computer with no internet. I came in and it's flashing 'ALERT! SECURITY BREACH!' Carlos installed that software in case someone specifically tried to hack into the computer."

"Are you sure?" she asked.

"It even says the time. 6:49 PM yesterday. That would have been after the RBG youth left, but before the homeless teens arrived. One of the only times the place has been empty."

"That's right. Since the church decided to let us use our office as a part-time shelter, there's always someone in there."

"I'm never out of here before seven. But my computer crashed yesterday, and I went out. Somebody's been waiting. I bet it's those motherfuckers from Randell. Something's up with this Anitra Jenkins thing."

"Did they take anything? Did they mess with the paper files?"

"I don't think so. I gave everything the once-over."

"Let's not jump to conclusions," Sharon said. "Let's talk to the teens about it this afternoon with Jimmy."

"You're damn right we're gonna talk about it. And then I'll ask the night shift what time they came in and I'm not leaving this goddamn office empty, even if I have to come in at seven thirty AM and leave at seven thirty PM."

"We're gonna figure this out, honey," Sharon said. "But I gotta go. Love you."

"Love you too."

The recording clicked, and Peterson shut off the machine.

"Vance, what's your take on this?" Campbell said. "Are they having an affair? 'Honey?' 'Love you?' Isn't she homosexual?" He flipped through the dossier on the group.

"She's definitely a lesbian," Yolanda said. "I don't think it's an affair, sir. They have a very . . ." she searched for the word. "Affectionate culture, sir. Everyone hugs each other. They all say 'I love you' quite often. I don't think it has a romantic connotation."

Rafferty made a face of distaste.

"Too bad," Campbell said. "Would have been a nice lever. What about this Carlos kid?" Campbell scanned the page of the young man's profile. "He obviously isn't really the one who installed the security system."

"With all due respect, sir," Peterson spoke up. "You'd be surprised what these kids can get their hands on through the internet."

"Seriously?" Campbell asked. "You want me to believe that a kid from the ghetto with an illiterate Mexican mother could detect an FBI device?"

As the moment stretched with no one speaking, Yolanda

could hear a faint buzz of the computer that was still running. Campbell glanced at Rafferty, but the case agent's face was blank.

"All right, Vance," Rafferty said. "Go through everything on Winters's hard drive and flag anything important. Also, now that the surveillance apparatus is up and working, we'll need you to review it daily."

"Yes, sir."

That evening, around eight PM, she logged onto the system to review the day's audio files that had been uploaded.

Marcus on the phone complaining about having been broken into. Marcus on the phone complaining he was stressed out. Marcus scheduling a psychotherapy appointment. She noted that in her report.

At 2:57 PM, Carlos came in and confirmed that an intruder had copied the hard drive. Later, the other teens came in and explained that they had all left just after six thirty.

"What about Yolanda?" Marcus asked.

"She left even before we did," one of the girls said.

For the next several days, the recordings were painfully routine. Marcus chatting up a funder about how important it was to invest in the next generation of leadership among people of color in the climate movement. Marcus making an appointment to take the van in for a tune-up.

Finally, she came across something.

"Marcus, this is David."

"Hey big Dave, how's the case going?"

"It looks good. We've got our exhumation hearing with Judge Greenlee, one of the most sympathetic judges we might have gotten."

"That's great," Marcus said. "He presided over that case

where the police wrongfully killed that pair of twin brothers, and the family got twenty mil."

"Hopefully, he'll be sympathetic about Anitra Jenkins," the lawyer said, and signed off.

The only other recording came from a listening device in the main room. Nakeesha and Sheena sat around on one of the couches. Supposedly, they were working on their articles for the newsletter, but mostly they gossiped. Yolanda learned more than she wanted to know about which friends had cheating boyfriends, who might be pregnant, and who had gotten arrested.

Then they gave out what they called "The Fashion Awards for the Week."

"Best dressed goes to KayLana, as always," Sheena said.

"That girl fitted every day cause her daddy the biggest drug dealer in town," Nakeesha agreed, rattling off several brand names. "But who got worst dressed this week?"

"Mrs. Lawton, my English teacher," Sheena said.

"Yassssss," Nakeesha agreed. "Whassup with the fake fur jacket? She look like she oughtta be on *The Muppets* with that shit."

Sheena cracked up.

"As always," Sheena said, "the award for most Afro-centric goes to Dana."

"Oh thank you," Nakeesha mimicked. "I'd like to thank my Blackness for making this moment possible."

"Don't be mean," Sheena said, but she still laughed.

"What else?" Nakeesha asked.

"I got a special award category this week," Sheena said. "Most Disappointing."

"For who?"

"Yolanda," Sheena said.

Yolanda blinked and ran the recording back to make sure she had heard correctly.

"Yolanda," Sheena's voice said in replay.

"Yolanda from here?" Nakeesha asked.

"Yeah," Sheena said. "She's cute, and she has a nice shape, but she dresses like . . . I don't know. She just has no style."

"You right about that," Nakeesha said. "She walks in the room and her clothes make me want to fall asleep."

They gave out several other awards, but Yolanda didn't pay attention. "Most disappointing"? She felt a burning in her chest, like when she was a kid at boarding school, so clearly outclassed by all those rich girls.

But what the hell was she supposed to wear? Bright pink sweat suits, and jeans so tight they rode up her butt? Years before, it had been Apple Bottoms. What was that? Comparing your ass to an apple?

The recording ended, and she rewound and played the section over again.

She's cute, and she has a nice shape . . .

No style . . .

Her clothes make me want to fall asleep . . .

She stood up and looked at herself in the mirror. Plain white t-shirt, navy blue sweats. No brand names. Not much color.

She had a specific suit she wore to interviews. Another suit for second interviews. As an attorney, she had a great wardrobe. The cashmere coat, the beautiful boots. As an FBI attorney working white-collar, she had bought several affordable dark suits. But as an FBI agent on assignment? She just sort of put together the casual dregs of old wardrobes.

In college, Yolanda had always seen fashion as something girls showed off for each other. A waste of time, since they weren't the ones who could really help you get ahead. *What do you call a girl with a designer outfit and bad grades? A receptionist.*

Yolanda scrolled through the audio file and played the clip of the recording again.

With Lester Johnakin in mind, Yolanda tried to find something positive. They were disappointed because they thought she was pretty. She wasn't making the most of her assets. Johnakin would say "look for the useful feedback." They thought her look was boring. She had the power to change that. She would change it.

After an hour of online shopping, she purchased a few sweat suits, in bright blue, purple and red. She wouldn't change everything at once. Just add a little more color each time she saw them.

She looked for t-shirts that would express something interesting. It seemed like all the trendy tees were white bands from the '80s and '90s. She finally found a shirt that said "trust black women," and bought that in a size smaller than she usually would wear.

But Yolanda couldn't stop thinking about the last time she had cared about fashion—in boarding school.

From her miserable Detroit middle school, she had dreamed that the Alice Lloyd Academy would be different. Smart kids wouldn't be jealous of her—she would find her place in the cream of the crop. She rode by herself on the plane, an unaccompanied minor, with friendly flight attendants offering her food and sodas. When she arrived at Alice Lloyd, it was just like a movie, with brick buildings and green lawns, smart girls and great sports facilities. But it wasn't as "diverse" as the brochures had implied. She was the only black girl in her grade.

When she arrived as a freshwoman, she made top spots on the junior varsity teams in soccer and volleyball. The coach praised her skill but warned her to be humble. Apparently a few of the girls from the lower school had returned from the summer break expecting those positions. "They might be jealous."

But Yolanda didn't encounter any jealousy. Only encouragement.

"You're so amazing," Dale, one of the girls on the team showered Yolanda with praise. "And you never had a personal trainer or anything?"

"Pure talent," another girl agreed.

They were two of the four most powerful freshwomen in school: pretty, smart, wealthy, and strong athletes. They had been friends since they had arrived at the Alice Lloyd lower school for seventh grade.

Over the next two months, they treated Yolanda like a favored pet. They even took her shopping and bought her designer clothes. "Retail therapy," Dale called it, as if Yolanda was doing her a favor by giving her a reason to shop more.

In some ways, those two months were magical. She could be smart and athletic and popular and glamorous.

In fact, she was wearing one of the outfits Dale had bought her when her history teacher confronted her in class.

"Miss Vance, where's your midterm paper?" she asked, her stern face looking over a stack of papers in her hand.

"I'll turn it in next week," she assured the teacher as another student walked in and handed in her paper.

"Next week? Miss Vance, it's due today."

"But I'll get it in by the end of the grace period," Yolanda faltered.

"There's no grace period, Miss Vance," the history teacher said sharply. "Is that what you had at your public school? This is a college preparatory school. We prepare you for college, where there is no grace period. There's a grading period, though. You'll get an F for that."

Yolanda flushed and headed to her seat bewildered. She tried to sort the jumble of her thoughts through the shame.

She had told Dale the night before that she was worried about her history midterm report, that she didn't think she was doing her best work. Dale had told her that it was an unspoken rule for freshwomen that you had a grace period of a week for the assignment. Had the rule changed? Had Yolanda misunderstood?

At dinner, she caught up with her friend. "Dale," Yolanda grabbed her shoulder. "The history teacher wouldn't let me use the unspoken rule."

"The what?" Dale asked coolly.

"The grace period," Yolanda insisted. "She didn't believe me."

"What grace period?" Dale blinked, as if confused.

"For turning in my midterm paper."

"Oh, that," Dale dismissed it. "I guess they've changed the unspoken rule."

"Well, can you talk to her? Tell her you told me about it? Let her know I was ready to turn in my paper?" Yolanda said. "I can finish it by tomorrow."

"You didn't turn it in?"

"You said I didn't need to."

"You must have misunderstood me," Dale insisted.

"But you—" Yolanda faltered. She knew it was all wrong. Not only had Dale assured her that she would have another week, she had also invited Yolanda to spend the rest of the evening watching movies on another friend's laptop, deliberately pressing her to leave the paper unfinished.

"Sorry sweetie," Dale shrugged. "Better luck next time."

As she walked away, Yolanda had a sick feeling in her stomach. Her mind spun. Was it a race thing? A money thing? Dale and her friends were second and third generation Alice Lloyd students. Was this some sort of insider rule that only applied to them?

Yolanda stayed up all night finishing her history paper,

her iron focus kept the feelings of anger and confusion at bay. The next morning, she suited up for an early soccer practice. She was uneasy about facing Dale and her friends on the field. Clearly Dale had turned on her, but were the other girls still Yolanda's friends?

Out on the field, the coach called her over.

"Sorry Vance," she explained. "You're on academic probation. No team sports til you clean that up. But you're my best player. If you get your grades back up, and work out every day, you'll be in shape when basketball season starts next term."

Yolanda looked over the coach's shoulder at her former friends. A tight knot of four heads, glossy with expensive haircare products, diamond and gem earrings glittering on each of their ears, skin still wearing the last traces of tans from their summer together in the south of France.

What a fool she'd been. With her downfall, each of them moved up on the team to the places they had considered their rightful positions by ascension.

Numb with rage, she went back to her room. Her roommate was just waking up, a girl from China who was practically pre-med already. Carefully, Yolanda folded up all the designer clothes that Dale had bought for her and put them in two paper bags that she left outside Dale's door.

She went out for a run, playing her "Aretha Sings the Blues" album in her headphones. When she was far out onto the trail, miles out of everybody's earshot, she blasted "Nobody Knows the Way I Feel This Morning," and was swept up by a wave of rage and grief so strong that her knees buckled and she collapsed. Out on the wooded grounds, no one could hear her fists pounding on the moist dirt, her feet kicking the trunk of a nearby tree, her screams of fury into the fabric of her jacket over her forearm. By the time she returned, the jacket was sodden, with a brackish mix of sweat and tears.

In the bathroom, she took off her shoes and socks and stepped into the shower with all her clothes on, peeling them off, piece by piece. She wrung each one out under the spray. She wanted nothing left of her tears, her defeat.

As she dried off, she hardened inside into a cold resolve. She would beat those white girls at everything: sports and academics.

Four years later, she walked out of Alice Lloyd with all the honors: class valedictorian, MVP on each of her teams, and a full scholarship to Cartwright College.

Her freshman history class was the only A- to mar her otherwise perfect record.

Chapter 12

The Wednesday morning after the break-in, Yolanda sat at on the tiny sofa in the apartment editing RBG's monthly newsletter.

"Hey Yolanda," Marcus had said at the previous Sunday meeting. "I know you're studying for the bar, but do you have a minute to proofread something?"

"No problem," Yolanda had smiled and reached for the draft copy. Marcus promised to email her the file so she could make corrections.

The Sunday general meeting had gone well, attended by more people than usual, as word had spread in the neighborhood about the break-in.

But Yolanda was beginning to see the pattern. People came to the big community meetings and showed up for particular events, but day-to-day, it was the same core of kids and sometimes a few of their friends. Which was good, because that meant it was unlikely that Kenya would show up.

Nothing notable had taken place during the week. The lawyer was waiting to hear back from the judge on the motion to exhume Anitra Jenkins.

As she scanned through the newsletter, she noted that most of the articles had been written by the kids.

Sheena had written an article about the Randell Executive Vice President Andrew Wentworth, and all the money he made. These kids were full of contradictions. On the one hand, they wanted to make money, but they seemed resentful of the rich.

Yolanda heard their rap music blasting every day with lyrics about nothing but money. Yolanda had even heard Sheena singing: "Peel Off Another Hunnit"

> *Come on nigga, peel off another hunnit*
> *spend my vacation on my yacht straight blunted*
> *relaxing in the Caribbean beach fronted*

Yolanda had wanted to ask why it was fine for this rap artist to relax in the Caribbean and smoke marijuana, but they complained about the Randell VP spending time in his fishing cabin at Lake Berryessa?

Johnakin would say that those who want to prosper shouldn't waste their energy envying or attacking those who have already achieved prosperity.

Proofing for errors took longer than she expected. Clearly, Marcus hadn't run the spell check on the different articles. Yolanda tried to let it auto correct, but *Nakeesha* became *Handshakes*, and *hella* became *hello,* so she had to do it manually.

It was fine to use a little slang, but some of the pieces were almost unintelligible. It took hours to correct. By the time she finished, she barely had time to run to the gym, before she needed to be at RBG for her Wednesday tutoring group. Dana, Sheena, and Nakeesha had expressed interest in becoming lawyers, and had named themselves Future Lawyers Of the Way, or FLOW. "The Way" was slang for Holloway. As in *I live in the Way,* or, old school, *I live around the Way.*

After her workout, Yolanda had showered and changed into her new form-fitting sweat suit and "trust black women" tee. Two young guys driving by in an old car honked at her. These clothes weren't going to make anyone fall asleep.

Yolanda arrived at the office and found Marcus on the phone. She waved at him and set the proofread newsletter on his desk.

"Listen," he was saying. "Planet Greener needs to stop nickel and diming us to death."

She dragged two of the couches out into the main room as Sheena and Dana walked in.

After they'd hugged her, Sheena said, "Somebody looks cute today. You been shopping?"

"I just wanted a change," Yolanda said. "Dana, where do you get all your t-shirts?"

"Mostly at the Ashby Flea Market in Berkeley," Dana said.

"Excuse me, Yolanda," Marcus came out of the office. "Can I speak to you for a minute?"

She followed Marcus into the office, and he closed the door behind them.

Her eyes flitted around the office where the bugs were, as a thin film of perspiration began forming on her forehead. His face was hard, a sharp line between his eyebrows. This was it.

"Yolanda," he said, his voice low. "I don't even know how to ask this question."

She swallowed. "Just ask, Marcus."

"Have you read any of our other newsletters?"

That wasn't the question she expected. But Yolanda nodded. "I've read them all."

"Then you should be familiar with the young people's voices."

"Their voices?" she asked.

"I asked you to proofread the newsletter. For typos. You completely rewrote it."

Her draft of the newsletter was covered with blue question marks next to most of the changes she'd made.

"I just cleaned up the errors," she explained.

Marcus sighed. "They're not errors. It's how they talk."

"Exactly," Yolanda said. "But it's not appropriate for the written word."

"Come on Yolanda," Marcus said. "These kids are about to give you all their money and all they're asking in return honey."

"Excuse me?" Yolanda asked.

"R-E-S-P-E-C-T," Marcus said. "Aretha Franklin."

Yolanda nodded. She knew that song.

"Bottom line, this is not an English class—" Marcus began, but then broke off. He crossed his arms and surveyed her. "Yolanda Vance, you're a very interesting sister, you know that?"

"What do you mean?"

"Sometimes I'm so glad to have you on board. And then other times, like this, you just don't seem to get it."

"I'm sorry, Marcus." She tried for an expression that was part confused, part contrite. "Can you explain it to me?"

"Where did you grow up?" he answered her question with a question.

"Sort of all over," Yolanda said.

"What I'm trying to ask," Marcus said. "Is did you grow up around black people?"

"Around all kinds of people."

"But in a neighborhood that looked like this? Like Holloway?"

How could she explain herself? In Georgia, she had been around all black people til she was five. But it was different. All houses. Clean streets. Everybody went to church. The other side of town was more like Holloway. Sometimes she visited. She recalled a woman in a tight orange flowered dress, and a thick shag carpet in a small apartment. Walls of cheap fake wood. The clink of alcohol in glasses. The sound of laughter, of music.

She recalled being in church, asking her mother for something. *Axing*. No, baby, it's *ask*, her mother had corrected. A-S-K, sounding out the *sk* sound with her.

Her mother had trained as a teacher at Howard University.

"I'm sorry," Marcus said into the silence. "That wasn't a fair question. I'm just trying to understand where you're coming from." He uncrossed his arms and put them in the pockets of his jeans. "I know you went to Cartwright, and to Harvard. Personally, I'm self-educated. I just—you need to understand RBG's values. We don't change the grammar of the young people's voices. Not in speech, not on the page. It's a political position. I thought you understood that."

Yolanda shook her head and swallowed against the knot in her chest.

"When I was little, I lived in Carson, Georgia," Yolanda said. "When I was in middle school I lived in Detroit. Both of those neighborhoods were pretty much all black. In between was California, which was a mix, and Colorado, which was mostly white people. And then prep school."

"I didn't mean to give you the blackness third degree," Marcus said. "I'm sorry. Can I start over?"

"Okay," Yolanda nodded, and the knot loosened slightly.

"Yolanda," he smiled broadly. "Thanks so much for proofing the newsletter for us. You did a great job. In fact, you did too great of a job. I can see that *I* wasn't clear enough about what I wanted. I should have explained that I wanted you to check for typos, not to change any of the grammar."

"I get it," she said, her voice clipped.

"I'm sorry I was hard on you," he said.

"My mistake," she said, reaching for the draft of the newsletter. "I'll fix it tonight."

"No," Marcus said. "I couldn't make you do it over."

Yolanda took hold of the paper, still in his hand. "Marcus," she said. "I always give my best. Sometimes I do it wrong if I don't know the rules, but once I know, I follow through."

"Okay," Marcus said, and let go of the draft. "I'm really sorry for what I said before. You make a big difference here—to the youth, to me, to the whole organization. You're a good sister, Yolanda."

She couldn't quite meet his eyes. She said, "no biggie," and walked out into the main room to tutor Nakeesha in social studies.

The memories of Georgia stung. She hadn't been there in twenty years, but it was the last time she had felt at home. Sometimes she would dream of the place, green and humid, the pecan tree outside her bedroom window, the woods behind their house.

Waking from those dreams was always the worst, to find herself in some cramped Los Angeles apartment with her mom. Or worse, living with one of her mother's idiot white boyfriends. Or as a teen in a boarding school or college dorm. All the green and comfort draining out of her, all the home.

Two months after her layoff from Van Dell, Meyers and Whitney, Yolanda had bundled most of her clothing and furniture into two giant green boxes on the sidewalk. She waited in front of her exclusive Chelsea apartment building, in full view of the doorman and the neighbors, for the storage people to come haul it away to somewhere upstate. Yolanda had smoothed her hand along the soft leather of the designer boots as she boxed them for storage, along with the cashmere coat and angora scarf as she downsized for the studio apartment in Queens.

Now she had nothing but regrets for staying in the Manhattan apartment after the layoff. She had just assumed she would be able to bounce back in corporate law. Before word got out that she was the one who wouldn't shred papers for her firm.

An immediate move to Queens could have meant a year to look for work. Toward the end, she had begun to apply for jobs in New Jersey, Ohio, even Vermont. She created a revised version of her resume, cut out Harvard law, and did temp work to stretch her dwindling savings, but it was hard to work and job hunt at the same time.

She recalled one afternoon, she knelt in a subterranean hospital basement in the Bronx, alphabetizing patient files, when her cell phone rang, a callback from a Connecticut law firm. She ran up the stairs to the lobby where her cell had decent reception, only to find out that they were calling to cancel her second interview. She dragged herself back down into the basement and got chewed out and fired by a supervisor for taking personal calls during work hours. It took her nearly three hours to get home to her apartment in Queens, on three trains and a bus.

By the time she walked in the door, she was so desperate that she dug out her old address book. She dialed the Boulder, Colorado, number that she had never bothered to transfer to her smart phone.

"Life of Bliss meditation center," a familiar, breathy voice floated across the line.

"Mama?"

"Yolanda," she could hear the smile in her mother's voice. "What a blessing to hear from you."

Yolanda's mother thought everything was a blessing: a delicious tangerine, the sunrise, hearing from her daughter for the first time in years.

"I'm—I'm not doing well, Mama."

"I'm sorry to hear that," her mother said with no change in her tone. "I've been praying for your happiness."

"Mama, I got laid off from my job, and I can't find any work."

"Yolanda, you'll never find contentment until you open space for your right livelihood."

"Mama, I'm out of money."

"Your attachment to material reality is the true cause of your suffering."

"I was wondering if you could possibly make me a loan."

"God will provide."

"So there's no way you'd loan me any money?"

"If you're not on your path, no amount of material energy will rectify the disharmony."

"Well, if it comes to it, could I—" Yolanda could barely force the words out. "Could I come to Colorado to stay with you? Just til I can get back on my feet."

"Of course, Yolanda. You're always welcome. Except next month, because I'm subletting the house and spending a month in India. I'm adopting twins, a boy and a girl. What a blessing."

"Mama, I'm afraid I'll end up on the street."

"Don't worry, Yolanda. I'm going to visualize a job for you."

"Mama, please. I need your help."

"I see you outside in nature, surrounded by lots of other people with strong energy."

"I don't know why I even bothered to call," Yolanda swallowed down the tears that threatened to form. Just like the time in college when she needed her birth certificate to get her passport, and her mother had said that borders were an illusion.

Yolanda had missed the trip with the basketball team to Italy. While the team was away, she sent for her birth certificate, vowing never again to ask her mother for help.

Sitting in the Queens apartment, she regretted breaking her vow.

"I see children," her mother continued. "I see you working with children. I see all your chakras opening."

"Mama, I have to go now."

"Don't worry Yolanda. You're going to be fine. All is well."

Yolanda had hung up the phone, refused to cry, put on her sneakers and jogged six miles.

It was the only time she'd spoken to her mother since college. The thought of it still burned in her chest.

By now her mother would be long back from India, and her new twins settled into their new life in Boulder. At least as twins they'd have each other.

The stab of the memory mixed with the disorienting revelation that her mother had also been right about working outside and with young people. She wouldn't, however, be holding her breath waiting for her chakras to open up.

Chapter 13

That Sunday at the meeting, Yolanda was sitting on one end of the couch, next to Nakeesha and Sheena. She was sharing a bag of blue potato chips with the two girls when Jimmy walked in late. The group had already done introductions and was moving on to announcements, when he sat down in the chair next to her.

"So we all need to go down and pack the school board meeting on Thursday," Dana was saying. "We're gonna let the board know that these racist teachers need to get fired or at least to be publicly held accountable."

Jimmy leaned over and murmured in Yolanda's ear. "So how you been?" he asked, smiling. "I'm still waiting at the runner's trail on campus."

"Fine, thank you," she said. She covered her mouth, which was full of potato chips. They might be lodged, bright blue, between her teeth.

With Jimmy sitting next to her, Yolanda was already feeling awkward when Marcus made an unexpected announcement: "I just want to take a minute to appreciate one of our newest members, Yolanda Vance." He stood up and detailed a number of things she had done: coming to the police station, the tutoring session, inspiring FLOW. "Finally," he said, "I really appreciate her for proofreading the newsletter. She did a great job with it and was our most thorough proofreader yet." As he spoke, he handed out the copies. "So let's give a round of applause to our newest adult ally!"

As they clapped, Yolanda was mortified, running her tongue across her teeth, hoping to remove any fragments of blue.

"Plus," Nakeesha added, "she been looking hella cute lately."

"Hear, hear," Jimmy murmured.

Yolanda felt her face flush. She wanted to sink into the chair. She was grateful to know that she would get a copy of the recordings from the rest of the meeting, because she was unable to pay attention. She was completely distracted by the chemistry between her and Jimmy, the feeling that everyone was watching her, and worrying about blue chip fragments.

When the meeting finally ended, she tried to leap up, but Jimmy caught her gently by the wrist.

"Yolanda, wait," Jimmy said. "Can we talk for a minute?"

"Sure, uh, how are you doing?" she asked lamely.

"I'm good," he said, and put a hand on her back to lead her away from the crowd. Even though his voice was low, she was aware of the spot above the window where the listening device would be recording everything. "You know I thought—I hoped really—that I would see you on the campus," Jimmy began. "But I've been swamped with midterms and haven't made it out of my office much."

"Sounds like you're really busy. Me too. I should really—"

"Yolanda, I would very much love to take you out sometime. I mean, when Marcus announced that you've been making so much time for RBG, I thought maybe you could make time in your busy bar-studying schedule for some dinner. You gotta eat, right?"

"I don't know," she said.

"I mean," he stumbled on, "I know it's awkward to talk here. And, well, I have your phone number from the phone list. But I didn't want to be inappropriate and use it for personal reasons if my call would be unwelcome, you know. In which case, I could just forget the number, and get an anchor or a rose or something over the place where I tattooed it on my heart."

She burst out laughing.

"Can I take that as a yes?"

"Why don't you just call," she suggested.

"Okay," Jimmy said, his smile luminous with delight.

As she walked away, she could still feel his smile beaming into her, and a mixture of elation and dread pooled in her intestines, thick like molasses, like tar.

"Good work, Vance," Rafferty offered a rare compliment in their special briefing the next day. She sat across from him at his desk with Peterson.

"It's no big deal, sir," Yolanda mumbled.

"Don't argue with success," Peterson said. "You've planted the bugs in less than a month."

Rafferty gave a noncommittal grunt. "Peterson will brief you for your contact with Thompson."

"You don't want to ask questions the first time out," Peterson was saying as they arrived at her cubicle. "Act like it's any regular date. Be charming. Get him to like you. Ask him about himself. Be honest about your life as much as possible. Lying means more things to remember."

"Will I need to wear a wire?" Yolanda asked.

"No need," Peterson said. "We'll see what develops."

On her way out, Yolanda peeked in the door of Agent Donnelly's office. Donnelly was huddled with three other agents, including Rafferty. She looked up and saw Yolanda, then walked out to greet her.

"Looks like a bad time," Yolanda said.

"Unfortunately, yes," she said in a loud, jovial voice. "But don't give up on me. We're gonna have lunch one of these days."

Donnelly patted her on the back and leaned close.

"Rafferty is such an ass," the senior agent murmured in her ear. "He's got you dating a subject? If things get dicey, you give me a call."

The next evening, Yolanda's cell phone rang. She picked it up when she saw the name "O. Thompson."

"The lovely Yolanda," Jimmy said, his voice softer and more intimate than on campus or at RBG.

"So the answer is yes," she said. "I'd love to go out with you sometime. Maybe next weekend? I was thinking of a day outing."

"Wow," Jimmy said. "I thought I'd have to spend the first twenty minutes convincing you to go out with me and the next twenty convincing you to pick a date before you take the bar in July."

"Nope," Yolanda said. "I'm a decisive woman."

"Okay Ms. Decisive," Jimmy laughed. "Did you have a destination in mind?"

"I was thinking maybe the Ashby Flea Market," Yolanda suggested.

"Sounds great," Jimmy said.

They agreed to go on BART, Saturday at noon.

Only after they said their goodbyes and hung up did she allow herself to lie back on the bed and let the excitement wash over her, her whole body tingling silently, secretly, unobserved and unrecorded.

On Wednesday, Yolanda walked into the RBG offices to do tutoring but the teens were already there. Dana was standing next to a large flip chart that said KNOW YOUR RIGHTS.

Underneath it was written "police" and "ICE" in Dana's neat block letters.

"We're not doing tutoring today," Sheena said. "We need to make a legal handout for a public services fair at school. If they're gonna have the police and social workers and all that, we're gonna present the other side."

"So far, we got the obvious stuff," Nakeesha said. "Know your rights when the police stop you. And know your rights when ICE comes to your house."

"Which basically both come down to don't open your door," Darnell said. "If they have a warrant for somebody's arrest, they need to show it to you. And it's only good at that person's house. Then you have to open the door by law. But otherwise, you don't need to do shit. Which is how my cousin got caught up. They had a warrant for his arrest, but they came and got him at my grandma's house."

"And even if ICE has a deportation warrant, they don't have the right to enter without your consent," Sheena said. "If you don't open the door voluntarily, they can't come in."

"Talk to them through the closed and locked door," Darnell said. "Ask the cops to slip the warrant under the door or hold it up to the window for you to see. Cause cops be lying."

Yolanda sat down on the couch. She had finally gotten into the groove with the tutoring, but now she wasn't sure what her role was supposed to be.

"Okay," Dana said. "We got the basics for our handout on the cops and ICE, but what else should we be talking about in terms of legal rights?"

"I think we need to talk about that emancipation proclamation," Nakeesha said. "Because I have this friend who got in trouble at school for forging her mama's name, but her mama is high all the time and won't sign nothing. So my friend basically got no rights."

"She has the right to get birth control in the state of

California without parental consent," Sheena said. She leaned over to Yolanda. "I used to be a peer sex educator."

"I think you mean your friend wants to be declared an 'emancipated minor,'" Yolanda said. "She needs to have an adult status, even though she's underage, because her parents aren't functioning as parents."

"Yeah," Nakeesha said.

Dana wrote "emancipated minor" on the paper.

"I've studied that law, but not in California," Yolanda said. She had researched it for herself in boarding school.

"Well, you need to look that up," Nakeesha said. "We want that for our handout."

Yolanda nodded and pulled out a yellow legal pad to take notes.

"And what about the point Sheena brought up," Dana said. "About not needing parental consent for birth control."

"Or abortion," Sheena said. "Some of these fake abortion places are up here lying to girls about all kinds of stuff. They need to listen to their baby's heartbeat. They need parental consent. Counselors telling them they'll never get over it if they have an abortion. You know what you really don't get over? Having a baby when you don't want to have a baby."

"And the baby don't never get over it, either," Nakeesha said.

"People never talk about these things when they talk about knowing your rights," Dana said. "I mean, stuff with ICE and the police is really important, but what about stuff that focuses on girls?"

Dana wrote "reproductive rights" on the paper.

"Our handout needs all this birth control stuff," Nakeesha said. "But we also need something about sexual harassment. This boy grabbed me in the hallway and I punched him, right? Then *I* got in trouble. The counselor told me 'boys will be boys.' Nah. Boys will get they ass kicked if they grab me in the hallway."

"That's right," Dana said. "We need to check the school policies about that." She misspelled "harassment" with two Rs and a single S, then rewrote it with the correct spelling.

"It's more than school policy," Yolanda said. "It's federal law through title nine."

"I thought that was about girls can play sports," Dana said, looking up from the paper.

"It's both," Yolanda said. "Title nine of the Education Amendments Act of 1972 says nobody can be discriminated against or excluded from anything in public education on the basis of sex. That includes sexual harassment in schools."

"Man," Nakeesha said. "I need to get me a baseball bat and carry it in the hallway. And when these boys try to mess with me, I'll hit them upside the head and be all 'Title nine, bitch!'"

Everyone laughed.

"That's not exactly how the law works," Yolanda said.

Nakeesha crossed her arms. "Nah. But it should."

Chapter 14

This is not a date. This is not a date. This is not a date. Yolanda kept repeating it to herself on Saturday at 11:45, as she stood on the plaza outside the Holloway BART subway station.

Yet she had taken extra care when she flatironed her hair after coming back from the gym. Halfway through, she had realized that maybe he wouldn't like it. The adults in RBG wore dreadlocks and afros. Only some of the teens wore their hair straight. Yolanda had never lived anywhere that black women didn't straighten their hair. It was something you just did. Her clothes were casual—jeans and a royal blue t-shirt. But her hair would show the effort, she told herself as the steam hissed from the hair between the hot surfaces of the flatiron. She wouldn't wear her usual ponytail. She would wear it loose.

At the BART station, a light wind blew her hair into her face. Maybe she should have just worn the ponytail, she thought to herself. She finger combed her hair out of her eyes, scanning the people for Jimmy's dark brown face and ready smile.

The Holloway station was part of the original BART system built in the seventies. It had a pavilion-style building above the ground and a brick plaza outside. A covered rack for bikes stretched along the far end, and a line of buses pulled up along the curb in front to pick up passengers who waited on wooden benches. On either side of the station, two busy parking lots attracted suburban commuters who paid to park their cars and beat the freeway commute into San Francisco.

One thing that had changed since she had lived there was the appearance of high-rise lofts. All around the BART station were gated apartments. They were cookie-cutter buildings with underground parking beneath a dozen floors of apartments that hardly anyone in Holloway could afford.

A trio of white guys came out of one of the buildings and jaywalked to the train station.

The BART plaza bustled with Saturday foot traffic, but Yolanda didn't see Jimmy anywhere. In the distance, she saw a figure cut through the front parking lot with the right broad shoulders and confident walk. The sudden spike in her heart rate unsettled her.

As the figure approached, his shiny blue jacket looked wrong. As he came nearer, he waved to someone else.

She felt her phone buzz, signaling a text. Jimmy saying he had to cancel? Would she be relieved? Disappointed?

It turned out it was Marcus. The judge had granted the exhumation order. He wanted her to join their legal observers. She texted back yes and would include that in her FBI report.

Yolanda pocketed her phone and looked up to see a young mother of three struggle out through the fare gates of the BART subway. A baby slept on one side of her double-stroller, which had to come out through the emergency exit.

"You need to get in there with your sister," she said to her toddler son, who was running back and forth in front of the ticket machines. "I ain't gonna carry you, and you too wild today." He began to scream as she buckled him in against his will. His sister slept through the tantrum.

The young woman called to her oldest, a preschool boy who had climbed up into one of the planters. "Git yo ass down from there and stay by me, you hear?"

The #37 bus pulled up to the stop at the station, and the woman queued up in line.

"Come on, now," she called to the little boy. "We gon miss our bus."

The boy tried to climb down, but couldn't find his footing. He began to whine.

"Need help, little man?" Jimmy asked, walking up to the child.

The boy nodded but didn't take his eyes off his mother who was struggling to get the stroller onto the bus.

Jimmy carried the boy over to his mother, who grabbed his hand.

"I'm a leave yo ass one of these days," she said to the boy. The she turned to Jimmy. "Thank you," she said, and offered him a tired smile as the bus door closed.

Jimmy walked over to Yolanda. "I paid them to make me look good for you. We rehearsed a lot yesterday. The kid did great, don't you think?"

"So nice of you to keep the community employed," Yolanda said.

"All in a day's work," he said, as they headed down into the station.

As they sat next to each other on the train, she could feel the warmth through his "Green New Deal" t-shirt where her shoulder touched his arm.

As they passed through Berkeley, Yolanda confessed that she'd never been in the city. Only the university for basketball games.

"I got a free ride to Cartwright, so I didn't bother to check out any other colleges."

"But didn't you come to Berkeley for parties?" He had to speak up as the train went underground. "There's nothing going on at Cartwright."

"Exactly," Yolanda said. "No distractions."

When the doors opened at Berkeley's downtown station, Jimmy grabbed her hand and rushed her off the train. "This is unacceptable. You've gotta see Berkeley today."

When they came up from the station, she immediately thought of Harvard Square. In the plaza, she saw the same fast-walking young students in jeans buying coffee and running to the bank. She also saw the same scruffy skateboarding teens and homeless people asking for spare change in grimy Starbucks cups.

"Reminds me of Cambridge," she said.

"Right," he said. "I forgot you were a Hah-vahd girl."

As they reached the next corner, he pointed down the street. "I'm a public school guy myself. McClymond's High in West Oakland. UC Berkeley undergrad."

"So, where'd you get your PhD?" she asked, as they walked past a movie theater with a long line for the latest superhero blockbuster.

"Columbia," he said.

"I almost went to Barnard," she said of Columbia's sister college for women. "I always wanted to be in New York City."

"So?" Jimmy asked. "Why didn't you?"

"Cartwright had better athletics," she said. "And too many men at Columbia. I didn't want a co-ed college experience."

"Co-education is part of the college experience," Jimmy explained. "It's one of the things about teaching at a women's college that I don't like. Half my students have crushes on me simply because I'm the only guy they ever see."

"Don't be so modest," Yolanda said. "You're an attractive guy."

"Food always looks more appealing to the starving," Jimmy said. "Sometimes I feel like Indiana Jones in that movie where the girl is batting her eyes at him and her eyelids say '*love*' '*you*.' I give my students flyers to co-ed social events so they can meet some guys their own age."

"Maybe they don't want to meet guys their own age. Maybe it's helpful to have a crush on their professor because it motivates them to do well in school and secure their future. Maybe the guys their age are knuckleheads who would just distract them from what's important."

"Relationships are important, too," Jimmy said.

"Sure," Yolanda agreed. "But not til after a woman is. . . . more established. I watched girls fail out of school behind stupid relationships with boys who certainly weren't losing any sleep over them."

Jimmy stopped and looked at her squarely. "I know your type, Yolanda Vance. You never think it's the right time to get involved. Not til I get my degree. Not til I finish law school. Not til I pass the bar. Not til I get through my first year at the firm." He began to walk again, and she fell into step with him.

"It's a good plan," she said.

"Then what are you doing out with me? Distracting yourself from studying for the California bar?"

They had passed the shops and bustle of downtown, and were moving through a section of Shattuck Avenue with big car dealerships and less foot traffic.

"I had a box for you, Jimmy," Yolanda confessed. "You were supposed to be my motivational crush."

"Your what?" he asked, eyebrows raised.

"You heard me," she said. "You were supposed to be the attractive guy that I looked forward to beating at the runner's path three days a week. A little flirtation, and a really good workout."

"So I was like your unpaid personal trainer," he said.

"I wouldn't quite say that," Yolanda said.

Jimmy affected a high pitched voice: "But what about my needs??"

"Please," Yolanda laughed. "I would've been *your* personal trainer. You needed somebody to motivate you on the track. Your form is sloppy, and you weren't giving your best."

"Oh," Jimmy said, laughing. "So you were doing me a favor?"

"More or less."

"So what changed your mind?" Jimmy asked. "Why are you out with me breathing Berkeley air on a perfectly gorgeous Saturday, when you could be in a gloomy library studying for the bar?"

They had veered onto Adeline Street, a broad, tree-lined boulevard with a wide, grassy strip in the middle that had more trees, even a picnic table on one block, kind of a mini park in the middle of the street.

"I broke form," Yolanda said. "I had a neat little place for you—the guy at the track. But you showed up somewhere else in my life and I . . ."

"You couldn't just jog off with your gorgeous self and leave me drooling after you," Jimmy said.

"I wasn't gonna quit RBG just because you showed up there. I believe in what those kids are doing. If we had met at RBG for the first time, I would have kept it strictly professional. But I couldn't act like we hadn't met before, and I couldn't act like I hadn't flirted with you. I tried to avoid you—"

"Yeah, I noticed."

"But you were persistent, so I decided to talk to you, to accept the inevitable."

"Damn, you make our date sound like the chicken pox," he said, laughing.

"It's not a date," she said.

"Whatever," he said. "We're almost there."

Yolanda could see what looked like a tent city in the Ashby BART station parking lot, with dozens of canopies of various colors that were visible. The actual station was underground.

As they got closer, Yolanda could hear the sound of drums in between bursts of traffic noise from the busy intersection. As she entered the market itself, Yolanda saw mostly brown faces as patrons strolled past booths selling used and new items.

"It reminds me a little of the church bazaars we used to have in the parking lot back in Georgia," she said.

"Georgia?" he asked. "I hadn't pegged you as a Southern girl."

"One of the many places I lived," she said.

She recalled summer days, running around with a pack of kids, begging tastes of pound cake and BBQ chicken from the church women. She always went home stuffed and falling asleep in the back seat of the car.

The Ashby flea market was more eclectic and Afrocentric than any Georgia church bazaar. Several vendors were selling brightly colored African textiles and beads, cowrie shell jewelry, and ebony statues. Nearby, a long line of patrons waited at a food truck selling West African cuisine.

Each booth was located in a numbered stall or two in the BART parking lot. Pedestrians wandered leisurely up and down the aisles that, on weekdays, would be crowded with cars of rush hour commuters.

Loud dancehall reggae music blared from a booth selling clothing in color combinations of green, yellow, red, and black. Incense burned in another booth that also sold black soap, shea butter lotion, and scented candles. A tiny glass bottle of Blue Nile scented oil blazed turquoise when Yolanda held it up to the light.

One booth had political t-shirts, with mug shots of different members of the Black Power Movement: Assata Shakur, Angela Davis, and Huey Newton. Yolanda recalled from her training at Quantico that the Black Panthers were one of the black identity extremist groups the Bureau had fought in the sixties.

"See anything you want?" Jimmy asked, as they passed a hardware booth with electrical equipment, phone cords, and gloves of every description. The Asian woman working there smiled at them.

"Just looking," Yolanda said. "How about you?"

"What I want isn't sold here at the market," he said, looking her in the face.

Yolanda looked beyond Jimmy at some of the other shoppers: the two gray-haired women walking ahead of them, a pair of young women pushing strollers in their direction, the young man with orange dreadlocks and gold teeth, his arm around a manicured young woman with a straight weave the same sandy brown color as her skin.

"Look," Yolanda said, pointing to a booth across the way. "Maybe those are the t-shirts I've been looking for."

Yolanda saw stacks of snug-fitting tees that said "Black Princess," "Sexy Queen," "Looking for a BMW—Black Man Working."

"I just got these in this week," the older black woman with the plaid wool cap offered. She held up a shirt with a black and yellow traffic-style sign. It had a silhouette of a female crossing the street. APPROACH WITH CAUTION, it said. BLACK WOMAN ON A MISSION.

"The perfect shirt for you," Jimmy said.

"Or maybe this one," the woman suggested, lifting up a shirt that said, DANGER: EDUCATED BLACK WOMAN.

"I like that," Yolanda said, and asked for a size small. She held the red shirt up to her chest and looked in the mirror. Jimmy looked over her shoulder.

"Will I offend you if I offer to buy you the shirt?" he asked.

"I got it," she said, handing the vendor a twenty-dollar bill.

They strolled back to the food truck, and Yolanda had African food for the first time.

Jimmy had suggested the jollof rice and plantains with chicken.

"These are so good," she said, digging into the spicy tomato-flavored rice, and nearly burning her mouth on the fried starchy bananas.

"So how are you enjoying our non-date?" Jimmy asked.

"Good so far," she said.

"You're kinda subtle with the feedback," he said. "I'm never really sure if I'm annoying you and you're just being polite. Like on the phone, you said yes, but your tone was—"

She cut him off: "You need to know I'm just not a phone person. I prefer to talk face to face."

"I can live with that," Jimmy said, taking a sip of his fruit punch with ginger.

"And I'm kind of shy in groups. So you really shouldn't expect a lot of conversation from me at RBG."

"I'd settle for eye contact," He said.

She shook her head. "I'm not sure how to say this," she said. "But when you flirt with me there, it makes me feel exposed in front of everyone."

"Can I flirt with you now?"

She just smiled and shrugged, as her mouth burned with the spice and scald of the food.

"Too hot for you?" he asked, indicating the chicken.

"Spicier than my usual diet," she said.

"Have a sip of this," he offered the fruit punch.

One sip sent her mouth from smoldering to blazing. She

gasped for air, half laughing, half choking. "Even the drink is spicy. My God. Are you trying to kill me?"

"Try some plain water," he said, and handed her his metal canteen.

She gulped it all down, and then had to wipe her eyes and nose with a napkin.

"Sorry," he said. "I'm half Nigerian, and eating spicy food is my superpower."

"My mom had a Nigerian boyfriend for a minute in Oakland," Yolanda said.

"Did he cook spicy food?"

"I have no idea," Yolanda said. "I never saw him set foot in the kitchen."

The boyfriend had been part of the Yoruba religion. Her mother's only attempt at anything Afrocentric. How old had she been? Eight? Nine? She remembered seeing her mother with cornrowed hair and a set of bright beaded necklaces. At the rituals, there were other black kids—some Nigerian, some African American, and some Afro-Latin—who played together. It was the only one of her mother's religious communities she was completely sorry to leave.

"Well, let me assure you," Jimmy said. "This African man cooks. And I clean. And can put the spicy stuff on the side. Just in case you'd like to come over for dinner tonight . . ."

She shook her head. "I should get back to studying," she said, chewing on the ice from the bottom of the fruit punch cup. "What are you up to for the rest of the day?"

"I thought I'd spend the afternoon daydreaming and writing in my journal," he said. "Dear Diary," he began in a high-pitched voice. "I had the super dreamiest non-date, just going to the flea market with princess charming. She loves me? She loves me not? Oh diary, will I ever get to eat a meal with her by candlelight?"

Yolanda laughed and shook her head as they headed down past the drummers to the station.

"But seriously," he said, taking her hand. "I know you're busy. I respect that you're so committed to your studies and your career. But if not tonight, I'm just hoping that maybe we could have dinner sometime."

"Okay," she agreed. "But no candlelight."

"I was joking," he said. "Nobody can afford candlelight in Holloway. Just streetlight, headlight, flashing police light, and daylight, cause that's free."

"Let's stick with daylight," Yolanda said.

Chapter 15

When Yolanda was in second grade, she and her mother were still in Los Angeles. Her mom was working at a new age bookstore and was taking night classes to get her teaching credential in the state of California. After school, Yolanda and her mother would go to the bookstore, and stay until closing at six. Yolanda sat on a little couch in the back and did her homework or read.

For the first time since losing Yolanda's father, the grief was starting to lift, and they seemed to be settling in. Then a new guy started coming into the bookstore. Hal. He was indistinguishable from the other thirty-something, balding, nondescript white guys who came into the store. But he stood out because Yolanda noticed him noticing her mother.

Hal eventually asked her mom out and she said yes. Yolanda was wary of this new stranger in their lives. Before she knew it, Hal was always around. Six months later, they moved from their small one bedroom into Hal's house.

"You'll get your own room," Hal said with a wide smile. It was like a bribe, but one she didn't want. Why would she prefer to sleep alone, when she had shared a bed with her mom?

But at Hal's house, her mom slept in Hal's bedroom and Yolanda had a tiny room that had once been a sun porch.

The second bedroom of the two-bedroom house was Hal's office. He distributed specialized martial arts gear, and within the year, Yolanda's mom had stopped working at the bookstore and was the office manager for Hal's business. Gone were all plans for getting her teaching credential. As Yolanda moved into third grade, she disappeared increasingly into reading books. And her mother disappeared increasingly into Hal's life.

Around Thanksgiving of that year, Hal lost one of his major contracts with a large martial arts school. It was supposed to just be a temporary setback, but they had a lot of trouble bouncing back. Over dinner, her mother and Hal would argue about money. Her mother began to insist that she needed a salary. Hal insisted that he couldn't afford it. Her mother said she wanted to go back to the bookstore, but Hal insisted that he needed her.

"Besides," he said. "I pay the rent for all of us. I buy the groceries."

"If I had my own job I could contribute," her mother said.

"What are you trying to do," Hal said. "Sabotage my business? You spent the last year making yourself indispensable, and now you want to leave?"

"What am I supposed to be then," her mother asked, "an indentured servant?"

That was when he slammed his fist on the table. "Is that what you think this is?" he asked. "After everything I've done for you?" And his outburst ended the discussion.

Yolanda did all her homework and read book after book. She couldn't get enough reading material. She checked books out from the school library and the public library. She had her head in a book from the time she woke up to the time she fell asleep.

And so her face was pressed against the book she'd fallen asleep over when her mother shook her awake late one night.

"Baby, we need to go," her mother whispered in her ear.

"Is it morning?" Yolanda grumbled.

"Shhhhh, baby," her mother hissed. "Keep your voice down."

As Yolanda allowed herself to get oriented, she saw that her mother had on a jacket and was holding Yolanda's own jacket and shoes.

"Where are we going?" Yolanda asked in a whisper.

Her mother was opening the bolt on the exterior door of the sunroom. It led out to the back yard. They never used it, so the bolt was rusty, stuck.

When it finally opened, it was with a shriek of metal on metal.

"Hurry now," her mother said.

"Will we be gone long?" Yolanda asked. "I need my book."

"No time for that, baby," her mother said, pulling her at a half-run up the driveway.

Behind them, they could hear Hal calling Yolanda's mother's name. "Mary?" he bellowed. "Mary, you come back here."

The windows lit up as Hal tore through the house looking for her mother.

Yolanda sped up, fully awake now.

Her mother packed her into the front seat of the VW bug and closed the door as quietly as she could. Then she walked up to Hal's car for a moment before circling to the driver's side of the VW. But in the dark, Yolanda couldn't see anything.

Her mother slipped in and started the Volkswagen with a roar. As she slammed the driver's side door, the porch light flipped on and Hal came running out in his boxers and a t-shirt, his face contorted with rage in the porch light.

Her mother pulled the car forward with a lurch. Yolanda struggled to put on her seat belt.

She turned and watched over her shoulder as Hal got into his car. The new model Toyota would certainly be able to catch up with them. But then, as he started it and pulled away from the curb, he stopped.

". . . slashed my fucking tires, you bitch . . ." was all Yolanda heard before they had sped out of earshot.

It was then, in the glow of the streetlight through the windshield that Yolanda could see the right side of her mother's face, the bruise over her eye still opening like a blossom.

At 9:45 on the following Wednesday morning, Yolanda was waiting to observe the exhumation. She and Marcus sat in David Weisberg's car outside the cemetery. The attorney was in his mid-thirties and wore a suit. The morning was cold and rainy, a bleak gray sky stretching over the dark ground. The cemetery was up in the hills, two miles north of Cartwright College.

Yolanda didn't like cemeteries.

Marcus dozed in the back seat while Yolanda sat in the passenger seat. She held a cup of coffee to warm her hands and talked shop with David.

"So what are the biggest differences you're finding between New York and California law?" David asked.

She had been studying her bar review materials this week. She needed to sound like a woman who spent eight to fourteen hours a day studying California law, not listening to wiretapped conversations and trying to understand the point of Twitter.

As they spoke, Yolanda stayed focused on the conversation, turning herself in the front seat to face David, turning away from the sweep of lawn and the gray sky and the rain out the window. Turning away from the headstones and the flowers and the small dark silhouette of a vehicle making its way toward them on the long road from the maintenance yard.

Yolanda focused the discussion on the nuances of jurisdiction between New York and California law, and the complexities of e-commerce in determining which laws should apply. Yolanda only took in the cemetery in her peripheral vision, the rain obscuring much of the view.

When the small flatbed truck bearing the Holloway Cemetery logo came to the other side of the black iron gate, a lone man stepped out into the rain, and unlocked it for them. As David turned on the wipers and eased the car into gear, Marcus roused himself and sat up. The car was quiet except for the whine of the engine and the swishing of the wipers as the car crept forward. Yolanda recalled the last time she had been in a cemetery.

Black girl, black dress, black hair in braids, black patent leather shoes, tiny matching black patent leather purse. She had lost the purse. Nobody cared. She didn't care. There had been nothing in the purse. What does a five-year-old need with a purse?

"A little lady. A brave little lady," the church women said. Black church women. Black church, black funeral. Black mama, black dress, black hat. Black daddy, black suit. Yolanda's white socks and her daddy's white shirt were the only things not black that she recalled anyone wearing at the funeral, the burial, and as they closed the casket, lowered the lid over the black suit, black daddy, she could feel the connection sever, like the socks and the shirt were the last of their connection, and she cried into the white handkerchief they gave her.

And she remembered thinking that she would have liked his shirt, instead. His white shirt. His white shirt, which she thought would smell like him.

Of course it wouldn't have. It would have smelled like starch and like face powder and embalming fluid, but you can't understand when you're five that your father has never really worn the shirt, that he has never sweated, mixing that cologne and daddy smell, the heat of his body breaking down the starch that your mother so carefully presses into the shirt, to make it crisp and white, just so he can turn it into a sodden, smelly rag in the pulpit on Sundays. You can't understand that your mother is crying because she will not miss starching those shirts, that she hated starching those shirts, that she would run the iron over the white fabric thinking she had not gotten her teaching credential at Howard so she could iron his shirts, before she left for work every morning, while he had much more leisure time. Let him iron his own damn shirts. But when she had left them to him, they came out uneven. Limp in some spots, crackling with too much starch in others.

The church women sucked their teeth at her bad housekeeping. A bold young woman even offered to help the minister, as she could see that his wife was so busy with teaching and all, that it was no trouble. Yolanda's mother could see that she had better be the one to starch and iron those shirts, that if she didn't, someone else would. That a minister in the South never needs to learn to iron.

But now. But now at the funeral her mother would starch every shirt in Georgia just to have him back, and she had her own white handkerchief and she was crying into it, just like Yolanda. They were nearly exact replicas in their grief, except for the scale—her mother was bigger—and except for the white socks.

And then they were in the cemetery, standing by the graveside on a day with no rain, a perfectly hot Georgia Spring day, crying into their handkerchiefs. Yolanda and her mother looked like twins, like bookends, each with the handkerchief in their outside hands, their inside hands clasped, leaning on each other, this pair of what was left of a family, watching her father's body lowered into the ground. Watching the now closed, now covered white shirt, black suit, black daddy lowered, when a scream pierced the air.

Yolanda looked up as her mother's hand clamped down on her own. Yolanda cried out in pain, trying to wriggle her hand free from her mother's iron grip. Why wouldn't her mother look at her? Didn't she see she was hurting her?

A second later, the grip slackened. Yolanda pulled her hand free and followed her mother's eyes. A young woman teetered at the edge of the grave. Shrieking like in church. Like in church when Yolanda saw some people shrieking with spirit, others just shrieking for attention, waving their own arms. She could always tell. Always had been able to feel the difference.

Why was this woman pretending she would throw herself in the grave? Why were two other church women holding her waist, holding her back, holding her up, when she had no intention of really letting herself fall? Fall down onto that dirt, onto that hard coffin, not in her best black dress.

Why was she screaming so loud, so loud? This woman whose house had purple flowers in the garden, this woman whose living room smelled like apples, this woman whose house Yolanda had visited so many times, this woman who wore a tight orange flowered dress sometimes when her daddy visited. Why was she screaming so loud when daddy always said his friendship with this woman was a secret?

The car braked to a halt, pulling Yolanda back to the rainy day and the Holloway Cemetery. She cleared her throat, as if to clear away the memory. Through the rain, she didn't have a very good view of what was happening. The workers had erected a sort of tent over the grave, and a bunch of men were digging, while another pair of workers approached with some kind of machine that Yolanda assumed would lift the casket from the earth.

Behind their car, the Independent Medical Examiner's van pulled up, and the IME stepped out and pulled his coat over his head to protect him from the rain.

Marcus leaned over and opened up the rear door for him.

"Good morning," the doctor said, climbing in and introducing himself. He was a fortyish guy with thick glasses and a slack handshake.

The four of them made small talk as they peered through the rain and attempted to watch the slow progress at the grave. Eventually, the workers seemed to have gotten the machine attached to the casket, and the engine roared to life.

"Looks like this is it," David said, and the four of them stepped out into the rain.

Yolanda and Marcus stood under one umbrella, David and the IME under another.

After a few moments, they could see the top of the coffin rising up above the ground. When they had lifted the casket all the way up, the medical examiner backed his van up to the edge of the tent, and the workers lifted the casket to load it into the van.

But as soon as they had gotten it off the ground, the man in charge of the workers stopped them.

He ordered them to set the casket back down on the earth beside the open grave. The men exchanged some words, and then the worker in charge opened the coffin.

"*Vacío!*" the man yelled to his colleagues.

"What?" Marcus said sharply.

He handed the umbrella to Yolanda and marched forward into the rain.

"*Vacío?*" Marcus yelled through downpour as he approached the casket. "*Está vacío?*"

"What the hell is he saying?" David asked Yolanda.

"I don't know," she said. "I don't speak Spanish." Neither did the doctor.

The man shrugged, lifted the lid again, and Marcus peered in.

"What the hell?" Marcus asked, as the man lowered the lid. "It's empty," he yelled to Yolanda, David, and the doctor. "It's fucking empty."

Chapter 16

An hour later, Yolanda, Marcus and David sat in a chain diner off the freeway, eating a late and mediocre breakfast.

"This shit is crazy," Marcus said through a mouthful of waffles and bacon. "I don't even know where to begin to understand what just happened."

Once the casket had come up empty, the medical examiner went back to his van and left the cemetery. Meanwhile, the other three of them had double-checked that it was the right grave. Along with one of the men of the work crew, they had traipsed, sodden and muddy, into the main office and spoken to the supervisor in charge of the cemetery.

"That's ridiculous," the neat, older woman in the overheated office had said. She looked at them as if they were purposely dripping and tracking dirt on the carpet to offend her.

"*Díle*," Marcus urged the man from the work crew to speak.

"Ees enty inside," he told the woman. "Nossing inside."

The woman looked flustered, her curled helmet of improbable ash blond hair unable to move independently as she shook her head. "How is that possible?"

"That's what I want to know," David said, waving a piece of paper in her face. "Especially when I have a court order to exhume the body of Anitra Jenkins. Not the coffin, not the former resting place, but the body. Signed by Judge Greenlee of the Superior Court. I'm not sure yet which laws have been violated, but somebody's gonna be looking at a civil suit if not criminal charges."

From the diner, David and Marcus had called the funeral home and Mrs. Jenkins to confirm that a coffin with Anitra Jenkins in it had definitely been buried that day.

Yolanda could hear the voice of a very upset Mrs. Jenkins all the way across the table: "No, I was with my baby from the minute they closed the coffin. I watched em put the coffin in the hearse and I was in the limo right behind em. Then I stayed at the cemetery til they finished burying her. The ground closed over my baby, and I left her flowers. Ain't no mix up, Marcus. These people ain't shamed to rob a grave."

"So what the hell do we do now?" David asked, draining his second cup of coffee.

"I see two angles," Marcus said, chewing on a piece of chicken apple sausage. "You should call Judge Greenlee's office. This'll get him good and pissed off. Then, why don't we call the press? Organize a protest. We wanna create a sense of public outcry."

"Good idea," David said.

"I'll also call Sharon and Carlos to organize the youth," Marcus added.

Yolanda finished the last bite of her scrambled eggs and toast, and then offered to call a friend of hers, a freelance reporter with a connection to the *New York Times*.

"Great!" David said. "National news is even better."

They paid the check and dashed back to the car. The rain was starting to let up a bit. As soon as they shut the doors, the three of them hit their cell phones.

Yolanda dialed a San Francisco cell phone number.

"Peterson," the agent answered.

"Hey girl, it's Yolanda Vance," Yolanda said conversationally. "Got a minute?"

"What's up, Vance?" Peterson asked cautiously.

"Are you still freelancing for the *New York Times*?"

"You in trouble, Vance?"

"No, nothing like that," Yolanda answered laughing. "Too bad you left New York, because I have a crazy story developing out here in California."

As they drove down from the hills, Yolanda saw a scattering of expensive houses on this side of the park. Situated on a west-facing hill, they looked out onto the bay. Yolanda had gone to that neighborhood to visit a professor's house once. As night fell, she was dazzled by the view of San Francisco, and the green hills of Marin.

"Should I alert Rafferty on this?" Peterson asked.

"Definitely," Yolanda said. "But to make a long story short, there's this sort of suspicious death out here in Holloway, and they got an order to exhume the body, and they brought up the coffin, and the body was gone."

"The Jenkins girl?"

"Exactly," Yolanda said. "There we were in the rain, looking into an empty coffin. Crazy, huh? So we're currently calling the press and getting organized to create a sense of public outcry."

"Okay, Vance," Peterson said. "I'm on it."

"Too bad you're not with the *Times* anymore, but the local press will probably pick it up. We're calling the media right now."

Yolanda finished her phone call, as David navigated a sharp turn. With expert handling, he maneuvered the car onto the two-lane road that cut through the narrow strip of the regional park system that bisected Holloway. This stripe of green separated the tiny, affluent section of Holloway near Cartwright from the rest of the town.

"There's so much more to this than an empty coffin," Marcus was saying into his phone. "Can we meet later today? I can come into San Francisco, no problem."

"Any idea when Judge Greenlee might break for lunch today?" David was asking. "Okay, I'll be waiting outside his chambers."

David drove a little too fast for the winding road. Momentarily, they had descended out of the hills to the other end of the park, where the meadow at the flatlands entrance was decorated with beer bottles, food wrappers, and as near as Yolanda could tell from a distance, a dirty diaper.

This area of Holloway was starting to get gentrified. Realtors called it "Park View." It was slowly expanding down the hill, but the flatlands below were much slower to change.

Yolanda's phone rang. She answered the "unknown" number.

"Hey Vance," Peterson said. "Stay on it with RBG today. Sit in on the interviews, if possible. Just keep us updated, okay?"

"Sure thing, honey," Yolanda said.

"Sounds good cutie pie," Peterson joked. "Also, Rafferty wants you in tomorrow morning for an in-person, around nine."

"You got it," Yolanda said.

When they arrived at the RBG office, they compared notes. The three of them sat at the table in the office with the heat on high. Yolanda shivered in her soggy shoes, and rainwater had turned her jeans a darker shade of indigo from the knees down.

"I got KPFA on board 100%," Marcus said, wiping the rain off his glasses. "Plus a freelancer who's gonna pitch it to the weeklies. She's gonna come to our Sunday meeting to do interviews."

"Great," David said. He looked far less professional with his hair plastered to his head. "I'll stay on Judge Greenlee."

"Okay," Marcus said. "Hold off on social media til we have the press release ready. I'll post it on our website. All social media needs to link back to the press release."

"I took photos of the empty coffin," David said. "I'll text them to you to include with the press release."

"My friend took a job in Cleveland," Yolanda lied smoothly. "But she has contacts. I'll send her the press release."

"Great," Marcus said. "Thanks, Yolanda."

"But what the hell do we do after we alert the media?" David asked. "Do we call the FBI?"

Yolanda felt a twinge in her chest.

"Are you kidding me?" Marcus asked. "The FBI is like, like calling in the wolf to protect the henhouse from the fox."

"Well who else can we call?" David asked. "It's gotta be better than nothing."

"Do you know the history of the Civil Rights Movement and the Black Power movement?" Marcus asked. "The FBI is never on the right side of these things, David."

"I know a guy in the FBI," David said. "He's a good guy. I worked with him on a case last year. I could just talk to him. Get his advice."

"Absolutely not," Marcus said. "I grew up with people who had been in the Black Panther Party. I heard how the FBI and COINTELPRO destroyed a movement. They killed people, David. They handed Fred Hampton to the Chicago police so they could shoot him in his bed."

"Marcus, it's not like you're keeping this a secret," David said. "You're going to the press. The FBI is gonna read it in the paper."

"How are you so naive, David," Marcus slammed his hand down on the table. "Whose side do you think the FBI will come down on? Randell is a huge biotech corporation. The FBI is not gonna rock the boat of an industry that lobbies our congress for billions, to find justice for one poor black woman who used to be on drugs. Black life doesn't mean shit to the FBI." Marcus's voice trembled as he spoke.

"Okay," David spoke gently to Marcus. "I won't call my guy at the FBI. We'll go with the press angle. I just—I'm scared, Marcus. I thought we'd pull up the body, get the autopsy, and find—I don't know what we'd find. This is just bigger than I thought. It's freaking me out a little."

"That freaked-out feeling?" Marcus said. "That's how black people feel every day."

"Of course you do," David said. "Sorry to show my white fragility."

"Big brother isn't gonna protect you David."

"I know you're right," David said. "What the fuck? We got a dead woman with an unexplained wound in her arm, and a disappeared body?"

"Scary shit," Marcus said. "Public outcry is our best protection."

"You've been pretty quiet there, Yolanda," David said. "This is sure more exciting than studying for the bar, eh?"

"It's been really . . ." Yolanda searched for the words. "Really eye-opening."

"Okay you two," David said, rising. "I'm off to stalk a judge."

After the lawyer left, the two of them sat in the quiet RBG office. Yolanda had no idea what to say.

Marcus spoke softly after a moment: "God, I thought I was gonna lose it when David talked about going to the FBI. He clearly had no idea what kind of violence the government has done in our community. I'm so glad you were here."

He looked her right in the face.

"Of course," she said.

"David's cool," Marcus went on. "But sometimes white people just don't get it, you know. If I had been alone with him, I might have really flipped out. But he's a good guy and we need him. Anyway, I just really appreciated your support."

"Anytime," Yolanda said. She kept her responses clipped, not betraying anything to him or to the recording devices.

"You're such a blessing," Marcus said. "Really, I mean it. You always seem to be in the right place at the right time. I'm sorry this has taken up so much of your day."

Later, after she left the office, Yolanda finally had a chance to think. The rain had stopped and she walked to the apartment, her sodden shoes sloshing on wet pavement.

Where was Anitra Jenkins's body? She understood that Randell had a classified contract with the US government, something to do with national security, probably the department of defense. But it didn't add up. And what was Marcus talking about? That wasn't the version she had heard about COINTELPRO. She couldn't google it, because the FBI would know. For the first time in the case, Yolanda Vance had no idea what to do.

To: Special Agent Rafferty
From: Special Agent ▮▮▮▮▮▮▮▮▮▮▮▮▮▮
Re: CRITICAL JUNCTURE

My Holloway street sources tell me that the exhumed coffin of Anitra Jenkins came up empty. I want to make sure The Bureau gets ahead of this. I am not sure how you plan to contextualize this with Agent Vance, given that she is an inexperienced agent, stepping into the middle of an operation that is

Is anyone reviewing her surveillance? If you don't have the manpower, I would offer myself as a reviewer, to make sure

██

██

To: Special Agent ███████████████
From: Special Agent Rafferty
Re: Re: CRITICAL JUNCTURE

I appreciate your concern. As I said, I want you strictly behind the scenes. However, I have no objection to you reviewing her audio files. I'll get that set up for you.

Chapter 17

"So I have the audio files from yesterday," Campbell was saying, "but I want your take on yesterday's events."

Yolanda was in her special briefing in the FBI San Francisco office at nine AM the next morning. Usually, her weekly briefing meetings were with Rafferty and Peterson. Today, she was meeting alone with the big boss, the ASAC, Campbell.

The Assistant Special Agent in Charge sat across from her, his hands making a church steeple under his chin.

"Agent Vance," Campbell said. "You've done a great job. I know you expected to work for the Bureau in a very different capacity. You've gone above and beyond, and I think you deserve some answers. RBG is trying to find out what happened to Anitra Jenkins," Campbell explained. "The police say it was a drug-related death, but her grandmother suspects something happened at RandellCorp. Both things are true. I regret to report that Anitra Jenkins died in an industrial accident at Randell. Jenkins was also under the influence of narcotics at the time—heroin—which was part of how the accident happened. As you may know, with an accidental death on the premises, the federal protocol is for a full investigation. However, Randell is at a very critical and sensitive point in their research on this government contract. And given certain factors that I am not at liberty to discuss, the government can't afford a delay. But I expect that in three to six months, when this particular project is over, we will be able to release the proper information to all interested parties." He stopped, eyebrows raised.

Yolanda nodded once. A quick nod.

"This is why your work is so important, Vance. We need you on the ground with RBG, sort of like with a baby who's playing on a bed. You don't want the child to get too close to the edge, because they might fall off and get hurt. So as they get to the edge, you sort of steer them away from it, closer to the center of the bed."

Campbell looked directly at her and gave her a smile that didn't quite reach his eyes.

"I know that the Bureau doesn't have the best reputation with the African American community," Campbell went on. "The Bureau has taken some tactics in the sixties and seventies which were, in my opinion, regrettable. We can just put that on the table. This is all public record. But that was a lifetime ago, and hindsight is twenty-twenty.

"In our operation here," Campbell was saying, "you'll notice that we're not disrupting the activities of RBG in any way. We're simply monitoring them so we can steer a little when they get close to the edges. I assure you that it's in the interest of everyone's safety."

Something in his eyes was different from last time they had met. He didn't trust her. She could see it.

Yolanda scanned back in her mind through the conversation in the RBG office from the day before. She had heard it once in real time, while it was happening, and had listened to it again when she received the files. Had she said anything to lead them to believe her loyalty was wavering? She was an agent, a professional. She had taken an oath. How dare he condescend to her like this?

"Thank you, sir," she said to Campbell. "I appreciate you taking the time to give me the big picture."

Campbell dismissed her from the meeting. She felt relieved.

As she walked through the FBI offices, everything looked as it always did. Yet somehow, it felt different.

She stepped outside into the overcast downtown San Francisco morning. But nothing Campbell said had fully released the tight feeling in her chest, a high-pressure system that had moved in and taken up residence since she had stood in the rain, splattered with mud, and watched the coffin come up empty.

Yolanda needed to think. The FBI office was located near the Tenderloin section of San Francisco, a neighborhood overlapping downtown. It was filled with single-room occupancy hotels and a few strip clubs, attracting homeless people and drug traffic. A man in a raggedy plaid blanket stood on a corner screaming at those who passed by. She crossed the street to avoid him, but as she came closer, she made out the words: "I don't believe you! I don't fucking believe you!"

She walked briskly from the Bureau office to Market Street in downtown San Francisco. She passed the Civic Center BART station and didn't walk down the cement steps into the subway as usual. She wasn't ready to return to Holloway.

The only place in her regular routine where she could think freely was in the gym. Whether or not they had her under any kind of surveillance, she felt free when she jogged on the treadmill or lifted weights. She got into the zone, sometimes while listening to recordings of RBG she had downloaded.

Curl. And breathe. Two. And breathe.

"My mom drinks sometimes," she heard Carlos saying as she welcomed the mild burn in her bicep. She felt a little guilty for listening in on their support group, their private conversations with each other, with Sharon. As she got to know the teens better, she felt protective. What would Rafferty and Campbell do with this information? Would tapes of Dana's teenage questions about sex pop up in twenty years when she was running for senate?

Yolanda needed to think.

She continued down Market, the wide main street in downtown San Francisco. A bicycle messenger sped by in black clothes and wraparound shades, with a heavy chain lock across his chest like a strip of bullets. He zipped easily past three slow buses, and turned left, narrowly avoiding an oncoming streetcar that looked like an antique trolley.

Yolanda continued down Market Street, past the brightly lit SF Shopping Centre with its fancy department stores and specialty boutiques. Past the less glamorous discount clothing shops. Past the drugstores with bright, crisp *Summer is Coming!* displays, and homeless people standing in front of the windows with their palms extended, brown with city grime.

Further down Market, Yolanda came across the blazing windows of Sally's Books. As a kid, the library had often been her refuge. She walked into the bright, warm store.

In the biography section, a large display caught her eye. They had made a pyramid with copies of the autobiography of Lester Johnakin, Yolanda's former guru of positive thinking, *Positive is a Lifelong Decision.*

What would Johnakin have to say about her current situation? Think positively about the FBI? She had stopped worshiping Johnakin's every word in high school when she couldn't reconcile his advice, "Assume other people want the best for you," and the way Dale and her clique had suckered her.

Yolanda pulled one of his books off the shelf, the *New Big Book of Positive Thinking*, and did what she had done as a young teen, opened to a random page to seek advice on her situation.

Misfortunes happen to everyone. We have had an
otherwise good and productive day, but the parking
ticket has "ruined" it. We don't even notice how our
minds look for an opportunity to emphasize the negative. Or we think, "Why does this always happen to
me?" as if we are the only ones in the world ever to
get parking tickets. We had a choice. We didn't put
enough money in the meter—or didn't put any! We
didn't pay attention to the time. Our parking ticket is
generally the result of our own actions, and yet we
feel victimized. Why? The meter clearly said how
much time we would be allotted for each amount of
money, and we know how to tell time.

I like to think of the parking meter attendants as
my personal trainers. They help me exercise my capacity for taking responsibility. Sometimes, I put a
dollar into a parking meter, when I am likely to only
need a quarter. That seventy-five cents allows me
freedom and relaxation while I run my errand and de-
lights the next person who parks in my space to find
twenty to thirty minutes already on the meter. Such a
small price to pay for a positive outcome.

Yolanda remembered reading the passage for the first time
at the age of thirteen. Recalled how she had decided to be
one of the people who put a dollar in the meter. It was a
catchy metaphor, but life wasn't really like parking.

How was Dorothea Jenkins's life like a parking space?
How did she fail to put enough money in the meter? What
would Johnakin have to say about Anitra Jenkins's death?
Was this a minor misfortune that Mrs. Jenkins was supposed
to look past and notice all the positive in her life? She had
lost her daughter and both of her grandchildren. Would
Johnakin blame them all for not thinking positively enough?

Johnakin never seemed to focus on people who came from places like the Stats projects. Or if he did, it was the one person who thought positively and became a success. Did that mean that the other 99% were to blame for not being able to make lemonade out of battery acid?

From the beginning with this case, she was uncertain if the FBI was listening in her apartment, and she knew they were listening in the RBG offices. In a wave of paranoia, she worried that they could overhear her thoughts. That was ridiculous. But they could have someone following her.

Did they?

She looked around at the nearby bookstore patrons. Two teen girls looking at a gossip magazine. A young black guy in a sweat suit flipping through a graphic novel. The girls were too young to be FBI and the young man could be cleared by a process of elimination. If he was on the local FBI's payroll, they would never have gone to the trouble to pull her from white collar to take this assignment.

Yolanda wandered into the magazine section and picked up a copy of *Vogue*. Everyone expected women to be fascinated by fashion. She flipped idly through the pages, and drifted into the political section, scanning book spines. She picked up *A G-Man's Life: The FBI, Being 'Deep Throat,' And the Struggle for Honor in Washington* by Mark Felt, the former FBI Associate Director. As she scanned the book, she looked around to see if anyone could see her. Satisfied that she was alone, she quickly slipped a thicker volume off the shelf about COINTELPRO, and slid it under the *Vogue*. She carried the three items, the magazine shielding the COINTELPRO book from anyone who might be watching, and settled herself in an armchair in an alcove between bookshelves, with her back to the wall. She opened the magazine and slid the COINTELPRO book in front of it and began to skim the book's pages.

Five minutes later, a young man came and sat in the chair across from her. Yolanda studied him in several quick glances. Neat haircut, starched collar, navy blue trench coat in case the rain started up again before he went back to his downtown office. Or he could be FBI.

If he was an agent, he would notice that she wasn't actually turning the pages of the magazine.

Yolanda slid down in the chair and put her knees up, sliding the book below the magazine and nestling the spines of each in the crack between her thighs. The magazine peeked out above her knees, but the COINTELPRO book was hidden below it.

COINTELPRO was the FBI's counter-intelligence program of the sixties and seventies, where they spied on their own citizens and used dirty tricks to destroy radical movements, especially the Black Panther Party.

Yolanda spent the next hour perfecting her technique of flipping the pages simultaneously. To any observer, Yolanda looked like a woman deeply absorbed in fashion.

And so it was that in her mind, the murder of Fred Hampton would always be juxtaposed with "What to Wear When Throwing the Perfect Spring Evening Party." The combination was so bizarre that she would recall the experience as a sort of surreal dream. The image of Fred Hampton, open mouth to microphone, with his circa-1969 kinky hair matching the pale nap of the faux sheepskin lining of his dark leather coat, would always be juxtaposed with the sleek and shiny fabrics of evening wear, his earnest, furious expression contrasting with the vapid, sullen faces of the models. The image of fourteen heavily-armed Chicago police officers storming into the apartment of the young Black Panther leader would always have the unexpected presence of white fashion models with inhumanly long eyelashes that extended beyond the thick black smudges of liner at the edges of their glassy eyes strutting through the runway of the frame with long, bony legs and pointy stiletto heels, carrying trays of canapés that none of them would be allowed to eat. *How to stand out when so many of your guests will be dressed alike?* The mental newsreel of the police in identical riot gear, busting into Hampton's bedroom and killing Hampton while he slept next to his wife who was expecting, would always coexist with the challenging questions of style. *Are you ready for the unexpected?* What does the well-dressed widow wear to her husband's murder? If she's eight months pregnant, which designers will offer their couture in maternity wear? So many unexpected guests, all so early for the party. 4:45 AM and the hostess is unprepared for company. But funeral black is perfect for all such occasions. Black dress, Black Panther, Black Power.

Mark Clark, the young Panther guarding Fred Hampton, fired only one bullet; one witness said it was accidental, as he fell from his chair, shot in the heart by police. Between eighty-two and ninety-nine shots were fired by police. The well-dressed hostess will hope it was ninety-nine. That plus the Panther shot makes a nice even one hundred. Parties thrive on even numbers.

What to do when some of your most influential guests exhibit such bad manners?

"That's Fred Hampton."

"Is he dead? . . . Bring him out."

"He's barely alive. He'll make it."

Two shots were heard, which, it was later discovered, were fired point blank in Hampton's head.

According to Deborah Johnson, one officer then said:

"He's good and dead now."

Parties are wonderful, but such a trial to clean up.

Hampton's body was dragged into the doorway of

the bedroom and left in a pool of blood. The raiders then directed their gunfire towards the remaining Panthers, who were hiding in another bedroom. They were wounded, then beaten and dragged into the street, where they were arrested on charges of aggravated assault and the attempted murder of the officers. They were held on $100,000 bail apiece.

What will people say about your party afterward?

Yolanda rubbed her eyes as the pages blurred into double vision. How could this be true? When Marcus mentioned Hampton, she had pictured him heavily armed. *Come and get me, motherfuckers!* Not asleep in bed with his pregnant wife. The book had a color photo of the blood-soaked bed he was lying in when the police killed him.

During her FBI training at Quantico, they had mentioned that there were books out there, books that distorted, exaggerated, and just plain lied about the FBI's activities.

The trainer had paced while he lectured, a tall, intense older man with a shaved head, striding up and down the rows of chairs in the lecture hall and looking at different students as he spoke.

"Hoover's decisions were sometimes controversial," he said. "But he made the best calls he could at the time and helped guide the country through an era of civil unrest. With cities burning and criminals looting, and leftist extremist hate groups running around rioting and shooting peace officers, Hoover wasn't about to send agents into the field offering Girl Scout Cookies. The Bureau showed strength. We played hard and used tough tactics. We got the job done."

The sports metaphors appealed to her. "Winner Language," Johnakin had called it. Her athletic teams had gotten similar pep talks:

"Here at the Alice Lloyd Prep School, we want you to be

young ladies," the lacrosse coach had said. "Except on the field. I want animals. Wild beasts. This is not the time to worry about being polite, looking cute, or breaking a nail. You're athletes. Bring us home a win, but if you can't win, come home sweaty, grimy, and knowing you gave your all."

But in the COINTELPRO book, Yolanda read account after account of FBI intervention in groups, sending fake memos to start fights between leaders, leaking lies to the press that ruined peoples' marriages, families, careers, and FBI agent infiltrators promoting and using violent tactics, even in peaceful organizations. The FBI operative had turned the floor plan of Fred Hampton's apartment over to the police for the purposes of the raid? Could all of this be true? Some of it must be accurate, if Campbell was assuring her that today's Bureau was so different now.

"Look, Daddy," a child shrieked as he ran by her. "I found my bunny book!"

"Great job, kiddo!" The man in the chair across from her stood and scooped up the small boy.

"The dentist said I didn't have any cavities, see?" The boy opened his mouth full of baby teeth and showed his father.

A woman walked up and kissed the man.

"I parked in the garage," the man said. "Let me just pay for this magazine before we go to your mom's for lunch."

"And my bunny book?" the kid asked. "We're gonna buy my bunny book too, right?"

"And your bunny book."

Yolanda looked up from her magazine and blinked at the light coming in from the plate-glass windows. It was noon. Bright. San Francisco. There were kids in the world who wanted bunny books.

Her wave of paranoia passed. Like Johnakin said, *nothing is inherently all good or all bad.* You had to hope for the good as well. She couldn't live thinking every dad waiting for his kid at the dentist was an agent watching her. It would make her crazy.

She headed to the register to purchase *A G-Man's Life*. On the way, she put the *Vogue* and the COINTELPRO book away. She put the magazine back on the rack, but first she slid the COINTELPRO book surreptitiously behind a row of cookbooks after wiping her prints from the cover.

Chapter 18

The regular Sunday meeting of RBG was packed. The photos of the empty coffin had gone viral on social media, and liberal outlets were covering the story. It seemed like every activist in the community wanted to express their outrage, every person who knew Anitra Jenkins wanted to share their grief and give their testimony that she had turned her life around, and every kid in the neighborhood wanted to get their picture in the paper. In the crowd, Yolanda was on alert for signs of Kenya.

Before the meeting even started, while it was still light, the photographer arranged all of them on the steps of the church. He was a scruffy white guy in torn jeans and a raggedy black jacket. He looked out of place as he arranged Mrs. Jenkins, decked out in another mourning suit, Marcus, Dana, and Sharon in their bright African fabrics, and the rest of the youth leaders of RBG, all wearing their trendiest "fits" in the front row.

Another forty or so people squeezed in behind them. Yolanda recognized a scattering of the faces from Sunday meetings, and a number of others from the community forum. There were representatives from Black Lives Matter, the Anti-Police Terror Project, Youth vs. Apocalypse and

The Sunrise Movement. One group had a sign that said "#SayHerName: Anitra Jenkins." Yolanda pressed in right behind them, letting the sign partially obscure her face.

Before they dispersed, people kept running up to the cameraman with their phones to take more photos. He took about five before Carlos yelled that he was uploading several shots to the RBG social media accounts right away, and they could get it from there.

After the photo shoot, the group filed into the building. Nakeesha and Sheena stood at the door, handing out copies of their YOUTH: KNOW YOUR RIGHTS flyer to all the teens that came in. The church had a program in the sanctuary, so nearly seventy-five people crammed into the basement main room for the RBG meeting. A lot of the teens ended up sitting on the floor.

In spite of the crowd, Yolanda knew the exact moment when Jimmy entered the room. The door opened, and she glanced up to see him walking quietly down the stairs.

"Tonight our meeting is gonna be a little different," Dana began. "We have several members of the press here." Dana outlined the details of the case for anyone who didn't know, right up to the empty casket.

Yolanda also knew the moment that Kenya entered the room. In preparation, Yolanda was wearing a baseball cap and had it pulled down a bit over her face. Getting rave fashion reviews from the teens was her lowest priority today. She was pleased to see Kenya find a spot on the other side of the room, facing away from her.

"So here's how we're gonna roll tonight," Dana continued. "We're gonna ask anyone who has anything to say, specific to the case of Anitra Jenkins, to speak up. Everybody gets a two-minute time limit, so please, think carefully about what you want to say, and be brief."

"Everyone gets two minutes, except Mrs. Jenkins," Marcus said. "We're gonna ask her to start it off."

"Oh, and one more thing," Dana added. "KPFA is recording tonight, so if you don't want to be recorded, please let us know."

Mrs. Jenkins sat on one of the faded couches between Sharon and Sheena. "I praise God for the Red, Black and GREEN!" she said. "Cause now the whole world is gonna listen to me. Ain't nothing nobody can do now to bring my baby back, but I want justice. I wanna know why my baby ain't laid to rest in the ground where she sposed to be. It ain't bad enough that they kilt her, but they won't even let her rest? Shame on you Randell! Shame on you Holloway police! Shame!" She leaned on her cane and sat down.

The room exploded with applause. As it finally died down, Marcus yelled out, "RBG is behind you one hundred percent, Mrs. Jenkins! We want justice for Anitra and we want the city of Holloway and Randell to show some respect! Black lives matter! Defund the police."

The cheering continued so loudly that Dana had to wait a minute before she continued.

Most of the speakers offered the same complaints from the community forum.

At one point, Dana stood up again. "There's a lot that needs to be done in Holloway, but if we can please focus on Anitra for tonight. I know Darnell has something specific to the case."

Darnell stood up. His long afro was braided back, and he had on a custom made RBG baseball cap.

"Don't nobody record this," Darnell called out, pointing to the reporter.

The short and sturdily built black woman had been listening quietly on headphones. When Darnell pointed to her, she leaped to life and fidgeted with her recorder.

"So me and some folks talked to all the drug dealers in Holloway to see if anybody sold heron to Anitra Jenkins during the week that she passed away. And we couldn't find nobody who woulda sold it to her. I'm not saying she couldn't of gone to Richmond or Oakland to get it, but why? Plenty of folks selling it in Holloway, but not to her."

Dana called on an older man next. "My name is Dante V., and I'm a drug addict and alcoholic."

"Hi Dante," about half the room chorused back.

He had a knife scar that that stretched from the side of his nose to his left ear. "I was in treatment with Anitra," Dante said. "We been in the rooms together—NA and AA—and let me tell you, Anitra was clean and sober from crack cocaine and proud of it. I saw Anitra at the meeting on Wednesday. She didn't have no abscess. She wasn't using no heron. Not even when she used to be out in these streets. It was never her drug of choice."

He stood up and pointed north toward where they had discovered her body. "I know that shooting gallery. I got my damn face cut in that shooting gallery. Ain't nobody been up in there for twenty years. They think they can put a needle in her arm and then won't nobody care about her. Just another junkie dead in the back alley. We care!"

"That's right!" somebody yelled back.

"Even if you clean and sober like Anitra J. was? Shit. Even if you dirty and drunk—excuse my language, Mrs. Jenkins— I meant shoot."

Mrs. Jenkins waved her cane at him to continue.

"I'm just trying to say we can't fall for that trap where they find some dirt on us—like some arrest record, or using drugs—and act like our lives ain't worth nothing!"

A young woman spoke next. She had brightly colored braids and several piercings. "We gotta care about every single person in our community. Whether they use drugs, whether they sell drugs, whether they been in prison, whether they still in prison. Whether they selling sex. Everybody. All black lives matter!"

The room pounded with applause again. This time the

loudest was from Dante's crew, who had a "Justice for Anitra J." sign.

The next speaker was an androgynous young person with a large red afro.

"I don't know what happened to Anitra Jenkins," they said. "But I know Randell is behind it. These corporations are desperate. Time is running out for the greenwashing corporations like Randell that are trying to convince people that we can save the planet while they still make mega profits. They're trying to squeeze every dollar out of a dying economy. It's just not sustainable. And they don't care who gets in their way. People disappear. People die in mysterious 'accidents.'" They made quote marks in the air. "These corporations are willing to bring the entire human race to extinction to keep making money. How can we expect them to care about any one individual human life? Let alone the lives of black females and femmes. They don't. Time is running out. Which is why we need to keep organizing to deal with this climate crisis in ways that prioritize our people and our solutions."

When the meeting finally broke up, Marcus stood on a chair and yelled, "If you need a ride to the Stats, the van is leaving."

A bunch of teens scrambled to follow Marcus.

Kenya was headed toward Yolanda, so she turned quickly to Marcus. "I need a ride."

"You live near the Stats?" Marcus asked.

"Close enough," Yolanda said, tracking Kenya in her peripheral vision.

A line of teens climbed into the car.

As Yolanda waited to get in the van, she heard a woman calling her name, "Yolanda Vance!"

She looked up to see Kenya. Yolanda's heart was pounding in her chest, but she pasted on a smile. It had been foolish to think she could avoid her indefinitely.

"Girl, I had no idea you were here in Holloway," Kenya said.

The two women embraced. Yolanda felt certain that Kenya would be able to feel her panic.

"I've been here for a couple of months now," Yolanda said, trying to stay cool. What did Kenya remember? Who did she know? Who would she be talking to?

"I tried to look you up after we ran into each other in New York," Kenya said. "But you must be the only person I know who's not on social media."

"Yeah," Yolanda said. "I'm old school. You have to call me or send an email."

"We should stay in touch," Kenya said. "What are you doing out here?"

"I got a new job," Yolanda said. "I'm here studying for the California bar,"

"That's right," Kenya said. "You had been working for that big New York firm that got indicted right? Or were they in New Jersey?"

"New York," Yolanda said.

Kenya's brow furrowed. For a long moment, Yolanda was certain she was busted.

Then Kenya shook her head. "No idea where I got Jersey from," she said. "I musta had more to drink that night than I thought. New York is such a drinking town."

"Yep," Yolanda said, feeling a rush of relief. "I miss the music, though."

"The Bay Area has great blues," Kenya said. "You gotta let me show you all the spots."

The two of them exchanged numbers, and Kenya joined a pair of teachers and a crew of students from the middle school.

Yolanda recalled the club in New York. Not only had Kenya been drinking, but the music had been loud that night.

It was a trumpet player. How much information could be retained between two women shouting to each other over blues horn lines?

Marcus walked over Yolanda. "Van's full," he said.

Now that Kenya had recognized her, it didn't matter anymore. She opened her mouth to tell him that she could just walk, but Marcus had already turned to the group's Wellness Coordinator. "Sharon, can you take Yolanda?"

"It's really not—" Yolanda began, but Sharon was too busy herding a group of girls into her car.

"I'm full up," Sharon said. "Jimmy!" she called through the crowd. "We need you on ride duty."

He walked over to where they all were. "I didn't bring my car," he said.

"You don't have to—" Yolanda began again, but Sharon didn't register her protest.

"Okay, well can you walk some young women home?" She barely waited for his nod. "Dana, Sheena, Yolanda, and Jasmine live in your general direction."

Jimmy walked over to Yolanda with a smile. "Can I carry your books?"

"I better go round up the other folks," Yolanda turned to catch Dana, who was handing the middle school teachers a stack of the KNOW YOUR RIGHTS flyers.

"Hey," Jimmy held her arm. "I don't care where you live, I'm dropping you last, okay?"

"Okay." She felt warm where his hand touched her arm.

"I can't wait to have a minute alone with you Yolanda," he murmured in her ear.

Yolanda felt her torso turn to liquid. Blinking, she looked around and had lost Dana in the crush of people. It took them another fifteen minutes to finally leave.

"I've never been in the paper before," Sheena said excitedly as they walked down Holloway Avenue.

"Me neither," Dana said.

The evening was cool and clear, with a bright crescent moon.

"Are you cold?" Jimmy asked Yolanda. He playfully pulled her hat off.

Yolanda smoothed back her pressed hair and tried not to feel too awkward.

"I been in the paper for basketball," Jasmine said. "But that's different. You don't get to smile. They always catch you when you're all—" she froze, with her hand above her head as if dunking and her mouth wide open in a lopsided yell.

Everyone laughed.

"I remember that," Yolanda said, recalling her own newspaper photos when she was a student athlete.

"You used to play ball?" Jasmine asked. "But you're so short."

"Skills before height," Yolanda laughed, and snatched her cap back from Jimmy.

"Ooooh, nice steal," Jasmine said.

"Candy from a baby," Yolanda grinned at Jimmy. "I played everything," she said, turning to Jasmine. "Basketball, volleyball, track, lacrosse . . ."

"Lacrosse?" Jasmine asked. "That's for white girls."

"Explain that to all the white girls whose asses I beat," Yolanda said.

"What about all the black men whose asses you beat at the track?" Jimmy said.

"You beat men in track?" Jasmine asked.

"Just me," Jimmy said, laughing. "That's how I met Yolanda. A month ago, she was beating my ass in sprinting. This brown blur that flashed by me."

"You guys met outside RBG?" Dana asked.

"Up at Cartwright," Jimmy said.

"Oh riiiiighht," Sheena said. "Cause you teach there and Yolanda used to go there."

"You went to Cartwright?" Jasmine asked. "You must be rich."

"No, I got scholarships," Yolanda said. "Basically, they paid me to go to college and play sports."

"Because title nine says girls have to be equal in schools," Sheena said.

"Maybe I wanna go to Cartwright," Jasmine said.

"You need to get your grades up," Sheena said.

"If somebody's gonna pay me to go to college, maybe I will," Jasmine said.

"You're an amazing role model for these girls," Jimmy said later, after they had dropped off all the teens.

Yolanda shook her head. "It's no big deal."

"No really," Jimmy leaned over and bumped her shoulder with his. "I don't think you really have any idea how . . . how amazing you are. You're beautiful. You're smart as hell. And you really make a difference to these girls. To RBG in general."

"And I can kick your ass in track."

"I wouldn't go that far," Jimmy said.

"But you just admitted it in front of witnesses."

"No, that was a pro-girl-power move," he said. "I just falsely admitted defeat to encourage them in their athletics."

"Well I'm an attorney," Yolanda said. "And an admission in front of witnesses is an admission. You can't recant your testimony now, Mr. Thompson."

"Permission to approach the bench," he said, and took a step closer.

Yolanda could feel her pulse pick up as he moved toward her. "Oh no," she said. "You haven't passed the bar. You need to stay in the witness box."

"What if I don't? Will you find me in contempt?"

He was close enough that she could smell the soap on his skin.

"Order!" Yolanda said. "Order in the court!"

"Okay, I'll behave," Jimmy said, taking a step to the side and putting a little more distance between them.

They passed a pink bungalow with magenta trim and a big palm tree in the yard, right next to a boarded-up old Victorian.

"So . . . how's the studying going?" Jimmy asked.

"This week is pretty much shot," Yolanda said. "But . . . I don't know . . . since joining RBG, my previous career path, career decisions don't seem as . . . important as they used to." She was trying to find the words. "I don't know if this job I took, this job that brought me out here is right for me."

"Really?" he asked.

"I'm just . . . I'm just questioning a lot of stuff. A lot of my values. When we met you sort of suggested that I wasn't suited for corporate law. I thought I was . . . a good fit for the job I'd gotten. But now I don't know."

"You'll figure it out, Yolanda," he said, encouragingly. "And whatever you decide, I really . . . I really like you. I want to keep getting to know you."

As they passed under the streetlight, she could see the earnestness in his face. He reached for her hand, twined his fingers with hers.

"It takes a while to really get to know me," she said.

"I've got a lot of patience."

"That was my building by the way," she said, pointing back to the towering apartment. "The one we just passed."

"Does that mean you're coming home with me?"

Yolanda laughed. "That really would be getting to know you."

"Hey, a guy can hope."

"Consider your hopes dashed," Yolanda said. "Can we just stay like this for a while?"

"Sure," he said gently.

They walked around the block four more times, fingers intertwined. When they finally walked up to her door, Jimmy put a hand on her shoulder.

"May I kiss you?"

Yolanda shook her head. "Not yet."

He pulled her into an embrace instead. She could feel the heat of his skin, the muscles under his sweatshirt.

After they let go, she walked into the house alone, the front of her body still tingling.

Chapter 19

Officer Joaquín Rodriguez sat at the coffee table in his Holloway bungalow staring at the photo of Dorothea Jenkins and RBG on the cover of the *East Bay Weekly*.

It was nearly seven AM, and he had read the article twice. He lifted his coffee mug off the paper, leaving a wet ring on the ad for LASIK surgery opposite Mrs. Jenkins's photo in the paper. He flipped the paper back to the beginning of the article, looking for the part where someone else would take care of it. The part where the kindly woodcutter was on his way to Red Riding Hood right now.

After the third read, he realized he was as close to a kindly woodcutter as they were gonna get. Rodriguez the would-be hero could see himself, frozen on the porch, axe in his less-than-beefy hand, peering through the tiny window at the monster beyond the glass.

Chief Evans, what big teeth you have.

"I'm at a loss," Yolanda said to Donnelly. "When that coffin came up empty, it totally changed the game."

"I'm not as worried about that as I am about their little debriefing," Donnelly said. "Campbell is a spin doctor because his approach can be so unscrupulous."

The two women were walking along the Embarcadero beside the San Francisco Bay. The Bay Bridge stretched out on one side of them, and cars sped by on the other.

"What should I do?" Yolanda asked.

"Document everything," Donnelly said. "Keep a paper journal with a log of all your actions for every day. Record every contact with the FBI that you can without attracting attention."

"What good will that do?" Yolanda asked.

"It'll protect you from being their scapegoat," she said. "If it blows up in the FBI's face, you can document that you were systematically misinformed and manipulated."

"Do you think that's what's happening?" Yolanda asked.

"I have no idea," Donnelly said. "But the FBI is a bunch of paper pushers. After the dust settles, the victory goes to the one with the best paper trail."

"I'm on it," Yolanda said.

"I don't mean to sound paranoid," Donnelly said. "But if Campbell's giving you loyalty pep talks, you can assume they're watching you along with the target group."

"How am I supposed to live like this?" Yolanda asked. "No privacy. No idea what I'm mixed up in."

"I don't blame you," Donnelly said. "If it's too much, you can resign. I'd be glad to write you a letter of recommendation."

"For what job?" Yolanda asked. "I got limited savings, no job prospects, no current bar card for any state. At least this is a temporary assignment. If I can close this case, I know I'll get a reasonable attorney position somewhere in the bureau."

"I don't blame you," Donnelly said. "My family threw me out when they found out I was gay. If I had some place to go home to, I might have quit myself. But I hung in there."

"Was it worth it?" Yolanda asked.

"Overall, yes," Donnelly said. "I got through the hard

times, and now I've got a great team where I call the shots. Assholes like Campbell are the type of colleagues I see once a week at most."

"That's what I want," Yolanda said.

"Then hang tough," Donnelly said. "Here's my home number. It's secure. If I'm not there, leave a message with my wife." She scrawled the number on a sticky note and handed it to Yolanda. "But if you do call, find a pay phone."

Yolanda stopped by Sally's Books on the way back from her walk with Donnelly. Her second visit, she avoided Johnakin and the political section. Instead, she wandered through the store at random. A familiar text caught her eye in the languages section, the book she had used in high school when she studied Japanese. *Kana and Kanji Writing Workbook, Vol. 2.* The workbook was large and heavy, and she recalled hours of copying the characters to fix them in her mind. However, there was also a portable version, *Learning Japanese Kanji on the Go.* This smallish, square book had a blue cover and several Japanese characters, or Kanji, running down below the title.

Impulsively, she grabbed the smaller book off the shelf and purchased it. On the way home on the BART train, she swung her legs up onto the seat and wrote in the book with her back to the train window.

Yolanda wrote in the lines beside the characters.

命 *My name is Yolanda Vance. I'm twenty-six years old, and I am currently an agent for the FBI, operating clandestinely as part of Red, Black and GREEN! in Holloway, California.*

勇 *As an operative, and as an attorney, I have become increasingly concerned about the ethics, integrity, and legality of this assignment.*

She had never understood why people kept diaries. Probably because she always associated them with romance. Why would you bother if you didn't put a lot of focus on your love life? But now that she had this huge secret, she understood better. She had to have some space to think, to make the words stand still for a moment to consider them. But most of all, she needed a release valve.

The night Jimmy walked her home, it had been such a delicious relief to even tell him a few partial truths. She felt an urge to pour out a complete confession to him, like a campy scene in an old black-and-white film. *Darling, I'm a spy!* She could imagine the fifties version of herself—matte lipstick, a vintage dress, hair in pin curls—she would tear off her hat, shouting: *But I didn't know what they would ask of me! I never meant to hurt anyone!*

She needed this three-by-five notebook. A tiny confessional where she wouldn't find absolution, but she could remind herself what was true.

The following week's Sunday night RBG meeting was huge. The *East Bay Weekly* article had attracted people from San Francisco, Berkeley, Oakland, and even Vallejo.

A contingent of senior citizens came out to support Mrs. Jenkins, so everyone under sixty was standing, except one guy in a wheelchair, and he had to be carried up and down the steps.

Yolanda stood against the wall in a crush of standing-room-only bodies, and Jimmy squeezed in next to her. He reached for her hand, and her pulse raced at the contact, the press of his fingers against hers.

Yolanda tried to ignore the buzz in her body from the contact with Jimmy, as she half-listened to RBG's big new plans. They intended to organize a rally at Randell, a teach-in at the high school, an RBG crew at Cartwright, a letter-writing campaign to Chief Evans and the mayor, a PR team to send updates to the press, a web media team—led by Carlos—to post updates to the RBG website and social media, as well as a phone-calling team to contact all the folks who didn't have internet access.

After the meeting, she and Jimmy were leaving to walk home with several teens, when a thirtyish Latino guy showed up. He pulled Marcus Winters aside and asked to speak with him. Yolanda and Jimmy didn't notice him in the rush of the meeting breaking up. He was lost among all the teens laughing on the church steps, the bus from the senior center beeping with the loading of a wheelchair and the various elders on canes and walkers boarding slowly. Yolanda and Jimmy were turning the corner off Holloway Avenue when Marcus asked Sharon if she could drive the van, telling her he needed to talk to this guy who was waiting on the steps of the church, could she take the youth home to the Stats? Sharon said sure, but she wanted Marcus to wait for her, and walk her to her car when she got back.

Yolanda and Jimmy were dropping Jasmine's cousin at his apartment building when the Latino guy introduced himself to Marcus on the steps of the church. He was Officer Rodriguez of the Holloway PD, one of the cops who had found the body of Anitra Jenkins, and he had something to tell Marcus, but he wouldn't talk in the office unless he checked it out first.

Yolanda and Jimmy were approaching Sheena's house when Rodriguez and Marcus walked quietly back into the office. Rodriguez didn't say a word, but began looking behind pictures, under tables, and in lampshades. Rodriguez silently rolled a chair below the windows and found the first of several listening devices.

Yolanda and Jimmy were each hugging Dana goodnight as Marcus made a call from RBG's landline to Sharon's cell, just to see how soon she thought she'd be back, complaining that their connection was breaking up. As he spoke, Rodriguez took apart the phone receiver and pointed out the bug.

"Listen Sharon, I'm just here waiting," Marcus lied into the phone. "The guy turned out to be some jerk from the Revolutionary Disruption Squad. I don't have time for that shit." Marcus continued as Rodriguez reassembled the phone receiver, "I'll see you when you get here."

Yolanda and Jimmy walked around a different block that night as Rodriguez and Marcus scanned the street for anyone who might be watching and climbed into Rodriguez's personal car, realizing that Marcus's car might be bugged. His house might be bugged. His cell might be bugged. Anyone associated with RBG might be bugged. Yolanda and Jimmy walked five times around the block, and this time arm in arm. The journal seemed to be working, and Yolanda felt no need to confess, as Rodriguez poured out his story about finding Anitra Jenkins: how everything looked wrong, but how his partner, the coroner, and the chief didn't seem to want to look any further than the carefully choreographed surface of this death.

"Do you think maybe one of these days we could spend time together inside of a building?" Jimmy asked Yolanda with a chuckle.

"You can't talk to anyone inside any building that isn't a public place," Rodriguez warned Winters.

"I don't feel comfortable talking inside," Yolanda said. "I'm sort of claustrophobic."

"I shouldn't even be talking to you now," Rodriguez said. "I could lose my job over this."

"Maybe I'm a little scared," Yolanda said.

"I'm fucking scared, man," Marcus said.

"Don't be afraid," Jimmy put an arm around her shoulder.

"You should be scared," Rodriguez said. "I don't know who the hell has your place bugged. Randell? Holloway Police? The

FBI? Fuck. Don't ever say my name out loud to anyone. Not in person not over the phone, you understand? Don't even talk in your sleep."

"Don't give me the runaround," Jimmy said. "If you don't really like me, promise you'll just let me know, okay?"

"It's not that, Jimmy," Yolanda said.

"What is it, then? Is there somebody else in the picture?"

"I get the picture," Marcus said. "But how the hell can we be in communication?"

"I'll contact you," Rodriguez said. "I might send someone else with a message."

Yolanda laughed. "No, Jimmy. There's nobody else. I've been single since . . . forever."

"Well, what is it?" Jimmy asked. "I mean, when we met at the runner's path, there was this incredible chemistry. You said you couldn't date me because you were so deep in your studies for the bar. But now that you're practically working for RBG, you don't seem to care if you pass the bar or not. You're not even sure that you want your law job. Can't you make room for me in this new life?"

"I don't know," Yolanda said. "I mean I've . . . dated a few guys. But I always fit them into the spaces between the work and school. I've never really let anyone get that close. But when I'm around you, it's like I could drown in this feeling."

"I'm in way over my head here," Marcus said. "What the hell do I tell all my folks?"

"Start with the bugs," Rodriguez advised. "Tell your folks individually. Say you're the one who found them. Tell them to act like nothing happened. You don't want whoever it is to know you know they're listening. Tell the adults, not the kids. Outside the office, outside the car. Go for a walk."

"Thank you for walking me home, Jimmy," Yolanda said, as they stood in her doorway. He propped the door open against his shoulder, the cool night air rushing into the dim hallway around them.

He squeezed her hand. "I'm not the kind of guy who fits into the tiny spaces between other things." He stared at the grimy, worn carpet, its diamond pattern dulled by years of dirt and wear.

"I mean, I've got a busy life, too," he went on, then looked in her face again. "But I want to inconvenience you. I want to lose sleep over you. I want to stand in front of my students, bleary eyed, and wonder if they can smell your goodbye kisses when I open my mouth to lecture about some biology concept I couldn't fucking care less about at that moment," he pulled her closer to him. "I want days that start and end with you."

Yolanda felt a spasm of desire in her belly and below. She wondered if she could stay standing.

He leaned in to her and kissed her softly, all lips, no tongue. He lingered for just a second, and then pulled back.

"I'll be patient," he assured her. "We can take our time. Just let me know when you're ready."

Yolanda couldn't speak, so she just nodded.

"Goodnight, Yolanda," he said, and ran his finger from her ear along her jawline before he turned and let the door shut behind him.

Marcus closed Rodriguez's car door and watched the cop drive away. He stood on the curb, waiting for Sharon to get back with the van. He would tell her as he walked her to her car. Maybe he would crash on her couch tonight. Her wife would probably be cool with that. He couldn't stand the thought of walking into his empty and cold house, wondering who the fuck might be listening.

Part 3

Chapter 20

Two days later, Yolanda left the apartment for the rally against RandellCorp, clutching her handbag to her chest. Ever since she'd started writing in her *Learning Japanese Kanji on the Go* book, she took it everywhere with her. She adjusted the strap tight on her bag and carried it messenger-style, over one shoulder and across her chest. She had bought the bag from a young woman at one of the RBG meetings. It was made out of thin, durable multicolored plastic from a recycled billboard ad.

She caught the #26 to ride the fifteen blocks to Randell. An easy walk. The kind of walk she liked on a warm day, with the few raggedy plum trees on her block with their wine-colored leaves and gnarled dark wooden branches. But lately she felt too agoraphobic to walk alone and exposed on the street. She pulled her baseball cap lower over her face and slouched into her bus seat.

Two blocks from Randell, the traffic began to slow. From a distance, Yolanda could see the high antennas of TV vans. Up ahead, rubberneckers gawked out of their car windows at the crowd. At 4:15 PM, the bus was packed with students, and several complained loudly as they crawled through the traffic.

Yolanda signaled for the driver to stop. She exited from the rear door, her messenger bag with the journal pressed between her breasts, keeping a firm grip on it with one hand.

RandellCorp was located up ahead and on the right-hand side of a two-lane, one-way street. There was only one entrance to the parking lot of the Randell facility, with the security of a military checkpoint. All individuals and vehicles entering RandellCorp needed to be approved at the guard hut. The exit had spikes that would shred the tires of any vehicle that tried to enter the wrong way.

A small cluster of protesters were picketing just outside the security gate on the RandellCorp side of the street, waving signs: JUSTICE FOR ANITRA, BLACK LIVES MATTER, CLIMATE JUSTICE NOW! and HONK IF YOU THINK RANDELL IS SHADY. One driver started honking, and the picketers cheered wildly.

The bulk of the protesters, however, had congregated in a small park next to Randell. But as the crowd had grown, they had spilled out into the sidewalk. The two lanes of traffic on the street had to squeeze into a single lane, because they were bottlenecked between the picketers and the battalion of news vans parked on the other side of the street.

Initially, the crowd had been mostly black and brown, with teens from RBG! and Youth vs. Apocalypse in Oakland. But then a huge contingent from the Sunrise Movement had marched over from the BART station—a racially mixed group of young adults in their black shirts with white letters and their signature yellow logo.

Meanwhile, Project Greener had brought out their base of supporters, a mostly white twenty-something crowd, heavy on the earth tone fabrics, tribal tattoos, and pale dreadlocks. A group called "Food Not Bombs" had set up a table and was giving out free organic vegan food.

An African American teenage boy was sampling their

chard, beans, and brown rice in a bowl made of pressed leaves with bio-degradable utensils.

"Ugh," he said to the young man next to him. "It ain't no meat in here."

"That's what vegetarian means, fool," his friend said. "And that shit is good."

Project Greener staff and volunteers circulated through the crowd handing out leaflets for their national fundraising campaign, emphasizing that RBG was sponsored by Project Greener.

On the far end of the park, several RBG! teens had created a makeshift stage by standing on a picnic table and were addressing the crowd through a bullhorn. Behind them, the concrete back of another building marked the unyielding perimeter of the park.

As Yolanda moved through the rally, she caught a glimpse of Marcus and Sharon, and worked her way toward them. At the same time, the teens on the bullhorn led the crowd in a more hip-hop version of an old protest chant:

> The people . . .
> *What?*
> United
> *What?*
> Will never be defeated
> *That's right!*
> The people . . .

They chanted on for a while, and then a young Latina climbed onto the picnic table and led the chant in Spanish:

> El pueblo . . .
> *What?*

Unido
What?
Jamás será vencido

I said the people
What? . . .

The young woman handed the bullhorn to Darnell who began to beatbox, vocalizing a rhythm to go with the chant, as she and another girl screamed the words from the picnic table.

When the crowd heard the beat, they roared with approval. Two young men next to Yolanda began to dance in an undulating break rhythm that made their bodies look boneless and impervious to gravity.

Yolanda pushed through the crowd to find Marcus and Sharon. "Hey there," she said when she finally caught up to them. "Great turnout. I've never seen this many white people—"

"We need to talk," Marcus said. "Sharon and I are calling a special meeting of the adults in RBG."

"Right now?" Yolanda asked.

"Let's get away from this crowd for a minute," Sharon said, and ushered them toward the edge of the park under a large pine tree.

"I don't know how to say this," Marcus began.

Yolanda turned and gave him her full attention.

"I know you don't have a lot of experience with political movements," Marcus said. "But sometimes, particularly when a movement is effective, it can attract attention from the government or the opposition."

Yolanda's mouth felt dry.

"RBG has been building our reputation for a while, but lately, with the Jenkins case, and the article, and everything—"

"Oh God, Marcus," Sharon interrupted. "Look at her

face. You're scaring the girl to death. Yolanda, the office is bugged."

"What?" Yolanda said.

"We don't know who did it," Sharon said. "We don't know what else is bugged, whose house, whose phone, what. But we want to tell all the adults today, and we'll have a meeting to figure out how to tell the young people."

As the words tumbled out of Sharon's mouth, Yolanda's mind spun, dizzy with relief. Everyone knew. She could stop pretending to be comfortable.

Another half-confession poured out of her. "It's so—so terrifying to think someone could be watching us, listening to everything we say," Yolanda said to Marcus and Sharon. "Not to have any privacy. Or—or not to know if you have any privacy or not." And her eyes welled up with the relief of it. She looked into their concerned faces, Marcus's furrowed brow, Sharon's open-eyed face nodding.

"All of us are really scared," Sharon said.

All of us. Yolanda felt more connected to them than she had to anyone since she left Georgia.

In the background, Yolanda could hear the crowd singing:

> *People gonna rise like the water, gonna calm this
>   crisis down.
> I hear the voice of my great-granddaughter saying
>   "keep it in the ground."*

"Yolanda," Marcus said, "I'm really sorry that we got you into this. I know you're new to political work. Worst case scenario, you might have an FBI file now. It could jeopardize your future. I feel like I pressured you to take on a big role in the organization really fast. None of us expected this. I would understand if you left RBG."

"No way, Marcus," Yolanda said. "I'm not leaving RBG just because we're effective. That's like leaving a winning team, just because the opponents pull a prank in your locker room."

"Okay," Sharon said with an anxious smile. "Then we should find Jimmy so we can have this meeting."

Yolanda scanned the crowd, looking for him. On the picnic table, the teens were leading a new chant:

> *Listen to the youth!*
> *We demand the truth!*

The crowd chanted along, waving their fists in the air.

As Yolanda, Marcus, and Sharon circulated through the protesters, Dana had the bullhorn and addressed the crowd.

"That's right, we demand the truth today," Dana said. "Did you know that Andrew Wentworth, the Executive Vice President of Randell who runs their operation in Holloway, makes ten million dollars a year? That's right people, ten million."

Yolanda squeezed past a man with a sign saying, "Randell can go to hell!"

"According to the property records," Dana said, "Wentworth lives in a twenty-five-acre estate in Blackhawk. His pool is bigger than most of our houses. On the weekends, Andrew Wentworth plays golf or goes to his cabin on Lake Berryessa." She made quote marks around the word cabin. "As in a five-bedroom, four-bathroom building. You know. A little cabin."

"Bullshit!" someone yelled from the crowd.

"Andrew Wentworth, are you kidding me?" Dana yelled. "People in Holloway are trying to hang on to one house! Our unhoused population is exploding. Young people in Holloway don't even have a ten-million-dollar budget for our high school. Every year our community has more and more climate refugees. We're sick of corporations like Randell getting rich off the destruction of the environment and the destruction of our people."

"Hell yeah!" a thin, bare-chested white guy in baggy burlap pants yelled.

"We don't care how much money you make or where you live. We demand that Andrew Wentworth be accountable for the death of Anitra Jenkins. Black lives matter!"

The crowd exploded with applause.

"Jimmy!" Sharon yelled, and waved her arm high over her head. Yolanda looked in the direction Sharon was facing, and saw Jimmy standing far back on the sidewalk outside the park with his video camera panning the crowd.

"Jimmy!" Marcus yelled, but his voice was drowned out by the crowd noise.

On the picnic table, Nakeesha took the mic and began to chant.

"What do we want?"

"Justice!" the crowd yelled back.

"When do we want it?"

"NOW!"

The three adults from RBG moved toward Jimmy through the masses of people.

"Hey," Jimmy said. His smile expanded when he saw Yolanda.

"Some serious shit going down, bruh," Marcus said.

Sharon took his arm and pulled him to the side of the crowd. Jimmy reached for Yolanda's hand, and the four adults walked even further from the park.

As Marcus told Jimmy about the bugs, Yolanda could see his jaw clench.

"We gotta figure out what to tell the youth, who to tell, how we tell them."

"They deserve to know," Sharon said. "But I don't know if they can keep their mouths shut. I know Nakeesha can't. But it doesn't seem right to tell some and not others."

"What the fuck?" Marcus said. "If we keep it from them and they find out later that we knew . . ."

"I just don't know what integrity looks like here," Sharon said. "But I'm most concerned about their safety."

"We don't even know what the hell to do to keep them safe!" Marcus exploded. "I've talked to their mamas. They're worried about their kids protesting, and I've looked in their eyes and promised them it would be okay. This shit is not okay!"

Jimmy put a hand on Marcus's shoulder. "Take it easy, man. We don't want to attract any attention right now. And we don't want the youth coming over and asking what's wrong."

As Marcus took several deep breaths and tried to calm down, they heard a booming voice over a loudspeaker coming from the RandellCorp side of the street.

"This is the Holloway Police Department," the cop in charge spoke through a much larger megaphone. "You are participating in an unlawful assembly and you need to disperse immediately. I repeat, DISPERSE IMMEDIATELY."

A cordon of police began to march from the Randell lot in full riot gear. Yolanda froze for a second. What the hell was happening? The police had vehicles barricading the street on both ends of the block.

The picketers were backing away from the cops, signs in hand. They moved across the street to the relative safety of the larger protest.

"Fuck the police," a young man's voice came over the RBG bullhorn, suddenly small and tinny compared to the police loudspeaker. The young black man—someone Yolanda didn't recognize—had grabbed the microphone from Nakeesha. She was fighting to get it back, two handfuls of his jacket in her fists, face contorted with the effort of pulling against him with all her strength.

"Oh shit," Marcus surged forward.

"Marcus," Sharon barked the order. "You and me should go deal with the youth. Jimmy and Yolanda, go talk to the police."

Jimmy and Yolanda crossed the street at a brisk walk to speak to the officer with the loudspeaker.

Yolanda put a hand on Jimmy's arm. "I'll handle this," she said as they approached the cop. "I'm a lawyer."

Jimmy nodded, and Yolanda could feel the tension in his body.

"Sir," Yolanda said to the officer in her most polite yet professional voice. "My name is Yolanda Vance. I'm an attorney. This is my colleague Jimmy Thompson, from the science faculty at Cartwright. What seems to be the trouble, sir? These people are just exercising their constitutional right to assembly."

"Ma'am," the cop said. "They're blocking traffic. They're loitering. We caught some individuals littering, jaywalking on the street, the food people don't have a permit, the protest doesn't have a permit."

"It's a public park, officer," Yolanda said.

"We received complaints from employees who say they can't get in or out because their way is blocked."

"You've broken up the picketing, sir," Yolanda said. "No one is blocked anymore. Why can't you just allow these citizens to continue with this lawful assembly in a public park?"

"Randell employees and other neighbors have complained that they feel intimidated by the protesters."

"The protesters aren't intimidating anybody," Jimmy said angrily. "Randell is the one killing people."

Yolanda had never seen him angry before. She squeezed his arm gently.

The cop looked squarely at both of them. "Tell these people that if they don't want to end up in jail, they need to disperse immediately. My team is ready to move in and make mass arrests."

Yolanda could see herself reflected in the cop's metallic shades, a distorted, convex version of herself, her eyes looking more imploring than she intended. She put on her most crisp businesslike face.

"If you insist, officer. But can we have ten minutes to get the crowd to disperse?"

"You can have one minute."

"That's crazy," Yolanda snapped. "You know we can't get four hundred people out of that park in one minute."

"That's not my problem, ma'am. I have instructions to disperse the crowd immediately or start making arrests."

"There are news cameras here. Reporters from the press," Jimmy heated up again.

"Would you like to be the first arrest?" the officer asked.

"No, sir, he would not," Yolanda said. She was itching to pull out her FBI credentials and show them to this asshole.

"This is a peaceful and nonviolent protest!" Marcus was yelling into the bullhorn microphone. "We didn't come here today to make any trouble with the police, we came to demand justice for Anitra Jenkins!"

Yolanda sucked up her rage and spoke in clipped syllables: "We're going to try to get the crowd to disperse. Please consider the impact on the reputation of your department if you use unreasonable tactics or excessive force, particularly with so much press in attendance."

Yolanda and Jimmy turned away from the cops and hurried across the street. They looped around the perimeter of the crowd, trying to get to the picnic table where RBG was congregated.

Over a hundred camera phones were out, recording everything.

"I'm not getting anyone to disperse," Jimmy said. "We have a right to protest here."

"At this point our right to protest is purely academic,"

Yolanda said to Jimmy and waved a hand in the direction of the police. "We better disperse before somebody gets hurt."

"What the fuck, Yolanda?" Jimmy asked angrily. "What fucking planet are you from? These are the Holloway fucking police. Every black man in this crowd has been slammed against an HPD cruiser. Including the one you're talking to now. We fucking get hurt every day. Our fucking office is bugged. It's not like there's a safe path for us here. We need to stand up to these assholes."

"Yes, but—" Yolanda began, when Jimmy grabbed her arm.

"Watch out," he said, and pulled her out of the path of the advancing line of blue.

The police crossed the street in a long row, then circled the crowd and moved in.

Yolanda and Jimmy stood outside the circle, watching helplessly as the crowd constricted in on itself.

"This is a peaceful and nonviolent protest," Marcus kept yelling into the microphone.

The young man who had yelled "Fuck the police!" began shoving his way through the crowd. The ripples pushed out toward the edges of the crush of people, sending one young white woman stumbling toward the police, her phone out and recording. An officer took out his nightstick and clubbed her in the head. The phone fell out of her hand as she threw her arms up to protect herself and the crowd surged back in panic, pushing back to the concrete wall at the far end of the park.

"The whole world is watching!" Marcus screamed into the bullhorn as several teens stood beside him on the table, phones out. Meanwhile, the news cameras rolled at the edge of the circle, capturing the panicked faces in the mob, the police moving in.

Yolanda watched, horrified, as she and Jimmy kept backing away.

They watched a police van roll up to the edge of the cor-don, and the cops began to grab people and put them in makeshift handcuffs, plastic zip-ties. They confiscated sev-eral phones. Once the protesters were cuffed, the police shoved them onto the van.

Yolanda and Jimmy began walking hurriedly out toward the end of the block, passing four sheriff's buses that rolled slowly down the street like tanks.

"Those motherfuckers," Jimmy muttered.

"Where are we going?" Yolanda asked.

"To the car. We need to follow the buses to see where they're taking everyone. Come on."

Once they passed the police barricade, Yolanda and Jimmy covered the eight blocks at a dead run. Yolanda's bag bounced roughly against her chest as she ran.

Jimmy had parked his old blue Mercedes on a side street and pulled out the key to unlock it.

"Wait," Yolanda whispered as she touched his arm. "The car might be bugged."

"Okay, no talking," Jimmy whispered back. "I probably have some paper if we need to write."

As he started the car, Yolanda was still in shock. Why hadn't they given the crowd time to disperse? Who the hell was that guy pushing everyone in the crowd?

When they got close to the barricaded corner, they saw that the police van had pulled forward and double-parked on the far end of the block. Other protesters who had avoided the cordon stood out on the street beyond the barricade, phones out. Four black teens in bright athletic gear stood talking agitatedly with a white Food Not Bombs volunteer who had a large empty pot dangling from her hand.

"I hope folks are able to post these videos on social media," Jimmy said.

Yolanda looked down at her phone and saw that she had

no signal. It had been just fine before the protest. She felt like she had swallowed a stone.

"I'm sorry," Jimmy said.

Yolanda widened her eyes, motioned to the ceiling and windows of the car.

"I don't care," Jimmy said. "I'm sorry I was so hard-headed. You were just trying to calm the situation down. Not that it mattered. The police were gonna fucking do whatever they were gonna do."

Her mind kept flashing to the image of Jimmy being slammed against a police car? A college professor? Darnell maybe. His drug dealer friends for sure. But Jimmy?

"Thanks. For the apology. I don't really know what to say." Yolanda shrugged again and fluttered her hands to indicate the possible bugs in the interior of the car.

Jimmy nodded and took her hands in his as the first bus filled with protesters rolled down the street and pulled up behind the full police van.

When Jimmy tried to edge the car closer, a motorcycle cop pulled up alongside him and demanded that he move on. They circled to the other end of the barricaded block, watching the growing caravan of law enforcement vehicles jammed with protesters.

Jimmy turned on the radio, tuned it to KPFA, and listened to a reporter tell them what they already knew about the protest, including the fact that cell reception had apparently been shut down in the area. When they reported that only a few people had been injured and that most of the crowd had gone willingly into the buses, Yolanda and Jimmy made eye contact.

"That's a relief," Jimmy said quietly.

Yolanda nodded and kept her eyes on the radio, as if she might be able to see the news in its unchanging digital face.

"Heaven help the roses when the bombs begin to fall," Jimmy said into the silence.

Yolanda knew this one. "Stevie Wonder," she replied. "Heaven help us all."

An hour later, the last bus pulled into the line, and the sun was dipping toward the horizon over the bay.

Jimmy maneuvered his car in line behind the caravan. By the time they arrived at the Holloway police station, it was dark.

Jimmy and Yolanda watched from outside the police lot as several individuals were taken off the buses and escorted into the building, including the young black man who had yelled "Fuck the police."

Jimmy motioned for them to get out of the car.

"I think he's a goddamn agent," he said to Yolanda on the street, a few paces from the car. "Mr. fuck-the-police."

"An agent?" Yolanda asked.

"A provocateur," Jimmy said. "Look at his behavior. He grabbed the mic and agitated the cops. He started the shoving in the crowd. That woman would never have gotten clubbed if he hadn't started the pushing."

"You don't know that," Yolanda said. "Crowds are unpredictable."

He turned to her accusingly: "Whose side are you on?"

"I just—I'm scared, Jimmy. I don't know what the hell any of this means."

He softened and took her hand. "Let me tell you what I think. I think they won't be locking anyone up tonight because they don't have the facilities here. I think they're gonna charge a few people, the ones who resisted arrest, plus their boy the provocateur. And then they'll just wait a little while and let everyone else go."

"What will they charge them with?"

"No charges."

"But they're supposed to charge them."

"Yolanda, these are protest tactics. It's not about a crime that took place, it's about the government protecting Randell's interests."

Protecting the baby from the edge of the bed? Protecting Randell from public scrutiny?

"I thought I knew the law," Yolanda said bitterly.

"You do know the law, Yolanda," Jimmy said. "You just don't know how it gets enforced."

Yolanda nodded, and he squeezed her hand tighter. Even though they had left the bugged car, she had nothing to say.

Chapter 21

Two hours later, the four adults of RBG, along with Carlos, Sheena, and Dana, sat in the emergency room.

Carlos had suffered a head injury. He had walked in with all of them but seemed unsteady on his feet.

"I don't need to go to the hospital," Carlos had said in the Holloway police parking lot. "I hate hospitals."

"When a cop clubs you in the head, you go to the hospital," Marcus said.

Sharon had looked in his eyes and determined that he might have some sort of concussion.

The seven of them had squeezed into Jimmy's car and headed to Kaiser emergency. As they arrived, a man was being rushed in on a gurney. There were already over a dozen people waiting, several of them bleeding, a few barely conscious, and a baby who kept screaming at the top of her lungs.

Carlos sat around dazed, watching sitcoms. The RBG members were glued to their phones. Yolanda still didn't have any of her own social media accounts, so she looked on with Jimmy.

Several of the protest videos had gone viral, but none of

the ones that really showed the excessive force used by the police.

"That guy right there," Marcus said. "I saw that guy. He had a perfect shot of the cop clubbing that woman. When he got arrested, they took his phone."

"You think they selectively targeted the people with the best video?" Jimmy asked.

"I'll bet they did," Marcus said. "I fucking hate the police."

"I thought you said law enforcement were just members of the working class who'd been manipulated to go against their people," Dana said.

"Some days I believe that," Marcus said. "On days I get arrested, I fucking hate them all."

"Amen," said Jimmy.

Yolanda ran her fingers across the exterior of her shoulder bag. She traced the ridges that defined the edges of her FBI credentials pressing against the vinyl from an interior pocket. Manipulated to go against their people?

In the background, the canned laughter from the sitcom died down, and the network aired their news preview clip, as they had done at every commercial break. They showed a brief clip of the rally, an image of the melee as the cops moved in, with the audio: "Mass arrests at a protest against Randell Corporation in Holloway today. Details at eleven."

Just before the second sitcom ended, they called in the woman with the baby, and the screaming finally stopped.

"Are they ever gonna call us?" Sheena asked.

"Eventually," Sharon said. Then she turned to Carlos: "*Cómo tás amor? Cómo tá tu cabeza? Quieres mas hielo?*"

Carlos had his face in his hands. "I told you I'm fine," he mumbled. "Leave me alone." They had given him a large bandage when he came in, which had stopped the bleeding, and an ice pack which had warmed to room temperature half an hour earlier.

The rally clip came on TV again. "Police had to break up a demonstration at Randell Corporation in Holloway. The story at eleven."

"They didn't have to break up the demonstration," Dana said. "That's bullshit."

"I was hella scared," Sheena said. "When those cops rolled up, I was like 'oh fuck!' But Sharon came and grabbed me and Nakeesha and Jasmine and held onto us in the crowd."

"I got separated from you guys," Dana said. "But I held onto Darnell and we did what you told us to do at that non-violent protest training we had last year. Don't panic. Don't run. Don't yell. Stay together as much as possible, and don't resist arrest."

"Thank god Darnell ain't on probation no more," Nakeesha said.

"We're lucky we had all those cameras there, or it would have been so much worse," Marcus said. He had finally surrendered the bullhorn to the police and hadn't gotten it back when they released him. The teens had been cuffed with their hands behind their backs. So even though many of their phones were never confiscated, they couldn't use them until after they were uncuffed and released.

"They wouldn't let us off the bus to pee or anything," Sheena said. "I had to go hella bad, because I'd been holding it at the rally. We were on those damn buses for three hours! I thought I was gonna pee my pants, for real."

"Watch," Marcus said. "When the news segment comes on, I'll be surprised if they don't interview Andrew Wentworth from Randell or Chief Evans. Turn this shit into some kind of PR opportunity."

"That'll be next week," Jimmy said. "You watch. Sometime soon, there'll be a news story on Randell's Pick Up the Bay Day activities with Holloway Elementary."

"My brother was in that," Sheena said. "All they did was have him pick up one piece of trash, give him a donut, and have him pose for a picture."

By ten PM, Jimmy had made a run to take Dana and Sheena home. Sharon had gone to the nurse's desk twice to see when they might call Carlos in, showing her badge and explaining that she was a Kaiser therapist.

The nurse seemed unimpressed.

"You do realize he has a head injury and is bleeding?" Sharon asked.

"Miz Martinez, we're doing everything we can," she said. "We have two gunshot wounds, and a cardiac arrest. And that's on top of the five-car pileup that happened nearby on 580 from earlier today."

By the time the Eleven O' Clock News came on, they were still waiting. During a news story about a celebrity wedding, the nurse came out.

"Carlos Moralow," she butchered Carlos's last name, Murillo.

"Finally," Carlos grumbled, standing up.

"You want me to come in with you?" Sharon asked.

Carlos tried to shake his head, winced, and waved her away.

On the television, a blonde woman with stiff hair and thick makeup wore a somber expression as she detailed the story on the protest. Above her shoulder was the Randell logo.

"In Holloway today, a demonstration against Randell Corporation, led by Project Greener and Red, Black, and GREEN! got out of control and police had to break up the crowd."

The story cut to the young man yelling "[Bleep!] the police!" Then they cut to a clip of the police on the loudspeaker: "This is the Holloway police department. This is an unlawful assembly and you need to disperse immediately. I repeat, DISPERSE IMMEDIATELY." The next shot was a quick cut to pushing and chaos in the crowd.

"Police arrested over three hundred protesters, but most were released this evening."

The next clip showed a line of protesters filing off the bus into the Holloway PD parking lot in the plastic handcuffs under dim light.

"However, several were charged with resisting arrest, and one had a warrant for a felony charge." The final clip showed police escorting a few demonstrators into the building with their heads down.

The anchorwoman smiled and turned to her co-anchor. "I guess he'll be spending the night in jail. So what's our weather looking like?"

"I knew it!" Marcus said, turning away from the television. "I knew they wouldn't even mention Anitra Jenkins."

"This is bad," Sharon said.

"MSNBC showed a few clips from protesters' phones," Jimmy said. "And Democracy Now is gonna run a story about the protest in the morning."

"Does it look like anyone got the video of the police clubbing that white girl?" Sharon asked.

"Not yet," Jimmy said.

"By then, it won't fucking matter," Marcus said. "They've already framed the story. Protesters were out of control. The police did what they had to do. By the time Democracy Now shows the real story, the mainstream press will have moved on."

"You're right," Jimmy said. "To the average TV viewer, it looks like another episode of COPS where they get the bad guy in the end."

"This is gonna make our organizing twice as hard," Sharon complained. "None of the black parents of Holloway will want their kids to go to RBG."

The door opened and Carlos came back out. The nurse came with him and spoke to the four adults.

"He has a mild concussion. He can take a pain reliever for the headache." She talked about Carlos like he wasn't there. "Which of you are the parents?"

"The guardians," Marcus volunteered quickly.

"Wake him up every two hours. If he won't wake up, call us, okay?" She handed them an information sheet and walked back to the desk.

"Is your mom home tonight?" Sharon asked after the nurse had left.

Carlos shrugged. "I think she's working graveyard."

"You're coming home with me," Sharon said.

"Oh joy," Carlos said in a deadpan.

"Or," Marcus said. "You could come home with me. I got a frozen pizza, some mix and pour brownies. A bunch of sci-fi movies. Maybe we won't even go to sleep."

Carlos gave a lopsided half smile, the first Yolanda had seen since he had stepped off the bus. He pointed at Marcus and gave a thumbs up.

In the Kaiser parking lot, they all squeezed into Jimmy's car.

"I'm gonna drop Carlos and Marcus first, okay?" Jimmy asked. "It's not the most efficient, but I want to get Carlos settled ASAP."

After everyone agreed, none of the adults said anything.

"Damn. you guys," Carlos said. "I'm not dying. I don't need a moment of silence or anything."

"Of course not," Yolanda said.

At the same time that Sharon said, "We were just so worried about you."

"Carlos could tell something was weird," Sharon said, after they'd dropped Marcus and Carlos. She, Yolanda, and

Jimmy were standing in the cold night outside Sharon's house. "We've gotta figure out how to handle this bugging thing."

"Maybe we should just go public," Jimmy suggested.

"Maybe we should," Yolanda agreed.

"I can't think clearly, I'm so tired," Sharon said.

Sharon hugged them both goodnight, and Jimmy and Yolanda drove in silence to Yolanda's house.

As they reached the corner at the end of her block, she tapped Jimmy on the shoulder and motioned for him to keep going. They passed her building and drove out onto Holloway Avenue.

Yolanda felt reckless, unleashed. Nobody else seemed to be playing by the rules. Where was the payoff for being good? Being the best? The best grades, the best test scores, the best law school didn't pay off when Van Dell Meyers and Whitney wasn't paying by the rules, and now it seemed like nobody was.

The empty casket in the Holloway cemetery? The sixty seconds for hundreds of people to get out of a park? Cell service suspended in the area? Phones confiscated? What if the young black kid really was a provocateur? Sent by the FBI?

Johnakin's words came into her head: "When we let fear make our decisions, we are rarely pleased with the outcome. Take a risk and see what happens."

She directed Jimmy to park the car downtown.

"Where the hell are we going?" he asked after they got out.

"I don't know," Yolanda said as they walked across the BART station plaza. "I can't go home. Not knowing if it might be bugged. I need—I don't know what I need. Let's just go."

"Okay," Jimmy said slowly, and they caught the last BART train out of Holloway.

They sat side by side, holding hands, not talking. As the train slid into the Transbay tunnel, Yolanda mustered her courage to speak, emboldened by the loud echo of the train in the tunnel that drowned out the music blaring from the headphones of the young man across the way, and the fussing child several seats back.

"Let's go to a hotel," Yolanda's heart pounded furiously as she spoke. "Somewhere we can be alone."

He blinked several times. "Are you sure?" he said. "I don't want you to make a decision you'll regret because of some sort of post-traumatic coping mechanism."

"Jimmy," she said sharply. "Don't psychoanalyze me. If you don't want to spend the night together—"

"Are you fucking kidding me?" he yelled against the noise of the train. "I been wanting you since that first day I saw you at the runner's path. I just don't want to fuck this up. I want you for more than just tonight."

Suddenly, Yolanda smiled. "*Geechee geechee yaya dada*," Yolanda said, looking him directly in the eyes.

"Well hey sister soul sister go sister," Jimmy said, grinning.

In high school, after Yolanda became disillusioned with Lester Johnakin, she briefly found solace in the words of her own father. She had sat through all of his sermons back in Georgia, but as a preschooler, she could never make anything of the content. She was happy to watch the rapidly changing expressions on his face and follow the rise and fall of his cadences.

But when she was fourteen, she had come across a recording of one of his sermons on the internet. When she played it, the theme was clearly about loyalty. She downloaded it into her computer and listened to it every night at bedtime. Her father's familiar voice sliding in through earbuds to soothe the slice of Dale's disloyalty.

"The world is full of shiny things," her father began. "We can get so distracted by them. You see me up here with my bling? A gift from my lovely wife. Praise God . . . I know it's a nice watch, but I'm up here promoting the word of God, not showcasing accessories. See, we get distracted. I get distracted sometimes. Lord have mercy! But I know where my loyalty lies. And it's not to any of these earthly distractions and pleasures. It is to God."

See, we get distracted. I get distracted sometimes.

At the time, Yolanda had taken the sermon to mean that she had gotten distracted by Dale and designer clothes from her real goal—success. Success was her god, and she vowed to serve faithfully.

She had listened to the recording every night for months. Her father's voice was the only way she could fall asleep. Feel protected again. This digital file, more than anything her father had actually said to her, became the memory she had of him. Even now, she could recall fragments, whole paragraphs, but not in any coherent order.

In the days leading up to the rally at Randell, she had searched again for the link online. She found it and downloaded the audio file into her phone. She listened to it as she worked out in the gym.

Yolanda saw that her understanding in high school had still been faulty. As a teen, she had shaped her father's message around her need to make sense of Dale's betrayal. But now she could see that he was talking about more than just God vs. material things.

"If you have your Bible with you today . . ." She could hear the rustling of papers as she worked with the free weights in the gym. "Yes, let's stand for the Word of God. Turn to Romans thirteen, verse one: 'Let every person be subject to the governing authorities. For there is no authority except from God, and those that exist have been instituted by God.'

"So we have the Bible telling us here that we are to obey

authority. That the government exists because it was instituted by God. But that was why we needed a New Testament, where Jesus came down and said that God was love. Not rules. Not rulers. But love. Somebody say Amen."

"Amen," the congregation responded.

"Even in the Old Testament." Again, the rustling of paper. "Proverbs three, verse three: 'Let not steadfast love and faithfulness forsake you; bind them around your neck; write them on the tablet of your heart.'

"The Bible is telling us that what is in our hearts is the ultimate authority. Oh I wish I had some saints up in here today to validate this holy word."

"Amen."

As a teenager, she had interpreted the love part as the ambition she had in her heart. But now she thought about loyalty in a different way.

"Oh thank you Jesus for your holy word. Because in Matthew six, verse twenty-four, the Bible says, 'No one can serve two masters, for either he will hate the one and love the other, or he will be devoted to the one and despise the other.'"

Yolanda met her own eyes in the weight room mirror. Wasn't that exactly where she was right now? The FBI had made a case for her to despise RBG, but then she had spent time with those people, and it became increasingly clear that the Bureau had painted a false picture. "Black Identity Extremists," is what the FBI had called them. But it was just a bunch of teenagers who wanted decent schools, safe air and water, and not to get shot by the police. What was so extreme about that?

"You see me up here with my bling? A gift from my lovely wife. Praise God . . ." And then there was a quiet moment in the recording where all she could hear was her father's throaty chuckle. He was flirting. Flirting with his wife from the pulpit. She remembered it now. How he would beam down at both of them, but a special look he had just for her mother.

"See, we get distracted. I get distracted sometimes. Lord have mercy! But I know where my loyalty lies." Yolanda had faltered, right there in the gym, right in the middle of her third set of reps and looked at her phone. As if the screen could tell her what she already knew. Her father was apologizing to her mother. Explaining his behavior. *I get distracted by other women, but I'll always be loyal to you.*

How had she never considered that possibility? That her mother knew? Knew *something.* Had she accepted the affairs because she thought they meant nothing? Didn't include children? Or was she just humiliated at the funeral that it had been such an open secret? Or maybe a woman doesn't have that much of a choice when she has a powerful husband and no local family of her own.

How had her father justified his affairs? If he was supposed to be such a man of God? She had wondered this in the gym.

But now, as she sat on the train, her fingers tangled in Jimmy's, for the first time she could imagine what her father might have felt. It wasn't the same. Her father had betrayed his wife, his daughter—women he loved and had vowed to cherish. But she was an FBI agent, barreling through a tunnel into an unfamiliar city to bed a man she was lying to—was spying on.

She couldn't even quite bring herself to say it to him. Had counted on Lady Marmalade to say it for her. But she wanted him in that way that says consequences be damned. Every pore in her skin hungered for him. "The Bible is telling us that what is in our hearts is the ultimate authority." She thought again about her father's loyalty sermon. She wasn't sure whom she was betraying: Jimmy or the FBI. Maybe both. But right now, the only loyalty she had was to the desire she felt. That longing had become her ultimate authority.

"Embarcadero," the driver's voice came over the loudspeaker. "Embarcadero station, our first San Francisco stop."

She took Jimmy's hand and exited the train, leading him up into the hotel above the ground.

She had always thought of herself as her mother's daughter—most of her life shaped entirely by her mother's choices and failures. Her father's only relevant act was dying and leaving a void, in which her mother could make mistakes. But in this moment of recklessness, she felt herself as her father's daughter for the first time in her adult life.

Chapter 22

Jimmy produced his credit card for the woman at the desk in the crisp suit. Was there a king room available? No, they didn't need any help with luggage. Could she see that their only belongings were a small messenger bag across the chest of the woman, and a twenty-four hour drugstore bag in the man's hand with a small square box in it?

The room was a big square box, decorated in muted peach and rose colors, with a king size bed, a desk, an armchair, and an armoire with a TV inside. A door with a full-length mirror led to the bathroom, and an alcove closet offered extra pillows and two terrycloth robes.

Once they stepped inside the room, and closed the door behind them, Yolanda felt shy. They tossed their jackets on the chair, and Jimmy reached to kiss her, but she pulled back.

"I feel gritty from the day," she said, shrugging off his touch.

"Then let's take a shower," Jimmy suggested.

"Okay," Yolanda reached for the top button of her blouse, but Jimmy stilled her hand, and took over. He carefully unbuttoned her top, fingering the baby blue fabric and pearl buttons. Her shyness dissolved with the undressing, and she wrapped her arms around his waist. He leaned forward and tasted her neck with an openmouthed kiss that made Yolanda wonder if she could hold out for the shower.

As they backed into the bathroom, she slid her hands under his dashiki, her palms gliding up his undershirt, feeling the smooth, lean muscles of his back, his ribs, pulling the bright orange fabric top over his head.

Jimmy reached past her waist to turn on the shower, lingered on the way back, caressing the curve of her firm hips, the taut muscles of her belly, running his finger along the top of her jeans.

He leaned down and kissed her, as she peeled off his ribbed undershirt, easing her hands slowly up his chest, stroking his nipples, rewarded with a gasp.

"Oh no," he whispered, pulling his mouth away from hers. "Not the secret weapon."

Yolanda laughed and pulled his tank top off, tossing it on the floor, and returned to sliding her hands back up and down his chest.

"Yolanda," he whispered. "If you don't stop, I'm gonna come in my pants."

"No you're not," she said, and unbuckled his belt.

The bathroom had filled with steam, obscuring the tangle of their limbs from the reflection of the mirror, a film of humidity coating their skin, making everything slick and moist.

He leaned forward to kiss the tops of each of her breasts that peeked out above her beige bra, while he reached around to unhook it. As the bra loosened, he leaned down and took her nipple in his mouth.

Yolanda moaned in his ear, taking the lobe between her teeth, using her hands to undo his pants and letting them drop around his ankles.

Jimmy unbuttoned and unzipped her jeans, sliding his hands down the back of her underwear, easing the two garments down together.

Jimmy squatted down and untied Yolanda's sneakers, sliding them off her feet, one after another, and peeled off her socks. She stepped out of the pile of clothes, as he took his own shoes and socks off, and stood up in his boxers.

Yolanda reached and caressed his erection through the dark maroon cotton fabric.

He ran his hands down her back, over the curve of her ass, and back up the front of her body, her hipbones, her ribs, her firm small breasts, their large brown nipples.

Finally, she slid off his boxers, and he lifted her up, hands under her ass, into the shower. She held the curtain rod to steady them, and he let her down slowly to her feet, sliding her body down the front of his.

The spray at their sides, she backed him against the wall of the shower, pressing his erection against her belly. Yolanda leaned forward and stroked Jimmy's left nipple with one hand, and put the right one in her mouth.

He tangled his hand in her hair and moaned, his knees nearly buckling with the pleasure of her.

"Yolanda, I'm serious. I'm gonna make a mess."

She moved her mouth from his nipple and continued to stroke it with her other hand, and kissed him, openmouthed and hungry, pressing her belly against him, her hips against the taut muscles of his thighs.

"It's okay," she murmured into his chin. "We're in the shower." She reached for the bar of soap and peeled off the paper.

"We can clean up as we go along," she lathered her hands and slid one onto his nipple and the other between his legs.

Jimmy gasped and fell back against the shower wall.

"Besides," Yolanda murmured into his neck as his muscles tightened and he grabbed her waist, moving against her in a rhythm. "This is only the first round."

Fifteen minutes later, as they were toweling off, he laughed softly through the fluffy white towel.

"Wow," he said. "I sure do feel extra clean."

"I told you we'd feel better if we freshened up." She finished drying herself and swung the towel over the shower rod.

"So when does round two begin?" he asked.

"Right now," she said, pulling him, half-dry into the bedroom.

He dropped his towel onto the floor and leaned down to kiss her again.

"So how should I pace myself for this next round, coach?" he asked, backing her up to the edge of the bed

"This is an endurance race," she said, sitting on the edge of the bed and sliding her hands down over his ass and back up his hips.

"Oh it's a race?" he asked, reaching down and taking her breasts in his hands.

"With many rounds on the track," she said, leaning back on the bed.

"Well for once, I finished first," Jimmy grinned. "But you can come in second."

Yolanda laughed and leaned back, ready for him to climb up onto the bed with her.

Instead, he knelt swiftly on the carpet at the foot of the bed and pulled her hips to the edge, clutching her ass and burying his face between her thighs.

Yolanda gasped as his tongue touched tender flesh, and buried her fingers in his hair.

The first two rounds had washed the voracity from their skin, cleared the agitation from between their legs, and left them each with a slow hunger.

Yolanda tried to sit up. "I should wash—"

"Oh no," Jimmy put a hand on her chest, and she fell back on the bed. He slipped into bed next to her, kissing her hairline, her eyelids, her lips.

They maneuvered up to the top of the bed and she pulled

him onto her, pulled his mouth into hers. He fumbled around on the nightstand for the condoms, and knelt between her legs, rolling one onto his erection.

She sat up and stroked his chest, slid her arms around his back and pulled him down onto her.

He teased her with the tip, and smiled at her moan.

"Yolanda Vance," he said. "May I come inside you?"

"Yes," she said in a heavy whisper.

Slowly, he entered her.

She cried out with the sharp, sweetness of it. How many years had it been? She unwound herself and just received him. Wrapped her arms around his neck and didn't try to control anything.

Slowly, they found their rhythm. She wrapped her thighs around his hips and buried her tongue in his mouth.

He moved gently inside her, looking in her eyes for confirmation of every stroke, the condom dulling enough of the sensation that he could be that patient.

The third round was lingering like that, all eye contact and slow burn, soft tongues and long strokes.

They made love all night, like athletes. Like that first day at the runner's path. Each one pressing the other to greater endurance, pushing from their bodies what they didn't think they could get. Teasing, taunting, pulling each other along when either one lagged.

Yolanda wanted every fiber of him. Had no idea when they could be this alone again. Refused to think about the bigger picture, the case, her job, surveillance. They fucked themselves into a stupor, finally falling asleep around the time the FBI office opened.

Yolanda lay alone in bed at noon, running her tongue across her lips. *I am savoring this moment. I am savoring this moment.* She repeated to herself, not yet ready to return to her real life.

She had tried to lure him to stay, but at 11:50, he left to teach a one thirty PM class at Cartwright.

"Cancel it," she said.

"Please Yolanda," he begged. "Don't tempt me. I'm a junior faculty member. I want to get tenure. I can't be disappearing when we have an exam coming,"

But a few minutes after he had left, there was a knock at the door of the hotel room.

Yolanda went to answer it, delighted. "You decided to cancel your—?" she broke off.

Agent Peterson stood in the hallway.

Yolanda's heart was in her throat. Suddenly, she felt naked and inappropriate, standing there in the hotel's fluffy white terrycloth robe. In contrast, Peterson wore a dark suit, sensible shoes, and a stern expression.

She walked in past Yolanda and closed the door behind her.

"What the hell are you doing, Vance?" she asked, sitting in the soft peach armchair.

Yolanda had no choice but to stand or to sit on the disheveled bed. She sat, and pulled her robe closed at the neck and the knees.

Yolanda reached to try to smooth her hair down a bit. Peterson had only ever seen her with her hair carefully flatironed. Now, the shower had made it wavy and wild, and the lovemaking had ratted it up in the back. The few hours of sleep had left it flattened in some parts and sticking out in others. She pulled the hood of the hotel's robe up over her head.

"I'm doing what you told me, Peterson." Why was Yolanda feeling embarrassed? The FBI had practically thrown her at Jimmy.

"I told you to spend the night with the subject?" the agent asked.

"You told me to go out with him, Peterson," Yolanda said. "And did you follow me here?"

"I saw you didn't go home last night," Peterson said.

"What do you mean, you saw?" Yolanda asked.

"The GPS in your cell," Peterson said exasperated.

Yolanda's mouth fell open.

"Rafferty didn't tell you?"

Yolanda shook her head.

"Holy shit," Peterson said. "Well, now you know. And you didn't hear it from me."

Yolanda put her head in her hands. She had assumed Rafferty was keeping tabs on her, but tracking the GPS in her cell phone? Peterson seemed to be on her side, but could she really trust her?

"Here's something else you didn't hear from me," Peterson said. "Some advice. You're in way over your head. Don't let yourself fall in love with a subject."

"That's ridiculous," Yolanda said. She didn't love him. She liked him, though. A lot. But there was no question of her trusting Peterson with that information.

"I saw your expression when you thought I was him," Peterson said.

"I'm putting on a face for the subject."

"You're full of shit, Vance, and we both know it," Peterson said, standing up suddenly. She advanced toward Yolanda, towering over her. "And Rafferty is just waiting for a woman to screw up, for an excuse not to promote a female for the next decade. I've put in too much time with that asshole. When he retires, I want his goddamn view."

How had Yolanda walked into this FBI office drama? All she wanted was to finish this assignment and get back to New Jersey. No. That wasn't the only thing she wanted. She wanted to go back to New Jersey, but she also wanted more of Jimmy.

"I'm not falling in love with the subject," Yolanda insisted.

"I'm gonna cover your ass Vance," Peterson said, slumping back into the armchair.

Yolanda could feel her body relax. Peterson couldn't afford to rat her out.

"I'm gonna expect a call from you on my cell in five minutes," Peterson said. "And I want you to act like this conversation never happened, but like you're calling in to tell me all about it. You need to sound professional, like an agent who has successfully seduced a subject to get information. And give me something good."

"They found the bugs," Yolanda said quietly. "That's why we're in a hotel."

"Oh shit," Peterson said.

"We're blown," Yolanda said. "They know somebody's listening, but they don't suspect me at all."

"Good work, Vance," Peterson said. "Maybe I misjudged you."

"Yeah, maybe you did," Yolanda said. "So when I call you and tell you we're blown, try to act surprised, okay?"

At 9:17 AM, Officer Joaquín Rodriguez pulled his car up in front of the Holloway cemetery. He had worked the night shift and regretted having taken a brief nap. He could have been running on adrenaline, but instead, he was foggy and jangled.

Taking a final sip of coffee, Rodriguez stepped out of the car. He had on the frayed jeans and stained shirt he wore when he mowed the lawn. He grabbed his cowboy hat off the dashboard and pulled it down over his eyes. Cowboy boots completed the look. But walking up the road, the cowboy boots pinched. They looked and felt too new, their shiny black leather and pristine stitching would give him away. He stepped over to the base of a pine tree and kicked them in the loose dirt a few times. His wife would kill him for that. The boots had been a gift.

By the time he approached the cemetery office, he had begun to work up a pair of blisters on his feet, and his mincing limp was authentic as he shuffled into the building.

"Good morning, *señora*," he approached the woman at the desk. "Is any work here?"

The blonde with the helmet of hair surveyed him with distaste. "Sorry. The positions have been filled." She spoke with finality and went back to the paperwork on her desk.

"Thank you," he said to the woman. She didn't even look up or acknowledge him.

Outside, he noticed a Latino worker pulling weeds from the flowerbed on the side of the building. The man was hunched over, his gray maintenance uniform smudged with dirt.

"*Oye*," he approached the worker, and when the man looked up, he was much younger than Rodriguez expected. He told him in Spanish that he was looking for work.

The man stood up and told him that there was no work. There had been three available positions, but not anymore.

Rodriguez asked how often positions came open.

The man shrugged. He was maybe in his early twenties, the top buttons of his uniform open on this warm day. He had only been working there six weeks. Every few months somebody left, but usually the guys would talk among themselves and someone already working there had a brother or cousin looking for a job. Before the guy even told the office they were leaving, the crew had a replacement ready to go.

Rodriguez asked what had happened the week before last.

"*Ellos desaparecieron*," the man said, his face clouding over. "*No sé adonde fueron. Quizás la migra?*"

Rodriguez knew folks who had disappeared like that, undocumented men who were gone one day, then weeks later would come out of the ICE holding facility, deported and dumped at the border of Mexico, whether they were Mexican or not.

Rodriguez asked for the names of the three men.

"Ernesto, Luis, y Juan Carlos."

A small vehicle that looked like a golf cart pulled up with another pair of Latino workers.

Rodriguez asked the younger man for the last names of the three workers who had left.

"*No sé*," he said, and turned to the men in the cart and repeated the question. The two older men's faces snapped shut when they heard the names. They shook their heads.

The younger man shrugged and climbed into the golf cart without a goodbye.

Through the open back of the cart, Rodriguez could see the older workers chastising the young man with a cuff to the head. The golf cart disappeared over a hill, and Rodriguez limped back to his car.

Chapter 23

Yolanda lay on her bed in a stupor. She kept her eyes closed. Hopefully the cameras—if there were cameras—would register her as sleeping. She drifted in and out of a doze, images of Jimmy Thompson in her mind, her body reliving the memory of his touch on her skin.

He was so different from her previous lovers—was lovers even the right word?—they were more like hired guns. Guys she dated and would sleep with sometimes. She could barely recall their faces now.

But she did have a clear memory of one guy who was supposed to be much more than sex. Ted. A young lawyer at the firm where she had interned the summer between sophomore and junior year: his sandy blond hair, his confident smirk, his toned, pale body.

Theodore Bradley Wilkerson, *call me Ted,* had cultivated her over that summer, had pursued her so relentlessly, taking her to dinner at upscale Chicago restaurants. He told her all about his family, told her a sob story about being nerdy and getting nicknamed "Thesis" by his jock older brothers. All of it leading her to believe she could be more than just a summer intern fuck. She was his first black girl. He was her first time. She had come into the office the next Monday thinking they were in a relationship. He came in thinking about the brunette from University of Hawaii.

Yolanda had cried about it all night, mostly blaming herself. She didn't really let herself sob, just lay there stiffly, tears leaking from the sides of her eyes. Why the hell had she trusted him? He was always so much cooler at the office than on their dates. She had told herself it was professionalism. Because he respected her. Stupid, stupid, stupid. Just like in boarding school. When was she going to stop falling for the charming rich white kids who were just using her?

She sat up half the night berating herself in that Chicago apartment. Finally, around four in the morning, she drifted off to sleep for a couple of hours. When she woke up, hazy light filtered into her room. She groaned at the possibility of the day, feeling her eyes fill with tears again.

She went in to the office that day, dry-eyed and rock-spined. She put in earbuds and played Aretha Franklin's blues album. She saw him flirting with another intern and willed herself to be steel.

That night, she stayed up, watching her tiny portable television. She found some old movie. It had a tall femme fatale character, which sparked an idea.

The following Monday, a young woman came into the office.

"Chlamydia!" the girl had shrieked, looming over Ted's desk, her breasts nearly falling out of the low-cut sundress. "You gave me chlamydia!"

"What are you talking about?" he had asked, horrified. "I don't even know you."

"Or don't fucking remember. Your drunk ass could barely get it up. Just enough to give me a goddamn disease."

Yolanda stood nearby, her errand by Ted's desk carefully timed with the young woman's entrance.

The raging girl pointed a finger in his chest. "Just call your doctor, *Thesis*, before you do any more damage." She threw a brochure about sexually transmitted infections onto his desk.

"I'm calling security," he said, reaching for the phone.

"Don't bother." She stalked out, firm ass in her tight skirt switching back and forth on high heels.

Yolanda forced her face to look horrified as she walked back to the interns' cubicle. The image in her mind of the woman striding off in her tight skirt was perfect fifties cinema. The actor had played it flawlessly. Yolanda had spent half her summer savings paying the girl, but it had been worth it.

She walked home with Aretha's "Trouble in Mind" in her ears.

Back at the police station, Rodriguez called over to the Holloway morgue, looking for homicide victims or unidentified male corpses that might fit the description of the missing Latino workers.

"All I got is three black guys," the morgue attendant explained. "Two young and one old. I think the old guy was homeless."

Rodriguez thanked him and hung up. Next he tried the city of Richmond. He had no contacts at the morgue, but called an old security buddy—McConnell—who now worked for Richmond PD. Half an hour later, the guy called back.

"Two bodies turned up a couple weeks ago, dead from gunshot wounds," McConnell said. "Juan Carlos Sanchez and Luis Garcia. We got a match on their prints from when they came over on short-term work visas for a company in Southern California. Both visas expired a couple years back."

"You sure there were only two?" Rodriguez asked.

"Yeah, and I checked a week before and after," McConnell said.

Rodriguez recalled the name of the third guy. What the hell had happened to Ernesto?

* * *

Yolanda woke up around five that same evening, completely disoriented. Her body felt heavy, alien. It took a moment to make sense of this unfamiliar place, and she had been dreaming that someone was calling her name.

She wiped the blur from her eyes, and the FBI apartment blinked into view.

"Yolanda!" Someone was *actually* calling her.

She grabbed her keys, and ran to the door of her apartment, stumbling into her jeans. She zipped them as she ran down the hall.

"Jimmy!" Yolanda bounded down the stairs, the plastic runner over the carpet slightly greasy beneath her bare feet. She sped to the door and flung it open.

Jimmy stood in front of the door. Hands in his pockets. When she saw him, she couldn't help but smile in spite of her irritation. "Hush up and come in."

"Hello Yolanda Vance. Beautiful sexy Yolanda Vance."

"How are you up here yelling like one of the kids in RBG?" she asked as they climbed the stairs.

"You bring out the randy teenager in me, woman," he leaned in and kissed her neck. "Besides, you didn't answer your cell phone."

"What are you doing here anyway?" she leaned in and gave him a proper kiss.

"I've come to swoop you up and take you to a hotel. Any hotel. The Ritz in Paris, the Four Seasons in New York."

"I'll settle for the 'It's Not Bugged' in Holloway," she said, and motioned for him to wait in the hallway.

She opened the door, and sure enough, the silent cell on the table announced nine missed calls. She grabbed a clean pair of underwear and a toothbrush and stuffed them into her bag with the kanji book, her gun, and her FBI credentials.

Earlier that day, she had recorded herself puttering around the apartment, opening the fridge, using the bathroom, and getting into bed. If the place was bugged, it would sound like she was at home. If there were cameras? Well, she couldn't do anything about that.

She left the cell on the table and slipped silently out into the hallway.

Forty minutes later, they checked into a chain hotel in downtown Oakland. As the door of the room closed behind them, Jimmy leaned back against the door pulled her to him.

"Mmmm," Yolanda smothered his Adam's apple with an openmouthed kiss.

Jimmy slid his hands down the back of her jeans, pulling her hips to his.

"Damn Yolanda," he said. "If I knew for sure the car wasn't bugged, we wouldn't have gotten past Richmond. Woman, I would have driven down to the marina and devoured you in the back seat."

"No way," she said. "I would have devoured you." She unbuttoned his shirt and pulled it down over his hard shoulders and smooth chest.

He fumbled with the buttons of her jeans, kneeling, pulling them down, along with her underwear.

As she stepped out of the clothes, he picked up her panties and buried his face in them.

Yolanda laughed out loud. "What are you doing?"

"I can't take the full dose just yet," he said. "I gotta build up my immunity so it doesn't kill me."

He carefully set the underwear on the chair and began to kiss her ankle. She reached down and ran her fingers across the burr of his hair. He kissed his way up her calf, licking the back of her knee. She moaned with the softness of his lips. He kissed his way up her thigh, planted his hands on the cheeks of her ass, and pulled her hips toward his mouth, burying his tongue between her lips.

She gasped with the sweet shock of it, started to pull back, but he held her, massaged her ass, entered her with his tongue. Her knees turned boneless, and sensing her lack of balance, he put his arms around her and lowered her onto the carpet. Pants still buttoned and zipped, he lay on his belly, sinking his tongue into the tender flesh of her until she quaked with the pleasure of it, and lay back, trembling with aftershocks.

"That's for the shower last night," he teased, climbing up onto her, and reaching his hands underneath her t-shirt, which was still on.

"You've always played dirty," she gasped. "But I've got something for you."

"Take a minute to catch your breath, baby. You ain't gotta rush."

She lay there for a moment. She could feel her heart rate cooling down. She took a deep breath, planted one foot and, with the full strength of her quads, flipped him over.

His eyes widened in surprise. He outweighed her by at least seventy pounds.

She planted her moist, naked hips on his belly and reached behind her to undo his pants.

"Let me help," he reached down, but she slid the fingers of one hand purposefully across his left nipple, and he gasped, and lay back, his hands suddenly slack.

Yolanda realized she was unprepared, but felt around in his pockets and produced a condom.

"How you gonna put it on?" he challenged.

"With both hands behind my back," she said, and slid down his body so that her ass was grazing his erection.

He reached around and she let him help. Between the two of them, they got the condom on, and Yolanda inspected it to confirm that they had done a proper job.

"We make a good team," he said.

Yolanda smiled, and planted her hands on his hips, slowly lowering herself onto him centimeter by centimeter, centering her full weight over his pelvis so he couldn't thrust yet.

But once she'd fully enveloped him, she freed his hips and slid her hands up his chest, stroking his nipples, and brought him to a climax, her tongue in his mouth, lapping up his moans as his hips shuddered into hers.

"You don't even give a brother a chance," he said, after he had caught his own breath.

"Excuse me?" she asked. "You didn't even let me get to the bed."

"I couldn't wait a second more," he said, kissing her jaw, her temple. "The car ride was so long, and the day without you was even longer."

"Can we get in bed now?" Yolanda asked, laughing.

"Assuming I can move."

They slowly peeled themselves off the floor and tumbled on top of the flowered bedspread. The hotel offered generic chain decor in beiges and mauves.

"You haven't heard the last of me, Yolanda Vance," he said, unhooking her bra, and sliding his hands under the soft nylon cups.

She patted his knee. "You just take a little nap and you'll be good as new."

"Uh-uh woman," he said with a grin. "Not this time."

He took his hands from underneath her bra and put them on his own chest, and took a deep breath.

"What are you doing?" she asked.

"I'm summoning my chi," he said with a half-smile. "Don't interrupt."

Yolanda watched as he took several deep breaths, held them, and then opened his eyes.

"How come you're so far away?" he asked, and rolled over toward her.

He had successfully summoned another erection, and before long he was inside her again, this time slow and steady and licking his thumb and sliding it across her clitoris in time with his strokes, only surrendering to his climax after hers.

He pulled out, in order to remove the condom safely, and then they both drifted off into a doze. Having slept for much of the day, she woke up an hour and a half later, but he slept soundly, breathing through an open mouth, his arm flung out over his head.

She was thirsty but didn't even want to leave the bed to go to the minibar. She had never felt like this before, so hungry to keep him in touching range.

It was nearly midnight when he woke up. His espresso eyes opening slowly, smiling to see her watching him. He wiped his mouth and kissed her.

"I was out cold," he said.

She just smiled and kissed him back.

"You hungry?" he asked, sitting up. "I've been running on coffee and love fumes all day."

He wandered into the bathroom. "Let's get some food. Denny's, if all else fails," he yelled through the door.

"God forbid," she murmured, as she heard the echo of him urinating.

"At least it's not Waffle House," he said.

After flushing and washing his hands, he walked back out, and began to put on his clothes.

"No shower before we go out?" she asked.

"Nah," he suggested. "Let's go raw like this."

"Maybe we could get something delivered," she suggested.

"Woman, this is Oakland, not New York," he said.

"Watch and learn," she said.

She made a call to the desk. An hour later, they were feasting on Mu Shu chicken, beef with broccoli, and hot and sour soup. They had pulled the covers back up and spread out their Chinese food feast picnic style on top of the bed.

As they ate, Yolanda kept absently rubbing a sore spot on her elbow.

"So what's up with your arm, Miss Vance?"

"What?" she asked, conscious of it for the first time. She tried to turn her elbow to look at it, but the spot was in an awkward location.

"I do believe we have a bit of matching carpet burn," he said, grinning through his Mu Shu chicken.

"No way," she said, leaping up to look at her arm in the mirror. "I would have felt something."

"Yeah, you were feeling something," he said.

Sure enough, there was a mild abrasion on her elbow.

"The scientific explanation is that the body releases endorphins at certain—ahem—key moments, and certain types of mild discomfort you may only feel after the fact."

"I don't believe it," Yolanda said. As an athlete, she was used to being supremely aware of her body, her form, her movement, at all times.

"Do you mean to tell me that I have the supreme honor of giving Miss Yolanda Vance her first rug burn?"

"Next time, I'm gonna insist we make it to the bed."

"I hope this is the first of many firsts, Yolanda Vance. Have you ever had multiple orgasms?"

"I don't think so," she said, on the verge of blushing. "Unless the other night counts."

"You're amazing, Yolanda. You're a grown woman, but there's something so fresh about you, too. You're not jaded like a lot of the other women I've known. They go into something new already prepared to be disappointed."

"You can't be disappointed by men if you're not depending on them to make your life complete," Yolanda said with a shrug between mouthfuls of broccoli beef.

"You're such a contradiction," Jimmy said. "I would have imagined you to be engaged to a stockbroker, or a doctor. Some guy who's just as busy and ambitious as you. A power couple. Both of you working long hours, and him definitely not coming by your place hollering up at your window, whisking you away to a hotel to have wild sex and fucking up your study schedule."

"Those guys don't want women like me. They want power wives who let them win at the track."

"Some guys are excited by women who can run faster than them," Jimmy said. "And even more excited when they slow down enough that we get a permanent spot in their workout routine."

"A permanent spot?" Yolanda said.

"I'm sorry," Jimmy said. "I know I promised not to pressure you, but I'm a lock-it-down type of guy. Take your time, whatever you need. But know that the girlfriend offer is out there."

She felt a spasm in her chest.

"I just need a little time, okay?" Yolanda said.

"I got nothing but time for you, Yolanda Vance," he said, licking a smudge of plum sauce off the tip of her index finger.

"Well what about you?" she asked. "Why isn't a lock-it-down guy like you married by now?"

"I was engaged for a long time," he said, fishing a piece of broccoli out of the container with his fingers. "She was a scientist, too. We both got jobs at Cartwright and moved out here from New York. But she didn't like it. She wanted to relocate to another city."

"Why didn't you?"

"Because she wanted to leave for all the wrong reasons. She was white. New York allowed us to move easily as a mixed race couple, but here it was harder. My parents were Black Nationalists from Oakland. That was easier to manage from three thousand miles away than a thirty-minute drive. Plus, living in Holloway pointed out how much I had learned to move in her world, and yet she was completely uneasy in mine."

Yolanda nodded. "I can see that."

"We fought about it for a long time, and eventually she

gave in, but not because she decided she was gonna make a home in the black community. She just gave in to living in an undesirable place, and made her life with the other academics on campus, or went to San Francisco with friends on the weekends. Holloway was an inconvenient address for her, not a place to live. We broke up a little over a year ago."

"I'm sorry," Yolanda said. "I mean it sounds painful. But I'm glad that her leaving made room for me."

"My parents were equally glad." Jimmy went on. "I need to warn you, though, my mom will be on you in the first five minutes to stop pressing your hair. I'm cool whatever you do: perm it, cut it, lock it, weave it, braid it, shave it off. You're gorgeous regardless. I have to admit, though, a jeri curl would be hard for me."

Yolanda laughed. "If you really cared about me, you wouldn't let that stand in our way."

"Seriously, though," he said. "My parents really are gonna love you. Both for you, and as the first black woman I've dated since grad school."

"Have you—" Yolanda searched for the words. "Have you mostly dated white women?" Yolanda asked.

"In college, I guess," Jimmy said. "But that's because I was recovering from my teens."

"Uh oh," Yolanda said. "How did the black girls do you wrong?"

Jimmy sighed. "When I was in high school, I was a nerd. A black science nerd. Before blerds was a thing. I had the glasses, the delayed growth spurt. The African name that kids made fun of. Wakanda was decades away."

"Your parents are Nigerian?"

"My dad's African American," he said. "But my mom is from Nigeria. I was just African enough to always be an outsider, just black American enough to care what my people thought of me. It was the worst of times, it was the worst of times."

"You don't have to talk about it if you don't want to," she said.

"I might as well tell you my sob story," he said. "So I was skinny and awkward my freshman and sophomore year of high school, and this really popular black girl wanted help with her homework and would ask me over to her house to study together. And I would go, and she would pretend to like me, or maybe in the privacy of her house she did like me—I don't know. But she would get what she wanted, the info on whatever math or biology test, and the next day at school, I was back to being nobody."

"That's awful," Yolanda said. She leaned forward and kissed him gently on his cheekbone just below his eye.

Jimmy lingered a moment receiving the kiss, and then stood up and began to clean up the containers from dinner.

"And the worst part was, that after she would dis me, I would vow to myself, 'never again! The next time I'm gonna turn her down flat.' But in February, I got a secret valentine from her. It said 'shhhhh!' There wasn't even a test coming up. She even smiled at me a few times when her friends couldn't see. So later I helped her, and then I was back to being nobody again. By the Spring she said she liked me. We even kissed a couple of times. Now that I say it, I think she did like me, but she couldn't let her cool friends know."

Having consolidated the leftovers, he put two of the containers into the mini fridge, and the empty ones into the trash.

"Black girls can be really cruel," Yolanda said.

"Summer before junior year, I had a big growth spurt," he said, setting the extra chopsticks and packets of sauces on top of the fridge. "I went to soccer camp. Came back looking like somebody her friends would approve of. Now she wanted to go out with me. I thought it would feel so good to turn her down, but I still felt a pang when I saw her. Other girls were interested in me. I moved on.

"In college, white girls just seemed to have a different thing going. They weren't so materialistic . . ."

She raised an eyebrow. "Or there was just a different kind of material they were after," Yolanda said.

Jimmy laughed and batted his eyes at her. "Oh Mandingo!" he said in a high falsetto. "Yes, Miss Anne?" Jimmy was playing both roles, as he flexed his muscles in imitation of the stereotype.

Yolanda was surprised. Jimmy seemed like such a brainy type, so talkative. How could any woman see him as a brainless hunk? A science major at UC Berkeley? A graduate student at Columbia?

"But Karen was different," he switched gears as they lay back on the bed. "I think she truly did love me just for me. As opposed to the girls who were into the novelty of my blackness."

Yolanda told him about her first time with Ted in college. And her revenge.

"Damn girl," Jimmy said, after he'd high fived her. "Remind me not to cross you."

Yolanda shook her head. "This will be your only warning."

"But seriously," Jimmy said, smoothing her hair off her face. "I'm sorry your first time was with such an asshole."

In the nearly suffocating gentleness of his arms, Yolanda realized she had never thought about it that way. Ted had wronged her and she got revenge. She had always thought of it that way: wronged. But the right word was hurt. Ted had hurt her. Jimmy's apology pierced something soft in her chest. She thought for an instant that she might cry, but instead she covered his mouth with hers and slid her hand down into his boxers.

Chapter 24

The night that her mother had escaped from Hal in Los Angeles, they simply drove and drove. She told Yolanda that she was aiming for Oregon, but the VW bug died in Milpitas, CA. She simply left it on the side of the road, and they caught a series of buses to Oakland.

"Why Oakland?" Yolanda asked.

"I don't have any money to fix the bug," her mom said. "And if we're gonna start over without a car, we need somewhere affordable with public transportation."

In Oakland, her mother changed her name from Mary to the Hindu name Madri. When Yolanda asked why, her mother said she had long wanted to find a spiritual name that fit her better. But later, she realized that her mother might also have wanted to hide from Hal. Madri had found work at a chiropractor's office and tried again to work on her California teaching credential. It was slow going as a single mom, especially when she skipped a lot of classes while she was dating the Nigerian guy. But then they broke up, and she got back on track. She was nearly a year in when she met Andrew, a white yoga teacher. Her mother and Andrew had been together another year when he announced he had gotten a job offer in Colorado. Yolanda's mom decided to follow him. So once again, Yolanda was uprooted. And this time—across state lines—her mother's educational credits didn't transfer. She stopped trying to become a school teacher and instead became a meditation teacher. Nine months after they arrived, her mother was fully "certified" by a local meditation center. She was headed to teach a class when Andrew informed her that he was leaving her for one of his yoga students. She was welcome to keep the apartment, because he was moving to Hawaii.

Yolanda's mother sunk into a deep depression. They lost the apartment and moved into a cramped studio. Her mother started working at a restaurant where they got most of their food.

At twelve, Yolanda asked her mother, "Aren't you going to figure out how to go back to school here in Colorado?"

They were sitting in the break room where Yolanda came after school and did homework. The two of them were eating twin Caesar salads before the dinner rush. Yolanda kept her salads interesting by mixing different dressings every day. Today's "Ranch Thousand" was proving to be edible, but not a favorite.

"Go back to school for what?" her mother asked.

"I thought you wanted to be a teacher," Yolanda said. She had always imagined her mother working the same hours that she went to school and they could finally have more time together.

"No, baby," her mother said, standing up and wiping her hands on her apron. "That ship has sailed."

As her mother gathered the plates and headed out into the restaurant, Yolanda recalled how everything was going fine until her mother met Hal. And things had finally gotten on track again until her mother met Andrew. She vowed never to have a boyfriend until she finished college.

A few months later, her mother met Terence at the meditation center. They bonded over being black folks in Colorado.

Being black folks in meditation circles. Soon, her mother followed him to Detroit. By then, Yolanda was completely soured on stepdads. She and Terence just stayed out of each other's way. But he had an extensive music collection, which she raided.

At first, she pulled a gospel CD—Mavis Staples—one that she recognized from her father's collection. Her dad had the recording on vinyl. The first time she played Terence's CD in her headphones, she felt her chest constrict with the first few notes of the organ. She scrabbled for the stop button and dropped the CD player. The headphones came unplugged and the music stopped. She sat down on her bed, winded, as if she'd just been running.

That day, she swore off church music, but continued to raid his collection for other types of music.

During the time they lived with him, she listened to all of the old Motown and Atlantic music, Columbia, even Stax. But it was the earlier music she loved the most, the blues. The sound was familiar but not too close to home.

The day her mother and Terence broke up, Yolanda had three of his contraband CDs in her case: The Staple Singers, Aretha Franklin's blues album and Stevie Wonder's greatest hits.

Apparently, Terence had cheated. Or her mother suspected him of cheating. "I wasn't going to stick around like a fool for him to dump me," she said. "I took my destiny into my own hands."

But after a few nights in a motel, her mother found out that she couldn't afford to rent any of the apartments in that same suburban town with Yolanda's well-funded public school. They had to move to an inner-city neighborhood where Yolanda found herself in a tough, urban middle school. Meanwhile, her mother sunk into an even deeper depression, doing only the bare minimum to keep her job as a waitress in a downtown restaurant. Sub minimum wage, no benefits, mediocre tips, with unpredictable shifts. And this time, no free food. That semester, Yolanda made two decisions: to do whatever it took to get herself into boarding school, and not to let any man distract her until after she'd made her first million.

The Staple Singers' "I'll Take You There," became Yolanda's anthem. She would get away from this place—this half-catatonic mother, these volatile black kids.

I'll take you there, she would promise herself. *I'll take you there.*

Officer Joaquín Rodriguez sat in Sunday Mass for the first time in over a decade. Nuestra Señora de la Asuncion was the church that served the Latinx immigrant and refugee population of Holloway. Ten minutes before the service began, he saw the older man from the funeral home walk in with his wife, a short, indigenous-looking woman, with a round face and ready smile.

He pointed the man out to his own wife, Isabel, who nodded. "*Sí, la conozco.* I'll talk to her after the service."

He hated to pull his wife into a case, but he had gone back to the cemetery and no one would talk to him. Not even the young man.

McConnell had gone up to the cemetery, as well. On behalf of the Richmond Police Department, he had confirmed the last names of the two dead men in the morgue. They sent next of kin to claim the two bodies for burial, but nobody knew a thing about any Ernesto.

At last, the priest said the benediction, and the congregation stood to go. As Isabel worked her way toward the guy's wife, Joaquín Rodriguez slipped out to the car to keep from being seen.

Twenty minutes later, Isabel slid into the passenger seat.

"What took you so long?"

"I had to say hello to a lot of people," she said chuckling.

"I'm not the same newcomer to this church from last time you came to Mass."

"Okay, what did she say?" he asked.

"I told her I wanted to talk about some concerns my husband and I had about the treatment of immigrants. She said she couldn't talk right now because she has to go to work, but we could come by on her break at four o'clock."

The woman worked in the kitchen at the Cartwright College faculty club. The staff had to come in to work a special luncheon and a reception that evening for a visiting scholar from Princeton. She got a thirty-minute break at four, between the clean-up from the luncheon and the set-up for the seven o'clock reception.

Isabel and Joaquín Rodriguez stood outside the kitchen entrance to the faculty club at 3:55.

At 4:03, the woman stepped out to meet them, wearing a white kitchen uniform with chocolate and raspberry stains.

"Thanks so much for agreeing to talk with us," Isabel said. They all spoke in Spanish, and Isabel introduced the woman as Mirta.

"It's nice to have a break," Mirta said. "I don't like to work on Sundays, but it's good to get the overtime pay."

The three of them walked across the garden behind the faculty club and over to a bench under a lemon tree.

"Joaquín is a police officer," Isabel explained. "He's very concerned about how the immigrant community in Holloway gets treated by the police, how we don't get the same services when we need help."

Mirta nodded. The late afternoon sun on her face showed lines of fatigue, making her look older than she had this morning in church. Was she thirty-five? Forty?

"We understand why so many in our community don't want to tell the police anything," Isabel continued. "Especially if they don't have papers."

Mirta looked sharply at Isabel. "I have papers," she said. "My whole family does."

"I know," Isabel reassured her. "But Joaquín is working on a case that involves the place where your husband works. Three men disappeared, and he's trying to find out what happened."

Mirta's dark eyes filled with tears, and she shook her head. "There is nothing that can be done now."

"Did you know the men who died?"

"Luis, I didn't know so well, but Juan Carlos was my cousin's husband," Mirta said through tears. "They just had a baby."

"This is wrong," Isabel said. "It's wrong that these men died."

"There's nothing that can be done."

"But what about Ernesto? Where is he?"

"Ernesto is gone."

"Gone where?"

"Back to Mexico." She didn't meet their eyes. "His mother was dying."

"But how?" Isabel asked gently. "How did he get the money to go back to Mexico?"

"He didn't get the money. We all got it. We worked. We saved up."

"When did he go?"

"I don't remember. It all happened so fast," Mirta said.

The sun came out from behind a cloud and made dappled shadows on them as it shone on the leaves of the lemon tree.

"Or are you working and saving right now to send him?" Isabel asked. "Is that why you're working the overtime shift? Where is he? We can help."

"I told you," Mirta said, anger constricting her voice. "He is in Mexico. *Se fué.*"

Isabel put a gentle hand on Mirta's cheek and tenderly

turned the woman's head, so they were face to face. "You can tell me. Please. Tell me what happened."

From inside the faculty club, Joaquín heard the clatter of metal on the floor. As if someone had dropped a pot or a tray.

"Why are you asking me this?" Mirta put her head in her hands. "They killed Luis and Juan Carlos. They'll kill him, too. Ernesto's my cousin. I promised my *tía* I would take care of him when he came to this country."

"Joaquín will protect him," Isabel promised.

"We just need him to make a statement to a lawyer and a police officer from another city," Rodriguez said.

"I was undocumented all through high school," Isabel said. "I know what it's like. You don't know who you can trust. But you can trust my husband."

"He can't talk to the police," Mirta said. "What about *la migra*?"

"We won't involve ICE," Rodriguez promised. "They can get his evidence on video, and then we can use that to investigate, maybe even in court."

"He hasn't left the house since that night," Mirta whispered.

"I can come to pick him up. Not in a police car, in my own car," Joaquín promised. "We can do it tomorrow. I won't object if he gets on a plane Tuesday. Maybe even Monday night. He can fly directly to Mexico City. From there, he can get on a bus to anywhere. No one will ever be able to find him unless he wants to be found."

Suddenly, Mirta deflated, the sharp angles of anger in her body slackened. She collapsed onto Isabel's lap and sobbed, as Isabel patted her back gently.

At 4:27, Mirta sat up and dried her eyes. She gave them her address and went back into the faculty club to finish her shift.

Chapter 25

Yolanda continued to check in with the FBI as if everything were normal. No one called her in for any special loyalty chat. Either they didn't know that she was sneaking out with Jimmy at night, or Peterson was covering for her. Or maybe the apartment wasn't even bugged.

The Wednesday after the rally, Yolanda got an urgent text from Marcus asking her to sit in on a meeting with Planet Greener. It was starting in twenty minutes at the RBG office:

Can you wear a suit and bring a legal pad?

What the hell is going on? she texted back, but didn't get an answer.

Fifteen minutes later she was at the church in a charcoal suit and white blouse.

The male and female representatives from Planet Greener were middle aged and white.

Marcus stood up when she walked in. "This is Yolanda Vance," he said to the Planet Greener folks. "From RBG's legal team."

As Yolanda shook hands with the two of them, she met Marcus's eyes. He obviously wanted them to think she was RGB's lawyer.

"I don't think we need legal representation at this meeting," said the man, with a slightly forced laugh. He had on a gray linen button-down shirt.

The woman wore a loose dress in earth tones and smiled awkwardly at Yolanda

They all sat back down, and Yolanda pulled out her legal pad.

"Marcus," the woman began, "we have no question as to whether your heart is in the right place."

"Look," Marcus said, "Planet Greener didn't call a special supervisory meeting to talk about my heart. Can you just cut to the chase here?"

The woman's smile didn't move, but the man jumped in.

"As you know, Marcus," he said. "We've been documenting our concerns about your job performance for a while."

Yolanda began to write down every word on her pad.

"And these have been documented in writing," Yolanda said. "Correct?"

"Some of them, yes," the man said. "But the bottom line here is that we were very clear—definitely in writing—that Planet Greener does not condone any illegal activities."

"You're referring to the police riot?" Yolanda asked.

"The what?" the woman asked.

"When the Holloway police deployed illegal force to break up a lawful assembly," Yolanda continued.

"Our board of directors—" the man began.

"Your board of directors can kiss my black ass," Marcus said.

"Marcus," Yolanda said, putting a hand on his arm.

"No, Yolanda," he said. "They came to fire me or shut RBG down or both. And I'll be damned if I'm gonna be fucking nice about it. So let me have my say, which I will be recording for social media." He stabbed a button on his phone.

"Planet Greener, which raises millions of dollars every

252 / Aya de León

year from people who want to make the world more sustainable, does not have a policy that prohibits investing that money into fossil fuels, and in fact does invest some of their money in dirty energy. And they also invested in buying huge tracts of land with endangered animals that they call nature preserves. But then Planet Greener went into business with fossil fuel companies to drill that land, killing off many of those endangered animals and making huge profits for their organization and their fossil fuel partners.

"And then, when those practices were exposed and their donors were disgusted, they tried to win back their good name by funding a bunch of 'green the hood' programs where they start a garden here and there, paying poverty wages to people of color to run them. And RBG actually builds a strong program by connecting to the issues that youth of color care about—issues that don't affect Planet Greener's board of directors, like police brutality and poverty and racism and ICE. So when we move beyond just planting some kale and go up against corporate polluters and greenwashers and start actually having an impact, they want to shut us down. Because it was never about helping our communities with our real problems. It was a white savior publicity stunt. And they always had their real allegiance to these fucking corporations and never to the people. So if you're gonna fire me for getting arrested during a police riot, please do it on social media."

Marcus turned the camera toward them.

The woman still looked frozen, but she wasn't smiling anymore.

The man cleared his throat. "I must respectfully disagree with a lot of your characterization here," he said.

"Nah, man," Marcus said. "Put the spin on it in your own PR materials. Am I fired or not? Is RBG disbanded or not?"

"In light of the illegal activities," the man said, "we have decided not to renew your contract for the next fiscal year."

"What about the RBG program?" Marcus asked. "Will the entire program be terminated or not?"

"Our board of directors has yet to decide how to handle the program moving forward," the woman said.

"Let's ask it this way," Marcus said. "Will you be continuing the leases on the church office space and the passenger van?"

"I'm not really—" the woman began.

"No," the man said. "They're up at the end of the fiscal year, as well. If the board moves forward with the program, it will be completely revamped."

"So the board really has already decided," Marcus said. He looked into the phone's camera. "Imagine that. They're shutting us down, y'all. A black woman is dead. We broke the story. And instead of giving us more resources, they're shutting us down. Ladies and gentlemen, your green philanthropy dollars at work."

"I think we're done here," the man said. He and the woman stood up.

"You mean you think RBG is done," Marcus said. "But you can't stop the power of the people!"

He filmed them walking out the door then turned and looked into the camera phone. "This movement was never about white saviors. It was always about young people of color rising up. We don't need their money, or their permission or their approval."

He shut down the phone and slumped down into his chair.

"Fuck!" he mouthed, his voice barely a hiss of air. He put his head down on his arms and stayed there for a few minutes.

Was he crying? Had he fallen asleep? What the hell was going on? Yolanda didn't know what to do. But eventually he lifted his head and suggested that they go out for a walk.

They headed down Holloway Avenue. She had on heels with the suit, so after a couple of blocks they sat on the front steps of a different church.

"I blew it," Marcus said. "I totally fucking blew it."

"How can you blame yourself?" Yolanda said. "It was a police riot. They were gonna arrest everyone no matter what."

"Not that," Marcus said, waving away her concern. "I shouldn't have made so much trouble before now. Before it really mattered."

"What do you mean?" Yolanda asked. "Aren't you basically a professional troublemaker?"

"That's exactly what I mean," he said. "I should have been more . . . more stealthy. Telling Planet Greener what they wanted to hear. Instead, I was always getting in their faces. I should have been more like—like a spy. Like the spook who sat by the door. If I had just been a little bit more accommodating, I wouldn't have ten conversations on my record when this shit all went down. They never could have fired me if I hadn't gotten any bad performance reviews up 'til now."

"There's no way you could have known about this," Yolanda said. "You can't know how things are gonna go in the future. Besides, that's not your style. The guy who could do that—who could be like that—would never have started this program. Kissing up to white people is not your strength."

Marcus let out a bark of laughter. "No, it's not," he said. "But apparently getting fired by them is."

"You've been fired before?" she asked.

"Definitely," he said.

"And RBG will continue," Yolanda said. "With or without the office and the van. And I know you aren't gonna stop working for the cause."

"Of course not," he said. "But it's gonna be a lot harder to do while I'm driving Lyft or whatever to pay the bills."

"Driving Lyft?" Yolanda said. "No way. We've got til the end of June to get you a new job."

"Oh really?" Marcus said. "Your superpower is finding jobs?"

"No," Yolanda said. "My superpower is bouncing back."

That Sunday night, the Red, Black and GREEN! meeting felt like a wake. As Marcus had predicted, the mass arrests and bad press had scared away some of the teens and soured many of the parents. Carlos, Nakeesha, and Darnell were the only attendees under thirty.

The news about Planet Greener yanking his salary, the rent, and the van had already gotten around via social media.

"Man, fuck those white people," Nakeesha said, but she was the lone voice of fire. The rest of the teens were shut down and didn't have much to say. The meeting was a sort of surreal check-in, since the four adults knew the place was bugged. They only offered generic platitudes about politics and cliché slogans about keeping hope alive and staying strong in the struggle.

Yolanda and Jimmy went to another hotel after dropping Jasmine at home. Yolanda's phone sat on her apartment table all night playing sound effects of a woman sleeping.

As they made love, Yolanda lay beneath him feeling the push and pull of him inside her, her body heating up to his friction, but behind her closed eyes, her mind wandered into worry. They had made it to the bed this time, and she lay on the white sheets, hearing the faint creak of the mattress beneath her.

Jimmy wanted her to be his woman? In spite of his promise not to rush her, he had brought it up again that

night. Be his woman. How enticing to belong with somebody, to say yes, lock it down.

Had she lost her mind? He had no idea that he was fucking an FBI agent. She couldn't let herself get so swept up in
this fantasy that she bid the hand before all the cards were on
the table.

His thrusting slowed to a halt and her eyes fluttered open.

"Baby where are you?" he asked. "It's like I can't feel you.
I mean, your body feels delicious, but it's like you're not
there mentally."

"I—I'm just a little distracted by work," she said.

"It's my fault," he said. "I promised not to throw off your
study schedule, and here I am, hounding you for another
night in a row. I'm sorry baby, but I can't help myself." He
leaned down and covered her nipple with his mouth.

"It's not that," Yolanda said. "I just notice how much less
I care about the bar, about my new job, being a lawyer."

"Let me distract you, Yolanda Vance," he looked directly
into her eyes and slowly slid into her. Her eyes closed, and
her lips parted with a slight exhale of air. "Yes, baby. Like
that. Stay here. Right here with me."

He thrust again, tender and hard at the same time. "Open
your eyes. Stay with me."

Yolanda swallowed hard and looked up at him. It was difficult to hold the eye contact now that she could feel the secret inside her, could feel the lie between them. She began to
thrust back, grabbed his ass and moved him faster, took over
and made it a match, a race. As an athlete, she could hold his
gaze. He smiled down at her, enjoying the game until he
closed his own eyes and slipped over the edge of their pleasure.

At noon on Monday, they checked out of the hotel, but
were unsure where to go. Jimmy didn't have any Monday
classes. Yolanda didn't have anywhere to be, either, but she

was anxious to go home and pick up her cell phone. On the one hand, she worried that the FBI would call. But she was more worried that they would barge in at her hotel if she brought it with her. She also wondered if they might have a GPS chip in Jimmy's car.

Finally, she and Jimmy decided to go up to Cartwright to study together. They swung by her apartment, and she picked up a bar review book and the cell. Next, they drove to pick up some things from Jimmy's house.

They walked up the concrete steps of his bungalow and Jimmy unlocked the door. As he swung it open, he nearly stepped on a piece of lined paper with an address and note that said, URGENT! COME ASAP!

Yolanda recognized Marcus's handwriting. As they walked back to the car, she dropped her cell phone into a planter on Jimmy's porch.

The address turned out to be a law office that David, the attorney, used for videotaping depositions. As Yolanda walked into the building followed by Jimmy, Marcus greeted them at the door.

"I'm so glad you guys made it," Marcus said, ushering them to the sixth floor.

As they entered the office, David broke from conferring with a somber gray-haired man in glasses. David introduced him as the translator.

Beside him stood a frightened young Latino man, wearing his best church clothes. He was scarcely out of his teens, his baby face not quite able to grow a mustache. David introduced him as Ernesto, and an older Latina woman as his cousin, Mirta. She stood just behind him in a kitchen uniform and held his hand. They had identical slanting eyes and the same straight, black hair.

The seven of them sat around a large oak table in the spare cube of a room, with a single window that didn't open.

From their sixth-floor view, they could see the corner of the Bay that touched Marin, with its green hills and harbor lights. Beside the window was the built-in camera, aimed at Ernesto.

"*Díganos, por favor*," the translator said to Ernesto in Spanish. "Tell us, just like you told the police."

The deposition took twice as long as usual, because everything had to be told in each of the languages. But over a couple of hours, with David's gentle questioning, the story emerged:

Deposition of Ernesto ▓▓▓▓▓▓▓▓▓
Spanish to English translation by ▓▓▓▓▓▓▓▓

A few weeks ago, on the evening in question, the three of us were out on the cemetery grounds at the end of the day. Two white men approached us—a tall one and a short one. They acted like they were coming from paying respects at one of the graves.

Would we be interested in picking up a little extra work? It would pay well. We said yes, we were interested, and they took us with them in their car. I got a little worried. I wanted to call my cousin so she wouldn't be scared that I was so late coming home. The two men promised us $500 each, but they said it might take all night. We said we wanted to call our families if we were going to be gone all night. They said we couldn't call anyone because their cells had no reception, but we should wait. They drove us out to a cabin near a lake. They put us in a room with some exercise equipment and told us to stay there. Not to track mud on their nice carpet. They said they would need a bigger vehicle to transport us, so they were going to get a van. We didn't like it, but we didn't know where we were, and there was no phone in the cabin, so we waited. We needed the money.

They came back a few hours later, after it was very dark, and told us it was time to go. They put us in the back of a van, and we looked out the rear window to try to figure out where they were taking us. When we got back on a big freeway with bigger towns, we figured there would be cell phone reception. We knocked on the little window between the cab of the van and the back and asked to call home. They said we could do it afterwards, that there wasn't time. Please sir, we asked, can you just hand us the cell phone and we can call? Only one call? Juan Carlos could call his wife and she would call the rest of our families.

When we kept asking, the men got mad. The tall one said they would let us call when the job was done and not before. We knew something was wrong. Why wouldn't they let us use the phone? Why didn't they want anyone to know that we were out all night on a job?

When they finally let us out, we were back at the cemetery. We were relieved. We guessed they had decided to let us go, not to do the work after all, but that's when they told us the job was *at* the cemetery. Why would they want us to do something in the middle of the night in a cemetery, and they wouldn't let us call home? We told them no. Whatever it was, we weren't going to do it.

The short one pulled out a gun and pointed it at us. They wanted us to dig up a grave or they would kill us. They marched us to the supply shed to get the digging equipment.

When we got to the door of the shed, I ran away and hid. They didn't want to turn on the lights to attract the attention of security. They were looking with just flashlights and they couldn't find me. I knew the place better than they did. I stayed all night and by the early morning, they were gone.

I came home just before dawn, and I haven't left the house until today.

Ernesto told it all with his face blank. He sat up straight and didn't make eye contact with anyone. He swore to the date in question, two nights before the excavation of Anitra Jenkins's body.

"Would you be able to identify the two men who held you at gunpoint?" David asked.

"*Sí*," Ernesto said through the translator.

They showed him several photographs of people who might be involved in the case. As he had done in the interview with the police, Ernesto identified Andrew Wentworth, Executive Vice President of RandellCorp, as the tall man, the one who gave the orders. Of the many photographs they showed Ernesto of RandellCorp staff and city officials, he couldn't identify the second man.

After the deposition, Yolanda sat in silence as Ernesto and Mirta left the office.

David made a call on his cell phone, and then turned back to Yolanda, Jimmy, and Marcus. "Richmond PD got the warrant, and I've got the new exhumation order."

"I can't believe he fingered Wentworth," David said. "He's so high up to be personally involved."

Marcus shrugged. "I can see it," he said. "He's notorious for micromanaging his employees and being a perfectionist. Fires people all the time and says they're incompetent."

"So what do we do now?" Jimmy asked.

David shrugged. "I go get the forensic pathologist. And then we wait."

After the deposition, Rodriguez met with Marcus at the law office.

"Where do you think they would hide Anitra Jenkins's body?"

"RandellCorp has all kinds of places to dispose of a

body," Marcus said. "But it has all kinds of workers, too. Somebody might stumble across it."

"Maybe they buried it somewhere on Wentworth's huge estate," Rodriguez suggested.

"Or what about the cabin?" Marcus replied. "Wentworth's fishing cabin? That's the most likely place that they took the three guys. Wouldn't that be the best place to hide a body?"

Chapter 26

At 5:23 PM, Officer Rodriguez sped Northeast down the 80 freeway toward the cabin in Lake Berryessa. He sat in the back seat of a Richmond squad car, with McConnell driving and a homicide detective named Banner riding shotgun. Following them was a crime scene unit team from RPD. Forty-five minutes behind them on the freeway, another van came from Holloway, with the forensic pathologist they had originally hired to autopsy Anitra Jenkins's body. The search warrant gave the Richmond PD permission to search the premises of Andrew Wentworth's house in Diablo Valley, his apartment in Point Richmond, his cabin in Lake Berryessa, and all of his vehicles.

Judge Greenlee had signed the search warrant. They had asked for permission to search all of RandellCorp, but Greenlee wouldn't grant it. There was probable cause to link Wentworth, but not enough evidence to link all of Randell.

Marcus was mad, but Rodriguez shrugged it off. They didn't have enough police power to make a thorough search of an operation as large as RandellCorp, anyway. The moment they arrived at the guard hut, the staff would have a heads up and they'd be able to conceal evidence.

Rodriguez didn't know what they would find at the cabin. They didn't have enough police power to thoroughly search all the residences simultaneously. They could have gotten more reinforcements from the Holloway police, but Rodriguez didn't trust anyone in the HPD.

The team decided to hit the lake cabin first, because it was the most remote, and because they would likely find forensic evidence of the three men who had been held. They reasoned that if they went to the Wentworth estate or the condo first, they'd certainly alert Wentworth.

"Take this next exit," Banner said. The homicide detective was a thickset guy with a sandy mustache and baseball cap.

McConnell steered the car off the multi-lane freeway and over the ramp, onto route 29, one of those wide, multi-lane roads with a traffic light every now and then. By the time they turned off onto the much smaller Route 121, it was so dark that Rodriguez couldn't see what was on either side of the car, just the blacktop ahead. He closed his eyes as they turned onto an unlit, rural road, and made their way toward the murky lake. The scattered cabins on Knoxville Berryessa Road by the lake were dark. As they neared Wentworth's cabin, Rodriguez could see several Richmond cops were in conversation with a pair of security guards. When the RPD had entered the building to search, they had tripped the burglar alarm. The security guys had responded and were examining the warrant.

The house was built into the side of a hill below the road. Rodriguez could see the balcony on one side of the house, and the deck on the other side.

After the local cops left, two more vehicles drove up, a white van, and a compact, its color indeterminate in the shadowy night. A white guy in a suit stepped out of the car and approached the cabin. The police officer at the door cautioned him to stay back.

"David Weisman, attorney," David flashed his bar card.

"We have an exhumation order for the body of Anitra Jenkins, signed by Judge Greenlee of the Contra Costa Superior Court. I'm here with an independent forensic pathologist and my legal associate, Yolanda Vance."

Yolanda stayed in the car as David approached the cops. The pathologist stayed in the van.

"We're investigating a possible crime scene sir," the cop at the door said. "Please stay on the public road and we'll inform you if anything we find is relevant to you."

They drove the two non-police vehicles up to the road and parked.

From the car's passenger seat, Yolanda could hear Banner, the plainclothes detective from Richmond, who was standing on the balcony. "The witness said they were held in a rec room," Banner said. "I want you guys to pick up every eyelash you find, every print on every surface you hear me?"

"Detective Banner!" one of the uniformed officers yelled up to him from the deck. "There's a big freezer down here with a padlock on it."

"Get the bolt cutters," Banner instructed.

A uniformed officer brought the tool from the crime scene unit van. He trooped back down to the deck again.

Yolanda slipped out of the car and moved closer to the edge of the road, leaning over the railing to get a better view of what was going on below. She could only see one corner of a stainless steel chest freezer that had to be at least ten feet long.

She heard the clank and thud of the lock giving way, and the clatter of the broken links and chain and lock falling onto the deck.

The sound of the freezer door opening sounded so ordinary, like a slightly louder version of the suction break of any refrigerator in any house, especially if it hadn't been opened in a while.

"Anything?" Banner shouted down.

"Nothing, sir," the cop yelled back.

Yolanda muttered a curse. And then, gazing unfocused out over the lake, she saw something. It was barely visible in the glow of the lights from the house, and it would be invisible to those in the house because their eyes were adjusted to the bright indoor lighting. Just a dark silhouette out on the inky expanse of the lake. A boat.

Yolanda crept back over to David's car and tapped on the window.

The attorney rolled it down, and a puff of warm air escaped, dissipating quickly in the cold night.

"The freezer came up empty," Yolanda said. "But I can see something they can't."

It took a minute for David's eyes to adjust, but finally, he did see the faint outline of something on the edge of the lake.

Five minutes later, David and Yolanda were examining the exact wording of the warrant.

"Says they have license to search the vehicles of Andrew Wentworth," David said.

"A boat is definitely a vehicle," Yolanda said.

David walked the warrant down to the cops. Through the windows, Yolanda could see Banner leave the crime scene crew in the house and take McConnell and the bolt cutters onto the boat.

Half an hour later, a local cop was knocking on the door of the forensic pathologist's van, asking if he had a stretcher.

David got out of the car and approached him. "Did they find the body?" he asked.

"Who the hell are you?" the cop asked. He was a short, dark-haired guy whose face was red with cold.

David identified himself. The cop examined the warrant and asked to see his bar card.

"So who's that in the car?" the cop asked. "Your girl-friend?"

"My legal associate," David said.

"Is that what you're calling them these days?" the cop asked. "She got a bar card, too?"

Yolanda itched to pull out her FBI credentials, but quelled the urge.

The pathologist pulled the stretcher out of the back of the van.

The cop turned to David. "By the time we get back up here, you and your *associate* need to be gone."

The cop trooped down the dark road with the stretcher.

"You should go," David said. "Take my car."

"Are you sure?" Yolanda asked.

"You don't have a California bar card," David said. "And that cop is looking for a reason to hassle you."

"But we need as many legal observers as possible," Yolanda said. "To make sure they don't try to pull anything shady."

"Rodriguez is down there," David said. "He vouched for Banner, too. I don't think Wentworth can squirm out of this one."

"I certainly hope not," Yolanda said, and took David's keys.

To: Special Agent Rafferty
From: Special Agent ███████████
Re: JENKINS DISCOVERY

My Holloway sources tell me that the police have discovered the body of Anitra Jenkins

Needless to say, my concerns about Agent Vance have
increased, given that ███████████████████████████
██
██

To: Special Agent ████████████████
From: Special Agent Rafferty
Re: Re: JENKINS DISCOVERY
   Stand down. We have a plan.

Chapter 27

It was nearly two AM when Marcus came and knocked on the window of Jimmy's house, rousing them from sleep.

Yolanda and Jimmy came out onto the porch to find a victorious Marcus along with their attorney, David. Standing on the street, David relayed that Mrs. Jenkins had positively identified the body from the giant freezer on the boat as Anitra Jenkins.

David and the forensic pathologist had argued with the Richmond and Napa County police over who had jurisdiction and would take the corpse. Finally, the law enforcement agencies had agreed that the independent pathologist could accompany the local coroner and participate in the autopsy.

A Polaroid photograph slid out from the Manila folder that David held.

It was a photo of a photo. In the picture, a foot in a sneaker peeked out from beneath a sheet. A woman's gold sneaker, made even shinier because it was covered by a sparkling sheen of ice. Not just the shoe, but the foot and ankle as well.

David scooped up the picture and slid it back into the file, covering the shoe, the sheen, the ice, the light. But Yolanda could still see the sinister glistening in her mind's eye.

By the time Marcus and David left, Yolanda was sitting huddled on the steps of Jimmy's house, shivering, her arms wrapped around her knees. The bag with her kanji book and gun and her FBI credentials was pressed between her knees and her chest.

None of this is news, she told herself. You knew she was in there dead when you left the cabin. You knew she was probably dead when you heard the deposition. You knew she had most likely been murdered when the coffin came up empty.

But that shoe. That foot. That ankle. That ice. They brought it all home to Yolanda. In a freezer. Like a caught fish or a slab of meat. Not human. It turned her stomach. Her teeth began to chatter.

"Baby, don't worry," Jimmy murmured. "Everything's out in the open now. They can't act like it didn't happen."

Even when he sat down beside her and wrapped his arms around her, even in her fleece-lined jacket, she continued to shake.

"Let me get you something warmer," he said and went back into the house, leaving her on the cement steps. His wooden porch might have been more comfortable, but it could have been bugged. A listening device could fit between the slats of the railings. In contrast, the cement steps below were unbroken slabs of concrete, surrounded by nothing but grass.

"Yolanda, what's going on, love?" he asked, after he had bundled her in his sleeping bag. He wrapped it around her shoulders like an oversized mink stole.

"I can't talk about it," she murmured, shaking her head. "It's just—I can't."

"Baby," Jimmy said. "You can tell me." He wrapped his arms around her in the bulky green nylon bag.

"I can't. I can't tell anyone." Her throat was tight. She could barely get the words out.

"I swear I won't tell. It'll just be between you and me."

Yolanda shook her head again.

"I saw how upset you were when you saw the photo. Have you . . . have you seen someone before who was . . ."

"It's something that I did," Yolanda barely managed to push the words out. "I got on the wrong side of something."

He stopped short. "Did you kill somebody?" he asked, his half-joking voice betraying a bit of unease.

"God no," she said, her voice nearly cracking.

"Whatever it is, I can handle it. You have to tell me." He slid his hand under the sleeping bag so that he could put his arm around her.

"I shouldn't have even said this much," she spoke in a choked whisper.

"Baby, you can't keep this bottled up inside you."

"I'm sorry I even mentioned it."

"Mentioned it?" Jimmy's frustration was rising. "Yolanda, baby. It's me you're talking to. Your lover. The man who loves you. I *love* you, Yolanda."

She could feel her eyes welling up, but she held the tears in check. "Don't say that," she struggled to take a breath through an airway constricted with tears. "You don't even know me. You don't know what I've done."

"Whatever it is, we'll work it out," he said. "And don't act like you don't love me back, woman. I know you do. Whatever this is, I got you, girl. I got you."

Like her father, when she was five. She had climbed up a tree, and gotten too high. "I got you," her dad had said. She had trust-fallen into his arms.

"I do love you, Jimmy," she whispered, then tried to clear her throat. "Which is why I can't lie to you anymore." She turned to him suddenly, eyes glistening. "Do you give me your word you won't tell, not until we figure it out?"

"You have my word, baby." He was all eyes and open hands.

"Your word?"

"Yes," he said. "Now just tell me what's going on."

"I'm . . ." Yolanda struggled to figure out where to begin. "I've never been involved in an organization like RBG before. I didn't know how it would be. I've changed since I got involved with RBG. You can tell that I've changed, right?"

"Of course I can tell. What are you trying to say? That you were a Republican before you got into RBG?" He laughed. "I know you were a corporate lawyer."

"Not a corporate lawyer," she opened her mouth but nothing came out at first. She took a deep breath and willed herself to pronounce the words. They came out as a whisper, a hiss of air. "An FBI lawyer. I work for the FBI, Jimmy."

As his hands went slack, she began to speak faster, to get it all out before those two brown hands disappeared for good. "They sent me to RBG on a special assignment. Because I went to Cartwright. Because I'm young and black. But I wasn't trained for this."

"The FBI? You work for the FBI?" he said as he withdrew his hands from her.

"I just got out of the FBI academy last year. I was working on a case in New Jersey as a lawyer, when they pulled me to do this assignment. I didn't know—"

"You planted the bugs," he said slowly, leaning his body away from hers.

"Yes," she breathed, resisting the urge to babble excuses.

"You came and found me at the track. You flirted with me."

"No!" she said. How could he believe that? "Baby, I had no idea. If I had known you were part of RBG I would never have flirted with you. You weren't in the file. I wouldn't have mixed business with—"

"What the fuck?" Slowly, he pulled away and stood up.

"Jimmy," she pleaded. "I do love you. Why would I tell you this if I didn't love you?"

"You've been spying on us?" he demanded. "How the hell am I supposed to know what to believe, Yolanda? Every fucking word is suspect. Every. Fucking. Word." Unconsciously, he wiped his hands on his thighs, as if to clean her off of him. Her father had made the same gesture once, long ago, when leaving a woman's house.

Inside her, the whirlwind of conversation, of pleading for understanding, screeched to a halt. What would have been her words became something snipped off like hair or nail clippings. They fell to the floor and lay inert.

"My mistake," she said, as she stood and gathered her purse, letting the sleeping bag slide off her shoulders. "Please don't tell the folks at RBG. I won't be back."

"What would I tell them? That I've been fucking a spy?"

"I'm sorry, Jimmy. I'll be turning in my resignation to the FBI tomorrow. I'll just disappear." Suddenly, she leaped up off the stairs and ran down the block. She didn't look back to see if he had tried to follow, but it didn't matter. She had always been faster.

Chapter 28

Yolanda lay on the bed in the apartment, covers pulled up under her chin. She was no longer cold. In fact, she felt nothing in her body but a familiar dull burning in her chest.

Even without benefit of a music player, Aretha's words drifted through her head.

Yolanda remembered her mother packing their stuff that evening of her father's funeral, ranting bitterly through her tears: "And you could tell those heifers knew!" she accused the other women in the church. "Why were you and me the only ones surprised when that tramp showed up acting like a widow?" She flew from room to room, haphazardly picking up items and piling them on the couch.

"They never liked me! Thought I was too Northern, too educated, too uppity for their goddamn backwater village, their handsome star preacher. Wanted him to go to Howard but expected him to come back and marry one of them. Probably encouraged him to screw their cousins Bertha and Mabel. Bunch of jealous bitches. Well they can all go to hell!" Yolanda's mother had opened the window. "Go to hell, I said!" she shouted into the empty courtyard between the pastor's house and the church, her voice bouncing off the carefully tended flower garden and neatly trimmed lawn. The

choir rehearsal singing floated up from the sanctuary, a surreal soundtrack to Yolanda's mother's rant: *I will trust in
Jesus with all my heart* . . .

Five-year-old Yolanda stood frozen, terrified of this new
mother, this enraged mother, entirely different from the proper
Boston woman who stuck out so much in this Georgia town.

Mary—she was still Mary then—packed all their stuff
from the pile on the couch into two blue suitcases. Cursing
all the way down the stairs and out through the courtyard,
she bundled the luggage and her daughter into her late husband's Cadillac and tore off with a screeching of tires and
gravel.

As Yolanda left the only life she had known, the choir's
voice floated behind her, as if mocking her: *He is my shelter,
my lighthouse, my home* . . .

The trip to the West Coast was mostly a blur of motels
and fast food that barely interrupted Mary's monologue,
which rattled back and forth between "those damn hyp-
ocrites!" and "how could he?"

Through the trip, Yolanda sat in the back in her car seat,
her chest burning dull and her limbs leaden.

By the time her mother steered the Cadillac, dirt-smeared
and dusty, across the state line into Texas, she had a plan.
"We're going to California," she said. "We need a new start.
I think God was trying to tell me something all this time. I
didn't want to see. God was telling me to go forwards and
not backwards. My grandmother came from a Southern hick
town like that, but she moved up North. I studied some meditation in college, some Eastern religion. I was on that path
when I met your father. It's been . . . a derailment. I got onto
his path. I'm gonna find my own path, and I have a vision of
us in California."

Yolanda didn't understand. Was she one of the "heifers"
who knew about her father and the lady in the orange dress,

or was she one of the "us" who was wronged—who'd been lied to? Questions swirled in her mind, while her mother's words flew around the car like crows, pecking at her, leaving her with no words of her own.

Yolanda arrived in California dazed and numb, not having spoken during the entire cross-country trip.

In Los Angeles, they needed money, so her mother traded the Cadillac for an old VW bug. As Yolanda watched them take the Caddy away, she recalled uneasily various trips she had taken with her father. Back in Georgia, she had ridden in that same Cadillac to different women's houses, and played with their children, while the mothers went with her daddy to have "Bible study."

One time, when her father went into someone's bedroom, the woman's seven-year-old son tried to have "Bible study" with her, and she started screaming. Her father came out of the room, tousled, but still clothed. He took one look at the boy, pressing Yolanda back onto the couch, pulling up her shirt, and demanded an explanation.

"He tried to have Bible study with me," Yolanda accused, trembling, one small brown finger pointed at the wide-eyed boy.

Her father stood for a moment, rigid. Then slowly, like a steam locomotive, he ground into motion, advancing toward the children. The boy cowered as if the preacher would strike him, but her father just scooped Yolanda up with one strong arm and headed for the door. In the midst of her crying and shaking, she could feel the solid beat of his heart beneath his suit jacket and white shirt.

"Come on, baby," the woman whined. "He didn't mean nothin.' I'll talk to him." She clawed at Yolanda's father, clinging desperately to his other arm. "Please, baby!"

"This ain't right," was all her father said as he shook the woman off. Yolanda never knew if he meant that the affair wasn't right or that what the boy tried to do wasn't right. But as her father walked out the woman's door, holding Yolanda in one arm, he absently wiped his other hand on the thigh of his trousers.

When Yolanda's phone rang sometime before seven, she had barely slept.

"Good morning Vance," Peterson said. "Have you heard the news?"

"About what?"

"About the discovery of Anitra Jenkins's body last night."

"The what?"

"Three corpses total," Peterson said. "I'm sending you a link to the story. Please read it on the way in to the office."

"Got it," Yolanda said.

"And where were you last night?" Peterson asked.

"In Holloway," Yolanda said. "I slept alone."

"You were at Thompson's house 'til late," Peterson said.

"He broke it off," Vance said. "It seems he takes up with the new girls in the organization and then moves on."

"You all right?" Peterson asked.

"I told you, it was only business," Vance said evenly. "I acted a little sad but agreed to be friends."

After she hung up, Yolanda put on some sweats and jogged down to the payphone at the liquor store, where the ex-con operative had been shot. She dialed Donnelly's number.

Donnelly picked up her cell on the second ring.

"I've seen the news," Donnelly said. "Is it as bad as it looks?"

"Probably worse," Yolanda said.

"What could be worse?" Donnelly asked. "I count three dead bodies and a grave robbery."

"The police aren't yet reporting that the Jenkins body was found on Wentworth's boat," Yolanda said. "And that an eyewitness has been deposed who identified Wentworth as the kidnapper of the two dead cemetery workers."

"You're fucking kidding me," Donnelly said. "Who else knows?"

"Local cops from a few different cities," Yolanda said. "Plus three of the main Operation HOLOGRAM activists, so this won't stay quiet long."

"What the hell is going on with Wentworth and Randell?" Donnelly asked. "Campbell really knows how to pick a winner."

Yolanda took in a breath to say she had to go, but impulsively said, "there's more."

She hadn't planned to say anything. But three people were dead. It might come out. She had to trust someone. "The subject I was sleeping with," Yolanda said. "I told him I'm FBI. When I saw the photo of Jenkins's body, I just lost it," Yolanda said, fighting back tears. "Now Rafferty wants me to come in for a meeting."

Yolanda could hear the hiss of the phone as Donnelly blew out a breath into the receiver. "I only have three words for you," Donnelly said. "Document. Document. Document."

At 8:51 AM, Yolanda walked in to the FBI building. She removed her watch, her belt, her cell phone, a mini digital recorder, and her FBI issue firearm and put them in the case to go through the metal detector. As Yolanda was gathering her belongings, she caught sight of Donnelly walking into the building. The two women made eye contact briefly, just before Yolanda turned and headed for the bank of elevators.

Donnelly had been helpful, but none of her strategies or advice could help the ache in Yolanda's chest for Jimmy. She pressed the button and rearranged the objects in her purse.

At 9:18 AM, Yolanda sat in Campbell's office with the Assistant Special Agent in Charge, plus Peterson and Rafferty.

"Vance, how the hell could you not know about this?" Campbell asked.

"Why was Anitra Jenkins's dead body in the freezer of the VP of RandellCorp?" she asked.

"Don't answer my question with a question," Campbell said.

"You told me it was an industrial accident," Yolanda said. "What cause of death is the forensic pathologist going to find? Somehow I doubt it's going to be a heroin overdose."

Campbell sighed. "She died of suffocation. She had been exposed to a fatal toxin. She was in excruciating pain. It was a mercy killing, Vance."

"Look, you don't need me in there anymore. The baby has fallen off the bed or whatever. The bugs are blown. They found the body. I want to go back to New Jersey."

Campbell paused for a moment and looked her straight in the eye. "You'll go where you're assigned, Vance. Is that clear?"

Yolanda said nothing.

Campbell sat forward in his seat and yelled in her face. "I said, IS THAT CLEAR?"

"Yes, sir," Yolanda said, as she wiped a speck of spittle from her cheek.

"So as of today, the FBI will be taking over the investigation into the homicides of Anitra Jenkins and the two Mexicans."

"Sir, how can you take over the investigation when this institution has a clear conflict of interest? The FBI doesn't want these murders solved if it's going to lead to any investigation of RandellCorp before the defense contract is finished."

"Vance, I don't need any legal advice from you, okay? You're on thin ice. The FBI will be taking jurisdiction on these murder cases and we will proceed at the pace that we see fit, and in the manner that we see fit, which will guarantee the completion of the project at RandellCorp that we have been assigned to protect. Is that clear?"

"Yes, sir."

"You will remain as an operative for a period of time. When I authorize it—not a day before or after—you will tell your RBG subjects that you've been 'fired' from your job at the law firm for not studying sufficiently and having low bar exam text scores. You will then be relocated."

"To my old job in New Jersey?" Yolanda asked.

Campbell shrugged. "Not for me to decide."

To: Special Agent ███████████

From: ASAC Campbell

Re: OPERATION HOLOGRAM

I am reassigning you to the RBG case. I have reason to doubt the loyalty of ████████████████████████████

████████████████████████████

████████████████████████████

████████████████████████ Report to my office immediately for details. ██████████████████████

Chapter 29

Yolanda had never felt at home in the studio apartment, but even still, the moment she walked in, she had the feeling someone had been in there. When she went to the closet to hang up her coat, she knew for sure. The door didn't close all the way and would open back up if you didn't lean on it til you heard it click. She had closed it the night before, but now it was open a crack.

Yolanda needed to get out. She changed into her running gear and examined the front door. There were no signs of a break-in, not even scratches by the lock.

She pulled on her running windbreaker. It had a big pocket in the back, in which she put her kanji book, her cell phone, her FBI credentials, and her keys.

She was nearly to the top of the hill when she realized that she was jogging toward Cartwright by default. She thought of Jimmy, then accelerated, the burn in her muscles driving the thought away, distracting from any feeling in her chest, except the rasp of her lungs as she breathed heavily.

She tried to empty her head as she ran. Focus only on the sensations in her body. Her lungs, her legs, the cool air on her face.

She was halfway around the path when he came up on her left side. "You come here looking for me?" he asked coolly.

"You said you jogged at noon," Yolanda said looking at the sunset. "If I had thought you'd be here, I would have gone to the gym."

"Well, I couldn't quite get it together today. I've been kind of fucked up since I broke up with my . . . I was gonna say girlfriend, but she wouldn't even agree to that, so I don't know why I'm so surprised it didn't work out."

"A piece of advice," Yolanda said. "Don't say 'whatever it is, we'll handle it together,' if you don't mean it."

"Lesson learned," he said. "Next time I'll add a disclaimer: 'unless you've completely betrayed me.'"

"You know what? Fuck you, Jimmy. That's the problem with you progressives or leftists or whatever you call yourselves. You act like anyone who doesn't agree with you is an idiot. What did Marcus say? Law enforcement were just members of the working class who'd been manipulated to go against their people? Maybe that was me. Maybe I was somebody who didn't have all the fucking information." She put on a burst of speed, but he caught up with her.

"You didn't realize you were lying?" he panted.

"I didn't realize the damn FBI was lying!" she said, exasperated. "We're not all from the Bay Area and so goddamn politically enlightened. We don't all have Black Nationalist parents who tell us what the government is really up to. Some people are from Midwestern towns where everyone watches Fox News and believe what the preacher tells them. Some people are from places where everyone doesn't have a goddamn 'question authority' bumper sticker on their car, from places where you get your ass kicked if you question authority, so you just do what you're told. And it doesn't make them stupid, it just makes them people in a bad situation."

"So what are you saying? That you didn't know any better? That you didn't know you were lying to me? Lying to people who trusted you?"

"My body didn't lie to you, Jimmy. I didn't lie about what I felt, only about who I was."

"Well who the hell are you? Are you some person from the Midwest who's in a bad situation?" he asked, sarcastically.

"No," she said. "Some people are from everywhere and nowhere and we just learned to be whatever people wanted us to be and we just focused on being the best at everything and hoped maybe we could get by without . . . without anybody. And maybe we finally let somebody in and showed somebody who we really were. And maybe we picked the wrong fucking guy."

"You lied to me, Yolanda."

"Yes, I fucking lied, but I was trying to remedy that. If you want honesty so much then be honest, yourself. Why did you bail on me?"

"It's so damn obvious," he said. "Why you gotta make me spell it out?"

Yolanda could feel tears rising. "Spell out what? What the hell are you talking about?"

"I *told* you!" Jimmy's face was tight and the words came out through clenched teeth. "About the girls in high school. The worst of times."

"Jimmy, what we have . . . what we had was totally different," Yolanda said.

"Was it? Or were you just fucking me to get information."

"What information?" she asked, exasperated. "What information was I supposed to get? I was fucking you because I was falling in love with you, and I told you I worked for the FBI because it had become obvious that I was on the wrong side. I tried to resign from the case the next day and they wouldn't let me."

"That's supposed to persuade me?" he asked incredulously. "That you tried to resign from the *case*. But you're still working for the FBI?"

"I got no net, Jimmy!" she yelled. "No savings. No family. And, without the FBI, no job references. My only other job was indicted by the feds. Without the FBI, I'm homeless and jobless."

"You didn't tell me any of that."

"You didn't hang around long enough to get any details. Filled in all the blanks with worst case scenarios and walked out."

The sun was setting as they came across the bridge, and their footfalls pounded in synch as they jogged across the resonant wooden planks.

Jimmy spoke quietly. She could just make out the words above the sound of their footsteps and heavy breathing. "In college, I promised myself that I'd never again be with a woman if I didn't know that she liked me for myself. I drive a beat-up car. I don't make a lot of money as a professor at a women's college. I don't attract gold diggers. Most adult women don't need help on biology tests. So finding out you were an agent just brought back that old teenage angst."

"I used to read this book that said ninety percent of success at anything is determined by your attitude." She leaned over and poked him hard in the chest with two fingers. "It's not that you don't trust me, you don't trust yourself. You know right in here that I was falling in love with you, but you don't trust it. My mistake."

She put on a burst of speed, thinking that was the final word on it. But then he sped up and grabbed her hand. "I'm sorry."

She stumbled, but he put his other hand on her shoulder to steady her. They both slowed to a walk. "You're a couple days too late," she said bitterly.

He reached to pull her close. She suddenly felt drained of energy, and the two of them stood in place.

He put his arms around her. "I'm sorry I let old insecurity get the better of me." He ran a hand through her damp hair. "I love you, Yolanda. I really do."

She could feel his heart still racing from running. "I'm sorry I lied," she said.

They stood in the clasp, both their heart rates that had just begun to slow from the run speeding up again.

"So what now?" he asked, as they started to walk, to give their muscles a chance to loosen and cool.

"I've gotta tell RBG."

"How?"

Yolanda shook her head. "I have no idea."

That night they made love in Jimmy's bed. Silently, both for fear of the FBI listening, and because there was nothing else to say. Yolanda the competitor was absent from the bedroom. She lay on her back and let her body melt into the bed beneath him. She wrapped her legs around his hips, her arms around his neck, and they hardly broke eye contact. He would lean down and give her the most tender of kisses, his tongue soft in her mouth, but then pull back and look in her eyes. He held himself up on his elbows, stayed tuned in to her every movement.

"I know it's not fair to ask you this," he whispered in her ear. "To ask you now, but I can't help myself. Be my woman, Yolanda. Please tell me you'll be my woman."

Yolanda knew it wasn't fair. Wasn't right to ask when she felt so defenseless, when she could feel him moving inside her and the heat between them would determine that the answer to anything would be yes. *Let's rob a bank. Let's buy a house. Does that feel good, baby? You like it like this?* But Yolanda had hungered since they left the jogging path, had wondered on the ride home, in the shower if he would reiterate his request to lock it down. She was too scared to ask, convinced that she was only barely back in his good graces.

So when he asked, his voice barely a murmur, his breath warm on her ear, his hips cradled between her open thighs, with him pulling in and out of her like a tide, she couldn't refuse, wouldn't have considered it even under the most sober conditions.

But she couldn't bring her vocal chords to engage, couldn't synchronize breath with articulation.

"Yes," she mouthed the word, their eyes locked, hips locked. Silent tears streamed down Yolanda's temples, pooled in her hair, her ears, stained the pillowcase a darker blue. She wrapped her legs around him and drew him into her as deeply as she could. *yes.* Her face wet. *yes.* Their eyes locked. *yes.* The heartbreaking tenderness of it. *yes. yes. yes.*

Yolanda woke slowly the next morning. Opening her eyes, the bright green numbers on the clock said 5:12.

Jimmy lay facing her on his side, snoring gently. As the dawn approached, a pale light stole into the room, illuminating the planes of his face. For a moment the beauty of him distracted her. She considered kissing him awake, pouring herself onto him, and initiating a replay of last night. Afterwards, they had lain pressed against each other, only untangling after several limbs had fallen asleep, and then, still feeling pins and needles in her arm, Yolanda dozed off, curled in against Jimmy's chest, her head on his arm, his knees pressing gently at the backs of her thighs. They were back together. No. They were really together for the first time.

By the time Jimmy finally woke up at 8:36 AM, she had the outline of a plan. She kissed him, despite their morning breath. He reached for her hips, but she planted her feet and pulled him out of bed. The time had come to truly figure things out. They put on sweats and went out onto the steps where they could talk.

Chapter 30

Clandestine surveillance cameras generally need to be monitored in a nearby van in order to pick up the signal. In contrast, the cameras in the studio apartment where Yolanda was staying were built in, so they had a live feed into the basement of the FBI office. The FBI had watched Yolanda as they had watched her predecessors, as a bit of a formality, a bureaucratic task that no one wanted. Peterson would usually fast forward the images. The first thing of interest that she found was the kanji book, but she still thought Campbell was making too much of it.

Peterson knew Yolanda had faked them out with the audio, but she also knew that Yolanda was with Jimmy.

However, at 10:47 AM on Thursday, Peterson was observing the monitors with the four different cameras in the studio apartment when Yolanda Vance had her first visitor in the apartment.

Peterson snapped to attention when she heard the doorbell ring. She had watched Yolanda on a single screen, sitting on the bed, writing in her kanji book for over an hour. But now Peterson's eyes flitted from screen to screen, as Yolanda stepped out of the frame of one camera and into another.

"Who's there?" Yolanda asked into the intercom.

"Sharon," the staticky woman's voice came through the system.

Yolanda buzzed her in and put her kanji book away in her purse on the desk and slid her FBI credentials into the bag as well.

When Yolanda answered Sharon's knock on the apartment door, the two women hugged each other, and Sharon walked in.

"Thanks so much for agreeing to proofread the newsletter," Sharon said, setting down the draft on the small desk.

"Thanks for dropping it by," Yolanda said. "I'm so far behind in my bar review studies, I think I'm gonna get fired from this job. The funny part is that I don't really care anymore. Do you want anything to drink?"

Peterson watched Yolanda step out of the frame of the living room camera, and into the kitchen area.

"Sure," Sharon said. "What you got?"

The kitchenette camera observed from an upper angle as Yolanda moved things around in the fridge. A half loaf of wheat bread, mayo, cold cuts, a bag of tomatoes, a few cans of soda. Meanwhile, the other camera observed Sharon, pulling at the edge of a leather wallet sticking out of Yolanda's bag on the desk.

"Girl," Sharon said. "You got to be careful, your wallet was about to fall out of your—"

"Cola or lemon lime?" Yolanda asked.

"The fuck is this?" Sharon asked.

"What?" The kitchen monitor observed Yolanda looking up from the fridge to see Sharon with her FBI credentials.

"Give me that," Yolanda rushed across room and grabbed the credentials. Peterson's eyes flitted from screen to screen, attempting to see both women's faces. She turned up the volume.

"You're FBI," Sharon yelled openmouthed. "*Coño!* You're a goddamn agent."

"It's not what you think," Yolanda snatched up the bag

and shoved the credentials back in. "I was assigned to the case for everyone's protection."

"Don't try to bullshit me, Yolanda. I'm going straight to the office and telling everyone that you're an agent." Sharon grabbed her purse and jacket.

"Please, just hear me out," Yolanda begged.

"Too late for that shit," Sharon said, and rushed out of the camera's frame. Peterson heard the door slam, as Yolanda grabbed her own purse off the desk and ran out after her, slamming the door again.

"Sharon, wait!" Peterson could hear Yolanda yell from the hallway, as the monitors all began to reveal empty rooms, including the light spilling out from the open refrigerator door.

Peterson turned to the computer console and brought up the screen with the wiretaps on the various RBG phones.

A minute later, Peterson picked up a call from Sharon's cell phone to Marcus's RBG landline.

"Marcus, it's Sharon. Are you sitting down?

"You sure you want to tell me this on the phone?"

"It doesn't matter anymore. Yolanda Vance is FBI."

"She's what?"

"She planted the bugs."

"This has got to be some kind of mistake."

"Think about it, Marcus. How come she was the only one who didn't get caught up in the arrests at the rally? The police must have known. How come the bugs showed up in the office after she started to work with us? A young black woman who went to Cartwright? They knew we would eat her up."

"Sharon, we can't start accusing each other—"

"Listen to me," Sharon yelled. "I saw her badge, Marcus! I SAW IT!"

For a second, no one spoke, but Peterson could hear the sound of Marcus's desk chair groaning.

Yolanda had sprinted the several blocks to the office, and arrived while Sharon was circling the block, looking for parking.

"Marcus!" Peterson heard Yolanda's voice in the background of the phone call, breathing heavily. "It's not what you think!"

"I can't believe you," Marcus said. "You're a fucking spy. A fucking infiltrator."

"I tried to explain to Sharon. It's just—" Yolanda tried to catch her breath.

"Get out! Get out of this office. Don't ever show your face here again!" Peterson heard the phone fall as Marcus lunged at Yolanda, and the agent's rapid footfalls as she ran out of the building.

Yolanda walked quickly down the street, not even seeing Sharon's white hatchback as it circled the block again, or the black Jeep that also hovered nearby. She picked up her cell phone to call Peterson, but in the basement of the FBI building, Peterson's cell didn't get reception.

"I'm blown," Yolanda told Peterson's voice mail, panting. "I just got thrown out of the RBG office. It's over. I don't know what the hell to do." As she hung up and reached to put the phone back in her purse, a young man grabbed the strap and tried to take it from her. Yolanda planted her feet, tightened her core and yanked back with all her might. The young man stumbled, not expecting so much pull back, and let the purse go.

He was nearly six feet. Dark brown skin, dark hair, dark denim jeans, white t-shirt, dark shoes, dark shades.

Yolanda backed away from him, swinging her purse behind her back. He ran off and jumped into a black Jeep that sped away. The vehicle had dealership plates.

Dazed, Yolanda walked into the drugstore on the corner.

She circled the store aimlessly for a minute, then she bought a roll of masking tape and a Manila envelope.

"Do you have any stamps?" she asked the cashier.

"Sorry."

Yolanda paid for her purchases and walked home, observing carefully around her, looking for the Jeep, and avoiding other pedestrians.

After she stepped into the apartment, she locked and chained the door behind her. The place felt surreal. She grabbed her gym bag, and stuffed her purse into it, with the kanji book, a pair of USB drives with a digital recorder, and her gun. She also shoved in the plastic bag from the drugstore with the masking tape and Manila envelope and left the apartment.

In the women's changing room of her gym, she put her clothes in a locker, but kept most of the contents of her purse with her. The gun, badge, wallet, and keys she put in a string bag for toiletries. She went into the toilet stall and used the masking tape to secure the USB drive into the kanji journal. Then she opened the book flat and taped it behind a toilet tank with the Manila envelope, checking carefully that it couldn't be seen from above or either side, unless someone was really looking for it.

After that, Yolanda took her mesh bag with the rest of her stuff and kept it within reach as she jogged on the treadmill.

Two hours later, after some weightlifting and a shower, her body felt loose and subdued. On her way out of the gym, she felt alert and prepared to make her next move.

As she stepped out onto the street, a young woman skateboarded up behind her and sliced the strap on her purse. The girl sped off, her long black hair flying behind her. Yolanda chased her into a mini mall, but the girl was too quick, cutting across traffic and into a crowded food court. Yolanda scanned quickly from the Manchu Express to the Pizza Blitz, but the girl was gone.

To: ASAC Campbell
CC: Special Agent Rafferty, Special Agent Peterson
From: Special Agent Yolanda Vance
Re: LETTER OF RESIGNATION
    As of this morning, my cover has been blown with all subjects. In addition, my handbag was stolen, including my FBI issued cellular phone. I am hereby resigning from the RBG surveillance case, as well as the Federal Bureau of Investigation. I am vacating the Bureau's apartment. I will be turning in my keys, gun, and credentials at my earliest opportunity.

Yolanda walked to a pay phone on Holloway Avenue and called Donnelly at home. She just wanted to leave word about her resignation on the woman's voice mail.

"Hello?" a woman's voice answered.

"Donnelly?" Yolanda asked.

"No, this is her wife, Helen," she said.

"My name is Yolanda Vance."

"She said you might call," Helen said. "She wanted me to connect you on the three-way calling. Hold on."

"Vance?" Donnelly's voice came through. "Are you okay?"

"I just resigned," Yolanda said.

"I know," Donnelly said. "I ran into Peterson on her way out. She said Campbell was in a rage after receiving your resignation letter. He sent her to Holloway to look for you."

"He sent Peterson?" Yolanda asked, incredulous. "To Holloway?" Yolanda pictured the agent with her pantsuit, red hair in a bun, and pale skin, driving around in a dark car.

"Her orders are to call him if she spots you," Donnelly said. "I don't know what's going on, but watch your back."

* * *

Taxis were hard to find in Holloway, and she didn't have a phone to catch a Lyft. Yolanda sat at the bus stop on Holloway Avenue waiting for the #36 bus up to Cartwright. The same bus she used to take when she worked at the Teen Center. She calculated that it would take Peterson at least another fifteen minutes to make it to Holloway. Hopefully the bus would arrive before then. The only things in her stolen purse were a roll of masking tape and her cell phone. Her keys, gun, wallet and credentials were all in her pockets.

Yolanda noticed a dark Jeep at the intersection and squinted through the glare on the window to see the driver. The young man at the wheel looked Asian or Latino, not the young black man who had tried to take her purse.

The light changed, and the Jeep took off. Still, perhaps because the Jeep had gotten her adrenaline pumping, she had a heightened sense of awareness, and noticed the charcoal gray sedan with tinted windows slow down slightly as it rolled up in front of the bus stop.

The passenger window was halfway open. He was in the center lane, so he wouldn't be turning right or left. But the light was green, so why was he slowing down?

There was no glint of metal, just an intuition, and Yolanda dropped into a crouch, her mind recording every sound during the second before the blast: the blare of car horns, the hiss of a bus stopping at the adjacent corner, the agitated cadence of Reggaeton music bumping out of a car a half-block away. And then there were the sounds immediately around her: the wail of the fussing toddler at the bus stop, his chubby brown hand reaching for the piece of the cookie, and the exasperated response from his grandmother. "Boy, I told you it fell on the ground. You can't eat it if—" The young woman next to them with the platinum blonde extensions, talking to an androgynous girl in boyish clothes:

"I told him, 'don't be calling me with that oh-baby-can-I-come-see-you-bullshit. You wanna go see somebody, go see your girlfriend—'" The young man next to Yolanda with the bass seeping out of his headphones, rapping along to the song:

> *A nigga like me*
> *wit a gun and a G*
> *on the run wit a key*
> *to the—*

The bus stop had not been quiet. The street had not been quiet. But the blast of the gun eclipsed all the sounds with its invasive, explosive fury, as the gunman shot a hole clear through the thick plastic of the bus shelter.

Everyone scrambled for cover: the grandmother screamed and scooped up the grandson, ducking behind a car. The young man dived behind a cement garbage can. The blonde hit the pavement with a shriek. The androgynous girl, however, pulled a gun from the waistband of her sagging jeans, and fired several shots at the gray sedan, nicking the bumper as it sped off. After firing, she jumped onto her scooter and headed off in the other direction.

For a brief second, the only sounds that registered were the ball-bearing rattle and the scooter's rubber wheels against sidewalk, and the departing engine of the gunman's car. Then slowly, the bus stop ground back to life, everyone checking themselves and each other for damage.

Yolanda stood on unsteady legs and looked at the location of the bullet hole. It had blasted through the spot right behind where she'd been standing.

As she slipped away from the crowd, the ground didn't quite feel level beneath her feet. As she came around the corner, she wandered into a busy supermarket parking lot, and was nearly hit by a car.

"Damn, bitch!" the young man yelled out the window. "Watch where the hell you going! You tryna get killed?"

Beyond the car, she saw a taxi, and sprinted across the parking lot to hail it. As she ran, she felt jittery and out of synch.

"Sorry miss, I'm waiting on somebody," the driver said. He was an African American man with salt and pepper hair peeking out from under an A's baseball cap.

"I'll give you fifty in cash to take me up to Cartwright College now," Yolanda said.

"Get in then," the driver said.

Yolanda spent the first five minutes of the ride making sure she wasn't being followed, sending the taxi on obscure turns and quiet streets. No sign of the gray sedan. No other cars seemed to be tailing her.

"Do you even know where you're going, miss?" the driver asked, irritably.

"I just wanted to drive past a couple of places on the way," she said.

"This is a cab, not a guided tour," he said. His dark face frowned back at her in the rearview mirror.

"Look, I'm paying you fifty dollars for an eight-dollar ride," she said, pulling the bills from her wallet.

As Yolanda sat back and buckled her seatbelt, he sucked his teeth. "Must be nice to be a college kid with money to burn," he muttered.

The science building had been renovated since her years at Cartwright. They had maintained the historical facade, with its tall cement columns and gargoyles, but expanded the interior, and built out into the lot behind the original structure to include bigger, more modern labs, and more faculty offices.

The Biology department was on the fifth floor of the new wing of the building. Jimmy's office was halfway down a long corridor, bright with florescent lighting and white linoleum. Yolanda wasn't quite sure how she'd gotten from the taxi to the hallway in front of his office, or even how long she had been standing there.

The door said "Dr. Olujimi Thompson," and the note on the bulletin board beside his door showed his office hours and class times and locations. It took Yolanda a moment to get her brain in motion, to figure out that it was Thursday afternoon at 2:41 PM. Another couple of minutes to put the current date and time together with his schedule, and to realize that he was in class from one thirty to three in a lecture hall in the old wing.

She found the room and peeked in through the little window in the auditorium door. Jimmy's back was turned to her. His lovely, broad-shouldered back. The sight of him comforted her, grounded her.

Yolanda sat down on the floor outside of his class. She found she still had her wallet in her hand from paying the cab driver. She went to put it in her pocket, and she realized her hands were shaking.

A sudden shriek of laughter made her whole body jump. *The cookie fell on the ground—wanna go see somebody, go see your girlfriend, cause—a nigga like me/with a gun and a G—*all ran through her head with the sound of Reggaeton music in the background and then the beginning of the blast sound. Like some abstract film montage. The echo of the blast stayed with her and left her slightly queasy.

Yolanda looked up to see a cluster of young women trooping past her down the hallway. Her body was clammy with perspiration. As the young women passed, Yolanda recognized their varsity sweats—bright magenta and gold—the college's colors.

"Post-traumatic stress," Sharon had explained. Yolanda had eavesdropped on a support group at RBG, and one of the teens had brought a friend who had witnessed a shooting. Yolanda began to shudder. A long, quivering tremor ran through her body, and she felt some of the fog lift from her mind. She needed a piece of paper.

A pair of young women walked by, and the closest one had a notebook in her hand. At Yolanda's request, she pulled out a few pages. Yolanda took them and began to scribble a note on one of the pages.

When Jimmy's class broke up, Yolanda slipped in the door to see students packing backpacks and chatting.

One young blonde woman was speaking earnestly to Jimmy. "Professor Thompson, our study group is gonna come by your office hours, okay? Because we've got the theory, but we still don't quite get the application. I heard you missed office hours last week, because no one was signed up, but I'll definitely be there."

"No problem," he smiled. "I'll see you all on Monday."

Yolanda saw the girl's crushed-out grin as she turned back to her friends.

"Have a good weekend, everyone," he called to the class, and headed for the door.

Yolanda stood between him and the exit.

He looked utterly startled to see her. "Is everything okay?" he murmured as he took her arm and they headed down the hallway.

"Outside," Yolanda hissed, as they walked out into the cool afternoon.

They sat on the grass in front of the science building, out of hearing range of everybody.

She took a deep breath. "Someone took a shot at me."

"What?" He moved toward her, as if to shield her body with his.

"Jimmy, please don't freak out. If we're gonna be partners, I need you to stay cool and listen."

"Okay," he stilled his body and his voice, but his eyes were still wide. "Yolanda, we shouldn't be outside in the open like this," he grabbed her hand. "Let's go to my office."

"It might be bugged," she said. "Besides, this is a gated women's college, with one entrance and a security guard. No one's gonna take a shot at me here. They wouldn't be able to get away clean. And I need to tell you about this plan I've been working on."

"Did your plan include you getting shot?"

"No, and it still doesn't."

"What the fuck are they after?"

"Something I need to put in the mail. What time do you get off work today?" she asked.

"I teach 'til four thirty."

"Can you give me a ride somewhere later tonight?"

"Of course. Where?"

"I dunno. Maybe Canada? Or Mexico? Whichever one is closer."

"You're crazy."

"I've gotta disappear, Jimmy. They'll come to you first to look for me, which is why I can't tell you anything."

"Which is why you need to tell me something. Shit. I thought we were partners."

"I'll think about it."

"You'll have a lot of time to be persuaded on the way to Mexico."

"We can't take your car," Yolanda said. "Unless we want the FBI to overhear our entire conversation. We need an out of the way Rent-a-Car."

"They can track a rental," Jimmy said. "But we can go by my parents' house and borrow one of their cars."

"Do they have something nondescript?" Yolanda asked.

"A battered old brown Toyota," Jimmy said.

"Perfect. Can you meet me at five o'clock today?" Yolanda asked. "Come pick me up at the post office in the Mercedes."

"If somebody took a shot at you, you should be waiting here, safe, until I can drive you someplace."

"No, Jimmy. If anything happens to me, I need to know that certain information is secure and in the right hands."

"Mail it from here."

"I don't have it with me," Yolanda thought of the book and USB drive taped behind the toilet tank in the gym.

"Let me go with you to get it," he suggested.

"The post office will be closed by the time you get off work, and I can't leave it in a mailbox. These folks won't let a little mail-tampering felony stand in their way. They'd just break in to the box and take everything. I need to get this in the slot in the actual post office building. There's no telling if they'll try to get it out of the post office, but they'll have a much harder time."

"Fuck it then," he said. "I'm gonna skip class and go with you."

"No baby, they know your car. I'm safer in a cab. Less likely to be spotted. Just pick me up afterwards and we'll get the Toyota and get the hell out of here."

"Yolanda, I'm not letting you out of my sight."

"No, Jimmy," her face was hard and serious.

"I don't like this, Yolanda. I do not fucking like this," he stood and began to pace. "Someone is shooting at my woman and I'm supposed to just be like, okay, see you in a couple hours at the post office."

"Right now, I'm not your woman," she stood and faced him squarely. "Right now I'm a trained FBI agent, a skilled athlete, and I'm armed."

"Yolanda—"

"Jimmy, don't argue with me. If you don't want to meet me at the post office, I can just do this by myself."

"You are so fucking hardheaded," he turned his back to her.

"That's right. Take it or leave it."

He turned to face her, clenching and unclenching his fists

several times. She looked at him with eyebrows raised, her face a carving of conviction.

"Okay," he conceded. "We'll meet in front of the Holloway post office at five PM."

"I'll be out front at five. If you're not there, I've gotta keep moving. I'll call you when I can on your cell. I don't have mine. They stole it."

"You won't need to call. I'll be there at five."

"Thank you. I—we can talk then."

They kissed once, briefly. Then he turned, and she watched him walk back into the building, spine straight, not looking back.

Yolanda walked over to the pay phones in the student center and called a cab. While she waited, she went to the student store and bought a booklet of stamps and a Ziploc bag.

Once at the gym, she tucked herself away in the bathroom stall, Yolanda carefully un-taped the book from behind the toilet tank. Into the Manila envelope, she put the kanji book, the USB drive with the digital recording, her FBI credentials, and the longhand letters and notes she had written on notebook paper at Cartwright. She addressed the envelope to David N. Wiseman, Attorney at Law and put all twenty of the first-class stamps in the booklet onto it. No return address.

On her way out, she was surprised to find everything she had left in her locker. But the scratches on the bottom of her lock let her know that someone had been there, and was uninterested in her digital recorder without the USB memory drive, her empty ankle holster, and the shades she wore sometimes when the glare through the windows of the storefront gym was too much. She plugged a duplicate USB drive into the machine and put the earbuds in her ears.

Everything between her and the mail slot was the enemy. Every square of sidewalk under her running sneakers, every traffic light, every insect that flew past, distracting her. Behind the dark wraparound glasses, her eyes scanned every car, every pedestrian. She ran against the traffic on a one-way street so no car could follow, and so fast that few could have kept up on foot. Her sneakers struck the ground in a rhythm that should have synchronized with the beat in her head- phones. But there was no music. Only conversation. She ran in time to the song of eavesdropping, surveillance.

"So as of today, the FBI will be taking over the investiga- tion into the homicides of Anitra Jenkins and the two Mexi- cans."

"Sir, how can you take over the investigation when this in- stitution has a clear conflict of interest. The FBI doesn't want these murders solved if it's going to lead to any investigation of RandellCorp before the defense contract is finished."

"Vance, I don't need any legal advice from you, okay? You're on thin ice. The FBI will be taking jurisdiction on these murder cases and we will proceed at the pace that we see fit, and in the manner that we see fit, which will guaran- tee the completion of the project at RandellCorp that we have been assigned to protect. Is that clear?"

"Yes, sir."

Sweat ran down her spine and pooled in a blister beneath the Ziploc bag that held the envelope. She had stuck the whole thing in the small of her back, down the waistband of her track pants.

As she ran, the wallet bounced awkwardly in her back pocket, and the gun in an ankle holster bit into the taut mus- cles of her calf with every step.

The back of the post office loomed a few blocks down, a white stone building crouching in the distance. She ran on, the skin at the base of her spine suffocating under the plastic, and cut through the post office parking lot, ignoring the "No Unauthorized Pedestrians" sign.

Once on Holloway Avenue, she began to sprint the final quarter block to the door of the long building, oblivious to the sweat that soaked the fabric of her shirt, athletic bra, pants, socks, underwear. Her throat burned as she gasped oxygen and bounded up the concrete stairs, through the revolving door.

Only once inside the post office, did she finally reach for the envelope. Before anyone else stepped into the building, she had snatched out the bag, slid out the envelope, and mailed it in the slot.

Chapter 31

As the handling agent on the case, Special Agent Peterson knew how to narrow down Yolanda Vance's location. At the start of the operation, Vance only went three places: the FBI apartment, RBG, and the gym. Peterson observed that Vance would pick up takeout or groceries on her routes in between those three points.

After Vance became involved with the scientist, she would disappear at night. But Peterson knew he was currently busy on the Cartwright campus, so that ruled him out. The FBI had both the apartment and the RBG office under surveillance. A colleague was monitoring both and would call if Vance was seen or heard in either location. So, Peterson drove to Holloway and parked across the street from Yolanda's gym.

Peterson had been sitting in the FBI car for nearly an hour when the yellow cab pulled up, and Vance hurried inside. She immediately phoned the location in to ASAC Campbell.

He thanked Peterson and asked her to stand by for further instructions from an operative they had in the field. Three minutes later, a young Latina woman on a skateboard came by and tapped on the window of the car.

"Special Agent Peterson," she said. "Campbell sent me.

He told me to commend you for your good work and ordered you to head back to SFHQ. I can take it from here."

"And you are?" Peterson asked, surveying the girl's scruffy clothes and messy ponytail. She didn't look like she could be over eighteen.

"I'm just a street kid asking you for spare change. Please hand me a few coins out of the window in case anyone's watching."

She handed two quarters to the girl, who took off on the skateboard.

Peterson felt uneasy. She had driven two blocks toward the freeway to San Francisco then decided to double-back. She parked down the street from Yolanda's location.

A charcoal gray sedan moved slowly down the street and idled across from the gym.

When Vance came out the door, it was at a full run, against the flow of traffic. The gray sedan made a U-turn, and sped to the corner, hoping to catch her, but Vance was already onto the next block. Peterson pulled hurriedly out from the curb, and followed the sedan following Vance.

Peterson hadn't expected Vance to move that fast, and both cars needed to loop around on another street going the right way to head her off. Both of their cars got stopped at a red light, and the gray sedan moved as if to run it, but there was a cop nearby, so when the cars finally got to the next intersection, Vance was gone.

The gray sedan went ahead and barreled the wrong way down the one-way for the length of a block. Peterson cut over to a parallel street and could hear car horns blaring at the sedan. At the next intersection, she could see the sedan turn off the one-way and cut up the block. She couldn't see Vance, but she assumed the driver of the gray sedan could. Both cars came around the corner in time to see the sprinting black woman disappearing into the parking lot behind the post office. The sedan U-turned in the middle of the block, among a cacophony of horns, epithets and obscene hand gestures, but he ran the light at the corner, narrowly missing a pair of teenagers, and swerved up the block in front of the post office.

Peterson followed Vance into the lot, and pulled in, parking her car and leaping out at a full run.

"Hey lady, you can't park here," a postal worker complained.

"FBI!" Peterson shouted, waving her credentials as she followed the path that Vance had taken.

Peterson made it around to the front of the building in time to see Yolanda running up the steps, nearly a blur.

Peterson turned and looked for the gray sedan. A large postal truck blocked her view of much of the street. In that moment, a battered blue Mercedes pulled up into the white loading zone in front of the post office. Peterson recognized the boyfriend. He had someone else in the car. Peterson squinted. Marcus Winters.

Peterson was still surveying the street when Vance ran out of the post office. As she sprinted down the steps, the postal truck lurched forward, and Peterson saw the gray sedan.

At that same time, Jimmy Thompson pulled the car forward and swung the rear door of the Mercedes open. In that split second of them both braking, the Mercedes and the woman, in the space of that hesitation, Peterson heard a shot that came from the gray sedan. Several pedestrians screamed as Yolanda Vance fell to the pavement, the left side of her lavender shirt blooming with blood.

Peterson was already in motion before Vance hit the ground, running back to her car. She leaped in and drove in pursuit of the gray sedan. She took off out the front driveway of the post office.

She barreled into the street, her peripheral vision revealing the agonized face of the boyfriend crouched over Vance, tears streaming down. Peterson sped after the gray sedan, but a red SUV cut her off and nearly ran into her. She swerved to avoid a collision and the sedan cut across two lanes and disappeared into the afternoon traffic.

She heard sirens headed toward the post office as she went back to see about Vance. On the way, she pulled out her phone to call Campbell. The sirens were so loud she could barely hear.

"Where the hell are you, Peterson?" he asked.

"Still in Holloway, sir. Special Agent Vance has been shot."

"What?"

"I tried to pursue the perpetrator. Gray sedan, eighties model, maybe a Lincoln or Ford. I'm returning to the scene to give the description and make sure she's okay."

"No way, Peterson," Campbell said. "I'll get that description to the local cops. I want you out of there, you hear me?"

"But sir, we've got an agent down. She's bleeding on the sidewalk!"

"A former agent," Campbell said, reminding Peterson of Yolanda's resignation. "Possibly rogue, and we have no idea who shot her or why. Do NOT return to the scene, and that's an order. Have I made myself clear?"

"Yes, sir."

Seething, Peterson came around the corner. Rescue vehicles and several police cars had already arrived. The boyfriend was holding Yolanda's hand as the paramedics bundled her into the back of an ambulance.

Marcus Winters was talking to a cop, loud and agitated. "A gray sedan," he said. "Took off up Birch Street."

With a prayer that Vance would be okay, and several curses at Campbell, Peterson headed into the rush hour traffic toward San Francisco.

* * *

At 5:08 PM, on his day off, Officer Joaquín Rodriguez felt a buzzing in his chest and looked at his cell phone.

"Marcus Winters," the digital readout informed him.

Rodriguez felt a jolt of panic. He had given Winters the number to call in case of emergency, but he had said to use some kind of code, and not to call from RBG or his own private number.

With a combination of dread and irritation, Rodriguez picked up.

"Who the hell is this?" he asked Winters. "This is a private number."

"Yolanda Vance has been shot in front of the post office. HPD is on the scene. Officer Rodriguez, I thought you might want to know."

Rodriguez hung up and ran out to his car.

Ten minutes later, he showed his badge and ducked under the yellow caution tape.

"I'm off duty today," Rodriguez told the detective in charge. "Heard there was a shooting. Came to see if you needed any help."

The detective sketched out what they knew, and invited Rodriguez to help question witnesses.

Rodriguez made eye contact with Marcus Winters and questioned an elderly lady for a few minutes before heading to Winters.

"What's your name sir?" Rodriguez asked. "Did you witness the shooting?" As they spoke, he made notes on his clipboard.

"The victim was Yolanda Vance," Marcus said just above a whisper. "She was FBI—just resigned. She had been infiltrating RBG. She planted the bugs."

"You think this is how the FBI decided to let her go?" Rodriguez asked quietly, nodding to the caution tape and the crime scene.

"Well they failed," Marcus said. "Shooter got her in the left shoulder, but she was breathing when she left. Jimmy went with her in the ambulance. I'm gonna drive his car over and meet them as soon as I'm done talking to you."

"Could this be a random shooting?" Rodriguez asked at full volume. "Mistaken identity? Innocent bystander? You know Holloway's murder rate."

"It's the second time someone shot at her today," Marcus said quietly. "First one just barely missed."

"*Carajo.*"

"Doesn't that mean 'oh shit'?" Marcus asked.

"Yeah," Rodriguez said. "*Mas o menos.*"

As Rodriguez was questioning a pair of postal workers, Marcus got into the Mercedes with Jimmy and drove off.

A moment later, an older African American man approached the police line. Rodriguez didn't recognize him, but he showed one of the cops some type of badge and stepped under the caution tape. Rodriguez excused himself from the witnesses and followed him.

"Who's that guy?" he asked another officer. "The tall black guy who just came in."

"Didn't catch his name," the cop said. "But he's FBI."

The tall black guy from the FBI was in conversation with the detective. "I have reason to believe the victim may be a witness to some homicides we're working on," the FBI agent said. "What hospital is she being taken to?"

"Kaiser emergency," the detective said, and the FBI guy thanked him and crossed back under the caution tape.

As he finished up with the postal workers, Rodriguez watched the FBI guy as he stood on the post office steps and made a phone call. Rodriguez hurried to hand his notes to the detective and was in his car ready to tail the guy when a young man in a black Jeep picked him up. The vehicle was brand new with dealership plates. Rodriguez followed them in his car, and they headed straight to Kaiser emergency.

When the young man stepped out of the Jeep, the older man kept going. Rodriguez decided to follow the young man into the hospital. The kid was maybe twenty and fit the description of a lot of the young black men in Holloway: dark brown skin, dark hair, white t-shirt, dark denim jeans, dark sneakers.

At the nurse's station, the young man inquired after his "Cousin" Yolanda Vance who had been shot. He was concerned. Was she okay? Could they tell him anything?

The nurse explained that she couldn't give out that information.

"Not even to family? That's my cousin. We was raised like brother and sister!"

The nurse shook her head.

"Can you at least tell me if she's here at this hospital? I need to tell her mama where to come."

"Sorry, young man. The police will notify the family about her condition and when they can come see her."

The young man sucked his teeth and looked to be on the verge of tears. "Please. That's my cousin, my blood," he said.

The nurse shook her head.

"Man, fuck this place. I done lost too many folks up in here anyway."

When Rodriguez followed the kid out to the street, the Jeep was gone, and the young man walked out to the bus stop. Ten minutes later, the kid boarded the bus with all the other passengers.

Rodriguez walked back into the hospital. At the desk, he showed his badge to the nurse.

"HPD. I'm looking for a gunshot wound victim, Yolanda Vance. She was brought in here maybe an hour ago."

"One moment, sir," the nurse said and made a brief call.

"Your name, sir?" she asked him.

"Joaquín Rodriguez," he said.

She repeated the name into the phone, listened briefly, and then hung up and gave him a room number.

The room turned out to be the lounge outside of emergency surgery, where he found two cops he didn't recognize guarding the door. Through the glass, he saw Marcus Winters pacing in front of a row of seats. On the end sat Jimmy Thompson, next to the Puerto Rican lesbian therapist from the group.

"Why won't they fucking tell me what's going on?" Jimmy raged loud enough that Rodriguez could hear through the glass.

"She's gonna be okay," the Latina therapist murmured. "The doctors are busy taking out the bullet, not reporting to us."

"She better be okay," Jimmy said. "She fucking better."

"The bullet didn't hit her heart or her lung," the therapist said. "That's the most important thing."

"Yeah, but he said she'd lost a lot of blood," Jimmy said.

"And if she needs a transfusion, they'll give her one," Sharon said. "I'm telling you, love, she's gonna be fine."

Marcus spotted Rodriguez and stepped outside.

"What you got?" Marcus asked.

"After you left, an FBI guy came to the crime scene. African American, fifties, maybe. Wiry, brusque. Didn't get his name. Not even sure if he's really FBI."

"You think he's the shooter?" Marcus asked.

"Something wasn't right about him," Rodriguez said. "I would've given anything to test his fingers for powder burns."

"What the fuck do we do now?" Marcus asked.

"I don't know, man, but we need to figure out something, because if they tried twice, then they really want to shut her up."

Chapter 32

That Friday, David N. Weisman received a package from Yolanda Vance, with the following handwritten cover letter.

Dear Mr. Weisman,

I am writing to you because my former employer, the Federal Bureau of Investigation, has violated my civil rights. They have taken over an investigation with the intention of delaying justice. Enclosed please find my field notes, and my FBI credentials, as well as a digital recording of the last meeting in which San Francisco Assistant Special Agent in Charge (ASAC) Campbell discloses his plan to conceal evidence from other law enforcement agencies in the murders of Anitra Jenkins, Juan Carlos Sanchez, and Luis Garcia.

Also, please find my last will and testament, in case anything happens to me, I will my only possessions of any value to Marcus Winters of RBG, my journal and my digital recording. Finally, enclosed, please find one dollar as a retainer.

"I thought you said your plan didn't include getting shot," Jimmy said Saturday morning, when Yolanda was finally stable enough to have a visitor. She was still in intensive care, but had been moved from critical to stable condition, the bullet having missed her heart and lung by less than an inch.

"Plan A was not to get shot," Yolanda said, her voice weak. "Plan B was not to get shot before I mailed the package." Her speech was still a little slurred from all the painkillers.

"I've got some good news for you," Jimmy said. "The independent forensic pathologist found morphine, not heroin in Anitra Jenkins's bloodstream. And the wound is definitely not an abscess, but an external wound, caused by some form of corrosive chemical. They're still not sure what caused it, but they think it's some sort of chemical weapon Randell was developing."

"I guess that was the top-secret government contract," Yolanda murmured.

"Shhhh," Jimmy put a finger to her lips. "Don't tell me anything else that might be classified."

"No more secrets," Yolanda said as she closed her eyes.

"I love you, Yolanda," she vaguely heard Jimmy say, then she drifted off again.

Two days later, she was moved out of intensive care. No longer doped up on pain relievers, and with the risk of infection passed, she was feeling more herself. She couldn't move her left arm, but they assured her that in time, she'd be fine, with just the bullet scar.

That day, Peterson came to visit. Jimmy was sitting on the end of the bed when the agent was admitted into the room.

"Hey Vance," she said, walking in with a bouquet of daisies. "Glad to see you still alive and kicking."

"And you are?" Jimmy asked.

"Special Agent Jeanne Peterson. San Francisco FBI." She put out a hand for him to shake, but he ignored it.

"Thanks for coming, Peterson," Yolanda said.

"Are you sure she should be here?" Jimmy asked Yolanda.

"Jimmy, it's okay," Yolanda caressed his forearm with her good hand.

"In fact," Peterson said. "I'd like to talk to Miss Vance alone for a few minutes."

"She's not an agent anymore," Jimmy said, pulling his arm away from Yolanda's touch. "You guys can't order her around." He turned to Yolanda. "Baby, I think I need to stay with you."

"Jimmy," she took his hand. "There are three cops in the hallway. You'll be right outside the door, and you're worth ten cops. I'll be fine."

He stood slowly to leave.

"Really," Yolanda said. "It's okay."

"I'll be right outside," he said, as he closed the door after himself.

"I thought he wasn't your boyfriend," Peterson said, one eyebrow raised.

"He wasn't until after I resigned."

"That's what I need to talk to you about," Peterson said, sobering. "HQ sent me to get your gun, keys, and credentials."

"Did they send the flowers, too?"

Peterson smiled. "No, that was from me to you. You didn't sign up for all of this shit, Vance. You did a good job."

Yolanda reached under the pillow and produced the gun—butt first—and handed it to Peterson. The agent unloaded it and put both the empty gun and the clip into her purse.

"The keys are in my jeans, I think." Yolanda waved to a hospital bag that contained her street clothes.

Peterson dug out the keys. "And the credentials?" she asked.

"They must have been in my purse that got stolen," Yolanda lied.

"Are you sure?" Peterson asked, raising an eyebrow. "Campbell seemed to think you had them."

"Why would there be any question?" Yolanda asked. "Unless Campbell was somehow involved in the theft of my purse."

"I don't know anything about that," Peterson said, pocketing the keys. "I just know Campbell was very specific in his request."

"I don't really care how specific Campbell was. Somebody shot me, Peterson. Right after I resigned. If Campbell isn't upset about a little grave robbing and a few dead Mexicans, what's a dead rookie FBI agent to him?"

Peterson turned and looked out the window. Yolanda followed her gaze. The small rectangle looked out on the parking lot. All asphalt and cars and white lines. A few spindly trees in cement planters between the rows of vehicles were dwarfed by tall metal floodlights.

Peterson fidgeted with a stray hair coming loose from her bun, then shook her head. "You didn't hear this from me, okay? If you ever bring it up, I'll deny it. But on the day you got shot, Campbell sent me to look for you after your phone got stolen. He was a lunatic, just insisting that I had to find you. And then, a few minutes after I called in your location to Campbell, the shooter's car came down the street and waited. Ten minutes later, you were on the ground."

"What?"

"I'm not repeating it, and I'll deny it if you tell anyone."

"Do you know who it was that shot me?"

"All I saw was the guy's car," Peterson said. "Oh, and Campbell also used a young Latina operative on a skateboard who couldn't have been more than twenty."

"The girl who stole my purse!" Yolanda said.

"Probably," the agent said. "I gotta go."

"Thanks, Peterson."

* * *

Jimmy canceled his classes and stayed at the hospital. By day two in the private room Yolanda began complaining that he needed to go home and take a shower. He only left briefly, when Marcus, Sharon, and several cops, including Rodriguez from Holloway and McConnell from Richmond, were all there at the same time.

"We can't keep up this level of security," Rodriguez explained later to Jimmy and Yolanda.

"This guy is trying to kill her. He's probably just waiting to make a move," Jimmy said. He was ragged and jumpy from lack of sleep and food.

"Yolanda's not the only the only person to get shot in Holloway," Rodriguez said.

"Yeah but probably the only one who got shot by an FBI agent," Jimmy said.

"Look Jimmy, I'm a rookie cop," Rodriguez explained. "I don't make the decisions. I'm just giving you the heads-up so you can prepare. I think this afternoon might be the last shift of the police detail."

"The FBI took her gun, and now HPD is gonna bail?" Jimmy was nearly yelling.

Yolanda put up a hand to stop him. "Okay, Rodriguez," she said. "What the hell are we supposed to do?"

"I would recommend that you hire a private security company and get a surveillance camera."

"That's the best we can do?" Jimmy asked.

"A rent-a-cop and a camera is a pretty big deterrent," Rodriguez said.

"And me," Jimmy said. "I'm not leaving."

"Sooner or later this guy is gonna make a move," Yolanda said. "I'm not the president. I don't have a whole Secret Service detail. We're gonna have to learn to live with risk."

"Fuck that!" Jimmy yelled. "We need to be able to protect you. I need to be able to protect you."

"You're a mess, Jimmy," Yolanda said. "You can't protect anyone. At this point, you're so crazy and sleep deprived, I feel more at risk with you around."

"You don't mean that," he said.

"She's right," Rodriguez said.

"You stay the fuck out of this," Jimmy pointed a finger right in Rodriguez's face.

"See what I mean?" Yolanda said. "You're out of control."

Rodriguez stood up. "I'm gonna leave you two alone for a minute. I'll be right outside."

Jimmy watched him exit and spoke the minute he closed the door. "My daddy taught me that a black man needs to protect his family," Jimmy said. "I'm not gonna leave you here alone."

"Are you saying I have to fucking break up with you to get you to go home and take care of yourself?" Yolanda asked.

"The last time I let you out of my sight you got shot."

"Fine," Yolanda said. "If you won't leave, I will." With a grimace of pain, she stood up from the bed.

"No, baby! You can't do that. Your wound isn't healed up."

"One of us is leaving this room tonight," Yolanda said. "It's either you or me."

"This is bullshit," Jimmy said. But once they stationed the security guard outside her door, and the technicians had installed a camera inside, he left Yolanda and Rodriguez talking quietly.

Chapter 33

At 1:23 AM that night, the gunman arrived at the nurse's station, dressed in dark clothes and a dark wool cap. He showed a convincing police badge to the nurse on the ward, and explained that he was here to see a witness.

"Certainly," the nurse said. She was petite, her blonde hair pulled up in a messy bun, and her scrubs were bright turquoise. "I'll just need to call my supervisor."

When the nurse turned to use the phone, the gunman grabbed her. He put one hand over her mouth and the other arm across her throat, choking her in the crook of his elbow until she passed out.

After she fell to the floor unconscious, he put on a pair of latex gloves, and pulled a gun from the waistband of his track pants. From the pocket, he drew out a silencer and attached it as he walked down the hall toward Yolanda Vance's room.

He moved like calligraphy, his long dark limbs striding down the bright corridor like brushstrokes.

"Excuse me, do you have a match?" he asked the young guard in front of her door.

"I'm sorry, there's no smoking in here," the guard said.

"But that sign right there said—" the gunman pointed

down the hall with his left hand. When the guard turned to look, the shooter cracked him in the head with the gun. The guard went down, thudding onto the pale linoleum in the bright, silent hallway. The gunman went through the guard's pockets for the room keys. He unlocked the door as he pulled the ski mask down over his face.

The camera in Yolanda Vance's room recorded a masked gunman entering through the door, gun drawn in his gloved hand. By the looks of his wrists, neck, and the skin visible around the eyes and mouth of the ski mask, he was African American. He advanced unceremoniously into the room and shot Yolanda, as she lay in bed, same left side, a cry escaping from her as the bullet hit.

As he stepped forward to take a second shot to her head, the camera turned and zoomed in on him. The whirring sound distracted him for a moment, and he turned to shoot out the camera.

The moment the gunman swung the weapon away from her, Yolanda Vance heaved herself up from beneath the sheet, the Kevlar vest, the layers of bandages. She moved surprisingly quickly, despite her freshly bruised skin and ribs, despite the aggravation of the gunshot wound. She sprang with all her strength and shot him twice in the chest. After his discreet entrance into the room, and the viciously polite cough of the silenced weapon, her gunfire was deafening.

She had practiced the move over and over with Donnelly, had drilled it into her body memory—to be able to raise herself, steady the gun, and shoot straight, despite the terror sending her heart clattering in her chest, the ragged surge of adrenaline in her bloodstream. Her aim was excellent, under the circumstances, and her body had expected to feel the gun recoiling in her clenched hand, just like on the firing range during FBI training. But neither Donnelly nor the silhouette targets at Quantico had prepared her for what it felt like to shoot a human being in a small hospital room—the heat of the bullets burning through the sheet, the sudden smell of blood and cordite in the claustrophobic air, the sickening thud of the gunman's body as the shots knocked him back, stunned, against the wall, not ten feet away, abrupt red stains on the pristine white paint.

Yolanda swung the gun back to the unmoving form of the gunman, a heap of brown skin and black fabric on the white hospital floor. Cautiously, awkwardly, she heaved herself out of the bed, and tiptoed over to the pile, peering at him for any sign of breath or movement. Seeing none, she slowly, carefully knelt down, gun still on him, to check for a pulse. His neck was warm but still.

Yolanda dropped the gun and stumbled to the door. Falling against it, her face pressed to the white painted metal, she sat frozen for a moment.

No. She couldn't let her guard down. They were determined to kill her. They might just send someone else. She turned the lock, and crawled back into the bed, barricading herself under the covers, shocked and numb.

The sound of the shots echoed in the room, alerting the hospital staff, and the camera alerted the security detail.

The security guards arrived first.

"Miss Vance!" they called. "We saw what happened on the monitors. Are you all right Miss Vance?"

Yolanda said nothing. The guards could see on the video monitor that she was unharmed.

"Miss Vance, please open the door!"

But she lay huddled on the bed, refusing to let them in.

At 3:07 AM, the police and hospital authorities allowed Sharon Martinez, a Kaiser employee and therapist, to enter the room. She stepped over the body of the fallen man and climbed into bed with Yolanda, who turned to her and began wailing. Yolanda sobbed all the while, as the Richmond police photographed, outlined, and removed the body of the gunman. Marcus Winters easily identified him as the man who had been around the Panthers, and who had briefly been part of RBG. His credentials identified him as a special agent with the FBI who went by a different name.

Yolanda continued sobbing as the police removed the crime scene tape and allowed Jimmy to enter the room. He climbed into bed with her as well, and Yolanda curled up between him and Sharon, still sobbing.

She heaved with the spilling of it, having both of them pressed on either side of her in the bed, the human contact undeniable, in the midst of the most brutal thing she'd ever done.

She couldn't get the image of the gunman out of her mind, him, the gun, the black and brown heap on the floor, the warm but still feel of his skin scalding her fingertips. The burning bruise of the bullet's force that couldn't penetrate the Kevlar.

Yolanda clung to Sharon, as Jimmy held her around the waist and let the sobs wash through her, wailing like a child at her father's funeral, holding nothing back.

Chapter 34

After she got out of the hospital, Yolanda moved in with Sharon and her wife. She got a job working with David on the civil suit against RandellCorp for the wrongful death of Anitra Jenkins and testified at various hearings about FBI wrongdoing in the case.

Despite her official address, she spent nearly every night at Jimmy's.

As part of her restorative justice to RBG, the youth demanded that Yolanda sit with them and answer all their questions. She expected it to be the Spanish Inquisition, but instead, she walked in to find all of them bright-eyed and suppressing grins.

"So we actually won you over?" Dana asked.

"Basically, yeah," Yolanda said.

"And then you went all double-agent," Darnell said. "And you all had to sneak around behind the FBI's back and stage a big drama on some, 'Oh snap! Sharon found my FBI ID.' 'You a damn spy!' 'No, wait it's not what you think!' 'Get the fuck out of here!' Man, I wish I could see that video."

"What did the FBI say about us?" Sheena asked.

Yolanda shook her head sheepishly. "They said that you all were totally manipulated by Marcus. They made him sound like some kind of puppet master."

The teens all laughed.

"And you believed that?" Dana asked.

"At first," Yolanda said. "But the more time I spent with you all, the less their explanations of everything made sense."

"Okay, but was it like on some romance, though?" Sheena asked. "Like you was feeling Jimmy so much you was like, 'Forget the FBI!'"

Yolanda blushed and put a hand over her face.

"Dang, Sheena!" Dana said. "How you gonna just put the personal questions on blast like that?"

"The restorative justice agreement is that we can ask whatever we want," Sheena said.

"It's okay," Yolanda said, steeling herself, and taking her hand from her face. "I met Jimmy outside RBG and I liked him."

"He says you flirted with him," Nakeesha said.

"Guilty as charged," Yolanda said. "And when I found out he was part of RBG I was mortified."

"Why?" Darnell asked. "That's a good thing when you like somebody. You know, be all up close and get personal."

"Nah," Nakeesha said. "I understand. Sometimes you need to have your school somebody. And your work somebody. And sometimes your neighborhood somebody, too."

"I definitely wasn't trying to have more than one—ah—somebody that I was flirting with—"

"Enough about your love life, Nakeesha," Sheena said. "So did you fall in love with Jimmy or what?"

Yolanda shook her head. "It wasn't just him," she said. "It was everybody. I ... I fell in love with ... the whole movement." And then, without any preamble, Yolanda started to cry.

"Awwww!" Sheena said, and she came around the table and hugged Yolanda. "We forgive you." Dana and Darnell also piled on to the hug.

"Speak for yourself," Nakeesha said. "I won't forgive her until she tells us all about how she shot that creepy old dude. Then I'll think about it."

As another part of her restorative justice to RBG, Yolanda had paid a specialist to find all the bugs in everybody's house, office, car, phone, and apartment. Other than the office and all of Marcus's phones, nothing else turned out to be bugged. From time to time, the adults in RBG would make what they called "the bug face," which usually consisted of an open mouth and eyes looking up and flitting back and forth. This also brought back the eighties hip-hop slang of "buggin" or "buggin out," which spread around the vocabularies of Holloway teens.

"Just talk to me baby," Jimmy said, as they lay in bed one night. "Say anything. It's just so good not to have to go outside in the damn cold to talk with my woman."

"I have a serious question, Jimmy," she said.

"Bring it on," he said.

They lay beneath the turquoise sheets in the queen-sized bed, Saturday's late morning sunshine filtering in through the rice paper blinds.

"Do you think the guy I killed really was a rogue agent like the FBI is saying, or do you think they set me up?" Yolanda asked. "I mean, at this point I'm not scared anymore. I've gotten everything I know on the record. Killing me now would only make them look worse."

"I think we'll never really know," Jimmy said, gently touching the scar on her left shoulder. "All we have is the ballistic evidence that the bullet they took out of you matches the one that killed the FBI's ex-con informant. Maybe that agent was just a mad dog operating on his own. Or maybe the FBI knew he was a mad dog, and that's why they sicced him on you, hoping he would do his mad dog thing."

"I just wanna know if Campbell really could look me in the eye while he was planning to murder me."

"That's why his ass had to resign. Baby, let's not talk about this anymore. Let's talk about how soon you're gonna move in with me for real."

"Jimmy," she pulled back from him slightly. "I told you I'm not ready."

"How can you not be ready to live with me, but you're in my bed every night? Answer me that, girl genius."

"I told you," she said. "I moved around a lot. I'm not used to staying in one place and having people so close to me."

"Well shoot, woman," he said squeezing her. "Get used to it."

On the evening after she completed the last day of the bar exam, Yolanda Vance stepped out of the Oakland Convention Center into the bright downtown afternoon, enjoying the warm July air.

She walked a few blocks uptown to a different type of bar and slid onto a tall stool next to Donnelly.

"Hail the conquering heroine," Donnelly said. "Back from three days of grueling legal battle. You think you passed?"

"Probably," Yolanda said, taking a sip of wine. "But the best part is that I can see that my life doesn't depend on it."

"It's good to have things in perspective," Donnelly said.

"I've got a job, a place to live—two, actually," Yolanda said. "Jimmy wants me to move in with him, but I'm taking my time."

"Well you're about to have two job offers as well," Donnelly said. "I've got an opening for an attorney in my division."

Yolanda opened her mouth to speak, but Donnelly held

up a hand. "Just hear me out. Campbell resigned in disgrace. He may face criminal charges."

"Dream on," Yolanda scoffed and ate a handful of peanuts.

"Andrew Wentworth from RandellCorp got indicted, and RandellCorp might even close up shop in Holloway."

"Thanks for your testimony on that," Yolanda said.

"You're a good agent," Donnelly said. "And we're a great team."

"Sorry, Claire, but I'm done with the bureau," Yolanda said.

Donnelly shrugged. "Say you'll think about it."

"I'll think about it," Yolanda said.

On her way to the subway, Yolanda got a text from Jimmy:

what's your ETA? U on the train yet? how'd it go? miss u

She joined a throng of professionals in suits as they descended into the BART station, heels clacking on the steps, briefcases swinging at their sides.

As she stepped through the fare gates, she texted Jimmy back. "Getting on at 12th Street," and added a smiley face and a shower of confetti.

"Richmond/Holloway train now arriving on platform four," the mechanical voice said over the public address system.

The train was packed. It had come from San Francisco and was already crowded with professionals headed home for the evening. The Oakland passengers squeezed in. Yolanda looked around and saw that there was an available window seat in the back corner, next to a young black man. As she made her way over to him, she could hear rap music blasting loud in his headphones.

She tapped him gently on the shoulder to get his attention. "Excuse me brother, can I squeeze in there?"

"Sure, miss," he said, and swung his legs to the side.

She sat down as the train moved haltingly and came above ground over a changing North Oakland. From the window of the slow-moving train, Yolanda saw two black women on the street recognize each other and embrace while a pair of boys with wild afros dashed across the street to the liquor store, pulling up their sagging jeans as they ran, flashing brightly-colored boxer shorts.

At Downtown Berkeley Station, the young man got off the train, and she moved out to the aisle seat.

"Excuse me, miss," someone tapped Yolanda on the shoulder.

Yolanda looked up to see Jimmy with a huge bouquet of blue irises and a wide smile. "Do you mind if I sit down?"

"Not at all," Yolanda said. "In fact, let me help you with those flowers. They seem very heavy."

"Thank you," he said. "A woman helping me with a heavy burden. I see chivalry is not dead."

Yolanda laughed. "How did you find me?"

"I tracked your train when you got on at 12th street."

"On what?" Yolanda asked. "Stalker.com?"

"Now that you've passed the bar—" Jimmy began.

"Taken the bar," Yolanda corrected.

"Will you move in with me?" Jimmy asked.

Yolanda looked down at the flowers. "I don't know," she said. "I was thinking maybe I'd get a place in Richmond."

"Richmond?" Jimmy asked. "What's wrong with Holloway?"

"Nothing," Yolanda said. "I just might not be ready to have my apartment, my job, my man, my man's job, and all my friends in the same small town."

"Bullshit," Jimmy said. "You were born a small town girl. Embrace your roots."

"I got a job offer today," Yolanda said. "There's an opening for a lawyer in the white-collar division at the Bureau. It's led by the one woman I trust at the FBI, and she reminded me that the benefits and retirement package are amazing."

"So what are you saying?" Jimmy asked. "That you'd go back to the FBI for the money?"

"I'm saying I got two tempting offers today," she said. "And I'm much more likely to say yes to yours."

"So I should be digging your scene with my gangsta lean," Jimmy asked.

"You should be what?" Yolanda asked.

"I should be grateful for what I've got," he said, and pulled her closer. "And I am. You have no idea."

"I might have some idea," she said.

She moved the flowers and leaned against him. "Diamond in the back," she murmured, as the train dipped into the Holloway tunnel to take them home.